Vines

A Killers Novel, Book 1

Brynne Asher

Dedications

To the Mister

Thank you for supporting my day dreams. After twenty-one years of marriage, it just gets better and better. Love you.

To Elle

What a year. It feels like just yesterday we were standing in a winery in Virginia doing a tasting when this new world popped into my head. The next thing I knew, Crew and Addy were born. Thank you for giving me the name Crew. He's perfect and I love creating characters with you. You'll always be the first to read my words.

To Layla Frost and Sarah Curtis

I can't remember the last time a day has gone by and we haven't connected. You've become the sweetest friends and I treasure you both. The Three T's *will* unite someday and when it happens, the world had better brace. Thank you for supporting me and always being there to straighten out my possessive/non-possessive issues.

To Rae Larand, Ivy, Laurie, Penny and Kristan

Time is one of the most precious gifts one human can give another. Thank you for yours and all your efforts in making Vines everything I dreamed. I adore you all.

And finally, to all my readers and bloggers

Thank you for taking a chance on my books. Without you, I couldn't do this.

Other Books by Brynne Asher

Overflow – The Carpino Series, Book 1
Beautiful Life – The Carpino Series Book 2
Athica Lane – The Carpino Series Book 3

Keep up with me on Facebook for news and upcoming books
https://www.facebook.com/BrynneAsherAuthor
<u>Email:</u> BrynneAsherBooks@gmail.com

Editing by Kristan Roetker at edit llc
Formatting by Formatting the affordable way
Cover design by Amy Queau at Q Design Cover and Brand Premades

A Note from the Author

When I moved to Virginia over two years ago, I had no idea I'd be living in wine country. It took one trip to a local winery to fall in love, and I have to admit, research was not chore. Whitetail is a beautiful blend of the region and history I was blessed to experience during my time there.

When I first put my fingers to a keyboard in 2013 to see if I could even manage a chapter, I never thought I'd end up where I am. As much as I'd love it to be, writing still isn't a full-time gig. Vines took almost a year for me to write since we were relocated *again*. Thank you, precious readers, for sticking with me and waiting over a year for a new book from this little author.

I hope you enjoy reading Vines as much as I loved writing it.

Prologue

"Are you sure I can't show you something in the District? Perhaps Georgetown or a brownstone in Arlington would better suit you. Your commute from way out here will be a bear."

I stare out the window from one of the top-floor bedrooms, wondering what I'll do with all this square footage. Shit. I wonder what I'll do staying put for more than a few days at a time. Looking over the snow-covered mountains, or what they consider mountains in Virginia, I think about space and privacy. I need both now more than ever.

She moves closer, her spiked heels clicking on the aged wood echoes through the empty room. "With your loan approval, you can afford a lovely penthouse overlooking the Potomac. Do you boat?"

Fuck. Do I look like I boat? I wish she'd shut up. I'm sick of her talking. My loan approval is a fake, because at this point, it's none of her business I'm paying cash.

"Mr. Vega?" she calls for me and I have to exhale to keep my patience.

Ignoring her, I deliberate on the only drawback to the property. I wanted three hundred and sixty acres so I don't have a neighbor. "You said this is two hundred and seventy acres. Who shares the section of land?"

It's her turn to exhale, her voice going bored. "A vineyard. I looked into it when you insisted on viewing this property. It's changed hands four times in the last nine years. Apparently everyone thinks they can make wine. The new owner has seen some success. There's no need for anxiety. The building and land are on the National Register because of its history and the age of the original structure. I believe it dates back to the sixteen hundreds. Properties such as these are hardly ever broken up. If you insist on the country life, your neighbor shouldn't be of concern."

I'll run that background myself.

Turning to her, I cross my arms. "You said the outbuildings have heat and water?"

She sighs, realizing she isn't going to sell me a penthouse in Georgetown. Not that her commission on this place won't be a mint.

"Yes. The previous owner was a mechanic specializing in large farm equipment. There's heat for the winter and air for summer months," she utters, flipping her jeweled hand toward the window.

We won't need much heat and absolutely no air in the summer. It's part of the program—they have to learn to live in the conditions.

I nod, looking back out over the countryside thinking this could be it. I'm ready for something different, ready to retire from the life I've lived the last ten years, even if it means I have to train my replacements.

"I need to make a phone call and look at the outbuildings." I turn back to her and raise an eyebrow, glancing down at her feet. "You want to trudge through the snow with me, or should I meet you back at the cars?"

Her look turns resigned, her voice bland when she replies, "Take your time. I'll draw up the paperwork."

I reach for my phone and start for the door mumbling, "Perfect."

When I reach the bottom of the stairs, my call has barely rung once when Asa answers, a smile in his voice. "Vega. What'd ya think of Stacey?"

"Fuck you, old man," I growl as I head out the front door to round the house.

"Me?" he feigns. "That was Stacey's job. You didn't like my welcome home gift?"

"Don't know if I'm home. It's been a long time." I crunch through the snow in my combat boots.

"You're home, boy. Don't question that," his voice turns serious.

I make my way through the barren woods that'll be perfect when it's thick with growth, toward the largest outbuilding. There're three, but I only need to make one comfortable or Grady'll be a thorn in my side.

"I need a favor," I say, my breath visible in the cold.

"Thought I was doing you a favor by sending Stacey," he grumbles.

I ignore him. "If these buildings check out, I'm making an offer today. Ready to get this shit done."

"Fine, what now?" he complains.

"I need a background check on the owner next door. It's a vineyard on a quarter section, adjacent to this property. I need it in an hour."

"Done. I'll hit you back." He's all business and abruptly disconnects.

As I make my way up the so-called mountain, I stop when I come into view of the neighboring property. The vines are bare like everything else, but there aren't any houses or buildings in view.

Vines

I turn and look back to my new house, thinking this is good. No direct sight—I can make use of the far side of the property for privacy. As long as the owner's background comes back clean—this is it.

A new chapter. A new start. And fuckin' finally, just maybe, a life.

Chapter One

Cows Are Girls

Addy

"Harry!"

"Moo." Scarlett nudges my shoulder roughly.

I push my hair out of my face. My naturally frizzy locks haven't been the same since I moved here. If I had known the humidity was this bad, I never would have settled in Virginia. It doesn't matter what the temps are, the humidity in the middle of summer is the worst. Heaven forbid it rains, not only is it bad for the vines, the humidity jumps to a gazillion percent.

I've got to get Morris to fix this section of fence. Harry has over forty acres to roam. You'd think forty acres would be more than enough for five cows. It's not like I have a herd. Harry's always the loner, poor girl.

I trudge up over the hill in my Hunter rain boots. The ticks are thick this time of year—no way am I going to risk walking with the cows in anything else. It gives me the heebie-jeebies just thinking about it. Over the last year, I've come to enjoy my morning walk with the girls. I don't get out here every day—it depends on the schedule. Today is Thursday and it's slow. The tasting room doesn't open until eleven and even though I have meetings, my first event isn't until late this afternoon.

"Harry!" I call again.

"Moo." Scarlett nudges me harder than before.

"No-no." I try and push her away. "You're so needy and it's too hot for you to crowd me. Go graze with your sisters."

Of course she ignores me and nuzzles my ear. Jimmy, Maria, and Jax act like normal cows, grazing the way a cow should while lazing their days away in the meadows. Scarlett lives up to her namesake—she's melodramatic and boisterous. And poor Harry, she only wants to be by herself, to the point of escaping to the neighbor's property. She knows her space—she's lived here longer than me and cows are smarter than I ever would have guessed.

I never thought I'd own a cow, let alone five, but I inherited them when I bought the vineyard. I also inherited my caretaker, Morris, and his wife Beverly. Oh, and there's the winemaker, Van, the tasting room manager, Evan—who's barely old enough to legally taste wine himself—and the chef, Maggie. I didn't know all these people came along with the vineyard when I bought it, but the day I signed my closing papers and walked into my new home and business, there they were waiting for me. They proceeded to tell me how things ran and why the previous three owners didn't work out for them.

That first day, I got the distinct impression I was interviewing to be their boss. It didn't matter whose name was on the loan or officially owned the establishment. When they explained to me all the reasons the past owners failed, I knew then and there if they didn't like me, I'd fall flat, too. It didn't matter that I'd sunk every penny to my name into a struggling winery.

Morris and Bev live on the property in the caretaker's home where they've been for eighteen years. I might own that teensy little house on the far side of my land, but it's very much theirs. Morris knows the land and vines well. No way could I get rid of them, even if he is ill-tempered.

Bev doesn't officially work for the winery, but she's usually around. Actually, she's always fussing about like she owns the place since they've lived here so long. She keeps all the flowers watered, the tables wiped, and when the spirit moves her—she'll wash a few dishes. I asked if I should make it official and put her on the payroll. She insists she likes to hang around when she feels like it but when she doesn't feel like it, she can go her own way. She quickly informed me I pay her plenty in wine and she's pretty sure that in the end we're—in her words—*Even-Steven*. I've learned to go with the flow and keep her in wine because she's as lovable as Morris is irritable.

I might've bought a vineyard, but I'm a beer girl who happens to be creative when it comes to business. I knew nothing about wine but when I found a great deal on a small struggling vineyard. All I saw was opportunity. I immediately knew how to turn it around.

As finicky as Van is about crafting wine, I knew I needed him. I try and ignore all the female customers whose sole reason for visiting is to lust after him. He's a manwhore in his forties who resembles a young Robert Redford. There's no other way to describe him. The women know he's a manwhore, but they don't seem to care one bit. I've never seen anything like it, but he brings in his share of business, so I've learned not to care, either.

Maggie is a young widow in her early fifties who can make a mean soup and sandwich. Her desserts are hit or miss. Well, mostly miss. I've started ordering from a local bakery even though it pisses her off. Lately she's been experimenting with fancy salads for summer— so far they've been a hit. Is she really a chef? No, but she runs an interesting deli out of the tasting room kitchen and customers seem to like her creativity. Even after a year, she still frightens me a tad.

Evan's been around slightly longer than me and though he's merely twenty-four, I'll never be as refined as the likes of him. Somehow, he can taste ripe apricots glazed with brown sugar butter in a white wine, and a woodsy fall day underlying a white pepper and smoky cheddar in a red. People ecstatically agree—wondering how they didn't taste it on their own to begin with. Customers eat that shit up. I don't get it— It all tastes like wine to me. But the customers love him and so do I.

There was no way I could get rid of any of these people when I took over. I had no choice but to work hard to make them like me. I think I've done okay. One thing's for sure, I've never had so many people in my life.

I climb up the hill, toward the old fence that's rotting away to look for her. "Harry!"

"You lookin' for someone?"

I shriek, jumping at the sound of a deep voice coming from my side. I must have startled Scarlett because she moves quickly, pushing me off balance. Letting out another yelp, I fall to my ass with a thud, landing in the morning dew-covered grass.

"Ouch," I mutter, twigs and rocks pressing into my palms where I tried to catch myself.

"Moo." Scarlett nudges the side of my head.

"You okay?" I hear and look up.

When I do, I have to squint. Blinded, I can't see his face so I bring my hand up to shield my eyes from the sun.

The man with the voice is standing across my dilapidated fence, looking down at me. I still can't see his face, but his body's covered in a sheen of sweat. He's wearing an old wife-beater and a pair of cargo shorts with running shoes. The tank is plastered to his tanned skin, covering muscles so distinct, every swell of his chest and abs is visible through the dirty, sweaty material.

"Need a hand?" he asks and starts to move my way, easily stepping over my broken fence.

He's tall and muscular, so when he moves his body blocks the sun, letting my eyes travel to his face. He's scruffy, to the point I wonder if he's starting to grow a beard. I bet he hasn't shaved in over a week, but underneath the scruff are facial features so rough and masculine, I let my eyes widen to take all of him in.

Standing over me, he extends his long sinewy arm, offering me a big callused hand. "Help up?"

"Uh, sure." I brush gravel and grass off my hands before putting my left in his right.

His big warm hand envelops mine, he gives me a yank and I'm instantly pulled to my feet. Steadying myself and looking up, I'm face to face with the sweaty stranger standing on my land.

His dark brown hair is sticking to him, falling onto his forehead where perspiration's dripping down his temples. I let my eyes travel to his lips. They're full, but frowning. This makes me yank my hand out of his and retreat quickly, pulling myself out of my surprised haze.

"Who are you?" I clip, putting space between us.

He tips his head ever so slightly, narrowing his deep brown eyes, matching the dark themed package he's got going on. They might be dark but what they are is sharp. In fact, now that I've stepped away to take him in all at once, I realize everything about him is razor sharp. His eyes, his expression, even how he holds his body. As much as he's sweating, he's not breathing hard as if he was working out. His breathing is relaxed, like he was lounging on the sofa. He appears to be a bevy of contradictions—aloof yet alert, tense yet relaxed, detached yet discerning. Everything about him is simple, but still, he's exceptionally complex.

I'm jerked out of my contemplation when his full lips form the words, "Your neighbor."

Oh, thank goodness. I let out a breath of relief. I don't care if he is tall, dark, and gorgeous, he's a tad scary looking. Plus, I feel like he snuck up on me. I'm glad to know he's my neighbor and not a creepy trespasser.

The tension leaves my body. "Sorry, you startled me. I didn't even hear you. You bought Mr. McCray's farm?"

Without taking his eyes off me, he simply answers, "Yeah."

"Okay, now I feel bad," I exclaim. "I knew it sold. Mr. McCray used to come over often. We even had a little going away thing for him in the tasting room. I knew he moved to be closer to his daughter, but I didn't know the new owner was in yet. Mr. McCray said the buyer would be doing some modifications before officially taking possession. I should've come over to introduce myself."

"No problem," he utters without a change in facial expression.

"Addy," I offer, stepping forward and extending my hand. "Addy Wentworth."

He offers me his big right hand again. When it folds around mine, engulfing me tightly, my breath catches.

"Vega," his deep voice informs me. Then he keeps on and strangely adds, "Crew."

I step back and frown. "Excuse me?"

"Crew. Crew Vega."

I frown deeper. "That's your name?"

Still no change in facial expression. "Yeah."

"Oh, sorry. That's just a little," I pause, raising my eyebrows. "Unusual."

"I know." He finally offers me a set of new words, but alas, not a new facial expression.

"Well," I breathe, finding him difficult to converse with. "Welcome to the neighborhood. I'm pretty new, as well, I've lived here a little over a year. I own the vineyard. Have you met the Kanes?"

He shakes his head. "Nope."

"They're great." Motioning in back of me, I blather on. "They own the horse farm across the highway. They have three kids, all teenagers. They seem okay, the teenagers, that is. Not that we would hear rowdy teenagers here with all this land around us. I'm still getting used to living in the country. What do you do?"

Finally, he raises his eyebrows. Not much of a facial shift, but at least I know he's alive when he answers, "Government contractor."

"Huh," I huff. "You and every other person around here. Everyone works for the government."

"They're a big employer." He strings a group of words together—more proof of brain activity.

"They are," I agree. "Do you drink wine?"

"Only to be polite. When I'm forced to be polite."

This makes me smile. "I was that way, too, until I bought a winery, of course. Now I love it. You should come by the tasting room—I'll give you the neighborly discount. One hundred percent off. All the neighbors love it and use it regularly."

"Free?" He reverts back to simple words.

"There's no money in wine tastings. My Buy-a-Barrel program, yes. The Wine Club, sure. Wedding receptions and private parties, absolutely. But a wine tasting? I barely break even. Plus, I hardly have any neighbors, so it's not a big deal," I explain.

"Thanks, but no."

Before I have a chance to talk him into it, I hear, "Moo," coming from afar.

I look toward my neighbor's property and here comes Harry, slow as a snail stuck in peanut butter.

"Moo!" Scarlet answers, bellowing from behind me.

"You raise cows?"

"What?" I ask distracted, as Scarlett starts to crowd me again. I try to push her back as I explain, "Well, I have cows, I don't raise them. They were cows when I got them."

"I meant raise to butcher."

"What? No, of course not." I frown. "Why would I do that?"

"You a vegetarian? Why else would you have cows?"

"I'm not a vegetarian, but I'd never butcher them. They came with the property and I guess I've come to like them. By the way, sorry about the fence. I'll try and get Morris out here today to do something about it."

He ignores my comment about the fence and frowns back. "They're pets?"

"No, they're not pets." I glare at him. "They came with the vineyard. I have forty acres of vines, forty of pasture and the other ten make up the farmhouse, tasting room, and other buildings, but they're scattered amongst the pasture. A dog is a pet, a cat is a pet. A cow is not a pet."

"Moo," Harry calls as she slowly steps over the broken fence to join us. The second she does, she comes straight to Scarlett and me, joining the crowd.

I give the little black mark on her white forehead a scratch and scold her, "You need to stay on this side of the fence, Harry."

"Harry?" I hear and look back over to my neighbor.

"Yes," I sigh, because someone else is about to give me shit for naming the cows. When I started walking with them, I had to name them. "This one's Harry because of the birthmark since it looks like Harry Potter's scar."

Crew's expression finally cracks, even if it is by only a touch. His eyes turning from sharp to amused. "You do know cows are females, right?"

I stand up straight and immediately become defensive. I'm tired of people mocking me about the cows.

"I know cows are girls. Do I look like an idiot? Look at her face," I say and point to Harry, the sweetest of them all. They're Black Baldies, all black with white heads, but Harry has a sweet little birthmark on her forehead. The minute I saw her the first time, she reminded me of Harry Potter. She's been Harry ever since.

+"See? Harry Potter. This is Scarlett, she's loud and obnoxious. I have Jax, Maria, and Jimmy, but they're off doing what cows are supposed to do—grazing."

Crew Vega moves, even if it is slightly, tipping his head and crossing his arms. A smirk spreads across his scruffy face, and as if out of nowhere, a dimple appears. Smack dab on his left cheek. A dimple. Proof there's soft under the sharp. Hell if that dimple isn't the hottest thing I've ever seen, even if it is covered in scruff, sweat, dirt, and hidden under a sharp toughness.

"Jax, Maria, and Jimmy?" the dimple asks.

I look up to his deep dark eyes, now creased because of his dimpled grin. "Well...yeah. I named them after my favorite characters. Besides Harry, I've got Scarlett O'Hara, Jax Teller, Maria von Trapp, and Jimmy Fallon."

His head tips the other way. "Jimmy Fallon's a person, not a character."

"I know, but he's funny," I spout.

He nods, letting his arms fall, probably tired of talking about my cows, but agrees. "True."

Okay, moving on.

"Sorry about the fence." I try to change the topic of conversation. "Like I said, I'll try and get my property manager to take a look at it today. I don't want Harry wandering onto your property again."

"We share the fence. I don't have a property manager, all I have is me and I'm busy. Send me a bill for half, we'll share the cost."

"It's really okay. I'm the one with the cows—you don't have a reason to fix the fence."

"It's both of our responsibilities," he keeps on.

"Yes, but you just moved in. I really don't mind."

"Send me a bill for half," he insists.

I sigh. "Well, it probably won't be much. Just consider it a 'welcome to the neighborhood' gift."

"Addison," he bites out, getting my attention because no one calls me Addison. Not even my mom when she was alive. And more specifically, I didn't introduce myself as Addison. "Send the bill."

I frown and cross my arms. "Fine, I'll send you a bill. Now that I'm thinking it through, I'm sure it'll be astronomical. At least what I've spent on molasses cubes for the cows in the past year. They really like their molasses."

He shakes his head with a half-smirk. "If it means I don't have to play fetch with your pet cows when they wander onto my property, I'll pay it."

Tired of talking about my cows, I decide I've stood here long enough. I've got purchases to process, bills to pay, and ordering to finish. I don't have time to stand here and argue about the cost of the fence with my new neighbor. I was only trying to be nice.

"If you decide to be neighborly, come for a tasting. If not, maybe I'll see you around, but I don't like being snuck up on, so don't do that again." I start to move out from between Scarlett and Harry. The instant I do, Scarlett crowds me but I have to make kissy noises to get Harry to follow.

"Send the bill," his deep voice demands.

"Don't hold your breath," I yell without looking back.

Marching off in my rain boots, I swipe the hair away from my face. It's only then do I realize during the whole encounter with my new neighbor, I'm not only wearing rain boots, but cut off shorts and my old UCLA Track and Field t-shirt I acquired years ago. And holy shit, I'm make-up free and my hair's a mess. Not my finest first impression, but we can't all look great covered in sweat and dirt.

What kind of name is Crew, anyway? I'm sure it's a stupid nickname his buddies bequeathed upon him.

"Come on, girls," I call for the cows. "I need to get Morris on that fence right away. I don't need our new neighbor complaining about you."

Chapter Two

The Country Life

Addy

"Why didn't I think of this sooner? We should have a grape-stomping station!" she says to her fiancé.

"What?" He looks at her like she's crazy and I would agree.

"Of course, can you imagine the pictures we'll get? It'll be priceless. We'll make the society page of The Post with grape stomping, for sure." Her eyes go dreamy, probably imagining herself plastered all over the District's society pages.

"Honey, people are going to be dressed up. No one's gonna want to stomp grapes in formal wear."

"Yes they will. They'll be drunk from the open bar and wine tasting. They won't care about their clothes."

"You're gonna stomp grapes in your dress?" he asks, exasperated.

"Why not? It's not like I'll ever wear it again." She looks over to me with a determined face. "I want the grapes in a trough, a big metal one. Like what your cows drink out of. Oh, we can put your cows in the background for pictures! None of my friends have had grape stomping at their weddings. I'll be one of a kind."

I look across the large coffee table at the engaged couple and mask my frustration. Our planning meeting has gone forty-five minutes over schedule, even with the extra time I allowed because I know from past meetings, she's high maintenance.

A grape-stomping station at a wedding reception?

And how am I supposed to get the cows to pose for pictures?

"Well," I start, putting a smile on my face as I search for patience. "We do have an annual grape stomping event every year after harvest, but I've never thought to add it to our reception package. We do like to keep things organic here at Whitetail Farms. I can certainly price that out for you."

"Price doesn't matter!" she shrieks with excitement, clapping her hands.

"Hannah," her fiancé scolds her.

"What? It doesn't. Daddy said to do what I wanted and I want to stomp grapes." She frowns at him before looking back to me. "Now, when shall I set up a meeting with the caterer?"

Hoping we're finally done, I pull up the calendar on my phone to set up our next exhausting meeting. The reception is planned for October. I'm counting down the days like a child at Christmas and cannot wait for it to be over.

After scheduling a meeting with the caterer—allotting twice the time necessary for such an appointment—I stand, needing to end the misery I've been forced to sit through in the basement inglenook. I make a note to meet in my office where the chairs are hard and uncomfortable, not to mention, it's downright ugly in there. The inglenook is comfy, inviting customers to stay for hours by the big huge fireplace, sunken deep into the lush sofa and chairs. I want people to be comfortable when they've just purchased a bottle, enjoying it over a delicious lunch. I have no desire to make Hannah Brown-soon-to-be-Hatfield any more comfortable than need be.

"This is going to be better than I ever dreamed," she delights. Reaching over, she threads her arm through mine, linking elbows as we walk to the stairs and make our way up to the main tasting room. "All my friends are doing it up huge, hosting their receptions at the Kennedy Center or International Trade Center. They'll all be copycat versions of one another. I can't tell you how happy I am we decided to go medium, you know, intimate. Large is so last year. A smaller wedding will make getting an invitation from us downright prestigious, and out here in the country? It'll be perfect—I'll be the talk for absolutely ages."

"We're just happy you chose us for your big day," I say with a forced voice and smile.

After more shallow pleasantries, Bradley Hatfield, III, drags his soon-to-be wife out the front door and toward the parking lot. I wonder what that marriage will look like in ten years, if it's still around at all. I've only lived here a year, but with a Washington elite offspring marrying another Washington elite offspring, it's anyone's guess. What I do know is having a Washington elite wedding reception at Whitetail is going to be great for business.

"Addy?" I hear my name yelled from across the room.

I turn and see Clara coming slowly as she has to make her way through the mingling guests. She looks frustrated since she never moves slowly doing anything. She's tiny, even five months pregnant. I've learned the farther along she gets, the grumpier she is.

She and her husband already have three boys, and they might be cute to look at, but they're little monsters. This pregnancy was an accident and she's not happy. She's less happy with her husband, who's over-the-top happy, because he wants a girl. She swears he impregnated her in her sleep. Routinely, she threatens him with murder in all kinds of creative forms, explaining the only reason she doesn't follow through is because she'd be stuck with four hellions to raise on her own. And just to piss him off, she refuses to find out the sex.

Clara Robertson has been with me since right after I bought the place. My turn-the-vineyard-around strategy centers solely on bringing events to the property. There's space in the basement and tasting room as well as the gardens and patios. If they don't mind the humidity—which I've learned locals don't—I can host large events outside in the spring, summer, and fall. With the views and scenery, it's a perfect locale for anything from a wedding reception to a business meeting to an organized girls-night-out. There's nothing we won't host and just like Hannah's grape-stomping station, we'll make anything happen for a client.

But to pull it off well, I needed help. Clara hadn't worked in years as she stayed home with her three little hellions. When the youngest started kindergarten, she wanted out of the house and after spending time around her kids, who can blame her? She practically begged me for the job, explaining she'd work the part-time position whenever I needed her—any day, any time.

She went on and on about how she needed an escape from runny noses and play dates and science projects. How she wanted to be an adult again, needing a reason to get up to fix her hair in the mornings and wear something that needed to be ironed, or maybe even dry cleaned. Finally, she explained how her husband landed a new job, allowing him to telecommute and keep his own hours. Her eyes then went a little whacky when she expounded, "It's his turn. He needs to build the next exploding volcano and endure the perfect moms at the bus stop, and possibly, clean a fucking toilet. And when you're surrounded by penises—it's not a fun job. I need these twenty hours a week to keep my sanity like I need my next breath. I don't care what you pay me. To be honest, I'll pay you. You have to let me work here for twenty hours a week, please!"

What could I do? She sounded so desperate, I put the three prior boring applicants out of my mind and cancelled the rest of the interviews. I hired her on the spot. It didn't hurt that before having hellions she worked as an event coordinator at the W Hotel in DC. As much as I've come to love my little winery, I'm no W. I knew I was lucky to find her.

She jumped across the table and tackled me with a huge hug, promising me she'd start the next day. She's proven to be the perfect choice, bringing in all kinds of events, and creating repeat business. I know I can be a control freak—I have a hand in all facets of the winery and still like to manage certain events myself, like the Hatfield wedding. But she handles a majority of it and we both kick in to help the other when needed.

When she finally gets to me, she rustles the bunch of papers in her hand while smiling, her shoulder length blonde hair swaying about. "I got it—it's done. The crazy horse-baby-making convention signed. It's going to be bigger than expected—almost double!"

I smile back. "They're the Eastern Horse Breeders Association. Quit calling our clients crazy, Clara. Just because you're a breeding association all on your own doesn't make everyone crazy like you."

"Shut up," she scoffs with a grin. "This is great. We were competing against two bigger venues. I'm pretty sure your neighbors helped seal the deal, but whatever. I'll take it."

"The Kanes are great. I'll send over a couple bottles to thank them. Do you need help with your event tonight?"

"Nope, I'm good. It's a client appreciation thing—easy. Evan will help me set up in a couple hours." She starts to rub her belly and goes on. "I've got to eat before I do anything else. I really need a burger, but I guess I'll have to make due with a Maggie sandwich."

Before I could ask to join her since I'm starving myself, I hear Evan call from behind the bar, "Addy!"

I glance over and he's pouring wine, but when I catch his eyes, his move to the front door. I cringe when I see what he's looking at.

"Hot damn, I can't believe he has the balls to come back. You've officially turned him down three times," Clara says from beside me.

I look to her and frown, thinking the same thing. I've turned down all his offers—each with more ferocity than the last. This has been going on for months. I'm over being polite. It doesn't matter how much he sweetens the deal, and each deal he brings to the table is pretty damn sweet. At this point it doesn't matter, he's starting to creep me out. I'm going to have to insist he stay off my property.

When I look back to Tobin DeCann, he tips his head to greet me from across the busy tasting room, and even that pisses me off. I hand Clara the Hatfield file and say in a low voice, "Do me a favor and call Morris. He's probably out in the meadow looking at the fence. Tell him DeCann is here and I want him shown off the property."

It doesn't matter how small Clara is or that she's waddling around pregnant, she crosses her arms and glares at Tobin while hissing, "I'll tell him to leave. He's an asshole sitting on piles of money who thinks he can wave it around and people will suck his tiny dick."

"Clara," I bite out. "Call Morris. Now."

"You want me to get Van? He's in the barrel room," she offers slyly.

"Are you kidding me? He'd make more of a scene than you."

She rolls her eyes. "Fine. I'll call Morris."

I turn back to the front door and square my shoulders, preparing mentally for the task ahead. I'm all of a sudden grateful for my exhausting meeting with the Hatfields to-be, I dressed up today and I rarely dress up. Even though it's a simple fitted cream dress hitting me at the knees, it'll do its job and act as my shield.

He's stopped right inside the front door. A show of power— waiting for me to make the first move. Damn him, this is my establishment. I'm the one who turned this business around. I'm operating in the black and started making money six months after I took over. I don't need the likes of Tobin DeCann walking through my front door making a power play.

Doing my best to make my face devoid of emotion, I walk in my spiked peek-a-boo blush heels, silently applauding myself. Not only do I pull off a look of pure boredom, but my shoes give me a boost, bringing me eye-to-eye with him. I'm standing at five-nine, maybe five-ten, and have to fight the urge to cross my arms. Crossing your arms is a sign of self-protection and I'm aiming for indifference.

When I arrive, I allow an acceptable amount of space required for a business greeting, but decide to say nothing. Instead, I tip my head and raise an eyebrow in question.

There. Silent, disinterested communication. Take that and shove it up your pretentious ass, Tobin-Fucking-DeCann.

A slow smile spreads across his arrogant face and his eyes travel the length of me. I couldn't care less and allow him the time to rake his light, sandy-brown eyes over my shield. If it wouldn't crack my defenses, I'd roll my eyes, but it would, so I don't. I remain perfectly bored, waiting on him to break the ice.

When he raises his eyes to mine, he also brings up a hand to greet me, but not in the manner a business associate would. Extending his hand, palm up, he clearly doesn't wish to shake mine. He wishes to kiss it.

I persevere, tipping my head the opposite way and raise both brows this time, not accepting his gesture.

His smile shrinks to a smirk as he runs his bereft hand through his floppy, dirty-blond hair.

"You're looking lovelier than your normal lovely today, Addy," he purrs.

It's plain weird for a man to purr.

"Lots of meetings," I blandly inform.

His eyes move around the room as he slowly nods his head in approval. "Business is booming, I see. I'm more impressed every time I visit."

"I'm pleased with the state of my company." I meet his pretentious with my own brand of pompous.

"You continue to astonish me, Addy. Not only is your business prowess exceedingly shrewd, but you've created an environment at Whitetail that is warm and inviting. Certainly you can think outside the box. If you've achieved all this in such a short time with limited funds, think of what you could do with a silent partner." He waves his male-manicured hand around to accentuate his point.

"Tobin, it's sad your recollection is starting to fade." My voice feigns sadness. "I do believe you should have that checked straight away. I'll do you the favor of jogging your memory—I've no interest in a partner, silent or otherwise. I learned from the best and I know silent partners don't always remain silent. Profits are exceeding my business plan. I'm pleased, my loan officer is pleased, and I could care less what anyone else thinks. My staff is hardworking and goal-oriented. I'm more than good with the state of my balance sheet. I'm thrilled."

"Your staff is incompetent," he accuses.

"I find my staff overly-proficient in their responsibilities," I defend.

"I have a new proposition for you. It would behoove you to consider it."

"No," I return. "It would behoove me to get back to work. My schedule is tight and my time precious. You're wasting it."

"Addy," his voice lowers, as if he's trying to calm me. He takes a step, closing the acceptable personal space between us, altering it from business to intimate. "This doesn't have to be so formal. Let's discuss it over dinner. Say, Claire's On The Depot? Clams on the half shell this time of year come from close to home, very fresh. Her She-

Crab soup is the best around."

And he does it again, but this time his intentions are more obvious than the last few. I hold my ground, fighting the impulse to retreat.

Just as I was about to refuse him, yet again, I hear from beside me, "Time to go, DeCann."

I look to my side at my big, burly knight. He's dirty, I smell the outside mixed with sweat, and he's probably traipsed mud through the tasting room. Normally that would set me on fire, but not today. If it wasn't an inappropriate moment, I'd reach up and kiss him.

Instead, I smile. "Hi, Morris. Fix the fence?"

Even if he is my knight, he still frowns. "Not yet. Gotta shop for supplies. Should be done in the next couple days."

"Harry's going to get out again," I point out.

"She'll come back, always does," he goes on, both of us ignoring the headache in front of us.

I look away from Morris and Tobin because the big wooden front door opens. The visitor is wearing an ugly, yellow polo shirt with the name of a courier company embroidered on the pocket.

"Can I help you?" I ask, since he doesn't look interested in wine or hosting a reception of any sorts.

"I have a delivery for Addison Wentworth," he says, holding a small envelope.

"That's me." I quickly sign for my delivery, only to watch him leave as fast as he entered.

"Addy," DeCann calls for my attention. "Have dinner with me."

I slide my finger under the flap of my envelope. "No."

"Time for you to go," Morris repeats, moving toward him.

"I'll stay for a tasting. You can look at the numbers," he insists at the same time my eyes bug out at the contents of my envelope.

"The nerve," I mutter, looking at a check written out to me for ten-thousand dollars.

"The only thing you're gonna be tastin' is gravel if I have to throw your ass outta here, DeCann," Morris threatens him like I knew he would.

"Addy—" Tobin tries again.

Between Tobin DeCann hitting on me and trying to weasel his way into my business—not to mention the ridiculous check in my hand—I've lost it.

"Don't come back," I snap, looking him straight in the eye. "I'm tired of this. I'm not interested in you or your money. Stay off my property." I don't wait for him to answer. I turn on my spiked heel and say to Morris over my shoulder, "Make sure he's gone. I have to visit my new neighbor."

Crew

I make my way from the largest of the outbuildings where I'm working on the plumbing. Everything's installed but the showers. I should be ready for the first round of recruits soon, Asa and Grady are working on a list for me to approve.

My phone alerts me, the cameras have picked her up on the surveillance system. This is a good test—Asa just got it up and working a few days ago. He's making adjustments, animals kept setting it off the first night. The system is intelligent enough to decipher between a deer and a human. Her Audi Q7 is easy to pick up. The system is more impressive than I thought—tracking and focusing in on the driver. I see the frown set in her deep brown eyes, but unlike yesterday morning when she was wearing her absurd boots and cut-offs, she's done herself up.

I don't know what I expected, although I did expect something. I have to give it to her, she's quick. The courier picked up the check less than an hour ago.

I round the corner and stand at the base of the porch that spans the front of my old farmhouse and wait. I hear tires on the gravel before I see her make the bend. She looks even more frustrated in person than she did over the cameras. I let my face crack into a small smile, because for some reason, I find the woman interesting.

She finally comes to a stop five feet in front of me. After throwing it in park and switching off the engine, her door is thrown open and a sexy as fuck pink shoe appears on the gravel. Then another, and when I look up, she's rounding her door before flinging it shut. Because of the sexy as fuck shoes, she's taller than she was yesterday and her hair is down, but now in the afternoon sun, hints of red shine through. As hot as she was in her university raggedy t-shirt and cut-offs, she's leaving nothing to my imagination in that dress with every curve on display.

"Mr. Vega—" she starts, but I interrupt.

"No need for formalities. You can call me Crew."

She tips her head. "Yes, I was surprised to see your check signed as 'Crew.'"

"Why?" I frown.

"Because it's not a real name. I assumed it was a call name, like something given to a fighter pilot or some sort of preposterous nickname your man buddies gave you," she spouts, waving my check toward me.

I let my brows raise. "My man buddies?"

"Whatever. Your friends, fraternity brothers, brethren, whatever support system you have," she huffs.

"I didn't lie. Told you it's my name and it is." I cross my arms, looking down at her.

"Okay, *Crew,*" she enunciates, her voice laced with frustration. "I explained to you yesterday, the fence isn't a big deal. I also told you it wouldn't be expensive. Further, I told you I need to keep my cows on my property so I'd take care of it. It won't even be close to this amount, let alone double if we were to split it. I can't accept this."

"I added some for labor."

"I told you I didn't want anything," she exhales.

"That's unacceptable."

Her eyes go big. "Unacceptable?"

"That's what I said."

She shakes her head, exasperated. "You can't make me take your money."

"Sure I can." I shrug back.

"What?" she yelps.

"I'll find a way."

"What the hell," she mutters, turning away from me and to the side. Now I get to admire her curves from a different view. I widen my stance, settling in for however long this takes as she keeps talking to herself. Finally, both arms flop to her side as she keeps on. "This is insane. Everyone wants to give me money. What are the odds? And on the same day."

I break in and point out, "You're gonna ruin those shoes, stomping around in the gravel like that."

That did it. She instantly turns to me frowning. Bringing her hands up in front of her, she dramatically rips my check—once, twice and so on, before tossing it in the air between us like confetti.

"The fence is on me. I'm not taking your money, let alone ten-thousand dollars," she huffs before turning to stomp through the gravel back to her car.

"We'll see," I call back.

She huffs one more time.

"Addison," I call as she reaches for her door. When she turns, I drag my eyes up from her ass to her eyes. "Nice dress."

Now I've pissed her off because she hitches a foot, putting a hand to her curvy hip. "No one calls me Addison. It's 'Addy.'"

That surprises me. I expected the dress comment to piss her off, not her name.

I give her a half grin, repeating, "We'll see."

That pisses her off more. She gives me a good glare before gracefully getting back in her car. I decide to stand here and watch her leave as she makes a quick U-turn, her Audi disappearing into the trees.

I instantly feel my phone vibrate in my pocket. When I see who it is, I greet him. "Grady."

"Fuck me, who was that?" he belts in my ear.

Then I do something for the first time in so long, I can't remember the last time I've done it. I smile big, and hell, I like the way it feels.

As I stand here in my gravel drive, watching the dust settle from Addison Wentworth throwing a fit as she drove off, I can't remember the last time I was this entertained. It's definitely been years since I've enjoyed anything as much as that.

I turn, making my way back to the outbuilding to finish the showers and drawl, "Just getting to know the neighbors, Grady. I think I might just like the country life."

Chapter Three

You Don't Look Like an Addy

Crew

"I don't like him," Asa declares.

"What the hell's wrong with this one?" Grady complains.

"You're shitting me, right? Did you read his background? What he's been through, what he lost? We don't need anyone with a vendetta. It creates emotion and emotion's your enemy. Did I teach you nothing?"

"That was a long time ago. Everything else checks out, Asa. He's solid, dedicated, and a loner, which is even better. He won't have to adjust."

"You'd know about that," Asa mutters to Grady. "Some days I still can't believe you made it through training. You were too fucking anxious for this job—I had you pegged as not surviving the second day of training. How you made it all these years, I have no idea."

I watch Grady shake his head at Asa before looking out the window of the downstairs bedroom I turned into a makeshift office. I dread it, but it looks like I need to go shopping for furniture. Leaning back in my folding chair, I study the last background Asa and Grady are arguing over. I'm used to them bickering, but today they've both made valid points. As valid as their opinions are, I'm sick of listening to them.

"This guy's outperformed top SEALs. The timing is right on both ends. We miss this window—we'll never get another shot at him. Not everyone's carrying around a fury of retribution, Asa," Grady chides. "Look at Crew. He could've and didn't."

"Enough." I toss the papers on the rickety card table I found in the basement with a bunch of other shit the previous owner left behind. I'm done. I don't need this conversation directed back at a younger me. "He's in. We'll see if his intensity works. If we think it'll get him killed, we'll cut him loose. That's ten, they won't all accept, maybe we'll get five. If two make it through to the end, we'll have a fucking tea party to celebrate. Get the communications started. If it's all a go, we'll start within two weeks."

Asa grumbles and stalks out, but Grady stays. He's leaning against the wall with his arms crossed, looking back out the window saying nothing. I stack all the recruit profiles together and when I move to stuff them in a file folder, I hear him mumble, "Sorry about that."

"About what?" I ask even though I know.

"Shouldn't have compared him to you," he sighs, not looking away from the window.

"Not a big deal. We'll see if this kid works out. He's too qualified to overlook him." I toss the file on the ever growing pile of papers and decide to order furniture today. There's no time to go shopping and I need something with a drawer, not to mention a real chair. "You good out there? The air working okay?"

"Yeah, I guess I need some furniture," he huffs my thoughts. Finally looking away from the window, he looks irritated. "I sleep on the bed, eat on the bed and work on the bed. I should get a chair. Maybe I'll go big and get a sofa."

I agree. "It sucks going from needing nothing for ten years to needing everything. I need a desk. I'm gonna take care of that today. Get some shit done before they get here."

"Well, Mr. Homemaker, if you start decorating do me a favor and rip this shit off the walls. These flowers are gonna make you grow a vagina. If you show up with a desk organizer with highlighters and shit, I'll know you've turned into a woman."

I barely look up to respond. "I'll paint the walls black if that'll make you sleep better."

"Black is good." He finally moves to leave. "I've got recruits to approach and a sofa to buy. Can I bring you anything besides black paint?"

"I'm good," I call and look up to the walls around me. He's right. I'm not sure how much longer I can look at this wallpaper. Maybe ripping it down will be punishment for the last man in.

Just as I'm wondering how creative I can get with the recruits, I hear Grady yelling through the house, "Crew, get out here!"

I make my way through the back hall and living room to the wide entryway. My front door is open and Grady is standing on my porch with his arms crossed, his back to me and facing outside. Before I have a chance to ask him what he's yelling about, I hear a low, "Moo."

When I walk out the door to stand next to Grady, he looks over at me and states, "It's a cow."

I narrow my eyes mumbling, "No shit."

Looking back at my neighbor's pet, I cross my own arms wondering how I'm going to get her home.

"You didn't tell me there'd be a cow," he accuses, irritated.

"Kiss my ass, man. It's not my cow."

"You know," Grady starts and his voice goes conversational as we both look at our visitor. "When you talked me into retiring with you, taking on this shit and moving to Virginia, you knew there was no way I'd turn you down. Working together all those years, you knew I couldn't say no, even if I wasn't ready to quit. But fuck, you sure didn't tell me we'd be livin' in the sticks where I couldn't get myself a furnished place to live. Now I'm on my way to buy furniture—and I don't even know where to go lookin' for furniture—for the glorified barn you've put me in. Don't get me started about having to drive a fucking age to find a restaurant. I've been eating cereal and microwave dinners for weeks—I'm fucking hungry. I'm dealing with Asa on a daily basis, face-to-face, not from halfway around the world which was bad enough." He pauses and I hear him move so I look over. He's frowning with one arm extended, pointing to the cow when he finishes, "Now we've got a bovine caller on your doorstep. I think I told you once I'd walk through the depths of hell for you, Crew, but I didn't mean it literally."

"Where'd you think this was gonna happen, in Arlington right next door to the bars and restaurants?" I frown.

He raises his eyebrows. "I didn't know there'd be cows."

As if she's being insulted, her tone turns sharper. "Moooo."

"Holy shit," he mutters.

"She belongs to my neighbor," I explain. "A section of fence is down. I talked to her about it—it should be fixed in a day or two."

"The Audi has a cow?" He's surprised since I know he saw her on the cameras.

"I think she's got a small herd," I mutter as I move down the steps. "Come on, help me get her up in the truck and I'll take her home."

"Now I'm a fucking farmer. What in the hell have I gotten myself into?" He continues talking to himself as I head to my old Ford, hoping she'll cooperate and walk up some boards. I don't have time to walk her back. Before I have a chance to move far, he keeps on, but with a warning. "You don't have time to be fucking around with the beauty queen neighbor. We've got shit to get done and not a lot of time to do it. Your focus needs to be here, Crew. Not in a pair of panties next door."

I stop abruptly, turning on my boot to find him right on my heels. This is good, because he's close when I get in his face. "You don't think I know the importance of the promises I made? The promises I've tied us all to when I made this happen? You think that after ten years I haven't learned that the people I made promises to don't fuck around? If you think I'd drag you and Asa along for the fuckin' fun of it without taking that seriously, then you don't know me. They don't give a shit about you, but I do and it was time. You were on the edge, Grady. I saw it and Asa saw it."

He narrows his eyes at me when he growls, "I was not on the edge."

"You fuckin' were. You can thank me someday when you finally open your eyes and see it for yourself. Until then, I know you'd walk through the depths of hell for me. What you don't know, is I'd do the same for you. Me moving you to the sticks of Virginia means having to deal with your ass until you figure it out." I exhale in a rush and take a step back, watching the anger set in his features and wait. Wait for him to argue, lash out or who knows, maybe open his damn eyes.

He works his jaw but says nothing. Finally, he shakes his head and looks to the side.

I guess today's not that day, so I bite out, "Are you gonna help me with the cow or not?"

His eyes shoot back and he's frustrated. He tips his head angrily as he swings his arm out, telling me to lead the way.

I turn away from him and call for her so we can get this done. "Come on, Harry."

Well, fuck me—Addison's cow is trained because she starts to follow.

That's when I hear Grady's irate scoff, "I don't know what surprises me more—that the cow has a name or you know it. Who in the hell are you and what have you done with Crew Vega?"

As I approach the entrance to Addison Wentworth's property, I see a simple black sign with stark white brush strokes, vaguely outlining a deer. It's modern art at its best. If It didn't say "Whitetail" underneath, I'd never know what it was.

"Moo," Addison's cow drawls in my ear since she's somehow managed to stick her head inside the sliding rear window of my truck.

I turn onto her property between the low-stacked stone border that looks as if it's been around longer than my house. I lean into my door as I creep up the drive looking like a freak show with a cow in the bed of my truck with her head tucked into the cab next to me like a dog. When I finally come up over the last hill, a large building comes into view with acres of vines in the distance. It must be the business since there's a parking lot that's mostly full. This is surprising since it's barely noon on a Saturday.

Beyond the business, there's a big-ass farmhouse. It's three stories and painted white with a one story red brick extension. Her property is all vines and wooded pasture. Farther out into the field is a barn with a silo, but the silo isn't one anymore since it has a tree growing out the top. From the top of the property, the view goes forever.

I don't bother parking and pull up to the front door. There's an older woman watering plants and lots of customers sitting at tables with wine and food. By the looks and stares I'm getting, it's confirmed that Addison's cow and I are the freak show I thought we were.

The older woman turns to me, but her eyes go to the back of my truck and she smiles big. Then I hear her start to cackle before I even open my door. When I get out, she looks me up and down, and for some reason starts to laugh even harder and louder.

I decide to wait for her to settle, watching the tall, graying woman hug her middle. Finally, she sets her watering can on the ground while wiping her eyes. Putting her hands on her hips, her breath is ragged from hysteria as she strangely says, "You're in trouble."

I cross my arms and frown. "Pardon?"

"I'm talking about Addy's Harry. You give her a lick of attention—she'll love you forever." She smiles.

Not finding anything funny, I try to move this on. "Is Addison here? Her cow was at my door step. I need to get back to work."

"Addison?" She seems surprised.

"Yes," I keep on. "Addison Wentworth? I believe she owns this place?"

She instantly sobers. "Wait, you're the new neighbor?"

"Yeah. Now about Addison—"

She smiles again. "You should stay for a glass."

"Thanks, but no. I'm busy. If she's not here, is there someone else who can take the cow?"

She ignores everything I've said. "I'm Beverly Shaw. You can call me Bev, everyone does. My husband, Morris, is the caretaker."

"Bev, good to meet you. Now," I sigh and try one more time. "What should I do with the cow?"

"You sure you don't want a glass? It's free for all the neighbors, and it wasn't always free for the neighbors—that's just been since Addy bought the place. Smart move, it's all word of mouth. That's how she sells the barrels and all that goes with it. I'm pretty sure it started with the neighbors playing 'keep up with the Joneses' with all their friends. Whatever it takes to keep me in wine, right?" She tips her head, finally stopping to take a much needed breath. She was rambling so much I was beginning to worry she'd pass out over the flowers.

"I guess." I bite my tongue and ignore her verbal barrage as I move to the back of the truck. If I have to leave the cow on the front door of her winery, I will. Pulling the tailgate, I grab the wide boards I had to bring to get her in the truck and slide them to the edge, making a ramp.

"Moooo." She stares me down, making it clear who's boss.

Shit. There's no other option, I'm gonna have to talk to her again. I cannot believe I'm talking to a cow.

"Come on," I call for her.

She doesn't budge.

"Harry," I call her by name.

This time, she steps back.

"It's scarier going down than up," Bev points out and when I look to her, she's still smiling.

I call to the cow three more times, and as cooperative as she was at my house, she's downright obstinate now.

"Maybe I should get Addy," Bev suggests, as if it were her idea.

I look to her and deadpan, "I'd appreciate it."

She disappears inside the building. Meanwhile, as I have a standoff with a cow, I realize everyone drinking wine is watching the show. I cross my arms and drop my head, looking at my boots. While I do this, I contemplate me driving a cow around in the back of my truck for a woman I've barely exchanged words with.

Grady is right. Who in the hell am I?

Addy

"Addy?"

"Hmm?" I hum without looking up from my screen.

I've got a huge meeting tomorrow. Massive. It could put my little Virginia winery on the big stage and I need to be prepared.

"Sweetie, our handsome new neighbor is here. He had to bring back poor Harry, she wandered. I think she likes him." I look up to see Bev peeking her head inside my office. "He's having a bit of trouble getting her out of his truck. I invited him to stay for a glass, but he said he had to work, which I don't understand. It's Saturday."

Pushing my chair back, I get up quickly. "She's in his truck?"

"Yes." She smiles as I move by her and rush through the back hall and toward the tasting room. "She's skittish and making quite a scene. I do find the whole thing funny."

She would find it funny.

When I push my way out the big heavy front door, I stop immediately. Pulled up right to the steps of the deep porch, where many guests are enjoying the late morning before the heat sets in, is a truck with my cow standing in the bed. The truck is old, like rusted, paint chipped, and missing some trim, old. My guess, it's been around for well over thirty years because the white is worn and there's a faded turquoise blue stripe running down the side. I'm sure this particular shade of turquoise hasn't been put on a vehicle for decades, and for good reason.

Harry greets me. "Moo."

I ignore her, allowing my eyes to wander, and there he is—my neighbor, leaning against the fender over the rear tire. His arms and legs are crossed. His arms, thick and powerful, are straining against his old white t-shirt. And he's in a pair of jeans that look as old as the truck my cow is standing in, fitting him perfectly, bunched at the bottom over a pair of work boots.

"You know," I hear, pulling me out of my stupor. When I glance up, I notice his hair is clean today but he still hasn't shaved. This is the third day in a row I've seen him—his beard is thicker, but I'd still categorize it as scruff. He's wearing a pair of aviators in the morning sun, so I can't see his dark eyes. From the tone of his voice and facial expression, I imagine those shades hide the sharpness he's proven to exhibit, inconsistent with his relaxed stance. Without moving a muscle, he goes on, "Never thought I'd find myself with a cow in my truck. Tried to make sure that didn't happen by helping to pay for the fence."

I bite my lip and raise my brows apologetically. "It, um, should be fixed tomorrow."

As if I didn't say anything, he adds, "You threw that in my face."

"It was too much." I frown.

This time his brows rise. "I don't like owing people."

"I'm sorry," I say in a way he can clearly tell I'm not. "I don't enjoy being indebted, either, and I would've been had I accepted your excessive gesture."

"My excessive gesture," he repeats.

"Yes, Crew. It was outrageous."

"Outrageous," he echoes.

I tip my head the other way. "Why do you keep repeating me?"

"Because," he pauses, jutting his thumb over his shoulder. "This is outrageous."

I roll my eyes and sigh. He's right. It is embarrassing he had to bring Harry home.

"Molasses," I hear and turn to see Bev smiling. "She'll come down for molasses."

"Of course, why didn't I think of that?" I look back to Crew. "Do you mind driving her down to the barn? I'm sure she'll come down for a treat."

"Why wouldn't she come for a treat, don't all pets?" he drawls and pushes off the truck. When he does, he extends his arm for me and keeps on sarcastically. "By all means, let's go get her a treat."

"Come back for a glass," Bev calls and when I look over, she's as happy as ever, waving at Crew. He simply shakes his head.

I hesitantly move off the porch and down the steps as he bends to pick up a board, sliding it into the bed of the truck. Slamming the tailgate, he follows me to the passenger side and when I push the ancient button on the handle to open the door, he moves in behind me to open it. I climb in to sit on the long, vinyl bench seat. My body jerks as he slams my rickety door closed, with what seems like all his might.

When he climbs in the driver's seat next to me, he's controlled, yet appears calmly put-out by the entire ordeal and I realize I feel smaller in his presence. The past two days when I've seen him, we've been outside in the wide open yonder. But here, in his rattley old truck, he seems larger and there's something about him that makes my stomach do a flip-flop, and not in a bad way, even with his underlying frustration over Harry.

"I'm sorry you have to deal with all this," I offer, looking out the windshield as we bounce along the gravel drive to my barn.

I hear him breathe in deep before responding on an exhale. "Don't worry about it."

"And I'm sorry about the check—even though it was exorbitant and I'd never accept it. I was in the middle of an exasperating moment when it was delivered. I could have declined more graciously."

We arrive, the trip to the barn being a short drive down the valley, and he puts the truck in park. Instead of getting out, he turns in his seat toward me. "Like I said, it's okay."

I finally relax and give in to a genuine smile before moving to open my door.

"Addison," he calls. When I turn back to look at him, he pulls off his aviators, his deep dark eyes are serious. "Just so you know—I'll find a way to pay you back for the fence. When I do, you won't rip it up and throw it in my face."

I scowl, ignoring his determination to pay me back. "Why do you insist on calling me Addison? No one has ever called me Addison. Ever. It's Addy."

He frowns in contemplation, his eyes moving over me but not as though he's checking me out, making me feel uncomfortable. Rather, he's thinking. Finally, tipping his head the other way, he says in a low voice as though he's talking to himself, "I don't know. For some reason you don't look like an 'Addy,' and I like the way 'Addison' sounds when I say it."

My body stills as I stare back at him.

I don't look like an Addy?

Not having the same paralysis issue, he moves from his truck, slamming the door. I stay where I am listening to him bang around in the back to deal with Harry.

Then, I realize I like the way it sounds when he calls me Addison. I like how his full lips move when his deep voice rumbles my name more than I should. So much so, I think maybe I need to stay far away from my new neighbor. Because me not looking like an Addy? That's too much. I don't know what to do with that.

Feeling my stomach flip in a whole different way, I take a deep breath and try to focus on what to do next.

I need molasses. I need to get Harry out of Crew's truck. Then I need to get back to work and get ready for tomorrow. And now more than ever, I need to get away from Crew. I slowly move to open my door, trying to focus on anything besides the fact he doesn't think I look like an Addy.

I head straight to the barn for molasses and decide my next task is to make sure the fence is fixed today. No way is Harry wandering onto Crew Vega's property again. Since he doesn't like wine, there's no reason for me to see him, let alone call me Addison.

Chapter Four

This Changes Everything

Crew

Stepping out of the shower, I barely have the chance to grab a towel as I try to get to my phone. All messages are important, but this text tone is different.

Dripping as I move across the room, I slide my finger over the message and my insides clench.

Rhonda – Don't forget to take out the trash.

Fuck.

Toweling myself off, I rush back to my room, dig through a drawer and pull out a never used prepaid cell. I punch in the number and grab some clothes so I can dress as I talk.

"Vega?" Carson bites out.

"What's happening?" Looking out my window, I hold the phone

between my ear and shoulder as I pull up my boxers. It's Sunday, Asa and Grady are gone. Grady should be in California by now and Asa's in El Paso, both approaching recruits.

"Fuck. I waited too long." He's breathless, speaking in a rush. "Got a high-level target we've been on for almost a year. Never thought he'd be comin' your way when he started driving west from Falls Church. No ties to you, but man, he's gettin' close and I have no fuckin' idea why. I thought it was a coincidence and he'd veer off, but he's not. He's a mile away from your camp."

I hurry and yank on my pants. "Who is it?"

"Shit," he hisses. "You know I can't say."

I stop for a split second before yelling, "You got a target coming at me and you're not gonna tell me who the fuck it is?"

"Damn it, three-quarters of a mile. He hasn't turned off," Carson growls.

I pull the phone away from my ear to tug a shirt over my head. "You've got two seconds to tell me who it is. You don't, I'll have your head."

"Fucking-A," he mutters. "Name's Sheldon O'Rourke. He's with the Department of Defense. We've had reason to track him for a year now. He's less than a quarter mile out, you ready?"

I pull up the security cameras on my phone and move to the safe in my closet. Swirling the combination, I quickly swing the door open and reach for two guns. I check both, making sure they're loaded and holster my compact backup to my ankle, sliding a forty-cal into the back of my pants.

"He alone? How many cars?" I ask.

"He's got a staffer with him, a guy named Marc Whittaker. Someone we've been lookin' at recently but don't know if he's connected. One car, a blue BMW crossover. It's only the two of 'em. He's approaching your entrance—I just switched to your cameras. I'll keep an eye on you. You want me to call for backup?"

I grab my other phone and jog down the stairs, watching the security feed on the screen. "I don't see them yet."

"Holy shit," he exhales, relieved. "He passed your entrance. He's not comin' for you. What are the fucking odds? He's turning into the next drive."

I'd barely relaxed a second. "The winery? What would he be doing there?"

"How should I know? It doesn't surprise me he'd be a wine drinker after watchin' him for a year. He's got a stick up his ass, an arrogant dickhead on top of everything else." Carson still sounds relieved.

Not feeling any relief at the moment, I demand, "Why's he a target?"

"You know I can't tell you. You're not a contractor anymore. I've given you too much as it is, but fuck, that was intense. I know Asa and Grady are gone."

"Carson, I'm goin' over there. Give me a background."

"You're not goin' over there. This guy's into some deep shit. You don't want him seeing your face." He's agitated again, ordering me to stand down, which he can't fucking do.

"You got a target anywhere near my camp, you better believe I'm checking it out. I'm going whether you give me a background or not." I run a hand through my wet hair to straighten it before I leave.

"You stay put, Vega. That's an order."

"Fuck your order. I'm retired."

I hear him huff into the phone and after a few moments he begrudgingly relents. "Fine. I'll send his mug to this line. I better not eat shit over this."

For the next ninety seconds, he gives me an overview of the Army Lieutenant Colonel who's visiting my neighbor's winery. When he's done, he asks, "What're you gonna do?"

I look out the back of my house toward Addison Wentworth's

property and think for two seconds before making an easy decision. "I'm gonna find out why he's there. Hopefully it's to taste the wine and be on his way, nothing more than a coincidence."

Not giving him a chance to respond, I end the call that's lasted too long, even on a prepaid line. Going to my kitchen, I pull out a trash bag and after taking a quick look at the surveillance photo of the target, toss the phone in. I bang through four drawers until finding what I need. Laying the trash bag on the counter with nothing but the phone inside, I take the hammer and decimate it with one hit. After tagging my keys, I toss the bag in the trash and stalk out my backdoor.

I can't believe I'm doing this, but I'm going to a wine tasting.

This place must always be busy. I had to park on the lane and double-time it up the hill. I'm pretty sure O'Rourke only beat me by five, maybe ten minutes, tops.

Opening the heavy door, I move inside. Quickly scanning the room, I instantly clock Addison. She's sitting at a far table on the perimeter, and hell if she isn't with two men. I look the other way before letting my eyes wander, as if I'm trying to decide where to settle. I glance back as someone places a bottle on their table with two wine glasses and a water. When the guy in a sports jacket looks up, I confirm he's the target. Different from his surveillance picture, he's smiling instead of scowling. Still, there's no doubt, it's him.

He thanks the server before returning his attention to Addison, like he's studying every feature of her face. It's only because I'm a practiced hand that I don't let my emotion show.

But that fucking pisses me off.

I choose a spot at the bar with his back to me. When I get there, a younger guy moves away from two couples to greet me. "Welcome to Whitetail."

I nod at the kid working at a bar.

He can't be much past twenty. His shaggy, sandy blond hair is a mess and he's dressed like a rich frat boy on his way to a Polo match. Since I can read people well, I know he's not full of shit when he asks, "How's your Sunday?"

I have a constant reminder of how my Sunday is going with the forty-cal pressed into my back. "Good, thanks."

He lifts his chin and reaches under the counter producing a dark brown leather portfolio, laying it in front of me. "What can I get you?"

I scan through the list of wines, five on each page with detailed descriptions under each. I have no idea what any of them are. Looking up, I see O'Rourke in the distance, deep in conversation with Addison.

"Surprise me," I say to the kid.

"You like reds or whites?"

My focus is on Addison, watching her speak, controlling the conversation. She's doing this with small gestures, nothing exaggerated or overdone. But the way she uses her body when she talks, any man would gladly sit for hours listening to her just for the privilege of watching her move.

"No preference," I answer.

"I knew he'd come back for a glass." I turn to see Bev walking up to the bar. Before I know it, she's settled herself on a stool next to where I'm standing. She explains to the kid, "This is our new neighbor, Evan. He gets the neighborly discount. His name is *Crew*." She looks to me. "I do like your name. Addy told me when she got back from getting Harry settled yesterday. It's one of a kind and quite masculine. I've decided it fits you."

I smirk at Bev the same time Addison pulls out a folder printed with her logo. She takes a sip of water as O'Rourke and his buddy pour themselves another glass of wine. Picking up her pen, she starts pointing at the papers when her other hand comes up. Then, as if my brain switched to slow motion, I watch her lightly swipe a piece of her thick dark hair out of her face, tucking it behind her ear. She looks across the table, her dark brown eyes lit with happiness as every feature on her fair-skinned face comes to life with a smile.

Fuck.

Damn if I don't feel that in my dick at the same time my chest seizes. When the muscles ripple up my back, I have to clench my jaw to overcome it. This strange sensation is foreign, something I've never experienced. I can appreciate a hot woman, but my entire body seizing? I'm fighting the urge to charge across the room to get her away from him, when I don't even know why he's here.

I pull my eyes away from her when the other man, probably around my age, leans back in his chair, swirling the wine in his glass. Hell if his eyes aren't glued to her and not the papers she's pointing at.

"Welcome to the neighborhood." Evan offers me a hand over the bar and I accept. "How about a tasting? See what you like."

"Sounds good."

"I'd like my usual," Bev orders before turning back to me. "I like reds, but only one glass a day. I read it's good for my heart and if I had more, I'd be a wino since I live on a winery. Now tell me, Crew, what do you do that you had to work on a Saturday?"

I hear Addison laugh from across the room, but I tear my eyes away and focus on Bev. I give her my fake occupation that no one in their right mind would find interesting. "Government contractor. I work for the Treasury as a programmer. Databases, some accounting programs."

"Oh," Bev responds with a frown. "That does sound tedious. What brings you all the way out here?"

"I'm able to telecommute. Grew up in the country, thought I wanted something different. I eventually got a job that was mostly travel. In the end, I got tired of the rat-race and decided I wanted to settle with some space. It's been good to be back in the fresh air." I tell her a half-truth as I watch Addison start to point out a window. I realize she's motioning toward the acres of vines as she speaks.

"All of our whites are aged in stainless steel drums," Evan starts as he places a glass in front of me. "This allows for greater temperature control during the fermentation process. It's favorable for lighter flavors, allowing the winemaker to retain the fruitiness and crisp taste desired in whites. First up is our Petit Manseng. It's the only grape we grow here at Whitetail. Their loose cluster and thick skins are well suited for the Virginia climate. We sell our grapes to other vineyards all over the region, and in turn, purchase to make the rest of our wines. Did you know our vines are the oldest in the state?" he asks as he pours a small amount in my glass.

"Nope."

Diverting my eyes back to Addison, my body instantly tightens as O'Rourke slides his chair, closing the distance between them, and leaning in to read whatever they're talking about. I find myself wanting to throw my glass across the room, but instead, pick it up and toss back the contents, barely tasting whatever it was he poured me.

"Um…" Evan stutters, frowning. "What, eh, do you think?"

"It's good," I say in a low voice and see the two men watch her carefully while Addison busily takes notes, O'Rourke still too fucking close. But he'd be too close if he was in the north forty.

"Crew," Bev whispers, leaning into me. "You're supposed to swirl it first, maybe even smell it."

I say nothing, but nod and realize I'm going to have to play along.

"Maybe you tasted the smooth lingering finish of citrus and ripe honeydew?" Evan asks.

I narrow my eyes as if to think and pause before offering, "Sorry. How about you tell me beforehand next time, that way I'll know to look for it."

I down three more samples and agreed that I tasted a mixture of white peaches, orange oil, guava and even fucking lemongrass. I also lied about noticing a hint of minerality, whatever in the hell that meant. During this time, Addison, O'Rourke, and the other guy continue their deep discussion.

"I think you're going to like this one." Evan moves on to the last of the whites. "Addy named it The Delaney, after her mom. It's a mix, or more appropriately, a blend of our whites. Our winemaker, Van Barrett, won Best in Show for this particular year by the Women of Mount Vernon. The group is partial to Whitetail because of the Ordinary."

"Ordinary?" I ask, distracted because Addison and the men move to get up as she collects her papers. The men grab their wine glasses and I see them all head toward the French doors off the back of the building, overlooking the vineyard.

"Ordinaries." Bev stresses the word. "They were scattered amongst the colonies. There were Ordinaries and there were Taverns. An Ordinary didn't serve alcohol, just a meal and a place to lay your head, for a price, of course. A Tavern was a bar. We all find it ironic a property that once housed an Ordinary is now a vineyard."

"This was an Ordinary?" I look at Evan, trying to maintain casual conversation while keeping an eye on Addison, but they've moved outside. If she goes farther, I'll have to make an excuse to break away. Not that anything would happen in front of all these people, but no way am I letting her out of my sight with him.

"No, not this building," Evan explains. "Addy's house. The brick portion was the Ordinary. Her house was added on in three different additions over four centuries. The Women of Mount Vernon are partial to Whitetail because George Washington is on record to have stopped over at Addy's Ordinary when he was in his early twenties. That's the main reason it's on the National Register. Plus, women like wine."

"You should come to poker night," Bev declares, slapping my arm.

I don't even know what poker night is, but there's no way I'm going.

"Yeah," Evan agrees. "Whitetail's closed on Mondays and every Monday is poker night in the Ordinary. It's not really haunted, but it's fun to freak Addy out."

"Haunted?" I ask as Addison walks down the steps from the stone patio, almost disappearing from my view.

"Yes," Bev insists seriously, at the same time Evan shakes his head disagreeing, "Of course not."

"It is, Evan. You haven't been here long enough. The past few owners have had," she pauses to widen her eyes at me, "*incidents.*"

Addison walks back up the patio and stops to shake their hands. O'Rourke holds hers longer than necessary, cupping both their hands with his other. They finally say goodbye and she waits while they walk around the outside of the building, disappearing out of sight.

I can't take my eyes off Addison. Fuck. As Bev and Evan argue on about ghostly incidents, I watch a smile creep over her features. A real smile, not even like yesterday in my truck when I had her close. Not only does she smile, but she fucking glows, her entire being radiating joy. I see it ripen by the second. The woman is beautiful, there's no doubt, but seeing her like this? It's like nothing else I've ever witnessed.

Then she shocks me. She throws her head back, flinging her arms in the air and while still holding her files, she lets out a high pitched, "Yaaay!"

"What on Earth?" Bev turns toward Addison's outburst.

She jumps, letting out a "whoop-whoop" before yanking open the French doors and yelling through the big room, "Ask me what just happened!"

Everyone in the building quiets and looks at her, but she's so excited, she doesn't care. It's Evan who finally gives and yells back across the room, "What just happened?"

"Who's not just a little winery anymore, huh? I don't need a slimy silent partner to make things happen. This is gonna put us on the map. The big-time-Virginia-winery map. Guess who's getting a big break?" she sings. Throwing her arms out dramatically, she goes on. "Huge break!"

"Us?" Bev asks.

"Yes!" She starts to move, looking around the room. "A glass on the house. Unless of course you're a designated driver. Then we'll get you a little coupon or something, you can come back and make your friend drive so you can have a glass on the house, too. We're celebrating—a glass for everyone!"

The room comes to life and when she finally gets to us, she stops abruptly. Seeing me breaks into her excitement.

"What are you doing here?" Her brows instantly furrow.

"Just drinkin' some wine," I casually respond, greeting her.

"He changed his mind about the tasting," Bev explains. "Now tell us, what's so great that you're celebrating by giving away wine?"

She huffs a breath before giving her head a little shake and focuses on Evan and Bev. "Do you know who that was?"

I do, but I'm not answering that question.

"Sheldon O'Rourke. He's some, I can't remember...Lieutenant-General-Colonel," she waves her hand around, "something-or-other from the Army. He's with the Defense Department and the other guy is sort of an assistant-Lieutenant-helper-lower-level person. Whatever. His name is Marc Whittaker. Anyway, there's going to be a dinner next week honoring disabled Vets who've given back and helped newly disabled Vets. I'm not even quite sure who all is invited, but it's a big deal. I guess they're doing a locally-grown, farm-to-table dinner. Everything on the menu will be from Virginia. They picked Whitetail for the wine. And do you know why it's such a big deal?"

"I bet you're going to tell us." Sarcasm leaks from Evans's voice.

"It's at the White House!" she screams.

"No," Bev breathes.

"Yes!" Addison yells.

"No!" Bev yells back.

"Yes!" Addison holds her arms out where Bev catches her in a big hug. "And guess what else?"

"There's more?" Bev pushes her back to look at her.

"I get to go, too!" She gives Bev a little shake to reiterate her excitement. "To the White House. And eat dinner. And watch my wine being served to big important people, even though I don't know who they are. Sheldon said he was going to pull some strings to get me on the list."

"I can't believe it." Bev mirrors her happiness.

"Me either." She smiles. "The dinner's on Thursday. I asked why they picked us on such short notice and he said another vineyard backed out, lack of supply or something. He liked that we have the oldest vines in the state and he really liked that we're on the National Register. You guys freaked me out about the Ordinary, but now I love it."

Bev turns serious. "It's haunted."

"Hush up," Addison quips, grinning, not allowing Bev to ruin her mood. "He said it's a smaller dinner—considering it's at the White House—around a hundred guests. It doesn't sound small to me, but who am I to know what kind of dinners they have at the White House. The dress is semi-formal—I need to go shopping."

As I watch her go on and on about the details of her news, I wonder what in the hell Sheldon O'Rourke and all he's into has to do with Addison Wentworth. I get it could be a fluke, but watching him with her, I doubt it is. Experience is telling me it's more, and whatever it is, can't be good. Because with the shit he's into, nothing he does can be good.

With all that's not good about O'Rourke and maybe Whittaker, I make a decision. Like so many of my decisions in work and life, it comes fast and it comes easy. Also, as soon as it comes, I believe in it wholly and know instinctively, it's spot on.

"I'm goin' to that dinner."

They all stop and turn to me, but I only have eyes for Addison when hers get big, looking right up at me, surprised. "You are?"

"Yep."

"Why?" she asks, frowning.

"I'm representing my company. We support the troops."

"Well..." she searches for words, her face etched with suspicion as she tips her head. "That's a coincidence. An uncanny coincidence, don't you think?"

I'd say so.

"Maybe." I give my shoulder a shrug.

"You can carpool," Bev announces from my side. When I look over, she goes on. "Addy always gets lost in the city. Takes her twice as long as it should to get anywhere. We won't worry about her if she's with you."

"No, no," Addison breaks in, frowning. "I can manage on my own. It's the White House. There's no way I won't be able to find the White House."

"A carpool. Sounds good to me." Needing to make my exit, I lightly slap my hand on the bar. "Evan, good to meet you. If you all don't mind, I'll finish the reds another day. Or better yet, at the White House. I've got wallpaper to strip. Addison, thanks for the wine."

Addison opens her mouth, probably to reject me again or tell me not to call her Addison, but Bev cuts her off as I walk away, "Come back soon!"

I give her a small wave on my way out and I swear I hear Addison say, "Would you stop?"

I push the door open while reaching for my cell. After finding his number and listening to it ring twice, Asa answers. "I've got one confirmed and one no-go."

I ignore him and demand, "What kind of background did you do on my neighbor?"

I hear silence before he finally answers. "A background."

"Damn it, I'm not talking parking tickets. I needed a fucking background. Did I get full clearance or did I get parking tickets?"

"I gave you what they gave me. You should've gotten more than parking tickets," he replies with an edge to his voice.

"Shit," I bite out. "She had a visitor. Someone we wouldn't want visiting us and, you know what I mean. I want her background. A complete fucking background, you get me? But first, call Rhonda and get filled in about what went down today. I want to know what our visitor has to do with my neighbor. I want a full fucking biography, I'm pissed this is the second time I've had to ask for it. I'd better not get something between jaywalking and a voting record."

"I gave you what they gave me," he reiterates.

"Well then you'd better have a talk with your friends and make sure they know the position we're in. From now on, if we don't get what we're asking for, we're out. They won't lay claim to us if shit goes bad, and we need to make sure shit doesn't go bad. We can't do that when someone's bein' a gatekeeper." I climb in my truck and turn it on before I add, "The full fucking biography, Asa. I'd better have it in my hands by tomorrow morning."

He sighs and I can tell he's as frustrated as me. "I'll be back at camp late tonight. We'll talk more and I'll make those calls now."

I'm pulling out of her property when I finish. "There's a dinner at the White House on Thursday night. I need to be on that guest list. When you talk to Rhonda, make that happen."

"What in the hell for? You of all people don't need to be showin' your face at the White House. Surely there's someone there who'll remember you. What happened to flying under the radar?" Now he's irritated with me, and rightly so. I did want to fly under the radar and this won't help.

"I'll explain tonight. Just make it happen."

Not giving him a chance to bitch more, I hang up. Damn it, I hate it when Asa's right. But there's something about Addison that makes me not give a shit. I shake my head at myself, because I know for a fact, this changes everything.

Chapter Five

Laffy Taffy

Crew

Standing in my kitchen, I toss her background—her real and complete background—to the counter. It's just Asa and me—Grady's still in California. Looking across the room at him, I cross my arms and sigh.

"Sorry. They said they thought they were giving you enough. They had no idea there'd be ties this old and deep—they know they fucked up. I know you're angry and I know this would've made you move on," he tries to calm me.

Would I have moved on?

That's a good question. I shake my head and look out at the dark of night. I don't answer because what I'm more concerned about right now is what's churning in my gut. I wonder how well I know myself, because for some fucking reason, I'm not angry. I'm relieved I didn't get the chance to make that decision.

I shouldn't be relieved. I should be pissed this has been laid at my feet and I wasn't given the truth from the beginning. I should not be feeling what I'm feeling, wanting to be nowhere but right here. I shouldn't be fucking grateful for half-truths and decisions that were ripped out from under me.

This complicates things, making what was supposed to be a private and safe compound, neither. When I settled on this place, her bio was her bio, even if I was given everything. At the time she didn't have a ghost from the past interested in her wine as a cover for what he's really interested in.

"She was five," Asa adds. "She must not have known him, surely she'd remember."

"They just flushed him out after all these years? Carson said they suspect this has been a career-long thing for him. He must be good."

"Must be. The guy's older than me. They're finding more as they build their case. He's been at it a long-ass time."

My mind goes back to this afternoon—him looking at her, casually touching her, studying her. Why in the fuck after all these years does he have an interest? Not only that, he must have his own level of clearance to even be able to find her.

What the hell? He doesn't need clearance. With what he's been doing the past twenty-five years, he'll find a way if he wants something bad enough.

Then, all of a sudden I think about him creating access to her in one of the safest buildings in the world. My head snaps up and I ask through a frown, "You get me into the dinner Thursday?"

Asa ignores my question and huffs, "You're a crazy motherfucker. I told Grady you had your head on straight—there was no need to worry about you chasin' tail."

I say nothing but glare at him. It's none of their fucking business and Addison Wentworth isn't a piece of tail. I'm running this show and don't owe anyone an explanation for anything I do.

"You have no business walkin' into your old place of employment ten years after disappearing off the face of the Earth—not when everyone there all but adopted you after what happened. You show your face, you're invitin' a mess of people back into your life."

He's right.

My gut told me this afternoon O'Rourke being there wasn't a fluke, even before I knew about Addison's past. Now that I know the truth, there's no way in hell Addison Wentworth is going to be in Sheldon O'Rourke's company without me by her side. Until the big guys get their shit together and take him out, I'm the only one who knows the connection that gives a shit.

"You get me in or not?"

Asa narrows his eyes at me and shakes his head. "I thought Carson was going to have a shit hemorrhage, but yeah, you're in."

I give him nothing else on that subject before demanding, "I want the cameras and sensors extended to her property and I want it started tonight. I don't care how many bodies it takes to get that done. By tomorrow morning I want eyes on her house, work your way out from there. It should be easy since they can maneuver their way over from here and it's only ninety acres. Between that and Carson's wiretaps, she'll be covered, even with the public coming and going from her business. I'll be there tomorrow night, there'll be some activity around her house, but you should be able to get it done. No one'll be the wiser."

"What's gonna be your excuse to be there tomorrow night?"

"Tomorrow's Monday, Asa," I say before starting my way out of the kitchen. Without looking back, I add, "It's poker night in the Ordinary."

Addy

I shouldn't have spent the entire day shopping. I have bids to get out for upcoming events and marketing material from my advertising agency to approve. I plan on using this White House dinner to pimp my little winery through the next century. I don't care what side of the political spectrum you're on, if my wine is good enough for the White House, everyone under the sun is going to know about it. It's going to be a marketing extravaganza.

But I didn't do any of that. Instead, I spent the entire day at the mall, driving all the way to Tyson's Corner. I only got lost twice when I missed my exits. All in all, that's a good day for me. I had to buy a dress, shoes, jewelry, and just because, I splurged on all kinds of new makeup when I didn't need any. Since I was there and it is Tyson's Corner—and everyone knows Tyson's has anything you could ever want in a mall—I did a tad more shopping than my White House dinner required. This included casual and dressy clothes for work, clothes for lounging, panties, bras, more shoes, and I even made a haul at Pottery Barn. Even though I have everything from my condo and my mom's house in California, it doesn't come close to filling up my huge farmhouse. But since I'm always busy with the winery and working most days, decorating hasn't been a priority. To say I took advantage of a day at the mall was an understatement.

And I missed my mom every single moment.

We shopped like queens my entire life, even when I was young when we _did not_ live like queens since we had nothing and my mom was starting from scratch. It didn't matter how little we had, even during the many trips where we bought nothing, there was always fun to be had with my mom at the mall.

But then again, she was simply fun in everything she did. Until she got sick, and as much as she tried for me, nothing was fun anymore.

Running up the two flights of stairs, I hurry to dump my bags on the bed and hang my dress. Just like always, by the time I get to the second staircase, I wonder what in the world I was thinking choosing the top floor bedroom when I moved in. However, between all the many staircases in this house and hiking around with the cows most days, there's no need for a gym membership. Not that there's a decent gym out here in the country, nor do I have the time to go to one, so it's good I have my own built-in Stairmaster. Not to mention, this is the best room in the whole house. I don't know this for a fact, but the way my house is situated on top of my mountain, one might be able to see way to West Virginia on a clear day. The windows were replaced during one of the more recent renovations. They're huge and I have a perfect northwest view. Even if this room wasn't the best in the house, which it is, the closet is a shrine to closets everywhere. There was no other option—this had to be my room.

I look at the clock and realize I'm late. Traffic was a bitch coming out of the city and everyone will be here in fifteen minutes for poker. Well, everyone but Clara and Maggie. Clara has a hard time finding a sitter given her boys' behavior and Maggie just plain hates card games.

I quickly move around the room, changing clothes into something comfortable to sit in all night. After throwing on a pair of lightweight yoga pants with a cami and loose tank, I hightail it back down to the kitchen. I knew I wouldn't have time to whip up any snacks, so I stopped at Maggiano's for pasta and dessert. I'm sure I walked miles at the mall and skipped lunch. I'm famished.

"Yoo-hoo, we're here," Bev sings from the back door where she lets herself in like normal.

Making it down the last few stairs, I turn the corner around the last bend into the kitchen where I find Bev and Morris making themselves at home. Morris has already cracked open a beer and Bev is plugging in a tiny crockpot.

"You two have a good day?" I ask.

"Great day, although I had to go back to the grocery store. Morrie decided he wanted lil' smokies late this afternoon. I'd only planned on bringing cookies," Bev says, stirring the contents of the crock.

"I should've called." I move to the oven where I put the pasta to keep warm. "I stopped to get dinner and dessert. You didn't need to bake cookies."

"Good," Morris gruffs. "We'll take 'em home. More cookies for us. She never makes cookies anymore."

"We're not taking them home, Morrie. Someone will want a cookie," she says, slapping him with her hot pad.

Morris grumbles, stalking out of the room at the same time the back door bangs open. Evan strides in with a soft-sided wine cooler thrown over his shoulder while carrying his poker table top and suitcase of clay chips.

Van's on his heels and announces, "Don't be a hater, but I've gotta cash out early. I'm telling you now so no one bitches when I do. I've got a date and there's no way I'm playing quarter poker with you all when I've got a woman waiting."

Evan doesn't stop, heading straight through the kitchen and down the hall to the Ordinary when he yells over his shoulder, "Why did you even come? It's bullshit to cash out early."

"This isn't a private table in Vegas. Get over it," Van yells back and drops his cooler looking at me. "Slice some limes, sweetheart. I'm mixing up Moscow mules. That smells good, what'd you make?"

"I've been out all day but had time to stop at Maggiano's. Pasta and dessert, I didn't think anyone would eat a salad." I pull the foil off the pasta and grab plates.

Van moves to my fridge and kisses the top of my head on his way. I'm used to this by now. At first it was strange, his demonstrative behavior, seeing as I'm his employer. But it's who he is and after a year and a half, I love him for it. He goes on as he pulls bottles and copper mugs out of his cooler. "You can't go wrong with Maggiano's. Good call on the salad, it'd go to waste."

"Who's the lucky young lady tonight?" Bev asks, as everyone is used to Van's parade of women. He's been at Whitetail for over ten years and it surprises me Bev is as accepting of his social life as she is, but even she isn't immune to his charms.

"Just another in a long line of lucky ladies. If it works out, maybe I'll bring her by soon. We'll see how tonight goes." He grins.

Before I get a word in, the door bursts open yet again. Mary blows in with her arms full, balancing two dishes covered in plastic wrap and bags hanging from her shoulders. "Hello, peeps. Make way, I'm about to drop this shit."

She pushes her way through Bev and Van to set her stuff on the kitchen table. My kitchen is big, square, and outdated. When I read through the records kept on the property, the last kitchen remodel was done almost three decades ago. It's not terrible, but it won't win any pretty kitchen awards, either. What it's not, is a priority. I put a table in the center which is hardly used to eat at, but it does serve as a makeshift island on poker night.

"Hey, Mary," Evan smiles as he returns to the kitchen with eyes only for her.

"Bite me, fancy boy," she mumbles without looking away from her task, unwrapping a dip and dumping crackers in a bowl.

Mary and I have been friends since the first moment I sat my bottom in her chair at the salon a year ago. I'm not spontaneous, even though I did purchase a winery out of the blue when I was here to spread my mother's ashes. I did this not liking wine or having romantic notions of owning a winery, but recognized it was a good business decision. My mom always taught me the best business is a struggling one run by imbeciles who don't know what they're doing.

She'd say to me, "If you come in with fresh ideas and energy, you'll win most every time."

Last year during my first summer living in the Virginia humidity, I lost it and decided to chop off my long hair. I couldn't deal with the frizz. I figured if it were shoulder length, it'd be easier to manage. My spontaneity took over and I drove to the closest salon I could find, walked in, and demanded a haircut with the first stylist available who could manage a pair of scissors. When I sat in Mary's chair a year ago, her hair was blonde with pink and purple tucked in, here and there. It was long, lush, and hung in soft, colorful curls down her back. How she pulled that off in the humidity, I'll never know.

Mary is everything I'm not, and I adore that about her. She's eight years younger than me, but even at the young age of twenty-three, she doesn't act it. She went to college for a couple years before deciding it wasn't for her, jumped right into cosmetology school and has been doing hair for two years. Mary's petite, but other than that, there's nothing small about her. From her ever changing hair color to her kick ass ink and piercings, she's full of life.

This is opposite of me. I'm boring. I've never highlighted my hair, I have no tattoos, and my ears are pierced. Once. Each. I've always tried to blend in, so I'm okay with boring.

When I told her that day I was sick of fighting the frizz and wanted it all lopped off, she looked at me like I was crazy. She started working her fingers through my hair and without looking away from my frizzies, asked, "Is this your natural color?"

I told her it was and to start chopping. Pronto.

She ignored me and kept fingering through my hair. Finally, she shook her head and questioned me through the mirror. "What's your budget?"

"Why, how much is a haircut?" I was shocked she'd even asked. I know some places can be pricey, but so far no one was giving me a foot-massage or handing me a martini. A haircut normally doesn't require a budget.

"Pay attention," she started and put her hands on my shoulders to lean in, looking at me in the mirror with grave seriousness. "A sister doesn't let another sister make a ginormous mistake. Now, hear me when I say, if I cut these luscious locks of hair, I'd go to Sister Prison for Stylists. This is your God-given color. I have clients who pay hundreds to try to achieve this look. With your dark eyes and the way it falls around your face, I refuse to go to Sister Prison for committing such a crime. I've lived in this humidity all my life—I know what you need. But it'll take a budget that's more than a haircut. Can you afford a couple hundred bucks? Three, tops?"

I could afford that, but what made me pause was what she said about my hair. I've always liked my hair—it's the same as my mom's was when she was younger. As I sat in her chair, the impulse was starting to wear off and I wondered what I was doing.

"I can do three hundred."

"Cool." She smiled before becoming a bundle of energy. "It's gonna take some time, I'll have to work you in around my other appointments. This is what we're gonna do. First up, a Keratin treatment. Then we'll deep condition you. Really, the Keratin is usually conditioner enough, but I'm dying to see how your hair responds to the special treatment we have. It'll shine you right up. And just because you'll be waiting in between my clients and trusting me with this beautiful head of hair without knowing me from boo, I'll throw in a trim for free. Sound fair?"

"Um...sure. I mean, thank you," I said, thinking I was going to lose an afternoon of work, but if I didn't frizz, I'd take it.

"We'll even have lunch together. Fun day," she announced as she pushed a tray on wheels across the room, disappearing into a doorway.

That day we got to know each other over four and a half hours of hair and had lunch from the pizza place next to her salon. I told her all about my mom and moving to Virginia to purchase a winery. Outside of my winery people, she's my only friend. She's become a part of my life and that means she's been adopted into our winery clan.

For some reason she doesn't find Evan cute or charming. For a twenty-four-year-old, I think he's a lot of both. Over the past couple months, we can all tell he's got the hots for her. From the way she treats him, I know for a fact she does not reciprocate his hots. This has made for some interesting poker nights recently, and I think Evan enjoys her attitude because he smiles as he moves to the table where she's standing.

He reaches around and scoops her dip with a chip when he leans in to the side of her face. There, he says softly, talking about her new hair color, "I like the turquoise." She turns to him, narrowing her eyes. He stands over her by a good bit, as he's probably just under six feet tall, making her look up as she glares. His smile turns into a wide grin, and I can see from here, that pisses her off. He holds his ground, saying, "I'll get you a glass. I picked out something new for you to try."

"Be fast about it," she accepts with attitude. "I'm thirsty and I'll need something to get through poker with you."

"All-righty then." My voice comes out chipper-like, breaking up the tense young-love moment. "Time to dish up some dinner so we can get started."

Everyone begins piling their plates full when the doorbell chimes. I set my plate down and walk out of the kitchen wondering who that could be since everyone's here.

I move toward the front door through the long center hall that separates the main floor rooms, running through the middle of the house. When I get there and open my antique door, I freeze.

Crew Vega is standing on my steps. He's holding a six pack of beer in one hand and a grocery sack in the other.

When I look up, his sharp eyes are on me. I'm not sure where else he'd be looking, as I'm the only one standing here, but they seem sharper than before, if that's possible. He's wearing a newer t-shirt and another pair of jeans that are just as old as the ones he had on yesterday. His dark hair looks a little damp like he just got out of the shower, and this makes me wonder what he smells like. Soap, shampoo, cologne, aftershave? No, he wouldn't smell like aftershave since he's still unshaven. I'm not surprised to see the scruff is thicker, and for some reason I'm fascinated by it.

"Addison," he greets me with a tip of his head.

"What are you doing here?" I ask, realizing I asked him that yesterday, too. I know this isn't polite or neighborly, but my goal was to keep my cows away from him so I wouldn't have to see him. And I don't see a stray cow, so I don't understand why he's here.

"Poker."

"Poker?"

"Yeah, poker."

"But…" I pause, not knowing what to say. "How do you know about poker?"

"Bev invited me. I hear it's in your haunted Ordinary." He tips his head the other way and one side of his mouth curves up. "Want to see it for myself. I'm hoping your ghosts don't wander as far as your cows, seein' as we're neighbors."

I stand up straighter and frown. "The Ordinary is *not* haunted."

"We'll see." He moves and I'm forced to step aside, allowing room for him to clear the doorway since he's entered without an invitation.

"Crew—"

He interrupts, holding up the beer in his hand. "Where's the fridge?"

When I don't answer, he gives up and turns, starting down the main hall. Quickly, he saunters straight toward the kitchen and Ordinary, eerily knowing exactly where to go. I sigh and bite my lip.

I want to curse Bev for inviting him to poker, but I don't. Instead, I thank her in my head, because I secretly like Crew in my old farmhouse.

Everyone must be settled because when I catch up with him, he's alone in the kitchen, helping himself to pasta and lil' smokies. Then he sets his plate down and reaches into his plastic grocery sack, pulling out a bag of barbecue potato chips. After ripping it open, I watch him dump a huge pile on top of his pasta and smokies.

I try not to make a face, but yuck. That's disgusting.

Reaching in the sack one more time, he utters, "Brought dessert."

My breath catches with what he tosses on my kitchen table.

"Ghost town this way? I've never met George Washington."

I don't look up from the kitchen table as he leaves, finding his way to the Ordinary without direction. I hear him clomp down the four wooden stairs into my large brick room that's listed on the Historical Register. Everyone greets Crew as I slowly move to the table.

When I get there, I pick up the bag he so casually tossed. More so, I wonder *why* he chose these. Further, I wonder *how* he could have known. I've eaten them my whole life and I still do. There's always a bowl on my desk at the winery and I keep a stash here at home, too. He's never been in my office or my home. And everyone, *everyone*, around me knows not to touch the green apples. They're the only ones I like.

I wish I had it in me to smile. To be giddy. To get all warm and fuzzy the way a woman should when a coincidence occurs with a beautiful but rugged man. I long to be normal, pondering the coincidence of him and my favorite candy, turning it into *everything*, when really, it's probably nothing.

But I've never been able to be that woman, and I never will be.

"Addy! I've got a date, you coming?" Van yells.

I quickly collect myself and rip open the bag, fishing out four green apples. Quickly, like I've done since I've moved here, I read the jokes and make sure they're not about cows. Ever since I purchased Whitetail, I save the cow jokes because they're funnier now that I own cows. No cow jokes, so I grab my plate and Moscow mule. Taking a deep breath, I head to my Ordinary—that *is not* haunted—and do my best to prepare myself for a night of poker with Crew.

I'll think about the Laffy Taffy later. I'm sure it's a happenstance, at best. Everyone likes Laffy Taffy, right? Especially the jokes.

Yes. It's a pure oddity. Nothing more.

Chapter Six

Flush

Addy

"Damn, I can't beat that. You got me."

From behind my mountain of chips, I glare across the table at Crew. It's late and I started scowling at him an hour and a half ago. Before that, I did my best to ignore his presence. Now I'm infuriated, and even though it's quarter poker, I know what he's doing.

Earlier this evening when I joined the rest of the group in the Ordinary, I found Crew in my spot. Everyone knows where I like my chair and place at the table, they know better than to disturb the seating arrangement.

When I saw him sitting in my spot, I informed him of this. "You're in my seat."

He replied with a mouth full of pasta, probably mixed with barbecue chips, "There's an empty seat across the table."

"But I always sit there."

He swallowed his mouthful of food with a swig of beer before refuting, "I'm settled."

Bev leaned into him and murmured under her breath, "She doesn't like change."

That was absolutely not true. I, of all people, have learned how to live with change. "I can do change."

"It's not so much change," Evan butted in. "She's a control freak."

Well that, unfortunately, was true. Still, I had to defend myself. "I can't help that I like what I like. And I've come to like my spot at the poker table."

Crew shrugged his shoulders. "It's just a chair. You'll be fine."

"No. I won't," I protested and started to move around the table.

"Addison," he called for me and when he did, my name glided out soft and smooth from his lips. When I stopped to look up, his eyes weren't sharp like they usually are. They matched his tone and he weirdly gave me a reassuring look when he tips his head toward the empty chair. "Sit down so we can get started."

I would've looked ridiculous had I kept arguing, not to mention his soft tone caught me off guard, so I sat across from my normal seat now occupied by Crew. I did this ill-tempered, wondering silently if Monday night poker will consistently include my new neighbor. The thought made me feel funny, in a good and bad way. There's something about him that makes me nervous, yet I find myself captivated. He's straightforward, but he's not. He is who he is, yet nevertheless, mysterious. What makes me nervous is the feeling he sees too much of me, and that, I do not like.

That's how the evening started. Not only did he show up uninvited—not invited by me anyway—but he grossed me out by mixing chips with pasta, freaked me out with the Laffy Taffy, and stole my poker spot. Once the game commenced and I finally ate something, I settled in, even if it was begrudgingly.

Until I started winning.

Even if the first couple hands were small, I was on a roll. Then I won huge during a game of No Peek. The winnings are always big in No Peek. I was thrilled and forgot all about Crew stealing my seat. I won again...then again...and again. Now, I'm not an idiot and have played poker for years. I knew what was happening, hence my reason for glaring across the table at our new guest.

"What did you have?" I demand after he informed the table he lost again without proving it.

Tossing his cards face down, he leans back. "You beat me—I don't have to show my cards."

"That's the third time you stuck it out to the end and said you lost."

"Thought I could pull it out. You can't win if you don't play, eventually my luck'll change." He starts to pile the cards together as Mary collects my winnings from the center of the table.

"You must really suck at poker," I chide. "Are you sure you've ever played?"

Shuffling the cards, his eyes narrow on me with a stony face. "Of course I've played. Just having an off night."

"I know what you're doing," I accuse.

"What am I doing, Addison?" His voice is sarcastic as he shuffles. He looks to me while handing the deck to Bev, who grins like a loon as she cuts the cards.

"You're paying me back."

He ignores me and starts to deal. "Texas Hold 'Em."

"For the fence," I add.

"Ante up," he keeps on ignoring me, but I don't ante. I sit back and cross my arms. Without taking my eyes off him, I sense Mary ante for me from my ever growing mass of chips.

If he's going to cheat and throw poker, I'll simply refuse to play.

Morris starts and the betting moves around the table. When it gets to me, I refuse to pick up my cards and grump, "I'm out."

"You can't be out." Evan frowns. "You haven't looked at your cards and the flop hasn't been laid."

"She's in," Crew announces and I frown deeper as Mary tosses my chips in to call the bet.

My cards lay unseen as I get back to the point I was trying to make. "You can't pay me back for the fence by throwing poker, Crew."

He calls, burns a card, and lays down the flop. Looking at the table, I see the Ace of diamonds, four of diamonds, and eight of spades. Nothing.

Betting commences.

Morris: I'm out.

Mary: Fifty cents.

Me: I'm out.

Evan: You still haven't looked at your cards.

Me: I don't care. I'm out.

Crew: She's in.

Me: I'm not.

Mary messes with my chips, and before I know it, she sees the bet for me.

Evan: I'm in.

Bev: I'm always in.

And she is. She plays to the end of every hand, no matter her cards. She says it's the law of poker, she'll win more that way—which she doesn't. She always loses.

Crew: I'm in.

Me: Of course you are.

That won me a scruffy grin and a dimple. Damn it.

The turn and the river are dealt, with more betting between each. Mary is out, however she keeps betting for me from my pile of clay while my cards remain face down. Through all this, the four of clubs and six of diamonds are added. A pair of fours show on the table. Abysmal.

The last round of betting ensues—it's down to Bev, Evan, Crew and me. When it gets around to Crew, he of course sees the bet and calls. "Show your cards."

"Straight," Evan announces with a smile.

Laying her cards out, Bev sighs. "I have a pair."

"Everyone has a pair, Bev," Morris scoffs. "There's a pair on the table."

"I was hoping for another four." She shakes her head in defeat.

"Show your cards, Addison," Crew demands.

I look at him, narrowing my eyes and refute, "You first."

"I dealt."

I tip my head the other way. "It's my house."

He says nothing but raises his eyebrows and shrugs as if to say, *that it is*, before flipping his cards over. "Flush."

I look at his cards, and coupled with the ones on the table, he has five diamonds. Finally, I smile. A flush is a decent hand, not at all common, especially without a wild card. Liking how I played this, finally making him show his cards, I realize my chances of winning are slim. Reaching out, I pick up my cards and flip them over in the middle of the table, landing on top of the pile of clay chips.

Then I slump in my chair.

Shit.

"You're on a winning streak!" Bev shrieks, clapping her hands in quick succession.

"What are the odds?" Evan grumbles.

"You thought you were all high and mighty with a straight," Mary gibes Evan.

I look up from the cards and all I see are Crew's deep dark eyes smiling. His lush lips surrounded by scruff tip when he says, "Full house beats a flush. You're having a good night."

He really makes winning not gratifying. At all.

"I'm beat. Time to go, Bevie." Morris pushes his chair back, scratching across my old hardwoods.

"I'll cash everyone out." Evan starts counting chips.

I don't even want to know how much I won. Deciding to ignore them all, I get up carrying dishes and cups on my way. When I get to the kitchen and start loading the dishwasher, Mary appears at my side.

"Who in the hell is that?" she asks under her breath while crowding me at the sink.

"Who?" I don't look away from my task, not wanting to talk about Crew. Especially right now.

She bumps me with the entire side of her body and frowns. "You know who. What's up with you and the new neighbor? He looked as comfortable as George Washington hanging out in the Ordinary and you looked scared of his ghost."

I whip my head to her and snap, "The Ordinary is not haunted. I'm not going to tell you again to quit talking about ghosts and George Washington. I'll ban you from poker."

She rolls her eyes and sounds bored. "Fine. It's not haunted, Georgie isn't floating around your house at night, and all the previous owners' stories are bullshit. Happy?"

"Stop it, Mary. You don't have to sleep here by yourself every night." I jab her with my elbow since my hands are wet from washing dishes.

"Whatever." She flips her long turquoise and blonde locks over her shoulder. "He's into you. Even if it is in a calm and cool way. He couldn't take his eyes off you all night, but how would you know— you spent the whole night ignoring him."

"I didn't ignore him. I'm plenty perturbed at him right now. He's trying to pay me back for fixing the fence that lines our properties. I refused him in the beginning, trying to be neighborly since the fence was rotted when he bought the place. I'm the one with cows—he doesn't have a reason to need a fence. Then he sent me a check, Mary. A ridiculous check for *ten-thousand dollars*."

"Wow." She frowns, her eyes go big.

"Yeah. I ripped it up and tossed it at him on his doorstep, no way am I taking money from him. I might not have been nice about it, but you know I don't like people having a hold on me and that's how it felt. He told me the other day he'd find a way of paying me back, now it's a matter of sheer will. The fence was barely over eight-hundred dollars in materials and Morris works on the property for a salary, there was nothing extra for labor. So you see, the man's infuriating and threw the game to pay me back for the fence."

"But you probably won thirty bucks at most. How's that paying you back for the fence?"

"It just is. I can tell." I slam my rickety dishwasher shut, flipping off the water and decide to leave it at that. It'll freak me out to talk about the Laffy Taffy or how he likes the sound of my full name.

She doesn't have the chance to interrogate me further. Bev comes in the kitchen announcing, "Fifty-two big ones for you. No one ever wins that much." She slaps my money down on the kitchen table before going to her crock pot. Morris goes straight for the cookies, bound and determined to keep them for himself.

"First Van cashes out early, which is bullshit, and then Addy wins twice as much as anyone normally wins. She even did it without looking at her cards," Evan gripes walking through the door with all his poker gear. Stopping to pick up his cooler, his face softens when he turns to Mary. "I'll walk you out."

"I don't need an escort." She puts her hands on her hips. "I'm parked right outside the door. What, is a deer going to get me?"

Evan ignores her and looks at me devilishly. "Probably not a deer, but maybe a ghost."

"Shut your mouth," I snap as Mary laughs out loud.

"Let's go," Morris says with cookies in his hand. "I've got workers coming tomorrow to prune. Gotta get up early."

Morris manages the care of the vines and they require pruning at least once a month. It's a big job and he hires a small group to help. It will take at least the rest of the week to get through all the acres.

Bev kisses me on the cheek. "See you tomorrow."

"Bye," I call as Bev follows Morris out. After more goodbyes, Evan finagles a way to leave with Mary. I shoot her a grin and get an eye roll in return. I'm not quite sure what her hang up is with Evan. Even though they don't look like they'd go together with her edgy, cool look versus his preppy persona, I think they're cute and wish she'd give him a chance. I wonder how I can help make that happen?

I'm snapped out of my matchmaking thoughts when I hear boots clomping up the steps from the Ordinary. I probably should've done something to stall them from leaving because now I'm alone with Crew. When I turn to him, he's carrying bottles and glasses in both hands.

I take the glasses and tip my head toward the other side of the kitchen. "Recycling is in the pantry."

The bottles make a crashing-clanking sound as I finish loading the dirty dishes. It's late and even though I don't have an early morning tomorrow, I've had a long day. I really don't want to be alone with Crew.

Preparing myself to walk him to the door and kick him out as politely as I can after he purposely threw poker all evening, I stop. He's digging through the bag of Laffy Taffy, grabbing a couple. When he steps back, he leans against the counter across the room from me.

Ripping open a banana flavored piece, he tosses the whole thing in his mouth. As he chews, I'm jerked out of my trance to catch the green one he tosses across the kitchen. I nab it out of the air quickly, just in time before it hits me.

Holding it up in my fingers, I frown at him in question.

Through his chewing, he mutters, "Thought you liked the green ones?"

"How do you know that?"

"Pretty easy to see, you've been eating them all night."

"Oh, right." I sigh, grateful that something finally makes sense. I rip open my candy and take a bite.

"What made you buy a vineyard?" he asks out of the blue.

I guess he's not leaving on his own. "I was here to visit almost two years ago. My mom is from this area and when she died, I thought it might be nice to spread her ashes here. My grandparents are buried here and she always talked about how she loved Virginia, even though we never visited. Anyway, when I was driving around the countryside, I happened upon Whitetail. It was for sale and had been for some time. Once I began looking into it, I realized it was a sound investment. Especially at the reduced price."

"What did you do before?"

"I was an assistant manager of a country club. Knowing the restaurant side of things along with managing large events made it easy to transfer that to the winery."

He tips his head to the side and changes the subject drastically. "Your mom died."

I take a breath and nod. "Cancer. Ovarian. It was progressed when they found it. She went through treatments for a while before it took over. At the end, she said she wanted her ashes spread at the shore where we lived in California, but for some reason it didn't seem right. I tried for months to do as she asked, but couldn't bring myself to follow through. One morning I woke up and decided she needed to be here—where she's from. You know the rest, I've been here a little over a year and a half."

"You just picked up and moved?"

"It wasn't that big of a deal, I thought I needed a change after she died. My mom was a real estate agent, and a good one. She purchased a brokerage firm ten years ago. Since I never got into real estate, she sold her firm near the end. That's where I got the money to put down on the winery."

He nods, his eyes narrowing slightly as he continues. "You must have family. What about your dad?"

I feel that down deep like I always do when I think about my dad. But after many years of practice, I hold steady. "My dad left when I was little. I don't have a lot of memories of him."

He looks at me for a second before slowly nodding again. This is far from small talk and getting too personal, it needs to end.

"I'm tired, Crew. I have an early morning," I lie.

He ignores me again. "Why the green ones?"

I sigh and lean back against the sink. "Green apple is my favorite. I don't like the others."

His mouth tips. "Banana's the best."

"Banana is gross. The worst." I wrinkle my nose because it's true.

He instantly smiles.

I cringe. "You would like banana. You eat barbeque chips on top of Maggiano's pasta."

He huffs a low chuckle and looks down to study the wrapper in his hand. Straightening away from the counter, he moves toward me. I try not to let my eyes widen as he approaches, standing straighter as I frown. When he gets to me, I'm forced to look up. He doesn't touch me, but he does put a hand to the sink at my side, leaning in close. *Very* close.

Without taking his eyes off me, he lowers his voice. "What did the boy chip say to the girl chip?"

I read all the jokes. Rather, I read all the jokes on the green apple pieces. I've been reading them for so long, I know a lot of them by heart, but I've never seen that one. Trying to keep my voice steady, I give my shoulders a slight shrug. "I don't know."

I look into his smoldering dark eyes and feel my heart pound.

When he leans in even closer, I feel the plastic of the wrapper lightly scraping my bare arm, giving me goose bumps. I congratulate myself for holding my ground, but I had to work for it. I want to push him away even though I want to touch him. I want to slide out from between him and the sink, yet I want to see how his lips and scruff feel on my face.

The next thing I know, he's holding the wrapper between his index and middle fingers. I lose his eyes when he leans in farther and I get what I wanted. His scruff scratches my cheek when his lips come to my ear, his voice coming out low and rumbly. "Let's dance and I'll dip you."

I whimper on an exhale. Holy shit. He can make a Laffy Taffy joke sound dirty.

He doesn't wait for me to reply and looks into my eyes. "Carpool Thursday. Be ready at five."

"I've decided to drive myself," I try, knowing if he makes me weak with a Laffy Taffy joke, there's no way I can be in the car with him for hours.

He doesn't say a thing, but shakes his head slowly.

"I'll see you there," I go on.

He keeps shaking his head. "Carpool at five. Don't be late."

I'll leave at four-thirty. I'm sure I'll get lost and need the extra time anyway.

"Fine, five o'clock," I lie, pleased with myself for sounding strong.

"Thanks for the poker night, Addison."

"You can't come back if you keep throwing the game. It's not fair."

He says nothing but he does smile, proving he threw the game.

His voice dips and he's so close, I feel it across my face when he promises, "Thursday."

My resolve starts to slip and I have to fight the urge to reach out for him, because right now I want nothing more. Finding it hard to stay in control, I decide it's best not to say anything and simply tip my head as a goodbye.

He pushes off the sink, tossing the wrapper to the counter before turning to leave. When he moves out of my sight, I slump in relief right before the front door slams. Quickly, I grab the wrapper and read the joke again. A joke for kids, that's clean and pure, but when read by Crew Vega, it's not only sexy and hot, but made me want to touch him all over.

I can't help myself. I cross the kitchen to the drawer where I keep my favorite jokes. After opening it, I toss the banana wrapper into a sea of nothing but green.

Chapter Seven

Carpool

Addy

Swiping mascara quickly over my lashes, I finish and screw the tube shut, tossing it on the vanity. It's a quarter to five and I planned on leaving fifteen minutes ago.

My day has been busy. The Hatfields-to-be were back and we met with their caterer. It was a long meeting, once again longer than needed. Between the caterer and me, we moved it along as efficiently as we were allowed, planning the sit-down dinner, table set-ups, and serving staff. Our kitchen should handle it all, as most things will be prepared ahead of time and finished off here.

All this put me behind and I need to get out of here before Crew shows up. The White House starts accepting guests at six-thirty with dinner being served an hour later. With traffic, the normal one-hour drive into the district could easily take two. There's no way I'm carpooling. Especially with Crew.

Giving myself one more look-over before racing out of the house, I say a prayer to the fashion gods that I'm dressed appropriately. I've obviously never been to a dinner at the White House—Sheldon O'Rourke said the dress was semi-formal. That's a fine line when it comes to dresses. I chose to go simple yet sexy. My dress isn't embellished and hits me at the knees—I hope that keeps it from being too formal. But it's fitted, the color of platinum, and the only way I'm able to walk is the slit reaching the middle of my left thigh. The neckline is low, draping into a cowl neck, framing my cleavage more demurely than it would otherwise. It sits on the caps of my shoulders and falls to the middle of my back.

There's nothing simple about my jewelry and shoes, though. I chose a lariat necklace, worn backwards to hang from my neck down the center of my back since it's bare. It's adorned with Swarovski crystals to catch a sparkle in the light. Since I pinned my hair up loosely, I chose long earrings, and my bracelet is wide, taking up at least a third of my forearm. Besides my silver clutch and pencil heels that hook around my ankle, that's it. I'm a shade of silver from head to toe.

But I've got to go, I'm cutting it too close. Grabbing my shoes and clutch, I scurry out my bedroom and down the two flights of stairs. Once I hit the main level, I turn toward the back of the house where the mudroom and garage were added eons ago.

"Yoo-hoo!"

Shit. What's she doing here?

"Addy?" Bev calls.

I stop at the door to the mudroom. I know I could run for it and she wouldn't be the wiser, but my conscience grips me. Bev is sweet and she's come to mean too much. She's a friend, yet a little maternal. No one could ever replace my mom, and Bev has her own family.

She's motherly and grandmotherly. Basically, she's too loving for me to skip out on her.

Turning back, I sigh. "Coming."

She meets me in the middle hall and shrieks, "Look at you!"

With my shoes in one hand and clutch in the other, I swing my arms out. "Do you like it?"

"Oh, you're a beauty," she beams. "You'll represent us splendidly this evening."

I smile, always loving how Bev has so much ownership over the vineyard. She's lived here for eighteen years, longer than anyone has ever owned the place in decades, so she would.

"Thanks, Bev, you're sweet. But I really need to go. I'm going to be late."

"But Crew isn't here yet," she says, a frown playing on her brow. "I came to take your picture."

"My picture?" I frown back.

"Yes. You're going to the White House, Addy. They're going to be featuring wine from our vineyard. A business you've worked hard to turn around in short order. A White House function isn't a common occurrence. You'll want to remember it forever so I'm going to take your picture," she explains, frustrated I even asked.

"Bev, I'm late."

"Crew's not here," she repeats.

"The carpool was cancelled," I quickly inform, because as the moments tick by, she'll soon find out the carpool was absolutely not cancelled.

She puts her hands to her hips and frowns deeper. "You're going to get lost."

"I'll be fine," I sigh and turn, looking for my escape.

"Addy!" she calls out for me at the same time the damn doorbell chimes. Shit. "Stop right there, I haven't taken your picture. Let me get the door."

I exhale and turn in surrender. Still standing barefoot and holding my shoes by the straps, I close my eyes cursing myself for not doing a better job escaping.

"You did come," I hear and pull in a deep breath before Bev keeps going. "Addy said the carpool was cancelled."

I look up and there he is. I'd say he doesn't look anything like himself, but he does. I've only ever seen him scruffy, sweaty, dirty, or at his best, in a clean t-shirt and worn jeans. And in all these states, he's been nothing short of gorgeous, sexy, and all man in every way he could be.

But now?

Now.

Standing on my doorstep, he's in all black. His single breasted black suit was molded to fit his body perfectly. He's a big guy, but it doesn't look too fitted or like a tent on his large frame. It's absolutely flawless. A black tie layered over his black dress shirt does all kinds of amazing things—making his dark eyes darker, his hair lusher, and skin even more rugged, if it's even possible.

And for the first time, I see him clean shaven.

"She did, did she?"

His voice pulls me out of my preoccupation of all that is him.

"You shaved." It pops out of my mouth before I know what I'm saying. In all honesty, I'm disappointed. As good as he looks—and he looks *really* good—I think I prefer the scruff.

Ignoring me, his eyes are again sharp and narrowed a bit, not at all happy to learn I was trying to give him the slip.

"There must've been a misunderstanding," Bev, ever so positive in everything, declares. "But now you're both here and I can take your picture. Come on, Addy. Put on your shoes."

Blinking myself back to reality, I say, "I'll put them on in the car. Which reminds me, we should take mine. I won't be able to climb up in your truck in this dress."

Vines

At the mention of my dress, his dark eyes drop to my body, traveling all the way to my toes. When they make their way back up, Crew steps through the door and swings it shut, capturing my gaze. "Since I'm only hauling you and not your cow, I didn't bring my truck. You'll be fine."

"You can't go to the White House barefoot. Put your shoes on, Addy," Bev keeps on.

Giving up, I step over to sit on the bench in the hall. I try and hurry with my shoes, but they're both waiting and watching. After stumbling with the first, I jerk, surprised when Crew is all of a sudden crouched at my feet. I didn't even hear him approach.

He doesn't say a word, but his big warm hands circle my ankle, making efficient and quick work of the delicate clasp. When he finishes, he doesn't stand, but slides a hand up the back of my calf, giving me a light squeeze. When I look up, he's got a smirk on his face. "We would've been here all night and missed the dinner."

"Sorry." The word falls from my lips in a breath, because his hand is searing into my skin, making the urge to touch him overwhelming. With Bev watching us, I need to get his hand off my leg before I throw myself at him. I quickly announce, "Let's go."

This buys me one more squeeze before he stands.

Holy shit, it's going to be a long night.

"Pictures!" Bev demands.

I turn slowly and tip my head, giving her a small smile.

Bev puts her hands up and flips them toward one another. "You too, Crew. Get in there—the two of you make one handsome couple. The White House won't know what hit 'em. Maybe you'll end up on the news."

The next thing I know, a large warm hand slides around my waist. I look up and there he is, pulling me to his side. He holds me snug and I warm all over. Trying not to think about it, but thinking about it all the same, I like how I fit against him. It's been a long time since I've been held close by a man, but I don't remember fitting like this. I've never been with anyone as tall as Crew. He looks down at me, our eyes a mere five inches apart. The side of his mouth tips before he looks back to our photographer.

I look back at Bev and she's grinning while pointing her camera at us, clicking away. After at least ten clicks, I pull away from the warmth of his body. "Thanks, I think you got it, Bev."

She kisses my cheek. "Have fun. I'll lock up after you leave."

I return her cheek kiss and slip through the door Crew's holding for me. But once I step outside, I stop, again surprised. "Is this your car?"

Crew moves around me and down the steps. When he reaches the passenger door, he opens it, sort of complaining, "Yeah. Let's get a move on, Addison. Traffic's gonna be a nightmare."

"You match his car!" Bev declares.

Holy shit. I do match his car.

Crew is standing with the door open to a sexy, silver sports coupe, but I don't recognize the model. Slowly, I move down the steps, listening to Bev clicking away, capturing the moment like the paparazzi.

"What kind of car is this?" I ask when I reach the opened door.

"Jag F-Type," he answers as I settle in as modestly as possible in the low seat. But modesty isn't promising when the slit up my thigh tightens, riding up my leg. I certainly didn't think about transportation when picking my outfit.

"Bye—" Bev's yell is broken off as he slams my door. Looking out my window, I smile as she waves excitedly from my doorstep.

When Crew bends to slide in next to me, I realize how small his car is by his nearness. And with his height, I'm surprised to see him fit comfortably behind the wheel. He presses a button and the engine purrs to life. I turn, waving at Bev one last time as he pulls out.

Silence engulfs us as the car come to a stop at the entrance of the winery. There's no traffic and I'm about to ask what's wrong, when I feel a warm touch on my bare knee. I look down and the tips of his fingers are barely caressing my skin, making my eyes dart up in surprise.

He slowly pulls his hand away, once again leaving goosebumps in their wake. His voice comes out low when he utters, "Never carpooled with anyone more beautiful than you, Addison."

I try to be flippant to lighten the heavy mood in the car. "Do you carpool a lot?"

A hint of a smile teases me, thinking might get the dimple, but I don't. "No, I guess I should correct myself and say, I've never done anything with anyone more beautiful than you. Ever."

I roll my lips in and exhale.

"Thank you," I whisper.

"You'll stay close to me tonight."

It's a statement, not a question, and it confuses as much as surprises me. Especially following his sweet compliment, making me frown.

"I'm sorry?"

"Stay close to me," he repeats.

"Why?" My voice comes out stronger and even more baffled.

His hand returns and this time his touch is firm, his big hand wrapping around the top of my knee, giving me a squeeze.

"I want you close. You'll stay at my side." Again, a statement. And, sort of an order.

"I don't understand."

His tone and expression aren't soft like before when he told me I was his most beautiful carpooler ever. Or his most beautiful anything ever. He's adamant, resolute and like I said—I don't understand.

His fingers press into my skin before letting go. Putting his hand back on the wheel, he raises his brows and gives me a single nod when he states, "Trust me, Addison."

When he looks to his rearview mirror, I realize we're backing up cars from the winery and he slowly pulls out. He doesn't say another word as he turns and heads east.

I have no idea what he meant or why he said it. But his tone and demeanor are back to sharp, making me nervous. I really wish I knew what to expect from him. I've trusted few people in this world, and the one I trusted most died of cancer two years ago. I'm not used to depending on people, and for the most part, I haven't had to. I've done okay on my own.

Do I trust Crew Vega?

I don't know. But something about him certainly makes me want to.

The drive to DC is a haul. Between my wine being served in the President's home and Crew demanding I stay by his side without reason, I think it's safe to say I was a tad bit on edge during the trip.

Or, barely hanging onto the edge with the skin of my fingertips, but whatever.

Crew set the music to a satellite station that was a good mix of the last three decades. It wasn't really rock, metal or pop, just the best of the best. This should've helped me relax—but knowing we might enjoy the same type of music on top of everything else, almost did me in.

Between being close enough to Crew to breathe in his clean-after-shave-manly-smell, the Laffy Taffy incident, feeling like he sees more in me than he should, liking the same music, him making weird demands, having dinner in the White House, and him touching my bare thigh, I did what I hate to do more than anything.

I rambled.

My mom taught me not to ramble. She explained haphazard

words are a sign of unorganized thoughts, coming across sloppy and inattentive to others. I used to do it all the time, but she made me mindful of this, and for the most part, I can control it.

Until I can't.

So, while trying not to think about how good he smelled or how I still had the itch to touch him, I gave in and started to ramble.

I worried out loud about guests liking my wine tonight. It didn't matter how much I spent on advertising, you can't beat the real deal when it comes to word-of-mouth. My little vineyard could use some positive chatter after the past four owners botched up the business.

During my ramblings, I had an epiphany. It occurred to me tonight could have the opposite effect. What if people hated it? What if they thought it tasted like Kool-Aid? Or worse—dry, bitter, acidic Kool-Aid? I'd been so excited about this opportunity to showcase my vineyard, I never imagined people hating it. If customers like your product, you pray they tell their friends. But when people hate something, they always seem to shout it from the rooftops. It's the law of practically *everything*.

I'd be out of business faster than Harry could say, "Moo."

Then, just because I was nervous and couldn't stop, I continued my thoughts verbally, brainstorming how I could play matchmaker to Mary and Evan. They're so cute, I really want them together.

Then it was nonstop, me going on about the intricacies of pulling off grape stomping at a wedding reception. I blabbered about how to clean people's feet without it turning into a backyard BBQ from hell.

I thought out loud for the first time to anyone about how I've been secretly thinking about getting another cow. I wanted a calf, maybe an orphan who didn't have its mom for some reason. I could bottle feed her and she could bond with the others.

Then I informed Crew—like he cared—that I was going to throw a surprise baby shower for Clara. Even though it's her fourth baby, she'd gotten rid of all her baby necessities, and a baby shower is always fun.

This brought me full circle, and I returned to freaking out about tonight. I explained to Crew how people were counting on me. I'm an employer and responsible for livelihoods, not to mention my enormous business loan that would set me on the path to bankruptcy if the business took a nosedive.

All through my ramblings, Crew settled back casually in his driver's seat, maneuvering us through traffic and commented when he could get a word in. He told me tonight would be fine, to leave Mary and Evan alone, how people will be too drunk to worry about cleaning their feet. He told me I should get a calf if I want one, but he didn't say boo about the baby shower.

Finally, he reached over and touched the bare skin of my thigh again, making me jump. He gave me a squeeze, his warm hand searing into my skin reminding me of my itch to touch him, when he smiled warmly, but looked amused. "Addison, calm."

Yeesh, easy for him to say.

I'm not sure I calmed, but I did bite my lip. It was plain to see I was making a fool of myself.

Traffic wasn't terrible, we made it in a little over an hour. Not too bad for rush hour. But once we turned from Pennsylvania Avenue, into the gated and probably most secure drive in the world, there was a guarded booth to our left and other uniformed officers on the right. Who knew how many invisible guards were watching.

Crew pulls up and lowers his window. "We're here for the Veterans Dinner."

The guard stoops low to look in the car as two other guards with dogs stalked around Crew's car, sniffing about. The officer's eyes are assessing, looking in the two-seater until his eyes come back to my carpooler and frowns. "Vega?"

Wait, he knows Crew?

"Hey, Jackson. It's been a while," Crew responds blandly.

"A while? Fuck. Forever. How long has it been?" he smiles big.

"Almost ten years."

"Damn, has it? You back in the area?"

"Yeah. My name should be on the list." Crew cuts him off and turns to me holding out his hand. "Need your ID."

"Of course," I mumble, digging through my clutch, wondering how Crew knows the guard at the White House.

I hand him my license and Crew gives them both to the guard.

He checks the list with our IDs and bends back down to look at me. Then he grins at Crew. "Nice. You're good to go. You know where to park—enter through the East Garden Room. You'll know where to go from there. But man, we've gotta get together. I can't wait to tell some of the others you're back. You took that job and disappeared. It's good to see you."

Crew hands me my license, but doesn't promise to get together with his long lost friend, simply offering, "It was good to see you, too."

How odd is that?

When he rolls up his window and pulls through the gate, I turn in my seat as best I can. "How do you know him?"

He slowly pulls up the drive, barely giving me a glance. "I used to work here."

I frown deeper. "You worked at the White House?"

He pulls into a parking spot, quite far away from where we're going. I'm glad my shoes aren't too uncomfortable. When he turns the car off, he moves a bit to look at me and explains. "I was with the Secret Service, but not as an Agent. I was uniformed police."

"Really?" That's...more than impressive. I'm kicking myself for using the hour we had in the car to ramble selfishly about myself rather than give him the third degree, maybe learning something about him. I'm such an idiot.

"It was a long time ago. I worked here for a year and a half before taking a job with my current company."

"What do Secret Service police do?" All of a sudden, I have to know everything about him.

He shrugs. "What you just saw, plus working the grounds and the roof. Basically all over the property. My dad was a cop and I always wanted to work in law enforcement, but I wanted to be an agent. Starting with uniformed police was a foot in the door."

"Why did you leave?"

After a small pause, he tips his head. "I got a different offer. My path changed. Sometimes things just drop in your lap."

"What did your dad think?"

I see his jaw lock and his eyes narrow, contemplating something. Actually, it feels like he's contemplating me.

"Crew?" I call for him.

He takes a breath and says on an exhale, "He never knew. He died before I quit."

I'm taken back by his words. "How?"

"He was killed on the job."

"Crew," I whisper, instinctively reaching out for his hand as my voice comes out soft and pained. I feel his anguish in a place he'll never know, but right now, I wish he knew how much I do understand. I want him to know more than anything.

"It was eleven years ago. I'm good, Addison." His voice is steady as always, but he does thread his fingers through mine.

"It doesn't matter how long it's been, I'm sorry."

"I've reconciled it," he says with conviction.

I tip my head frowning, wondering what that means. Do men reconcile hurt and loss? I've dated, but I've never been close enough to any man to truly understand how they tick. As a woman and daughter, I understand loss better than I should. But to reconcile it?

That's a strange description when dealing with such an emotion.

He gives my hand a squeeze and his eyes go from sharp to soft.

"Let's go. I'm sure you want to see people drink your wine. We don't want to miss that."

And before I know it, I've lost his touch and he's rounded the car to open my door. I give him my hand so I can maybe make a graceful exit. He helps by hauling me up and out, pulling me close to him. It wasn't completely graceful but it wasn't a fail, either.

I put my hand over his tie, smoothing it down his chest before looking into his eyes. There, I keep on in a whisper. "Thank you for telling me about your dad."

He doesn't respond, but his eyes heat before he finally lets me go. Placing his warm, firm hand to the small of my back, Crew led me in the direction of the East Garden Room. With an emotional start to our evening, I let him take me to see my wine served at the White House.

Standing in the East Room of the White House, I'm awestruck being here. I caught a glimpse of the President earlier, but he's already ducked out. Who knows what world emergency he had to deal with.

I've been able to relax into the evening as no one gagged on their wine. I've met many interesting guests and even handed out business cards to those interested in visiting the vineyard. Who knew I'd be networking in the White House when I started this venture a year and a half ago?

The significance of this very room isn't lost on me as I swirl a glass of The Delaney in my hand. I do this while tipping my head way back to look at the enormous painted portrait of President George Washington. I also do this frowning.

I never had anything against George Washington until I moved to Whitetail and those around me told tales of my Ordinary being haunted. I've never believed in ghosts, but I also didn't live alone in a massive, centuries-old farmhouse attached to a historic building, said to host our first president for a night.

Do I believe in ghosts now? I haven't decided. But do I go into the Ordinary at night by myself? No way, no how.

I do wonder what he was like, though. The portrait hanging in front of me depicts him as an older man, wearing a long black cloak, holding a sword in one hand and his other arm extended. Sipping my wine, I frown deeper, wondering what he's beckoning in this painting.

"Dolley Madison rescued him."

Startled, I look to my side and Sheldon O'Rourke is standing next to me, also looking up at George Washington.

"Sheldon," I greet him, extending my hand. We've had dinner, presentations were made and guests are now milling about. "It's nice to see you again. Thank you for arranging everything. It might not be a big deal for anyone else, but it's quite something to see my wine served at the White House. I'm grateful to experience it."

"I apologize I haven't been a better host. I've been busy with business this evening. But I see you've been preoccupied, as well." His hand and eyes linger before looking back to our first President. "This is a replica of the Lansdowne painting. The original is hanging in the National Portrait Gallery. Dolley Madison is credited for saving this national treasure just prior to the mansion being taken over by the British during the War of 1812. Brave woman. Otherwise it would have been burned to the ground with everything else."

"I didn't know that." I look up, thinking it's enormous and wonder how they wrestled it out in the chaos.

"You've never visited the White House?" he asks.

I turn to him, happy to take my mind off George Washington. "Never."

"I obviously don't have access to everything, but would you like me to show you the state parlors? Most people know them as the color rooms. They're right next door."

I can't think of anything better and look across the room. Crew excused himself to take a call and said he'd be right back. He's across the room, now involved in a conversation. This shouldn't take long—I'll just be next door. "I'd love that."

He takes my almost empty wine glass and sets it on a table before leading me to the next room. I get a private tour of the Green Room, Blue Room and when we finally get to the Red Room, the buzz of the conversation from guests is muted by the distance. Sheldon's told me what he knows of some of the furnishings and artwork.

As I stand at the fireplace admiring the antique gilded candelabras on the mantle, thinking very few people probably get a private tour of the President's home, I hear his voice dip lower from behind me. "You look like Anne."

I gasp and then freeze.

My vision goes fuzzy as I feel like I've been hit by a Mack truck. Pulling in a deep breath of air, I try to overcome the shock of his words, turning slowly to look at him. He's standing in the middle of the room with his head tipped, studying me.

I do my best to look confused, which isn't hard because I am, even with my heart beating a mile a minute. "Pardon me?"

"Yes." He tips his head the other way. "As a child, I thought you resembled Wes. But you've grown into a beauty, just like your mother."

With that, I fight my legs from buckling and force myself to breathe. All of a sudden, the room is warm, though the tingles down my bare back resemble an arctic blast blowing through the Red Room.

"You must be mistaken. I don't know what you're talking about." I force my voice to set at steady. Trying to relax my stance, the only tension visible in my body would be my white knuckles, fisting the clutch at my side. "My mother's name is Delaney. You have me confused with someone else."

It's everything I can do to stand strong when he shakes his head and takes a step, closing the distance between us. "No, I'm not mistaken. You're Anne and Wesley's daughter. I knew you as a child, but you were too young to remember me."

"Sheldon." I pause, my voice quivering with the pounding of my heart and my mind begs my body to pull itself together. There have been times I've had to remain composed in life, but not like this. "I've no idea what you're talking about."

"You're just like Anne," he keeps on. "I was friends with your parents before your father's death."

The blood instantly drains from my head. I can't hide the tremor in my voice when I lie, "You have me confused with someone else. My father's very much alive."

He simply shakes his head, his voice dipping and he's not friendly anymore. "Now, now. We both know that's not true."

I say nothing, but do feel myself start to shake.

"You were there when he was killed." My heart drops as his words shoot through me like daggers. He takes another step toward me and narrows his eyes. "Do you remember, Addy? As unfortunate as it was, I do hope you remember every detail. Those memories should serve you well. It would be a shame for you to meet the same demise as your father."

My insides clench and my head spins. I've no idea what he has to do with my parents, but I do know the door to the Blue Room is behind me and the Green beyond that. This happened to my mom once, someone from the past approached her—threatened her. We moved on immediately, but she didn't explain it to me until I was older.

It's never happened to me. I need to get out. I don't know his intentions, but I don't think there's anything he can do to me in the White House. I'll scream bloody murder if I have to and we'd be instantly surrounded, I'm sure of it.

Oh shit. All of a sudden, things are hitting me all at once. Crew told me not to leave him and thinking back to the look on his face, he knew something. This must've been what he meant, but how could he know anything?

I can't think about what he knows or why he told me to stay at his side. But for some reason, I want to trust him. At this moment, I've never needed anyone like I need Crew Vega. I need to find him and get away from here as fast as I possibly can. It's all I can handle right now—I'll worry about everything else later.

Crew

Watching her look up at our first President's portrait, I find her amusing. I stepped away to take a call from Asa, but never took my eyes off her. She's got a frown playing on her face and after finding out she's freaked about her Ordinary being haunted, I wonder what she's thinking.

Being at her side all night has been an experience. I don't remember the last time I've enjoyed a car ride so much, listening to her blather on about everything. Since we got here, I've done everything I could to steer her away from O'Rourke and Whittaker, even though I've seen them both watching her.

Focusing on what I need to while being with her has been difficult. Being alert isn't something I've ever had to work at. It's always come natural—it's also been a necessity to stay alive. With Addison at my side, I find myself wanting nothing more than to fall into some sort of normal with her. I've never had normal, whatever that is. She's mesmerizing to look at, talk to, and be with. When she reached out for me after I told her about my dad, I'd never experienced a touch like that.

Her simple touch, something that should've been insignificant and casual, wasn't. It was beautiful, weighty, and even healing. Maybe it's because I know more than I should, that she lost her dad as tragically as I did, but I do know I didn't want to lose the way she made me feel. If I could've held her hand there forever, I would've. It felt perfect, right over my heart where I didn't even know I needed it. Fuck me, but I've had a hard time focusing all night because I'm thinking of ways to get her touch back and never lose it.

Yeah, I've had to work to keep my focus around Addison Wentworth.

"Vega?" I hear and bite back my scowl. Shit.

Turning, I see an officer I used to work with, but he isn't an officer anymore. He's in a suit, it's easy to see he's an agent from his earpiece trailing into his suit jacket.

I back up two steps and turn so I can see Addison as I greet him. "Landon."

"What're you doing here?" He reaches out to shake my hand and I'm forced to turn away from her to reciprocate.

I've found it strange being here after so long. It's almost surreal after doing what I've done for ten years.

"I'm here for work." My attempt to shift away is cut off when he slaps my opposite shoulder with his other hand. I squeeze his to let go. He's trying my patience—I don't have time for small talk. I need to get back to Addison. "I see you're an agent. Congratulations."

"Thanks. I've been at it six years. Lots of travel, but it's good. Where've you been?"

"I've traveled some in my job too, but I'm back. Able to telecommute, I won't have to be in the city much." I start to turn, but he grabs my forearm.

"Wait, I've got to show you something." He digs into his pocket and pulls out his phone. I grit my teeth as I have to look at pictures of his wife and kids.

Barely sixty seconds pass before I break into his one-sided conversation. "Sorry, I need to get back to someone. We'll catch up soon."

I don't wait for him to respond and turn to Addison.

Fuck.

One second she was there and the next she's disappeared. Why I felt the need to be polite, I have no idea, but she's gone. After doing a quick scan of the room, O'Rourke is gone, too, but Whittaker's still across the expanse.

Damn it.

Unless she's in the restroom, which for some reason I doubt she is, there's not many places she could be. In past administrations, they'd leave the parlors open for people to walk through.

As I advance quickly through the Green Room and half way through the Blue, I hear her voice. I slow my stride to casual when I arrive at the Red and control myself when I see her standing with her back to me, but facing him. Fuck if they aren't alone.

"There you are," I calmly call and when I do, she instantly turns to me. Her body is composed but her eyes aren't. When they settle on me, they flare. I've seen fear in a lot of eyes over the last ten years, but nothing like hers. This is different. I don't know her well, but the look on her face is nothing but pure panic.

I don't like that expression etched on her beautiful face.

I move to her and when I do, I stop fighting it. With her back to O'Rourke, I tag her around the waist and tug her to me. I barely hear her surprised breath when she looks at me with her big brown eyes full of fear.

Then I pull her into my arms.

Addy

His lips land on mine like he's kissed me a million times in the Red Room of the White House. His other arm encircles me, his hand is hot and searing on the bare skin of my back. My body is frantic—I can't help but whimper. When I do, his tongue dips in and I taste him for the first time. He tastes like my Whitetail Cabernet mixed with something else all his own.

Forgetting where I am or who I'm with, I give in, letting all my anxiety sink into Crew Vega. I wrap an arm around his back still holding my clutch and fist his suit jacket in my other. I tip my head for him, wanting more.

He takes what I give, in a way he's been fighting an itch, just like me. Our kiss intensifies when he drops his hand from my waist to my ass, gripping me over my dress. He kisses me fiercely, possessing me, and the moment. My body, which was chilled just moments ago, warms all over. He deepens our embrace, arching my back while holding me tight, letting his lips linger on mine. As his kiss slows, his arms convulse around me, causing my lariat necklace to bite into the skin of my throat. My eyes barely open when he pulls away and gently kisses the tip of my nose.

Looking intently into my eyes, he murmurs, "You left me, baby. I missed you."

Even coming down from his kiss, I still caught the meaning of "you left me" and grip him tighter. He told me not to leave him, and now I'm not only confused, but scared out of my mind.

I look up and don't lie when I respond breathlessly, "I missed you, too."

"You ready for me to take you home?" His voice comes out soft, his eyes searching my face for an answer.

My hands fist him, no doubt giving away my fear. "Please."

He gives my ass one more squeeze before dragging his hand to my waist, slightly pulling at the material. Looking up and over my head, he gives Sheldon a bland stare. "I need to get my woman home. I'm sure you can understand how I barely let her out of the house tonight in this dress. If you'll excuse us, we have a drive."

Pulling in a deep, calming breath, I smooth my dress with my hands and turn to Sheldon. It's apparent he's angry and I try to comprehend all that's happened, what he knows, and more importantly, what it means. Crew threads his fingers through mine as I muster the words, "Thank you for the tour."

Sheldon says nothing, but nods tersely.

I hold on tight as Crew Vega saves me from I don't know what, walking me out of what's supposed to be the safest home on the planet. Which is strange, because I've never felt as unsafe and exposed as I had tonight.

I'm going to have to do something about that the moment I get home. The thought is gut wrenching. At least I have an hour to think on it, plan, and figure out how to make it happen.

Chapter Eight

Disintegrated

Addy

The brisk walk out of the White House to Crew's Jag was just enough to calm my body, preparing for the trip home. He held my hand all the way to the car and I let him. I tried not to think about Sheldon, or Crew and his searing kiss that practically swept me off my fect. I tried not thinking about anything besides my next task. And it's a big one, requiring all the mind space I could manage.

As we left the District, Crew asked if I enjoyed myself. He asked if I was okay. He asked who the man was in the Red Room. Then he asked what we were talking about and more specifically, what he was saying to me. His questions started out bland, but became more and more intense with each one.

Finally, he was agitated when he asked why I left his side when he explicitly told me not to. I looked at him and after giving him multiple non-answers, frowned. "Need I remind you, Crew Vega, it was you who left me standing under the portrait of George Washington."

This, thankfully, shut him up. His jaw turned hard as he fisted his steering wheel with brute force. At least he quit asking questions, leaving me to my thoughts so I could focus and plan.

But as much as I tried, I couldn't. It was all I could do to concentrate on the dark of night outside my window, barely keeping it together. If I let my mind think about what needed to be done, a weight fell over me that was so substantial, it was dreadful.

I absolutely couldn't take it. I did everything in my power not to think about Bev and Morris, or Van, Evan, Clara and Maggie. I didn't think about Mary, or my cows, or the business I've come to love and a house that's slowly become a home. I did everything I could not to think about the countryside that was lonely and secluded, but has become a peaceful and lovely place to be.

It was impossible not to wonder about Crew as he drove me home. I'd barely known him a week, but his mysterious aura couldn't be ignored, confusing me to no end. I shouldn't have felt safe with a man I hardly know. I should've questioned him as to why he commanded I stay by his side and how he knew about my obsession with Laffy Taffy. I should've demanded to know why it feels like he *knows* me when no one really knows me at all. Especially, most importantly, why he kissed me when he did at the White House.

Because his kiss wasn't merely a kiss. Crew staked his claim, unrestrained, unable to hold back another second. Damn it if I didn't like both. A lot. Way more than I should, especially now since I'll never have it again.

I'm immediately pulled out of my thoughts when Crew hits the gas and I'm jerked back into my seat with the sudden force. Simultaneously, he roughly grabs my thigh, rumbling, "Hang on."

"What?" I barely get the word out of my mouth when we're hit from behind. Our bodies jerk forward in our seatbelts, but he must have sped up enough to deflect a lot of the impact since the airbags don't deploy.

"Fuck me," Crew mutters, releasing my leg to fist the steering wheel as he quickly changes lanes.

I've been in such a fog after what happened in the Red Room, I have to look around to see where we are. We're far enough out of the metro where the interstate isn't too busy.

I grab my door and the console to steady myself when Crew changes lanes so quickly, the car jerks dramatically to the left.

"Aren't you going to stop?" I ask.

Crew, looking intently between the road ahead of us and his mirrors, growls, "We're not stopping, Addison. That was no accident."

I turn to look out my side window just in time to see a black sedan veer toward us so sharply, I scream.

"They're *trying* to hit us?" I exclaim, but he doesn't answer. I can't even think about who's trying to hit us or why. Because I don't think it's *us*. After tonight, I'm sure it's *me*.

Crew must have accelerated again, swerving to the left. When we hit the highway guardrail, sparks fly. Crew speeds around another car where the black sedan can't keep up and we swiftly cross two lanes to the right across traffic.

"Turn around and get your head down," Crew demands.

I'm not sure if he's forgotten how small his car is, but I lean down in my seat as far as I can. We're racing by cars so quickly—they appear to be at a crawl on the interstate.

"Stay down—I'm getting off."

Perfectly timed, he changes lanes just in time to exit the highway. I turn and see the black sedan force another car out of their lane, causing it to spin. Another car T-bones it so forcefully, they skid across the highway.

"Oh shit! They crashed. We have to do something." I turn back to Crew and when I do, he swings his arm out, pinning me to my seat like an iron bar. When I look forward, we're heading full speed to an intersection off the highway. I scream the second he hits the brakes and cranks the wheel hard to the left.

The rear of Crew's Jag spins to the right and we fishtail, back and forth, until he punches the gas again and we dart down a two lane highway that's dark and barren. I turn and barely breathe a sigh of relief before I see headlights careening around the corner after us.

The words, "Oh fuck," scarcely pass my lips when he guns it again, but the black sedan does, too. Crew's Jag, which was a smooth and comfortable ride on the way into the city, is proving its image isn't just for show. It's handling the hills and valleys like a superstar.

"I told you to turn around and get down, Addison," he bites out, frustrated.

I pivot back to the front and mutter as my heart goes a mile a minute, "What's happening?"

"Damn it! Get your head down." He hits his brakes so hard, my body is thrown forward. I not only feel it, but hear the tires on the road squeal.

We're yanked to the left and I realize he's changed lanes. When I look over, he's hunched as low as he can get, and just in time. Gun shots ring out in the night, and I scream again, hearing one catch the back of Crew's Jag.

Peeking out my window, I see the sedan zoom past us, trying to slow down.

But Crew's faster. He doesn't even come to a complete stop, spinning the back of the car and we turn right, down a dirt road, even darker than the one we were on because the forest's encompassing it. The second I hear gravel flying, pinging against the car, Crew flips his lights off. I have no idea how he can see where we're going with the darkness besieging us.

He takes a left, and then another quick right, down more gravel roads. I turn to look out the rear window between us. Nothing.

Jerking the car one last time, he flips us left into a drive that's made of merely two tire tracks and quickly maneuvers us into the middle of a field. Just as quickly and deftly as he's done so far, he turns off his car.

I hadn't even noticed but all this time, the music continued to play. *Jumper* by Third Eye Blind breaks through the heavy silence. That is, until Crew bangs the dashboard so hard, I'm sure he broke the controls, right before hitting the steering wheel. With his voice bellowing through his small car, he shouts, "Fuck!"

My chest is heaving—my breaths out of control. I hear my heart pounding in my ears. I've got one hand on the window next to me and the other is gripping the console. The weight bearing down on me from this evening's events are so heavy, I can scarcely keep it at bay. All I see is the dark field in front of us, lit only by the stars.

Just when I close my eyes, praying Crew outran them—whoever *they* are—I yelp, jerking when I feel a hand on me.

"Shh," he tries to calm me when he turns my face to his. His eyes roam my features and I realize he's not breathing hard at all while I'm practically hyperventilating. His voice, so different than just a few seconds ago, comes at me soft and soothing. "It's okay. You're okay."

I instantly shake my head in his hand. No, nothing is okay. But he doesn't know that.

His eyes narrow slightly, but his tone stays the same. "Do you know what that was about?"

Probably too quickly, I refute, "No. I've no idea."

He looks at me, assessing me, probably trying to figure out how to get rid of me, and quickly. I've been nothing but trouble all night. I'm sure he's regretting the carpool.

Then he slides his hand up and under my jaw and into my hair, pulling my forehead to his lips. Staying there, I have to squeeze my eyes shut when he whispers, "Relax, Addison. I'll take you home. You're safe."

He has no idea what he's talking about. I squeeze my eyes tighter to keep my tears at bay, breathing deeply to find control.

When he lets me go, I open my eyes. He strangely doesn't speak about the car chase, being shot at, his Jag being hit, scuffed, or driven to its limits. He says nothing about the Red Room, our kiss, or why he demanded I not leave his side tonight. He simply says, "Let's get you home."

I don't know whether to be confused or relieved. I do know I want this night to be over. For some reason someone is after me, and it has everything to do with my dad.

When Crew's Jag rolls to a stop at my front door, I waste no time climbing out. My heels are clicking up the stone steps when I hear him call for me.

"Addison, wait."

Ignoring him, my hands tremble as I search for my key. When I pull it out of my clutch, trying to steady myself to unlock the door, it's swiped out of my hand.

I whip around to face him, scarcely steadying my voice. "Give that back."

He doesn't say anything, but pulls his hand through his hair and looks at me intently. "Let me come in. We can talk."

I shake my head, putting space between us until my back hits the door. "I'm tired."

He moves into me, barely allowing any space between us, and as firm as his hand is on my hip, his voice is just as gentle. "Please. This's been a crazy night and you're scared. Let me come in so you're not by yourself."

Biting the inside of my lip, I swallow over the lump in my throat, holding myself together. "I'm sorry, not tonight. I'm fine."

"Addison," he calls, his voice gravely, coming out as a plea.

I give my head a little shake, whispering, "I'm sorry."

His eyes slowly close as he drops his head. When he finally opens them, he looks up and to the side, as if he's thinking. His hand at my hip grips me tighter when he finally looks me in the eyes, shaking his head.

I tense when he leans in, thinking he's going to kiss me again, but he doesn't. His freshly shaved, smooth face brushes my cheek, sending tingles down my spine. He steps forward, his firm body presses into mine. Inhaling deeply, he breathes into my ear, "I'm sorry I left you. I'll never do it again. Ever."

His simple words aren't only an apology, they're a vow. I hear it in his whisper so I nod against the side of his face, even though it won't matter because he won't have a chance to prove it. He brushes his lips against the sensitive skin under my ear and I have to squeeze my eyes to overcome his touch.

When he pulls away to look at me, he says in a low voice, "I'll come back tomorrow. We'll talk."

That's not going to happen. "Okay."

My hip gets another squeeze and he leans in, this time firmly planting a kiss on my forehead. I fight the urge to tip my head, inviting him to really kiss me, to lay claim to me like he did earlier, just one more time.

But I don't and he backs away, unlocking my door. When he turns the knob, the beeps of the security system pull me back to reality.

Crew stays where he is as I step inside to punch in my code.

"I'll be by tomorrow," he promises when I turn to him.

I say nothing, but simply look at him. Doing my best, I let my eyes drag over his body. He blends in with the night sky in his black suit as I memorize every beautiful inch—his dark eyes and hair, his broad frame, and long powerful legs. When I look down, I'm hypnotized by his hands, remembering how they felt on me, commanding, strong, and warm.

"You okay? You didn't get banged up in the car?" His voice cuts through the quiet and I look up quickly.

I ignore him, my voice coming out short and clipped. "Thank you. For tonight."

"You're welcome."

"Goodbye, Crew."

"Tomorrow," he reiterates.

With that, I inch the door closed until I lose sight of him. I lean my forehead to the door, needing to calm myself. Taking a moment, a much needed pause, I wait for Crew to leave and prepare for the painful task I'm dreading. I dread it to my toes, my insides twisted and turned with torment. As much as I don't want to, after what happened tonight, I know what I must do. Forcing my body to move, quietly, I lock the knob and deadbolt and arm the security system before ripping at my shoes.

All of a sudden—I'm in such a state—I break the clasp on one silver heel trying to get it off my ankle. Leaving them by the front door, I sprint up the stairs to the second floor bedroom I use for storage. Heaven knows I don't need all these extra rooms—I never have overnight company. Rushing to the closet, I grab my two largest suitcases plus another small one, doing my best to manage them up to the third floor.

Running to my large walk-in closet, I reach on my tippy toes for my mom's box. I have loads of my mom's things around the house, but I can't leave without this. It has everything important to me in this world. My favorite pictures of us together, a few of all three of us before my dad died, her wedding ring, a tattered copy of *Gone with the Wind* that she read more times than I'll ever know, and every single postcard she sent while I was in college. She never missed a day. Not one. She always said she had fun looking for the silliest and most obscure cards she could find. And every day the mail was delivered while I was at UCLA for four years, I knew she was thinking of me. Now that she's gone, I'm so thankful I kept them all.

Needless to say, the box is big as I heave it down off the shelf. I set it in the middle of the room and dash back for clothes and shoes. I pack fast, throwing only the essentials in the largest of the suitcases and head to my bathroom. Snatching a tote out of the linen closet, I mindlessly shovel in all the makeup and bath necessities that will fit. It's bulging out the top, but it'll do for now.

It's after midnight. I wonder how far I can get tonight before I'll need to stop for sleep. The thought makes my eyes sting, but I fight it back, needing to concentrate on what I'm doing.

Finally, I grab the last suitcase and go to my dresser, tossing armfuls of clothes inside.

"You goin' somewhere?"

I shriek at the deep voice breaking into my freak-out, spinning around instantly. When I see him, I back into my dresser violently, my hands grasping in an effort to steady myself. Picture frames, jewelry holders and perfume bottles rock, something behind me crashes to the floor from the force of my body.

He's standing in my doorway, leaning casually against the jamb. My heart beats desperately making my head spin, my lungs barely catching up with my frenzied body.

The control I normally hold so dear is gone.

Disintegrated.

Desperately, my eyes comb the room realizing I have no escape.

There's only one way out and he's blocking it.

"Well?"

My eyes dart back at the sound of his voice. The jacket and tie are gone—his black shirt is rolled at the cuffs and unbuttoned at the collar. Where he was sweet and tender on my doorstep just minutes ago, he's sharp as he stands in the entrance of my bedroom, looking anything but relaxed.

"How did you get in here?" I whisper, barely hearing my own voice.

"Where are you going, Addison?"

Pulling my lips between my teeth, I ignore his question and try to remember how he made me feel safe just a short time ago. Swallowing hard, realization washes over me and I panic.

"I set the alarm. How did you get in?"

Since he hasn't moved a muscle, it's easy to see his eyes narrow. "I have my ways. Tell me what happened at the White House. What did O'Rourke say to you?"

I shake my head quickly. "Nothing."

"He knows you."

"Get out of my house," I try to demand, but it doesn't sound convincing. It sounds feeble and weak, which is how I feel, down to my toes.

My eyes pool with tears as I keep shaking my head. "I have no idea who he is. I've never laid eyes on him before this week."

"I didn't say you knew him. I said he knows you." His head tips the other way. "Did he threaten you?"

"I don't know what's going on," I tell him the truth.

"Is there a reason someone was chasing and shooting at us tonight?"

I keep shaking my head and beg, "Please, leave."

"I want to know what he said to you, what happened on the way home, and why you're so scared you think you're leaving. Because I promise you, Addison, you're not going anywhere."

My tears spill over as the anxiety crawls through me, the way it does when I lose control. Between the Red Room incident and being chased and shot at on the way home, I can't handle it. It's happened since I was five. I've controlled it for years, probably since I was in high school, but I recognize it like it was yesterday. The panic is seeping in, beginning to strangle me.

"You don't know what you're talking about," I cry.

His piercing eyes soften, transforming his rugged, beautiful face. There's no edge to his deep rumbly voice as he informs me, "I do know what I'm talking about. I know more than you think I do. In fact, I know more than you. There's no way I'm letting you go anywhere."

"You don't know anything," I throw my words at him, my tears coming strong.

"I do," he insists. "I promise, if they found you here, they'll find you again. I not only know more than you, but I know more than them. This means, I know more than everyone and trust me when I say, you're safest here."

"What are you talking about? Who are they, and...and why should I trust you? I don't understand what's going on. What do you know? How do you know anything?" My voice rises with each question, laced with terror. He can't know anything. Especially about my parents, my past, the part of my life Sheldon O'Rourke clearly knows something about. Although I have no idea why or how he knows anything, I do know I'm not sticking around to find out. I have no idea why we were chased home, but I can only assume it has something to do with O'Rourke.

He doesn't answer but he does push away from the jamb heading straight for me. I'm paralyzed in my spot. There's no use in trying, I know I won't get away, even if I wanted to.

When he reaches me, his eyes are compassionate, almost

sympathetic. His hand comes to my chin, lifting my tear-stained face to his.

"I'm not letting you go anywhere. What I'm trying to tell you, is that I know everything. Everything," he stresses before turning my world upside-down. "*Abby*."

Holy! Fuck!

<u>Crew</u>

The instant I say her name, her real name, she lets out a choked sob and her whole body jolts. The color drains from her face when she gasps, "What did you say?"

I can tell she's about to lose it and pull her to me. Her arms are pinned between us when I give her a squeeze and soften my voice. "You heard me."

Her body goes limp and her tears keep on as she slowly shakes her head, before whispering as if she's talking to herself, "No."

"Yes," I counter immediately, looking into her terrified eyes. "I know it all."

Her head keeps shaking and she slowly looks down, away from me. Her eyes go unfocused, jumpy, and searching.

"No." She stares at my chest, chewing on her lip. Fisting my shirt, she keeps on, "This can't be. This isn't happening."

"Addison," I try again, giving her a squeeze.

This gets her attention—her body turning rigid in my arms. Looking up at me, she screams, "No!"

I don't have a chance to respond because her body bucks. She pushes, she pulls, she wrestles. Still in her dress, the material falls away from her shoulder on one side as she fights violently in my arms. I hold her easily as she uses all her might to get away, but there's no way I'm giving her what she wants. Especially now.

"Let me go," she cries, struggling in my arms.

"Calm down. I'm not going to hurt you." I grasp both her wrists in one hand, pulling her away from me long enough to turn her back to my front. When Addison's legs attempt to kick, I wrap my other arm around her waist, lifting her off the ground.

"Please," she begs through her sobs. Her body thrashes and twists, trying to get away from me. "I need to leave. I need to go—I can't be here. I never thought this would happen—it's been too long. Please let me go."

Putting my lips to her ear, I whisper, "Stop, baby, you're going to hurt yourself."

Eventually, her struggling slows as her sobs become deeper. She finally turns limp in my arms where I can loosen my hold so as not to hurt her. Sliding her down my body, her legs give out when her feet hit the floor. Quickly, I reach down and scoop her up under her knees. Going to the only place in the room to sit, I move to her bed and settle her in my lap as she continues to cry. Pulling her dress back up her shoulder, I hold her tight, letting her do what she needs to do.

Minutes go by, my shirt is soaked with her tears when she finally starts to calm. Through her struggles, her hair's a mess and falling from where she had it up earlier. I try to pull out as many pins as I can, running my fingers through her thick hair as it falls over my arm and shoulder. I keep at this until her breathing evens and her tears slow.

"I barely know you," she mumbles into my neck after a hiccup, trying to catch her breath.

I sigh and give her a squeeze. "I know."

"How do you know me?" she asks, gripping my shirt. "No one knows me. I don't remember the last time anyone knew me besides my mom."

I look over her head, deciding what to say, but I don't stop with her hair. It's heavy and thick and feels good on my skin.

"Crew?"

She shifts, looking up at me.

Taking a big breath, I start carefully. "I have a fair amount of clearance."

Her face is red, splotchy, and her eyes are swollen. Smeared makeup clouds her face. But even as she frowns at me, sitting here in my arms in her twisted and wrinkled dress, she's beautiful.

"I thought you were a government contractor." Her voice is rough and scratchy from crying.

I let my eyes narrow. "Sort of."

"Sort of?" she asks, confused.

I shift her in my lap to see her better and change the subject. "You're not leaving."

Her face starts to twist again. "I can't stay."

"You won't be safe if you leave."

"I'm not safe here," she counters.

"You're safer here than anywhere. And after what happened tonight, there's no denying it," I insist. "Trust me on this."

She quickly shakes her head frowning. "How do you know who I am?"

I don't answer. I'm not ready to answer that yet, even if I knew how. Instead, I fall back and to the side, taking her with me.

"What are you doing?" she exclaims, trying to push away.

I hold her close, settling us, Addison tight to my side. There's no way I'm leaving or risking her going somewhere. Not that she could with the surveillance—but this is easier and I'm tired. I push my shoes off, kicking them to the end of her bed thinking I could get used to this.

She tries to pull away from me one more time, complaining, "If you aren't going to tell me, you need to go."

Rolling, I pull her up so we're eye-to-eye. Her face is still etched with fear, but now since I've situated us in her bed, it's mixed with confusion. Looking at her, I decide I'd better give her something so she'll stop fighting me and this fucking night will be over. I'll figure the rest out in the morning after we've slept.

"I told you, I have clearance in my job. I had to know who my neighbors were before I bought. It came about differently than it normally does, but I've read your background and we'll talk about that tomorrow. For now, you're not going anywhere. You've had a rough night—we both need some sleep."

"Sleep? You're staying?" She frowns deeper.

"Do you trust me?"

She doesn't say anything for a beat and then answers quietly. "I did, but now I'm not sure."

With my hand in her hair, I pull her to me as I meet her, putting my mouth on hers. This time I kiss her slow. She tastes and feels like she did earlier—perfect—but salty from her tears.

"You can trust me. I'll prove it to you," I say against her lips.

"I want to." She pauses, breathing deep before continuing. "But I'm scared. I don't know what to believe."

"All you have to know is you're safest here with me." I give her a squeeze to echo my words. "Believe in that for tonight. But for now, get that I know what happened to your dad, I know all about you and your mom, and I know Sheldon O'Rourke had a hand in it all. He's not a good man, Addison. I don't want you anywhere near him. The White House dinner tonight was no coincidence, nor was that shit on the drive home. O'Rourke somehow learned you were close and lured you out. There's a whole lot more I can't tell you, but realize this won't go on forever. Until then, you're without a doubt safest here."

"You came to the dinner tonight because of me," she guesses.

"I did."

"You somehow arranged to be at a White House dinner because you knew it might not be safe for me to be there on my own."

"I absolutely knew it wouldn't be safe for you to be there on your own. I'm mad at myself I stepped away to take a call. I had my eye on you until someone pulled me into a fucking conversation." I frown at the memory of my mistake.

"You've only known me a week," she goes on.

I breathe deep, careful with my answer. "I don't like bad guys."

It's easy to feel her let a bit of tension go from her body when she sighs. "Me either."

Shifting her closer to settle us in, my voice dips when I add, "I'm developing a real soft spot for the good guys. I don't deal with the good guys, Addison. Only the bad guys." Her swollen eyes flare at my words. "You're not leaving. And I want you to trust me. Trust me for tonight and I'll prove it to you later."

She throws me a bone after thinking it over for a moment. "For tonight, until you can explain more tomorrow. I'm too exhausted to go anywhere."

I shake my head, not looking forward to convincing her tomorrow. I'm not sure how to make that happen, but I'll figure it out.

I lean in to kiss her forehead, even though what I really want to do is roll her over, take her mouth and eventually her, proving I'll protect her from anything. "Sleep."

Some of the tension leaves her body—I feel it as she sinks into me. Minutes later when I finally close my eyes, waiting for her to find sleep, I hear her call softly, "Crew?"

Without moving, I answer, "Hmm?"

"I'm sorry about your car."

I sigh. "It's just a car. Not a big deal."

Then she fists my shirt as she whispers, "And I'm sorry about your dad."

Fuck. It's my turn to tense.

Turning my head, I bury my face in her hair, responding in my own whisper, "Addison."

"I wanted to tell you earlier that I understood. Now I get to tell you."

"Baby."

She turns her head, nuzzling her face in my neck. "You shaved."

Finally, I relax because I've felt the way she's looked at me. I can't say I haven't enjoyed the hell out of it and I plan on enjoying more of it soon. As soon as I can. Letting my hand work its way from her lower back to her ass, I give her a squeeze, leaving my hand there.

"Went to the White House with you on my arm, Addison. That called for shaving."

"Oh...um...of course," she stutters.

I can't fight my smile any longer. "It'll grow back."

Her body once again tenses against mine.

"Go to sleep," I whisper.

"Thank you," she says quickly into my neck before her voice turns soft. "For tonight. For everything."

"Always," I promise.

Chapter Nine

Innocent

Addy

Coming down the last staircase, I hear voices—a loud, high pitched female's mingling with the low rumbly one of my neighbor. I hadn't thought about having a drama like last night's or my new neighbor sleeping in my bed when I invited my employees, who have become my friends, to come on in whenever they pleased.

It didn't take me long to pass out last night. I haven't had a panic attack in years, well over a decade, but they always exhaust me. Plus, I was lying in Crew's arms, I was warm and it felt good. I slept hard, but had no trouble remembering last night's disturbing events the second my eyes opened. Even if I hadn't, the mess created from my escape plan was enough to jolt me back to reality. I'm not sure when Crew left my bed, but the moment I looked in the mirror, I was mortified he slept with me.

Horrid. I looked absolutely horrid.

I'm not one of those women who cry elegantly, or even delicately, for that matter. Maybe that's just in movies and books, but even so, horrid doesn't even begin to describe it. My eyes are swollen, red, and my face is still puffy from my crying jag. My hair was a mess. I brushed it into a low ponytail, which helped a little, but I'm going to need cucumbers or tea bags for my eyes. Who knows when they'll deflate. Brushing my teeth and washing my face helped a bit, but not much. I was still in my dress so I changed into a pair of shorts and a t-shirt.

"I can't believe you've lived here for a couple months and I'm just now meeting you," Clara declares as I hit the bottom step and wonder if I should go back up to my room to take a shower. I'm not sure I'm up for Clara this morning, especially since she's talking to Crew. Not only will she demand to know what's wrong the second she sees me, but she'll also demand to know why I have a man in my house.

I haven't dated since I moved here, but she's tried to set me up with one of her husband's co-workers a few times. I wasn't interested and really, I never wanted to take the time. Whitetail is more than a full time job. I work at least six days a week, sometimes seven if we're slammed. I'm too preoccupied protecting my investment to worry about adding a man to the mix.

"I'm busy with work," I hear him say and that makes me wonder what he's really busy with, since I'm pretty sure after last night, he's not clicking away at a keyboard creating accounting programs.

I should turn around and take a shower, but my curiosity gets the best of me. I need to know what's going on. I need to decide if I can really trust Crew. Most importantly, I need to make the decision if I have to leave or if I get to stay. A decision like this requires a clear head and all the facts, so I'm grateful for my decent night's sleep. If

Crew hadn't broken into my house, I'm sure I'd be gone right now. My instinct to flee would've gotten the best of me, I'm sure.

I also need to figure out how he broke into my house without triggering the alarm. I did my best not to think about that one last night when he held me tight in his arms. I didn't need anything else to stress me out.

All eyes come to me when I turn the corner. My old farmhouse is built hell for stout, there're no squeaks or creaks in the old wood floors and stairs. Although, I could've used a creak or two last night when Crew snuck up on me like a stealth ninja.

"Holy shit. What's wrong with you?" I knew that was coming and Clara certainly didn't let me down.

I'm forced to look away from her. This is because Crew is standing against my counter holding a coffee cup. If my eyes weren't so swollen, I'm sure they'd pop out of my head at the sight of my neighbor. His shirt is unbuttoned and hanging open, giving me a glimpse of his chest and abs. He has a smidgen of chest hair trailing down his tanned skin, disappearing into his now wrinkled suit pants. When I look down, his large feet are bare and crossed at the ankles.

It's crazy, but even his feet look strong.

"You sleep okay?" I look up and he's tipping his mug to his full lips. Lips that've been on mine—in the White House of all places. Oh, and in my bedroom. And my bed. His dark eyes are narrowed, and if I had to guess, he's trying to figure out what he'll get from me after last night.

"Addy, what happened to you?" Clara interjects, demanding an answer. She's sitting in a kitchen chair leaned back, making room for her growing belly.

Trying to ignore Crew, I answer her, "Nothing. I'm fine."

"Did he do that to you? Your face is swollen and puffy," she snaps. Then she turns to Crew and pointing a finger straight at him, not letting the fact that he's built like a brick house compared to her petite pregnant frame frighten her. "What in the hell did you do to her? You were obviously with her last night and she's been crying. Why was she crying—"

"Clara, enough," I have to raise my voice to get her attention. After last night and how Crew proved he'd do anything to keep me safe, I don't like her accusation, and I really don't like her yelling at him. I go on firmly, "Lower your voice. You don't know him yet, but Crew wouldn't hurt me. I don't want you speaking to him like that."

At my defense of Crew, her eyes get big and she looks taken aback. Her voice dips when she asks, "What?"

I sigh, still tired. I look over at Crew whose head is tipped with his eyes on me. They're sharp with a hint of surprise, too. Looking back to Clara, I reiterate, "You'll see in time. He'd never do anything to upset me. This," I flip my hand toward my face as I move to get coffee, "is nothing. I must've had an allergic reaction last night."

"I didn't know you were allergic to anything." She frowns as she stares, confused by everything, I'm sure.

"Me either. Maybe it's just the White House. I'm probably allergic to politicians." Of course Crew is standing in front of my coffee cups. I do my best to ignore his bare chest and abs when I bite my lip while saying, "You're...in my way."

He doesn't move, but his free hand comes around my lower back, hauling me to him. When my body is plastered to the front of his, he holds me tight. He doesn't look away when he sets his mug down on the counter while pressing in on my back. The next thing I know, he's leaning in to kiss me, and not at all chastely, right in front of Clara.

Just like last night, both at the White House and in my room, I melt into him.

When he finally breaks his kiss, he leans away just enough where I can only see his eyes.

"Thank you," he murmurs.

I don't say anything, but give him a ghost of a smile.

He gives me a squeeze. "You didn't answer me."

Putting my hands to his shirt, I try to push away and my voice comes out small. "I need coffee."

"How did you sleep?" he repeats, and damn if he doesn't sound as if he really cares.

Looking up into his dark brown eyes, I give up. He's not going to let me go until I answer. "Better than I thought I would."

He finally pulls away a bit, still keeping me close. "I'm glad you slept. How do you take your coffee? I'll get it for you."

I tip my head and raise my brows. "I thought you knew everything."

He smiles big enough that his dimple greets me. "I know a lot, but I don't know that."

This brings my thoughts back to last night, wondering about his so-called clearance and what he actually does know. For now, if he wants to get me coffee, I'll let him. I can't remember the last time someone got me a cup of coffee.

"Lots of cream and a half-teaspoon of sugar."

He grins and kisses my forehead before releasing me.

When I turn, Clara's eyes are bugged out of her head. Shrugging, I give her the look that threatens, *not now*. She frowns, unhappy as she likes to be kept abreast of all juicy details in life, no matter the subject. I shouldn't be surprised when she keeps at me. "Politicians might be jackasses, but no one's allergic to them. Why do you look like that?"

"It's not a big deal. I'll be fine." I try to appease her so she'll quit badgering me and decide to change the subject. "Why're you here? I can't remember your schedule—do you need help?"

"No." She starts as she rubs her belly and continues to be the in-your-face friend I know her to be. Usually I love it, but today it's annoying. "I wanted to see how last night went. When I saw the cows without you this morning, I couldn't wait any longer. That's when I found hunka-hunka burning love here, making coffee in your kitchen. I gave him the what-for, he explained he's your neighbor. I bought it, deciding not to kick his ass until you came down looking like that. But just sayin'," she raises her brows, giving me her serious face, "he didn't have a shirt on when I got here."

Huh, I don't remember him taking his shirt off last night.

"Anyhoots," she continues, "Mr. Fancy Pants convinced me he was A-okay. I figured you hooked up with someone at the White House. I was all excited for you until he told me he was your neighbor and you were still in bed. Then I find out he's not only your neighbor, but he's the smoochie kind of neighbor who you're a *teensy bit* protective of. So, I want to know—why haven't I met him? And if everyone else knows about the smooches but me, I'm gonna be pissed."

I hear a chuckle when a steaming cup of coffee appears in front of me at the same moment I feel his lips on the top of my head. I ignore him and glare at her. "You're fired."

"Ha!" she belts. "I'm not fired. You're already worried what's going to happen when I pop this next monster out and I'm down for the count. You know I'll bring the baby to work just to get out of the house. Trust me—kids have you snowed for at least the first fifteen months before they turn on you."

"You want coffee?" Crew asks Clara.

She smirks. "No thanks, Hot Lips." Looking back at me, she adds, "He hasn't met my children. They don't need any caffeine in the womb to spur them on, do they?"

Well, at least she speaks the truth.

"How was last night? Did you see the President? Or get close to him? Did people fawn over our wine? Please tell me you drummed me up some business," she rapid fires questions at me.

I sit back in my chair and sigh, angry my big night for the winery was ruined by Sheldon O'Rourke or whoever he is, and whatever he's trying to do. Thinking back before the drama in the Red Room, I look at her across the table. "It was great. Everything was from the region. Obviously, there wasn't any fanfare about the wine, that wasn't what the night was about. But there was a write-up about it in the program and menu. I stole a copy, it's in my purse. I'll find it later—we'll have it framed or something."

"So cool. I still can't believe our goods were served at the White House." She smiles, hauling herself up to her feet. "I can't wait to get the marketing materials back—I plan on slapping potential clients silly with it. I've gotta go, I have an appointment in thirty and I walked up that damn hill. I should've driven."

"I—" but stop myself. Not knowing what's going on, I decide to finish carefully. "Maybe I'll be in later, but I might work from here. Call if you need anything."

Clara looks at Crew and then back to me, smiling with big eyes. "If I wasn't married with three monsters and one on the way, I'd work from here, too. Especially if he's all you made him out to be."

"You're fired again." I finally smile.

She waddles to the back door of the kitchen, but on her way she leans in close to me and whispers, "Put some ice on your face. Later, I'll send Evan down with some cucumbers for your eyes. You need a little...um...rejuvenation." When she stands, she gives me a serious as shit look, telling me I look as bad as I thought I did.

When the door slams, my chest instantly tightens. I'm alone again with Crew. I came down this morning, planning to demand answers, but now I'm afraid to ask and more afraid of what I might find out.

I huff once and shake my head. Leaning my elbows on the table, I rub my swollen eyes. "I look like shit."

"Addison," he calls for me. I look up and to the side. He's standing at the counter again, this time with his arms crossed, his voice soft. "You don't look like shit."

"I feel like shit. I'm sorry about last night. And I'm really sorry about your car."

"Nothing to be sorry about."

"I haven't had a panic attack in years. I learned to cope as I got older, but last night I...lost it. Controlling my environment is the only way I can keep it in check. I haven't had one like that in a long time."

He doesn't respond, but moves to me and yanks out a chair. Before I know it, my hands are in his where I'm forced to turn and face him. Leaning in to rest his elbows to his knees, he pulls us close, nothing in my sight but Crew.

He continues with his soft tone and ignores everything I just said when he states, "You were five."

I pull in a breath, realizing he's not wasting any time or letting me drink my coffee first. I nod, but don't utter a word.

He tips his head, his deep dark eyes searching my face. My house is eerily silent but his voice is low and soothing, cutting through the quiet, when he asks, "Do you remember?"

My eyes burn thinking of it, because yes. I remember everything. Every second.

I sound rough and hoarse when I answer. "Yes."

I'm not sure at what age you start remembering every detail of your life, but for me, it was that moment. From then on, I've remembered everything in grave detail. Before my dad was killed, my recollection was hazy. When I got older, I spent years searching out details in my brain. I remember little things about happier times with both my parents, but it's like comparing a snapshot to a feature film. Glimpses, hints, images. Up until that day, my life was flashes of memories. But from the instant my dad fell to the ground next to me on that bright, sunny, winter day, I remember everything like it happened two minutes ago.

Blood seeping out of a gunshot wound to the head on stark white snow would be enough to brand anyone's memory, though.

"You were so little," he says, pulling me back to the present. "It was just you and your dad when it happened?"

I nod. "We were running errands for my mom. It was right after he got off work, during rush hour. It was so busy, people everywhere. There was so much commotion when it happened. People were running and at the time I didn't understand, but when I was older I got it. They thought there'd be more shots, a mass incident. Everyone was racing for cover, but I just stood there, confused. I had no idea what happened, why my dad fell to the ground and all the blood."

"I'm sorry, Addison," he whispers.

"They never figured out who killed him. Army investigators came up with some retaliation story when the allegations against my dad began. Even the FBI was involved. They said information was being leaked to some former KGB from where he worked at Ft. Meade and all fingers pointed to him. They finally concluded the Russians were afraid their mole was getting cold feet and needed to eliminate him to protect themselves. My mom was adamant he didn't do what they said. She said he would never act against his country. He went to West Point, Crew. Duty, Honor, Country. He lived by the Coat of Arms."

"You don't remember O'Rourke?"

I shake my head adamantly. "I told you that last night."

With my hands still in his, he keeps on, gently. "He worked with your dad." At that, I try to sit up straight and pull away from him, but he holds firm, not letting me go. "They served together in the Army and, at the time of your dad's death, were both stationed at Ft. Meade. You don't remember him at all?"

I shake my head. "No. He said last night he knew my parents— that I used to favor my dad but grew up to look like my mom. No one's ever talked to me about my dad. No one but my mom. And he *knew* my mom, Crew. The *real* her. Like you know me."

His eyes turn sharp again and even though I've only been around him a week, I realize he falls into a mode when he does this. His stature doesn't change, but his demeanor does, I see it in his eyes. He exudes it. It's assessing, imposing, and with all that happened last night, as much as it confused me before, right now it scares me. I don't know what it means and I don't like it one bit.

He considers me carefully, as if he's trying to make a decision. "How much do you know about your dad?"

My answer comes quickly. "I know everything about my dad."

It's true. I was five when it happened and it was horrendous. It would've been terrifying for anyone, but especially a five-year-old child. My mom made sure I knew the truth.

Pausing, he narrows his sharp eyes before giving my hands a squeeze. His voice is low when he informs me, "Your dad wasn't guilty of espionage like they claimed. He was framed."

"I know that," I respond, quick and firm.

His head jerks as he frowns, surprised by my response. "You do?"

"I told you, my mom was adamant. She knew he didn't do what they said he did. She knew he would never betray his country. When I was old enough, she told me everything. She even told me more right before she died. I know that's why we left, why she went to the lengths she went through protecting me. She told me how hard it was changing our identities, but she managed it all by herself. She also knew she made a mistake right after he was killed, fighting for his name to be cleared because they came after her."

"No." He keeps frowning. "What I'm saying to you is they know he was framed and didn't commit treason. And when I say 'they,' I mean the government. I shouldn't be telling you this, but you have a right to know. I can't go into details because it's classified, but what I will tell you is there's an ongoing federal investigation that could eventually clear your dad's name. Officially."

My eyes immediately fill with tears thinking about my dad's name being cleared. And more, what it would've meant to my mom. But the fear seeps in again and I whisper, "How do you know this?"

After another pause, he continues, but carefully. "I told you, I have a certain amount of clearance. My people alerted me when O'Rourke was headed this way. When I found out he was at your winery, I came to see what he was up to. I saw him with you and demanded to know everything about him. He's a high level target who's tied to your father's death."

Even though he's not giving me any real information, I realize how he must know all this. I try to rip my hands out of his, wondering how I missed it. My mom warned me for years. It doesn't matter how overwhelming his dimple and scruff are, I should have doubted him. He looks nothing like your run-of-the-mill computer programmer. I might've just made the biggest mistake ever by trusting my new neighbor.

I'm such an idiot.

Panic starts to creep back in as I accuse, barely able to hear myself. "You're CIA."

Chapter Ten

Work For It

Addy

He frowns at my accusation, squeezing my hands to hold me in my spot.

My mom told me about the months after my dad was killed. How she was harassed, not only by the media, but their friends, and most specifically, the CIA. They investigated her, claiming they had to rule out she had anything to do with my dad's so-called traitorous acts. She was put through hell, mainly by intelligence officials, describing most of them to be on a witch hunt, wanting and needing to close the case because of public and media pressure. My mom described those months—dealing with her husband's murder, her child witnessing it, and being investigated herself—as nothing less than living in the depths of hell.

When the CIA couldn't find anything on her and declared all the information false that proved my dad innocent, she did the only thing she could do. She ran. And she used all the money she had left to buy new identities for the both of us.

To say that my mom didn't trust the government, especially the CIA, is a gross understatement.

"No," he answers, resolutely. "I'm not CIA."

"What are you, then?" I raise my voice, fear creeping through me, hoping against hope I haven't made a mistake trusting him.

His face quickly turns hard as he holds my hands in his firm grip. Regarding me carefully, he's bordering on angry when he says, "This is me proving myself to you, Addison. Last night and just now. I wish I could tell you more, but that can't happen. I'm letting you in on sensitive information about your dad. Information that isn't mine to share. I did it so you'd trust me enough to know I can keep you safe. I have the means and the skills to do it. I've been doing it since Sunday when O'Rourke approached you the first time. I said it last night and I'll say it again—you're safer here than anywhere. I'll even go out on a limb and venture you're safer now than you've ever been in your entire life."

"What are you talking about?" Protecting me? How has he been protecting me since Sunday?

He sighs. "Because of my work, my property is vastly secure. After O'Rourke visited you Sunday, I extended that to you. Your home, business, and entire property are being constantly monitored. How do you think I knew you were packing last night? Your blinds were open—I could see you running around in a panic."

This time I do rip my hands out of his, exclaiming, "You can see in my house? You've been watching me? You can't do that!"

My mind does a quick inventory—thinking back on my week. Please, let me have closed my blinds every day. Holy shit, he's looking into my freaking windows. I just let a crazy man sleep in my bed.

Lips tightened, he tips his head, looking at me like I'm unreasonable for complaining about him stalking me. "Yeah, I watched you last night. I can read you, Addison. When I found you with O'Rourke, you were freaked the fuck out. You wouldn't let me come in and I had a feeling you'd do something stupid. But I haven't been 'watching' you. I've been keeping an eye on you—that's different. I had a feeling you'd do something to put yourself in danger and I was right. I checked the cameras and saw you running around in a fit."

"Cameras?" I yell.

He leans back in his seat and crosses his arms, looking frustrated. "Relax, you make it sound weird. I'm not sneaking around in your trees. The system alerts me if cars or people approach your property. Specifically at night, since you have so many people coming and going during the day with the winery. I had a feeling you'd do something stupid when you wouldn't let me in, so I watched you. I was right. Where would you be right now had I not stopped you?"

My eyes widen, shocked by his nonchalant-ness of spying on me. He's got to be breaking some kind of law or something. Suddenly I'm defensive and stand, my chair scratching across the floor.

"If you have me on twenty-four hour watch status, why was it necessary for you to stay the night?"

He stands, towering over me. When he takes a step, I have to tip my head to see him—there's got to be at least eight inches separating us as we stand in my kitchen, both of us on bare feet. He surprises me when his hands come up to cup my face, his sharp eyes connecting with mine.

"You didn't see you," he utters in a gravelly voice.

I say nothing, but I pull in a sharp intake of air. Even I know I was a mess last night.

He goes on. "When I met you a week ago, walking with your cows, I knew none of this. I just knew you were my neighbor. That day, I knew I wanted to know you. I wanted to know the woman who would take on cows for pets and throw attitude back at me as fast as I could dish it out and who gives her wine away to neighbors. Then I learned you were meeting with a high level target and that target was lookin' at you like he was interested in everything but your wine. On top of all that, for the first time in my life, I find myself having to work to stay focused. I'm *always* focused, but it slips when I'm around you."

I exhale through parted lips. "What are you saying?"

His answer comes instantly. "I'm saying when that focus slips, I feel it everywhere. So yeah, you were safe with the sensors and the cameras alerting me of a threat, but you're fucking crazy if you think I could've left you last night. Not after you cried in my arms and I saw the fear in your eyes. No way could I leave you."

"Crew," I breathe and sink into him. When I do, his hands slide down my neck and shoulders, circling my back. When he draws me in, I hope he means what I think he does. Because my instinct is fighting my head, telling me to trust him with everything—my safety and my heart.

Even if the cameras do weird me out.

His hands separate—one going into my hair, the other to my ass where he holds me tight. "I'm saying, I thought I wanted you when I met you, but now I couldn't stay away if you made me. In my work, I need to be sharp and focused. Working for it is not something I'm used to. I'm not letting you go anywhere, but I'll tell you, I'd appreciate it if you'd cooperate. If I can rest easy and know you aren't gonna run off, you'll make my life a lot easier."

A moment goes by as his words penetrate, warming me all over. It's all too much—Sheldon O'Rourke, learning that Crew knows everything about me, my dad, and him telling me he couldn't stay away if he wanted. My eyelids droop and I exhale, planting my face in his bare chest where his shirt is hanging open. He's warm and smells rugged, if that's even a scent. I sink into him further, the bare skin of his chest feeling good on my face and I wonder how the rest of him would feel on me.

Even as I'm thinking about the rest of him bare, I still mumble, "The cameras freak me out."

He gives me a squeeze and I feel his lips at the top of my head. "They're there to keep you safe."

"What have you seen?" I dread knowing, but I have to ask.

He pulls away from me and when I'm forced to look up, the side of his mouth is tipped. "I'm not a Peeping Tom. If I want to see you, I'll work for it because when I see you for the first time, I plan on being there to touch you. I have no desire to see you over a camera. Starting now, I plan on working for it."

The thought of that makes me quiver because I want that, but I don't lie when I say, "This is all too much."

"I agree. I'd rather just be working for it rather than worrying about CIA targets at the same time. I can handle both and I plan to start immediately. After last night, you shouldn't leave the vineyard by yourself. Please make it easy on me. You'll stay put and cooperate?"

"The thought of leaving is gut-wrenching," I tell him the truth. "I don't want to leave my business and everyone in my life."

His full lips form a small smile. "That's good to hear."

I soften my voice and add, "Plus, I'm curious to find out how you're going to work for it."

His smile grows into a grin as it comes closer. When his mouth hits mine, I circle his back to hold on as he turns us. With the table at my back, he grabs my hips and before I know it I'm plopped on top. Stepping between my legs, he leans in to kiss me.

His kiss is deep and intense. So much so, I have to lean back on my hands to keep my balance as he comes over me, sliding his hands up my sides. This is like last night in the Red Room, but better. Better because I'm not scared, better because he's in my house, and finally, better because of what he told me, allowing myself to trust someone outside of my mom for the first time in almost twenty-five years.

But everything else makes it great. Well, everything is better but the cameras.

I've got a grasp on my life again and that feels good. That sense of security feels like a gift and Crew gave that to me by making me feel safe.

And he makes me feel wanted. I haven't put myself out there to feel wanted for so long. I like how it feels, especially when I want him.

Despite those fucking cameras.

Just when his hand dives in my hair, pulling my head back for better access, the doorbell chimes. I tense and our lips stop moving, but we stay where we are.

"Is that another employee?" he asks against my lips.

"No," I exhale to catch my breath. "My employees just walk in. They all have a key."

His head jerks back, frowning at me. "Why?"

"I don't know," I tell him the truth. "I guess my house feels like an extension of the winery and they're the only people in my life. They all have keys."

His frown deepens when he opens his mouth, probably to grumble about so many people having access to my house, but whoever's at the door is impatient. It rings again, then impatiently, again.

"I'd better get that." I try to move, but he gives me a squeeze.

Giving me a quick kiss, he stops me. "I'll get it."

He heads out of the kitchen, but this is my house. I hop down and follow through the main hall.

When Crew unlocks and swings my extra wide, heavy door open, a man is standing on my porch with his arms crossed. And he doesn't look happy to be standing on my doorstep.

His hair is rich brown, but since he's standing in the morning sun, layers of rich color from chestnut to gold are shining through. He's well over six feet and all bulk. He's dressed in cargos and a navy blue tee. But his eyes, as angry as they appear, are perfectly silver-blue.

Oh, and they're on me.

"What do you want?" Crew bites out.

It seems he's not here for me.

This draws his attention, his blue eyes moving to Crew before he turns and looks at Crew's poor Jag. It shouldn't surprise me that it looks worse this morning, and this makes me cringe. Seeing the after effects of what we endured is plain scary. "What the fuck happened to your car?"

Sounding like it's no big deal, Crew shrugs. "A scuffle. I'll explain later."

He thinks last night was a scuffle? He is definitely *not* a computer programmer.

The guy turns back to Crew. "You're not answering your phone."

"I'm busy. Told you where I was and when I'd be back," Crew clips.

The guy smirks. "You need to finish up being busy. We've got shit to do and something's come up."

Crew sighs and looks over at me. "This is Grady Cain. We work together. The clean air out here in the country isn't good for his system. It makes him irritable."

"No," Grady breaks in, still smirking. "I'm irritable because I'm hungry and I'm in the country with no restaurants close by."

I extend my hand. "I'm Addy."

"I know," he says, accepting my hand.

Of course he does.

"There's a deli in the tasting room. It's not a restaurant, but Maggie makes great sandwiches, soups, and salads," I tell him.

Grady frowns at me. "Really?"

"And cheese, meats, and baguettes, but that's not really a meal for someone like you. You might like the sandwiches," I keep trying. "She's open from eleven to six Wednesday through Sunday. We're closed Monday's and offer limited items on Tuesday's since she's off."

"I've been here for months and I could've eaten a sandwich next door five days a week? I'm going today for lunch." He pauses and looks at Crew before finishing, "and dinner."

Crew ignores him. "Give me ten minutes."

Grady raises a brow and shakes his head before shooting me a grin. "Thanks for letting me know about the deli. Good to meet you, Addison."

"No-no," I say quickly, halting him. I'm firm when I explain, "It's Addy. I don't care what Crew says. Don't call me Addison."

His grin gets bigger. "I like not listening to Crew. Addy it is."

I smile at him in relief, but don't get a chance to thank him because Crew throws the front door shut in his face.

He grabs my hand, pulling me to him. One hand goes around me and his other cups my face. "I've gotta go. Things are ramping up—we've got a lot to do."

"Are you going to tell me what you do?"

He says nothing and presses his lips together, shaking his head. "That's not a good idea."

"That doesn't really seem fair, Crew. You know everything about me."

He sighs. "I know, and I'm sorry."

I don't push it, because really, he does sound sorry. And even though I've only known him a week, there's something about him that's making him easy to trust.

I get back to the matter at hand. "I have all kinds of questions."

"I'm sure you do. You can ask me tonight when I come over to start working at it. Ask me what you want and I'll answer everything I can. But Addison, there'll be things I can't answer. You're going to have to be okay with that."

My insides turn funny thinking about the answers he could have for me. If he can tell me anything about my dad, I'll take it. Now more than ever, I'm desperate for information. "I think I can do that."

"Come here," he murmurs, pulling me closer. His mouth lands on mine and before I know it, his tongue is delving in.

He holds me tight, but kisses me slowly this time. His lips are soft moving on me, using his tongue to taste, letting it linger. Even though this is different, it's just as good and I let my fingers drag down his bare chest. I haven't been with anyone since before my mom got sick. This feels good, to be wanted and held in a man's arms. But having Crew's arms around me, Crew's lips on mine?

Yes, this is good. Really good, and he feels even better.

I lightly drag my nails over his nipples, and the second I do, he groans into my mouth. Before I know it, I'm turned and pushed up against the door.

There's not one thing soft about his kiss anymore. He's devouring me, pressing me into the antique wood. His hips press into my stomach, where I feel him long and hard.

I feel a tingle in my nipples and wetness between my legs. I feel it everywhere. Even though it's been a long time for me, no one's ever made my body hum the way Crew does. That's all him and I throw every care out the window that I've only known him a week. This week has been like none other, so I put that out of my head and let myself want him. All of him.

We're both breathing hard, our mouths still touching when he rests his forehead on mine. He exhales as he squeezes my hip. "I've gotta go."

I dip my head into his neck and feel his lips touch my forehead. "Okay."

"Are you going to work from here today or the tasting room?"

I tip my head back to look at him, asking sarcastically, "Why do I have to tell you when you can just check your cameras?"

"You know," he starts with a smile forming, meeting my sarcastic tone with his own. "You make it sound strange."

My eyes go big. "That's because it is."

"Not for me. Part of my business is information. I'm not watching you, I'm watching for those I don't want to get near you."

"You watched me last night."

He shrugs unapologetically. "True, but I got to sleep with you in my arms and you're here now, so it worked. I'll change my answer. I'm not only watching for those I don't want near you, but I'm also making sure you don't put yourself in danger by doing stupid shit."

"I've done okay up until now, and I'm thirty-one," I throw back at him.

He presses his groin into my stomach for emphasis. "You're not happy right here? When I had my mouth on you, you didn't seem like a woman wanting to run out the front door."

At that I say nothing but do roll my eyes, because he's right. I'd be scared to death right now had I left in haste like I planned last night. Plus, I have to squeeze my thighs as he presses into me, because right now, I don't want to be anywhere but right here. In fact, the only thing that would make it better would be more of Crew's bare skin.

"I'll see you tonight," he smiles.

I return his smile, but mine is smaller. "I guess I won't need to tell you when I get home, since you can see for yourself."

At this, he laughs.

I don't say anything else about him watching me, because to see Crew Vega—who can be brooding, sharp, and intense—laugh for the first time, is a sight to see.

And I let every second of it soak in.

Chapter Eleven

A Game Without Rules

Marc Whittaker

Sitting at the far end of the bar where I can see the door, I pick up my beer and take a sip. It's late, but not late for Washington Harbour and Georgetown. I'm too old for this crowd—they're just getting started.

Into my second beer, he walks through the doors of the Orange Anchor. I don't hail him or draw attention to myself. He'll find me.

He finally sees me and wedges his way through the crowd to order a drink straight from the bartender. It's Friday night and the place is a rush. The Washington bar crowd has filled the place, as well as the entire harbor, with boats lined up and docked on the Potomac getting ready for the weekend.

Eventually, the stool next to me becomes vacant. Casually,

O'Rourke slides into it.

He doesn't look at me when he speaks, barely loud enough where I can hear him over the crowd. "I don't like being beckoned."

I pick at the popcorn in front of me, seasoned with Old Bay, and say into my beer, "They want an update and you didn't reach out. You know better than me—when you reach out, you won't be summoned."

"There's no reason for communication. She was surprised like I thought she'd be. She has no motive to do *anything*. Judging by the look on her face last night, they've whipped up a shit storm and thrown me in the middle of it. I did what they wanted and she was so fucking thrown by my reveal, I know there's no way she's up to anything. At this point, if she's anything like her mom, I doubt she's still in town. Especially with the shit they pulled after the dinner last week. Trying to run them off the road and shoot them down? They can't do that shit in the States."

I sit relaxed while concentrating on my drink, listening to his frustration. Giving a chin lift to the bartender who set a fresh bowl of popcorn in front of me, I continue. "You know not to keep them waiting."

"I've been doing this for decades. Don't tell me how to handle them. I know what I'm doing, but they're digging where they don't need to dig." It's easy to hear the defensiveness in his tone.

I've been with O'Rourke for five years—I know he knows the score. Hell, he taught me the score. But they're getting restless and have wanted him to check into her for almost a year since they located her again. O'Rourke only relented to do it himself when I stepped up and said I'd get it done.

"They're not happy," I mutter.

"If you're their new messenger, tell them what I just told you, then leave it the fuck alone. I'll get in touch with them next week about the next installment. They know there's a new system to work around, it'll take me longer than usual." He sighs through his words.

"They're losing patience and want to know if she's still here. You insisted on doing this instead of me and didn't finish the task. Considering your background with her parents," I pause, looking around to make sure no one's paying attention to us, "especially your feelings for her mother, they question if you can be objective. If I had taken care of this like I wanted, it would've been done by now."

I let my eyes jump right, and when I do, he's furious.

"It's pointless. And what happened twenty-five years ago didn't have one fucking thing to do with Anne," he growls.

"Like you said," I shift to stand, reaching for my wallet, "I'm nothing but the messenger. You know they want to be assured she's not here for anything more than peddling her wine. You make sure ghosts stay buried where they belong, they'll back off. Until then, they want more convincing." I pull a couple bills from my wallet. Catching the eye of the bartender, I toss it on the counter.

"I need time." His voice is as tense as his body.

"I'll let them know. After all, I am the new messenger," I drawl, not able to fight back the sarcasm. Finding my valet ticket, I don't look at him when I add before leaving him at the bar, "Enjoy your weekend, Sheldon."

When I walk out of the restaurant, I do it knowing he's stewing. He should be. He's in deep, but he's been thoroughly compensated for it. They'll allow him to continue on with the status quo if he follows orders, but they were resolute. They want to be convinced, and from my conversation with them, that's not going to happen easily.

Yeah, edging my way in as the messenger is proving advantageous. I've sat back and watched for five years, I'm ready to move myself up the food chain and this is my chance. The way I see it, it's a game without rules.

Chapter Twelve

Blame it All on the Dimple

Crew

It's not late, but later than I wanted it to be before I got to Addison. There's still shit that needs to get done, but we're almost squared away for next week.

I thought we'd have five accept and I was right, but today we had a guy back out. I've never been on this end of business like Asa, who assured me it's fine and it happens. Although, he said not as often as one would think. When men get an opportunity like this, they usually jump, never looking back. Then again, the profiling process is arduous, the targets are usually spot on.

We'll have four trainees, not five, but that's okay for a first go. At least I brought Asa on with me, he's done this before. If I fuck anything up, it won't be as bad with a smaller group. I thought my conscience would grip me, recruiting others into something they had no clue of before we approached them, but it doesn't. They're men and we aren't hiding anything. They've been told what they're getting into.

I toss my papers on the card table, thinking the furniture I ordered can't get here soon enough. It should be delivered next week.

When I move out of my office to get to Addison, Grady meets me coming in.

"You done for the day?" I ask.

He doesn't look happy and also ignores my question. "I just got off the phone with Carson. It's official. Your neighbor's bad guy's little wine-drinking friend is on the list. Counter Terrorism just started tapping his phones. A call was intercepted thirty minutes ago and they barely had to minimize it. He went straight into talking about Addy."

My body turns tight and I take an easy guess. "Whittaker?"

"Yeah," he answers quickly. "He got a call from a guy in London. Whoever he's involved with wants more proof your neighbor isn't here under any circumstances besides selling wine. The conversation was short and sweet, but from reading between the lines, they suspect she's here to avenge her dad's death. Or at the very least, learn more about it."

From my experience doing this job, I'd bet all my bank accounts they've been keeping tabs on her and her mom all these years. "I'm sure the move here threw up a red flag."

"Most likely. They've got their fingers in too much, no way they just found her after all this time," Grady asserts, echoing my thoughts. "I'll tell you what though, Carson is around the bend about you—and now us—dirtyin' our hands with this shit. Especially after you getting shot at last night. He's not pleased."

I narrow my eyes. We're not getting involved for shits and giggles.

Even though Carson doesn't know why I can't step away, Grady sure does. "Last night was no big deal. They were amateurs, and Carson can kiss my ass. Who's in London?"

"Don't know. They're looking into him now. He's got political connections, both old school and current." Grady crosses his arms and sighs, frustrated. "Only you would settle next door to a woman being targeted by ancient KGB."

"What does that mean?"

"It means, I know you and I know you're all in. It doesn't have one fuck of a thing to do with how beautiful or single she is. Though, I'm sure it didn't hurt and now that I've seen you with her, I can see you're *all in*."

"Even if I wasn't *all in*, would you be able to look away? Leave her to it? You're the one who grew up in a henhouse," I shoot back. Grady's the oldest of five and the only boy. He's fiercely protective of the women in his family, and for good reason.

"What I'm sayin'," he continues, ignoring me, "is you're screwed. I've known you for ten years. I know you'd be all in to protect someone being threatened by the assholes you're used to taking out. I also know you can appreciate a beautiful woman, but I know you and I can tell this is different. It's easy to see she can dish back your shit but still be all woman for you to enjoy, protect, and love on. You put that together with being targeted by old KGB, there's no hope. You're a fuckin' goner."

I cross my arms and shake my head, because Grady's a freak. "Love on?"

His brows rise. "Hell yeah."

I sigh, ready to finish with this and get to Addison. "Has Carson sent a transcript of the call yet? I told him I wanted to know everything they've got on O'Rourke and Whittaker."

"It's being transcribed now. He said he'll send it."

I ignore his grin and move quickly around him, heading to the kitchen. I pull a pizza out of the freezer and six-pack out of the fridge.

"What are you doin'?" Grady asks.

"Taking dinner to Addison." I grab my keys off the counter and look to him over my shoulder. "I'd say lock up when you leave, but we're so secure here, it doesn't matter."

"You're bringing her a frozen pizza?"

"Yep."

He huffs, "I hope your charm outweighs your effort. We need to learn how to cook. I need to eat and you're not gonna win a woman by bringing her frozen food."

I raise an eyebrow at him. "I've got other skills, Grady. I don't need to know how to cook."

"Please tell me she can cook," he goes on. The man has always been obsessed with food.

I'm losing patience with this conversation. "I could care less if she cooks."

His eyes widen, surprised. "Shit, you are a goner. But for my sake, I hope the woman can cook. Maybe if she cooks for you, she'll feel sorry for me. If I have to put up with watchin' you go soft, at least I'll do it on a full stomach."

"Trust me, Grady." I turn to him one last time before leaving. "There's nothing soft on me when it comes to Addison Wentworth."

His lip curls as his face scrunches. He looks put-out when he grumbles, "I guess I'll see you tomorrow."

"Yeah," I call before shutting the door behind me with the cold pizza box and six-pack dangling from a finger. "I'm not coming home tonight."

Addy

I lean back in my chair at the kitchen table, sitting kitty-corner from Crew. We just finished dinner and as anxious as I might be, I'm still tired from last night.

As promised, Crew returned late this evening. He texted me this afternoon telling me he'd bring dinner, but he'd be late, as he was busy finishing up a project. At first this freaked me out, since I never gave him my number.

Then, of course, I remembered.

He knows everything about me besides how I take my coffee. Then again, I gave up that bit of information this morning, too, making it official. The man knows absolutely everything there is to know about me.

This made me feel all kinds of emotions. I was nervous, excited, anxious, and yes, even frustrated. I couldn't help but wonder all day about what he does for a living and how he knows...well...*everything*. I became more frustrated when I thought about the very expensive security system I had installed after moving in, which he magically disarmed without the code. And finally, after all that happened last night, he even demanded I blindly give him my trust.

I've never blindly trusted anyone. It's not who I am.

Hell, I've hardly trusted anyone with my eyes wide open, given all the facts.

There's just something about him. Everything in me is telling me he's real, he's good, and he's different. Where I've a hard time trusting anyone, my mind, heart, and gut is begging me to go with it. To go in blind. To trust him.

He's seen me at my worst. I'm not sure I can remember a lower point in my adult life than the fear I felt last night.

Other than the moment I lost my mom forever.

I've been preoccupied with it all day, fighting the urge to trust him. I fought it as I made phone calls to clients about upcoming events. As I paid bills and approved marketing materials. When I took a bath, soaking away the stress from last night while praying the cucumber slices would reduce the swelling in my eyes. And I thought over all my options as I applied a mask, with hopes of diminishing the puffiness in my face.

I thought through it all, because this is what I do. I analyze. It's how I've always managed. This was me searching for the control I need to function.

Hell, I need it to breathe.

I also went to these extremes because Clara was being kind by saying I needed rejuvenation. I looked like shit. And if Crew was coming back tonight, I didn't want to look like shit for him.

So I worked from home, sort of, and did everything a girl could do to pull herself back together.

I primped.

It worked for the most part, and for the rest, thank the makeup goddesses for concealer and tinted moisturizer. I didn't want to look like I was working too hard, even though I made monumental efforts to pull myself back to a state of normalcy. I let my minimal makeup do its job and dressed in a pair of perfectly faded jeans and a tee.

As much as I fought my urge all day, I finally gave in because I *really* wanted to trust Crew. I wanted it more than anything because I want him— and I want him to be real. If I give him my trust, I have a feeling he can help me learn everything I need to know about my dad's death. After the shock of last night, there's nothing more I want.

Well, that and Crew himself.

It was just an hour ago when the man who consumed my mind stalked through my kitchen door without so much as a knock. I shouldn't have been surprised even though I was. I was about to say something about his lack of etiquette, but he didn't give me the chance.

Tossing a frozen pizza on my table with a six-pack of beer, he advanced upon me quickly and purposefully. Without a word or warning, I was pressed up against my refrigerator by Crew's big strong body, his hands deep in my hair, and his mouth on mine.

It was such a surprise, I almost forgot to breathe as he kissed me crazy.

When he finally slowed, his hips pressed harder into my stomach when he murmured the same words as last night.

"Missed you."

Holy shit.

I would've fallen to the floor had I not been squished up against a kitchen appliance.

Still, I couldn't keep my voice from being small. "Really?"

His mouth returned to mine, but softer and slower this time, before he breathed against my lips. "Yeah."

I didn't ask anything further. His body and sweet words were enough to convince me. Plus, I was afraid of what he might do to prove how much he missed me. I was already a pile of goo, or I would've been had he not had me pinned against my fridge.

While the frozen pizza baked in my oven, he helped himself to my pantry and refrigerator. He found the partially eaten bag of BBQ chips leftover from poker night and a bowl of grapes.

How odd. I had no idea what to expect when he said he'd bring me dinner, but it wasn't this.

The next time he offers to feed me, I'll insist it's my turn. I'm no Martha Stewart, but I can do better than this. I hadn't had to cook much since moving here, usually eating whatever Maggie has left over from the day, but I thought it might be time to hone my skills in the kitchen.

That was an hour ago.

When I pop the last grape in my mouth, I grin, pushing my plate away. "Thanks for dinner. That was interesting."

He says nothing, but smiles big enough to tease me with his dimple.

I try to ignore the dimple, even though every time it comes out to play, it reminds me of his soft side hidden under the sharp. I try to focus on what's been nagging at me all day and move us past the casual conversation he's led since he kissed me crazy.

I don't beat around the bush when I start. "How did you turn off my alarm and get into my house last night?"

I don't lose the dimple completely, but it does fade when he narrows his eyes. It's his turn to push his plate away, and leaning back in his chair, he says nothing.

"You have to tell me." The seriousness in my voice rings through. "This is a huge house and I'm here alone. I spent a ton of money on my system—I need to know it's doing what it's supposed to do. You proved last night it's a piece of shit."

"It's not a piece of shit," he counters quickly.

"It didn't do its job. When something doesn't do what it's supposed to do, it's a piece of shit, Crew."

He frowns and gives his head a little shake. "Not many would be able to get around it."

"You got around it, which is one person too many."

He sort of changes the subject. "I asked you to trust me and you said you would. With my surveillance of your property, added to your security system, you're covered."

My eyes go big at the mention of his so-called surveillance of my home and business.

"Crew," I lean forward, stressing my words, "I said I'd trust you last night because I was exhausted and freaked. You said we'd talk today and it's time to talk. Especially about your cameras. I don't like them and I don't want them. What in the hell do you do that requires such a set up?"

He exhales deeply before leaning to me, taking my hands in his over the corner of the table. Pulling me closer, he says in a voice that grabs my heart, "I wish I could tell you, even though I don't want to tell you." I tip my head to the side in question before he gives my hands a squeeze. When he goes on, his voice dips. "I'm sorry."

"You want my trust?" I ask immediately.

"You have to trust me, Addison. There's a storm swirlin' around you. You don't have a choice."

I pull back a bit, biting my lip because I'm afraid he's right. My options are limited right now. I have but one—and he's it. Not a bad option, but it sucks not having choices.

Still, I counter, speaking my words with conviction. "Then trust *me.*"

"It's not that simple. Not with the people I work for, even the people I work with. Me not telling you isn't me not trusting you, it's me keeping that part of my life separate from you."

It's my turn to change the subject. "You slept in my bed last night."

His eyes flare at the mention of being in my bed, and the look on his face makes my nipples harden. Instantly grateful for the padded bra under my thin tee, I persevere.

"I liked you there," I go on in a whisper.

His voice is rough when he murmurs, "Addison."

"You're asking me to go in blind, Crew."

"You're right. I am."

"I need control," I add. "You saw what happens when I lose that."

All of a sudden, I'm not in my chair any longer. I'm up and yanked around the corner of the table where Crew pulls me onto his lap.

"Hey—" I cry out in surprise as he buries a hand in my hair, his other arm clamping around my thigh with a hand on my bottom. He brings my face close to his where he's a breath away.

I don't have time to say anymore because he interrupts me. "You let me take care of you—you can let that go."

I shake my head. "There's no way. I've suffered from panic attacks for years. I can't survive without knowing I have some sense of control."

"You'll learn to. I'll help you." He states this with conviction, like he knows for a fact he can best the challenge. I've been trying to best that challenge for years—I can't seem to get over it. "I promise, this shit with O'Rourke won't last forever. In fact, it shouldn't last long at all. What they're doin' is bad, but from what I've learned, the government is closin' in and wants to wrap this up as soon as possible. It's gone on too long. If you trust me, you won't need that control. I promise to take care of you, Addison."

I sigh, barely shaking my head, mulling it over. I know what I need, but I also know what I want.

I think he sees victory ahead, the finish line in sight, because he keeps talking as he gives me a squeeze. "You'll go in blind. For me."

I frown, throwing my words back quickly. "You're overly confident, you know that, right?"

I get a smirk. And a cocky one, at that.

Bringing my hands up to the side of his neck, I hold on. I don't say anything but feel my face fall in defeat when I finally nod my answer. This buys me a slow growing smile, which, from this proximity, is downright beautiful.

I guess I'm going in blind, trusting Crew after barely knowing him a week. Apparently, I'm going to do it not knowing anything about him when he knows absolutely everything about me.

Right before he pulls me in tighter to kiss me crazy for the second time tonight, I melt into him, giving in completely.

I'd say I hope it's worth it—that he won't let me down—that in the end it will be worth following my heart instead of my head.

But at that moment, it was. It totally was.

And I've decided to blame it all on the dimple.

Chapter Thirteen

Tuesday Nightie on Friday

Addy

For the second night in a row, Crew is in my bed. And just like last night, having him here makes my heart stir.

It hadn't taken long to clean up the kitchen from his simple, but odd, dinner. Since it was already late when we started, it was late-late by the time his dimple talked me into trusting him. With everything.

When he took me by the hand leading me out of the kitchen, I asked what he was doing. He answered with a question as he pulled me along. "You liked me in your bed last night?"

My eyes flared and I bit my lip. I said nothing because he already knew the answer.

His eyes heated when he responded to my silence as he led me up the two flights of stairs to my room. "You can like me there again tonight."

I had to fight against becoming a pile of mush, again. I didn't fight him because he was right. I liked him in my bed.

I wash my face and brush my teeth. I have no idea what to wear, but after sleeping in my dress last night, it's time to make a good showing.

Going to my closet, I shut myself in and strip down to my panties. I decide on a simple, but slightly skimpy, heather gray cotton nightie. It hits the middle of my thighs, has spaghetti straps and dips low in the front. It's not lacy or racy, screaming, "Make me your sex slave, pretty-please." What it is, is comfortable and cute with a side of sexy, even if it is sexy in a Tuesday-night sort of way. Friday-night-sexy would look like I was trying too hard.

Here I am, dressed in a Tuesday nightie with Crew waiting for me in my bed. When I finally open my closet door to find him lying there, he's bare chested with the covers barely pulled up to his hips. The lights are dim with only my bedside lamp casting a dull glow.

This is different. Settling in bed with him last night because I was upset from all that happened seemed oddly natural. Tonight, going to bed with my neighbor whom I've only known a week is awkward, and I don't like awkward.

He flips back the covers and he's wearing nothing but a pair of boxers. All of a sudden, I'm no longer ill at ease. Seeing him practically bare takes my breath away. His muscles are molded into one another and ripple down his body, doing that V-thingy before disappearing into his underwear. And his legs are thick and long, attesting to the fact he runs, works out, or does a shitload of squats every day. Although, I doubt he does squats. He probably leaps to the tops of trees, setting up cameras to spy on me. Either way, the results are delicious.

Realizing my eyes are everywhere but his, I look up and his are heated, dragging his gaze over me from top to bottom. I even hear the heat in his gravelly voice, ordering, "Come to bed."

I shouldn't be nervous. I slept with him last night, but when I reach the side of my bed, I have to tell him because I won't be able to sleep otherwise. "You're on my side."

He frowns. "You have a side?"

I only move to tip my head. "You don't? Everyone has a side."

"I don't."

"Well, I do and you're on it."

"You didn't have a side last night."

"I was upset last night. I wasn't in the mindset to think about it."

One side of his mouth tips as he keeps on, "If you get in, I'll make sure you won't think about it tonight, either."

"Crew," I drawl his name, complaining with my tone.

"Baby," his voice softens even as he sounds frustrated. "You said yourself you liked me here, but I'll bet your sweet ass I liked being here more than you liked having me here. It's late and even though tomorrow's Saturday, I've got a shitload to do. Now, come to bed. You look tired."

Maybe it's his tone or letting on he thinks my ass is sweet. Or maybe it's him telling me he liked being in my bed more than I liked him there—which is impossible, but the sentiment is sweet all the same. Whatever it is, I find myself once again relenting to Crew Vega.

Perseverance must be his middle name.

Crew Perseverance Vega.

It's strange, but it fits. It also doesn't bode well for me.

So I crawl into bed, on the side I never sleep on and Crew pulls me into his arms. Then, he kisses me crazy, and since I'm lying prone, I actually do turn to mush.

When he finally slows and looks down at me, his big hard body partly covers mine.

I decide to speak first. "Why can't I have my side if you don't have one?"

"You don't give up, do you?"

I raise my brows at him. "Well?"

He completely rolls on top of me and I separate my legs to make room for him. His voice dips, becoming as intimate as our new position.

"I've traveled for almost ten years with my work. Unless I'm visiting my mom or my brother, I've rarely slept in the same place for more than a few nights at a time. It's become habit to sleep on the side by the door. Your door's over there." He tips his head toward the entrance of my room. "I sleep on that side. Simple."

There's so much there. His family, him not having a home or hardly sleeping in the same place for ten years. I forget all about our sleeping arrangements, asking, "Do your mom and brother live here?"

He shakes his head. "He lives in Florida and my mom's outside of Atlanta. She moved a few years after my dad died. She wanted a new start. I see 'em a few times a year."

I give him a small smile because I'm happy he has them. I'm not sure why I say what I do next, but it pops out before I can make myself stop. "I don't have any family."

His grin disintegrates as he leans in to kiss me slowly. His hand comes to the top of my head, stroking my hair, whispering, "I know."

My body melts into his when I keep talking because I want to know more. "You have a brother?"

"Yeah."

"Older or younger?" I've always wanted a sibling. It obviously never happened, but I love that he has that.

"Younger. Twenty-nine. His name's Steele."

I raise my brows and smile. "That's as strange as Crew."

He returns my smile. "I know."

"Is there a reason your parents named you such strange names?"

He gives me a shrug. "You'd think it was my dad, but it was my mom. She said she wanted us to stand out—be different. She also said the best way to do that is giving a child a name they have to live up to. Strong names make strong individuals. Or so she says."

I run my hands down his thick arms. "She must be onto something."

Shaking his head with a smirk, he replies, "I don't think that's what she meant."

"Your mom sounds like a smart woman."

"She is." It's not only his words, but also his expression, that tells me he believes this wholly. Just when I was feeling pretty damn good right where I am, that makes me feel even better.

"Wait," I start. This has been the strangest week of my adult life— bar none. There's so much I don't know, especially about him. "How old are you?"

"Thirty-four."

"Oh," I breathe. I'm not sure how old I thought he was, but for some reason I'm relieved. "I'm thirty-one."

His smile slowly spreads into a grin. "I know that, too."

I roll my eyes, looking away from him, perturbed. "Of course you do." When I finally look back, I ask, "Is there anything you *don't* know about me?"

"Addison," his voice dips as he gives me more of his weight. To feel him against me, pressing me into my bed, is more than good. Knowing I don't have to be anyone but me with him? I don't even know how to describe it. I've never had that with anyone but my mom. It's impossible not to feel him everywhere when he wraps me up tight as he keeps talking. "What I know of you is on paper. Your family, where you've lived, things you buy. Anything that has a paper trail, I know. But you?" He presses his hips in between my legs, making my nipples harden. I pull in a breath when he continues on a whisper. "There's a world of you I don't know. I get to figure that out for myself. For now, you're tired, I'm tired and when I do explore every bit of you, I want us to be rested. I want all of you and I don't want you to be sleepy when I get it."

Oh.

So, wait. We're just going to sleep?

I tip my head and can't help my body from shifting under his. Maybe in confusion or objection, but definitely with disappointment.

I can tell he doesn't miss this when he gives me a small smile. "Trust me."

I don't answer when I narrow my eyes, frustrated. I'm flat out tired of him telling me to trust him.

He must see this on my face because he starts to laugh, but does it silently. As his body moves against mine, it feels good. Really good. Which makes me more perturbed because I can't lie to myself that I'm not disappointed we're simply going to sleep. I guess I wasted my Tuesday night nightie on him for nothing. I should have gone all out and done something with lace, a weekend nightie, for sure.

I exhale as he presses into me further, his hand dragging up the side of my body. Opening my mouth to say something, probably to lie about not being disappointed like I know I am, he takes it for a searing kiss. For the first time, I let my hands explore the bare skin of his back. Hard muscle over smooth, warm skin. Like magnets, one of my hands floats north into his thick, dark hair as the other drifts south. As soon as I hit the rock hard muscle of his ass, his hips press into me where I'm warm, wet, and wanting.

Oh, he's big, and he feels good. And oh so big.

I pull my knees up for more, but he breaks his kiss, breathing against my swollen lips. His dark eyes search my face and his voice turns ragged. "Was it just a week ago I met you walking your cows?"

I'm pretty sure this is a rhetorical question, but I get what he means. So much has happened in the past week, it feels like a blur.

My only answer is to lift my hips where his cock rubs against my clit.

He gives me what I want, pressing into me as his words keep coming against my lips. "Never wanted something so much. Can't stay away from you, can't even get you out of my head. I've never had a shot at anything good, let alone someone like you."

I wrap him up tighter in my arms. "Your words seem honest and real, but I have no idea what you're talking about."

"I didn't realize it back then, but I put my life on pause. For almost ten years, I've been in a holding pattern. Circling, doing what I needed but not knowing what was next. This shit swirlin' around you landed me in your life and your bed in record time. I won't lie, Addison, the first time I saw you, I couldn't help but wonder what it would be like bein' right here." He presses his cock against me harder, emphasizing his words. "I was going to wait 'til your shit settled to make my move, but after you fell apart in my arms last night, I can't be anywhere but here. I fought it, but I'm done. This feels right. We'll figure us out while we wait for them to take down O'Rourke. You okay with that?"

I don't have to think about it. I want that more than anything, but I'm honest when I answer. "I'd be more okay with it if I knew why your life was on hold the last ten years."

Looking down at me, he exhales before rolling, taking us to our sides. There, he gathers me up and kisses my forehead—something I'm learning is common for him. This is good for me, because I think I'm becoming addicted to it.

"Go to sleep," he whispers as he slowly fingers my hair, all the while, ignoring my comment.

I yawn as I complain into his chest. "I'm pretty sure with all your cameras, sensors, and my security system—that no one can get through but you—you won't need the side of the bed by the door. I'm not going to be able to sleep on this side, Crew."

I feel his chest move with laughter when I hear him smile. "Baby, we're in the middle. Let it go."

"If we flip, I'll be able to sleep."

This time, I feel him sigh. Then his hand drops and he yanks my Tuesday nightie up around my waist. Cupping my ass over my panties, he squeezes me tight when his lips come to my ear. "I like this. You always wear stuff like this to bed?"

"Well…" I take in a breath, smelling him. "Sometimes. Sometimes a t-shirt, but I have other things, too."

He pulls away enough to look down at me. "Yeah?"

I raise an eyebrow and smirk. "Yeah. I promise to show you if you switch sides with me."

His smile slowly grows, the dimple appearing as he shakes his head. Grabbing my ass again, he hauls me close and starts to slowly draw random patterns there with his fingers.

"I'm never going to be able to go to sleep if you do that, Crew."

"We'll see," he whispers into the side of my head.

I sigh, realizing I'm not going to get my side back. As I take a deep breath and try to relax, which truthfully isn't hard in Crew's arms, I start rearranging my room in my head. If I move my bed to the other side of the room, I'd get my side and Crew can have his by the door.

Just as I'm measuring wall space in my head, I drop off. Proving something else that I'm sure doesn't bode well for me.

Crew can talk me into anything.

Crew

With her back to me, she starts to stir.

It's eight-thirty, I don't know the last time I slept this late. I've got a shitload to do, but I can't make myself leave her. Unlike yesterday morning when I heard someone entering the house, today I get the opportunity to wake up with her. I'm not giving that up.

Her sweet nightgown rode up on her, right below her tits, and I woke up with my hand on her stomach, her back pressed into my chest. As she stirs, she presses into me farther, wiggling her ass into my crotch.

Well, fuck. Now I'm really glad I stayed in bed.

With a mind of its own, my hand drifts up to cup her tit as I use my chin to move her hair, putting my lips to her neck. Hell if she doesn't give me exactly what I want, tipping her head to give me access, at the same time arching her back. This thrusts her tit into my hand at the same time she grinds back onto my throbbing dick.

I twist her hard nipple just enough for her to groan before putting a hand to her belly. Moving away, I press her back to the bed and find her face sleepy but turned on. Feeling like I've waited a decade for her—since I have but didn't know it until this week—I can't wait another second. Fisting the bottom of her nightgown, I yank until it's up, over her head, tossing it to the floor.

She whispers my name, and just like every time she does, I feel it deep in my chest. Pushed up on one arm hovering over her, I take a second to drink in her mostly bare body for the first time. I grasp her hip over her tiny panties and barely hear myself mutter, "Fuck, you made it all worth it."

She reaches for my face and I give her what she wants, taking her mouth and feeling her skin against mine. Covering half of her, I explore her body while her nails lightly scrape down my back. I feel a hand dip into the back of my boxers where her small hand grabs my ass.

No hesitation, no shyness.

There's nothing more for me to want. She's everything.

"You're rock hard everywhere," she breathes against my lips.

I smile and knead her tit again, rolling her nipple between my thumb and index finger. She presses her chest into my hand, but before I know it, she plants a foot to the bed, trying to roll me.

I decide to allow her what she wants and roll, letting her climb over me. She rocks her pussy against my dick and I delve my hands into the back of her panties, cupping her ass. I wasn't lying when I said it was sweet, but it's sweeter in my hands. She rocks one more time before scooting down my thighs and when I look, she's reaching for my cock.

"Unh-unh," I growl, grabbing her hips, lifting her easily.

I flip her to her back and she complains, startled by my quick move

"Why did you do that?"

I crawl over her, raised on all fours, and give her a small frown. "Slow down, baby."

She exhales in a huff, a look mixed with confusion and regret bleeds over her features when her voice dips. "What's wrong?"

"Addison," I start quietly and lower my body to hers. I partly cover her, pinning her to the bed so I can still run my hand down the center of her body as I look into her eyes. "I like everything with you. Even though I look forward to taking you fast and hard at times, our first time'll be anything but. You're not getting your hands on me before I get mine on you. You need to relax for me."

I run my fingers down her stomach and trace the top of her panties barely dipping my fingers inside the hem. She closes her eyes and tries to bury her face in my neck. "I find it hard to relax, Crew."

"Ever?" I ask against her temple as my fingers move slowly, feeling how wet she is over her panties. I circle her clit through the material, giving her barely a touch.

"Pretty much," she whispers, her lips moving on my skin.

I dip my fingers inside to find her dripping and her body jerks at my touch. She's running hot, but I have no idea what's going on with her. The sooner I find out, the better. I keep whispering against her hair. "No one's ever taken their time with you?"

Her hand clamps my forearm as her body tenses. "Please quit talking."

I run my index finger lightly through her wet core, bound and determined to figure out what's going on with her. "Addison, look at me—"

But the moment I speak, the beeps to her security system break into the moment, alerting the fact a door has been opened. Ringing loud from the keypad on the wall by the threshold, I thought she was tense before, but nothing compared to now.

"What the hell," I start and begin climb from the bed. The beeps stop and we hear, "Yoo-hoo!" calling from far away in the house.

Addison grasps my shoulders, pulling me toward her bare body, whispering, "It's Bev."

I drop to her, completely covering her as I turn my head to yell over my shoulder, "We'll be down in a minute!" When I look back to Addison, I bite out, "I'm changing your locks."

"Get off. I need to get up." She tries to push me off.

"No."

Her voice turns frustrated as she drawls my name. "Crew."

"I'll let you up, but be prepared for a discussion. Tonight. I can read your body, and it's saying it wants me as much as I want you. But I can't make it good for you when you're trying to wrestle me. I promise it won't be anything but good for you—and if you let go, it'll be fucking great."

I see her building up her walls that were down two minutes ago. "I was not wrestling you, and there's nothing to talk about."

"I think you just proved there is. I've gotta get you to relax, baby. We'll figure that out tonight."

There's a hint of attitude in her voice when she says, "I might be busy tonight."

I grin. "With what? And before you lie to me, remember I have cameras everywhere. I'll know if you have a party going on."

Her eyes narrow with annoyance. "There's no event, but that doesn't mean I might not have plans."

I lean in to kiss her quickly. "You have plans all right. With me. Get dinner from Maggie and I'll be here at seven. We're getting an early start."

I shift my weight, but she grabs my arm, stopping me, and I see her eyes go big. "An early start to what?"

I pull away and reach for my clothes on the floor. Not taking my eyes off her, I adjust my raging hard-on, which is gonna suck. Her eyes dance up and down my body as I do. When I begin to yank on my jeans, I say with complete determination, "Tonight, my complicated Addison, I'm gonna figure you out. Before you fall asleep in my arms again, you'll be nothing but relaxed."

Her eyes widen as she fists the covers over her tits. I bend to grab my shirt and shoes, regretting leaving her practically naked in bed. I've got to count how many locks need to be replaced and add the hardware store on my long list of shit to do today. No one's walking in on us again.

I need uninterrupted time with Addison Wentworth.

And it's gonna happen. Tonight.

Chapter Fourteen

I Can Keep a Secret

Addy

I stand in the spacious entryway of my old farmhouse that acts as a corridor to every room on the main floor of my home. It's flanked by the front and back doors with the ornate stairway at the back of the house.

Ignoring the centuries of old charm surrounding me, I frown as Crew stands from where he's been crouched, working on my doorknob. He tests my new key before slamming the antique door shut. His eyes come to me at the same time I hear my deadbolt flip easily into place.

"There."

I frown deeper and cross my arms. "That wasn't necessary."

"Too many people have access to your home, Addison," he says resolutely. "Next up, you need to change your security code."

"Only my small circle of employees knows it. I trust them."

"I don't care if they are trustworthy. It's too many people." He starts packing up the small box of tools he brought over two hours ago.

In fact, I wasn't even here yet when he helped himself to changing my locks. We were finishing up from a small event late this afternoon when I saw him drive by in his old pickup truck. We had three events today and it was busy. I had to square up some things in the main building and Crew was here for an entire hour before I got home. He got into my house, disarmed my security system—even though I still haven't given him a key or the code—and he's worried about the people I'm closest to and trust?

I've been feeling petulant all day after he left me in bed this morning when he threatened to "figure me out," leaving me in a state of horny I hadn't seen in...ever, really. So much so, I almost brought him a salad with no meat for dinner. He's a big guy—no way would a salad fill him up. I'm all out of barbeque chips, and besides my Laffy Taffy, I don't keep a lot of snack food in the house. I'm barely here as it is.

As irritable as I was, I couldn't make him eat only a salad. So I ordered enormous turkey sandwiches layered with brie, thinly sliced green apples, and spring mix with honey mustard on cranberry wheat bread. It's a new Maggie creation this summer and one of my favorites. She added sides of fruit. When I told her it was for Crew and me, she threw in pastries and a container of meats and cheeses. Over the past few days, Crew, Grady, and Asa have been eating at the Café daily. Not to mention, Clara has a big mouth. Everyone knows who Crew is and what he is to me, even though I'm still trying to define what we are in my head.

Currently, he's my locksmith whom I'm not too happy with.

He took a break from his locksmith duties to eat, scarfing down his dinner in record time. He thanked me as he kissed me on the forehead and left to finish his task before I was halfway done with my meal.

By the time I finished eating and found him at my front door, he was finishing up.

"It's only five people, Crew. I'm going to have to give Morris a new key anyway. He's not only the caretaker of the property, but I pay him extra to maintain this house since there's so much I can't do myself. He'll need a key."

He sets his toolbox by my front door and shrugs. "I can help you with the house."

"What I'm trying to explain to you, Crew Vega," I stress his name, "is that I've managed just fine for the last year-and-a-half. I don't mind my employees coming in when they need to, or even want to. In fact, I like that they want to be here."

"That's fair." He moves to me and tags my hand, heading toward my stairs. "But you like me here, too. Right?"

I raise an eyebrow and can't keep the snark out of my voice when I mutter, "I thought I did, but I'm rethinking it."

He smiles. "Well, when I have you like I had you this morning, it would be nice if they knocked. Now they'll have to knock."

"What are you doing?" I ask, even though I know what he's doing since he did the same thing last night, pulling me up to my bedroom.

"I'm going to figure you out, Addison. I've been thinking about it all day, and I told you I had a lot to do. I need to focus and the sooner we get this hashed out, the better."

We make the turn to the second staircase and everything I've been feeling all day is coming to a head. I don't know what more he wants to figure out—he knows everything there is to know about me. The simple fact he looks at me differently than any man ever has before makes me crazy nervous. I do know I've thought about it all day and decided if he's going to demand anything more from me, I'm going to demand more, too.

I just decided to give everyone a new key. It'll show him, I'll just ask them to knock before using it. He can spin his wheels changing locks, my friends are welcome in my home all the time. He'll just have to suck it up and get used to it.

He pulls me around the corner to my room. As much as he's perturbed me with the locks, I like him everywhere in my house.

I sweep through the door, letting go of his hand. Putting a few feet between us, he stops in the middle of my room, between the door and me. I'm not sure what he's going to say, so I stay silent. I mean, he's kissed me in the White House, set up surveillance of my home and business, broken into my house twice, and now changed my locks. I didn't ask, but I'm sure he kept a key for himself. Not that he needs one—he seems to get in just fine all on his own. He's seen me mostly naked and knows all he has to do is lay a hand on my body for me to turn to mush in a heartbeat.

Oh yeah, and he knows my entire life history and all the secrets I've held dear for as long as I can remember. But here he is, thinking he has more "figuring out" to do.

Honestly. This has been the most bizarre week ever.

He crosses his arms and aims his dark eyes on me. Out of the blue, he starts with, "Tell me about the control."

I frown. "What do you mean?"

"Yesterday morning, you said you needed it to cope. Tell me more about that."

I shrug my shoulders, giving my head a little shake. "There's nothing more to tell. I need to have a grasp on things to function. What happened the other night hasn't happened in a long time, Crew. Probably not since my late teens. I don't know why you're asking about this."

"Because you don't need it with me. Because I know all there is to know, Addison. With me, you can let it go."

"You're expecting an awful lot, Crew." I tip my head before stressing my words. "Especially when you give me nothing in return."

I know he knows what I'm talking about, because he narrows his eyes and the sharp takes over. His body doesn't give it away, but his dark eyes do. Even though I've barely known him a week, I see it. It's startling because he's been nothing but warm with me since the night of the White House dinner.

"See?" I say softly. "I might not know you well, but I see what just happened. That shield has disappeared with me the last couple of days, but there it is again. You're guarded and closed off when you want me to be everything but. I've got an issue with that."

He doesn't take his eyes off me, but he scarcely shakes his head.

There's no beating around the bush, I have to know. "Why do you have clearance with the CIA?"

"Addison—"

"What have you been doing the past ten years?"

His voice turns as sharp as his eyes when he tries to squash my efforts. "I've told you I can't—"

"You said I made it all worth it," I quickly cut in, not giving up.

This statement not only makes his mouth go tight, but his whole body as well. The sharp from his eyes leaks out, tension spreading through his strong arms crossed over his chest, slipping over his body. In all the ways I've seen Crew Vega in the last week, this is new.

"Addison." His voice comes out rough, almost pained.

"I want to be worth it," I whisper. "Let me be that for you, but let me be it completely."

He says nothing, but his sharp eyes slowly close, shutting me out.

Crew

Fuck.

That's a surprise. I squeeze my eyes tight and think. I wasn't expecting this.

I wanted to figure out why she was wound like a spring in bed this morning. Hell if she didn't turn it back on me. Why I let that slip about her making it all worth it, I have no idea.

"You have a secret?" I hear her say.

I let my head drop and exhale.

"I can keep a secret, Crew."

Her voice, soft and smooth, breaks through to me and I look up.

Not taking a break, she keeps hitting me in the gut.

"I think I've proven that over the last twenty-five years, don't you?"

I shake my head at her relentlessness.

She even has the nerve to flip her hand out and half grin when she keeps on. "And since you know everything there is to know about me, you know it's true."

"Enough," I counter on a sigh.

"Well?"

"It's not only that I shouldn't tell you, but I don't want to tell you, Addison. I don't want you to know that part of me."

It's true. I'm not afraid of anything, but with what I've done and what I'm training others to do, I don't want to risk her knowing. It could only go two ways. With her past and what she's lived through, she could high-five me. Or, she could be disgusted and tell me to get the fuck out, never wanting to lay eyes on me again. I don't gamble. I'm calculated, measure every risk I face. I want her too much, it's a fifty-fifty shot I'm not anxious to take.

"Why?" She tips her head with a look of confusion. "In the past few days, you've gone out of your way to protect me, show me you want me, and tell me things I didn't know about my father. I've given you my trust for no other reason than because it felt right. But something you don't know about me, Crew, is I don't enter into things lightly. I grew up having to look over my shoulder as a necessity. As fast as things have happened between you and me, you're standing right here because I want you here. You might be pushy, but I'm no pushover. No way would you be here if I didn't want you."

I even my breathing before responding. "You can say that now. You don't know."

"Maybe it's time you give me a little blind trust, then. Try me, Crew. I dare you," she says with attitude.

My face cracks from her remark. "You dare me?"

She says nothing but raises her eyebrows, as if to silently double-dog-dare me.

I sigh, giving her an ultimatum. "You can't tell me to get the fuck out without me explaining."

Her face turns surprised. "Is it that bad?"

"Give me your word, Addison. I'll give you what you want, but I won't let you end what we've started over this. No fucking way."

"Fine," she breathes, giving her head a little shake. "You have my word."

She'd better mean it, there's no fucking way I'm gonna let her kick me out now. Not for this anyway. I planned to tell her down the road, when things progressed. I wanted her in deep, where there was no way she could walk away from me.

One thing's for fucking sure, it never occurred to me I'd be standing here after ten years, questioning my decisions for the first time ever. I've never questioned a decision in my life.

"Crew?" She breaks into my thoughts, becoming restless.

I decide there's nothing to do but throw it out there. "I don't have an official title, but some would call me a Soldier of Fortune."

She looks perplexed. "I don't know what that is."

"I contracted with governments. Ours and our foreign allies. I only worked abroad, never here in the States."

"Okay," she adds carefully. "Why couldn't you tell me that?"

"Because I did for them what they couldn't do, not even their troops, and they paid me well to do it. I didn't get into it for the money, I did it because at that time in my life, a long time ago when I signed on, it was important to me."

It's the truth. Nothing was more important to me at the age of twenty-three. There've been many days over the years I wondered where I'd be if the opportunity never arose. But I never regretted it, never imagined this moment. A day I'd have to explain myself— maybe defend myself—and hope to God a good woman would forgive me for it.

In ten years, I never conceived today. But here I am.

And here it goes. When I see the color leave her face and her eyes widen, I take a step closer, but she instinctively steps back.

Her words come out in a rush. "Wait, what did they pay you to do?"

"Addison," I start as I reach for her.

"What did they pay you to do?" she repeats, louder than the last.

I pull my hand back and try to even my tone, explaining calmly. "I was paid to eliminate threats. All kinds of threats, but in the past few years, mostly terrorism."

"Eliminate?" Her voice disappears into a whisper.

My jaw goes hard, answering in a single clipped word. "Yes."

She keeps whispering. "You didn't arrest them, did you?"

I exhale and say firmly, "No."

Surprisingly she stands her ground, not wavering. There's no doubt in my mind she now understands what I've done the past ten years.

"You killed them," she states.

"Yes."

"You were a contract killer," she goes on.

I pause, trying to figure out what she's thinking. "Yes."

"You worked for governments to kill people?" her voice comes louder.

"No," I quickly refute. "I never officially worked for anyone. Like I said, some might call me a Soldier of Fortune, but I wasn't a soldier for anyone. If I was caught or captured, not one person would lay claim to me. Those who contracted my services would deny any connection, including our own CIA. I worked at my own risk, but I did it knowing it was the right thing to do. I knew it then, and I know it now."

Her face falls. "Were you ever captured?"

I sigh and take a step closer, needing to touch her. Needing her to let me touch her. I reach out, dipping my hand around her neck and give her a squeeze when I soften my voice. "No. I was very good at what I did."

She doesn't pull away from me—which is a good sign—even if she still looks confused and surprised. I go on, hoping she'll let me explain more.

"My dad was killed in an explosion. Police were called to a home in a run-down neighborhood in the District where citizens reported unusual activity. Three other officers reported to the house with my dad. When they started to investigate, a bomb went off. The area was booby-trapped, most likely to protect whatever was going on inside. Killed three of the four, one being my dad. Later, they proved it was terrorist recruits, building shit to plant here in the States."

She reaches up, grasping my forearm, her face pained for me, for my loss. I hate that look on her face, but I keep going.

"The story was huge in the media—a fallen officer always is. Multiply that times three and throw in terrorist activity, it was off the charts. The families were thrown into the public eye—the funerals were enormous and there was no privacy. I was twenty-three, fresh out of college and following my dad's footsteps in law enforcement. I was made to be the perfect son by the public, comforting my mom and younger brother. I was forced to be in the limelight, something I loathed. I was even fucking celebrated because my dad was killed in the line of duty and I was carrying on his legacy by serving myself. I fucking hated it."

Her brow furrows and she takes a step closer, placing her hand on my chest over my heart, just like she did at the White House. Even with what I'm rehashing, it feels just as good as it did then. If possible, it feels even better. Anxious to finish this for good, I keep talking.

"The network of people I worked with recruited me a couple months later. They targeted me because of what happened to my dad and because I had skills they wanted. I'm a good shot, Addison. Even back then, I worked the roof of the White House because I was the best. Now, after years of training, I'm even better. They taught me hand-to-hand combat, how to disappear in a crowd, surveillance, how to survive in any and every condition. I'm fluent in six languages. They taught me *everything*, but that was only for backup. I never needed it. My shot is that good."

"You...um, only..." She bites her lip, trying to find her words. "*Targeted*...bad guys?"

I grimace and squeeze her neck. "Fuck yes, Addison. I'm not gonna kill the good guys. Holy shit, who do you think I am?"

She tries to pull away but I hold steady when she brings up her defenses, turning frustrated. "I'm just making sure. Don't talk to me that way. I'm sorry to offend you—I've never heard of a Fortune Soldier before, let alone met one. How was I supposed to know?"

I look down into her pissed off face, her dark brown eyes narrowed. Cupping the back of her head, I fist her chestnut hair and slowly close my eyes, tipping my forehead to hers.

"Baby," I whisper with nothing but relief. "It's Soldier of Fortune, and even I don't call myself that. You make me sound like a Fortune

Teller."

"Sorry," she lowers her voice and I open my eyes to look at her. "If you have a business card, I'll try and get it right when I introduce you to people."

I narrow my eyes at her sarcasm.

"It was dangerous?" she asks. I purse my lips before answering, wanting to be as vague as possible when it comes to the details of my past life. Impatient, a new look falls over her face, a look mixed with panic and concern. "It was really dangerous, wasn't it? Of course, how could it not be?"

"Sometimes," I answer quickly, wanting to put her at ease since it doesn't matter anyway.

"But you're done?" she pushes. "Done with it for good?"

I take a breath before explaining. "I've retired, so yeah. I'm done. I could officially retire and never work another day, but that's not me. I can't not work—I wouldn't know what to do with myself. The people I contracted for don't let you out easily. My way out was to train others to do what I did."

"You're training killers," she states, her eyes going big as if she's trying to get a grasp on all I've just told her.

I give her a squeeze. "Yeah."

She pulls her soft lip between her teeth again, mulling all this over. Then, quickly, her eyes dart back to mine and her voice comes out in a rush. "You'll never go back, right?"

My voice drops hearing the fear laced in hers. "I'm done."

"I'm glad you're done." She gives me a squeeze. "Not because I'm judging what you did, but because of the danger. I think it would make me crazy to think about you putting yourself out there like that now. I don't know if I could handle that, Crew."

She exhales and relief spreads over her beautiful face. That look settles in my gut like nothing I've ever experienced. Not only for her to know the truth, but to accept me, and now I don't have to worry about keeping anything from her.

"You see what's happened here, right?" I start.

"What?"

I turn her, walking her backwards to her bed. "I've given you what you wanted—I trusted you. You've got complete control over me now. I all but disappeared for ten years. I was a ghost. I wanted to be after what happened to my dad—I had to be. There're people in this world who want me dead for what I've done. I've crippled organizations, taken out entire cells, broken up networks. I told you everything because I want you."

"I can't say it doesn't kind of freak me out, but you can trust me, Crew."

"Because of what you've been through, the way you've had to live your life, and from what I've seen of you the past week, I don't doubt that. I never would've told you otherwise."

I've got her pinned against her bed when she smiles a small smile. "I'm glad."

"Now I need something from you."

Her smile disappears. "What?"

I look intently into her eyes, wanting what I'm about to suggest to happen more than anything. I even need it, but more, I want it so she can let go. I want to do it for her, give that to her, and make it great for us.

"I want you to give up another kind of control, Addison. I want you to give it all to me, completely and wholly."

Chapter Fifteen

Comply

Addy

I inhale deeply.

"What are you talking about?"

He looks at me, his body flush with mine. With his hand buried in my hair, he tips my head farther, looking deep in my eyes. "When we're like this, you and me, I want you to give you to me."

Confused, I insist, "I'm here aren't I?"

"No, Addison." His voice dips and his deep dark eyes flare. "I want you completely."

"I don't understand."

His hands start to roam my body as he gently tugs, untucking my blouse. "You were wrestling me this morning."

"I was not." I slap his hand away, because now he's pissing me off. I was only doing what I wanted, he was the one who made it wrestling.

"You were," he keeps on, ignoring my slap. "I want you to let go, let me handle it, and when we're like this, comply."

Wait. What?

Comply?

"Comply?" My body goes stiff and I manage to stop his hands this time. I'm even able to push him back a step.

"Comply," he confirms.

My eyes go big, because I cannot believe what I think I'm hearing. Shocked, I keep asking for details. "Do you mean...submit?"

The side of his mouth tips, giving me a hint of the dimple. "Now you're just getting technical, baby."

I put my hand up, palm to him and say firmly, "I've read about that shit and I am *not* a submissive."

His brows rise, the full dimple appearing when he replies, "Oh, I know you're not."

"Then what are you asking?"

He takes my hands in his, closing the distance I managed to create. Ever so gently, he pulls my hands behind my back, closing in on me. Holding me tight in this weird hug where it's clear he's proving I can't move—my heart picks up speed.

"I'm asking you to try," he whispers. "Try and give me that control when we're right here. When it's you and me and I've got you bared. I can take care of you, Addison, but you've got to hand it over. Let me take over."

My breath comes quick and my nipples harden listening to him speak so softly, so gently, about something so foreign. I don't understand it or why he wants it.

"Do you," I pause, searching for the words since I've never talked about this before with anyone. "Do you want to hurt me?"

He shakes his head. "Trust me—I don't have to hurt you to make you feel good. Later, you want to explore and add some kink, we can talk about that. Even then, I'd never hurt you."

Well, shit. For some reason I believe that, down to my bones. Oddly enough, tingles slither over my skin just thinking about this. I've worked hard to keep my mind in control all these years. I don't think I can turn that off.

Still, it makes me crazy he's asked me to trust him. Again. It's getting old.

"How many times have you asked me to trust you?" I spout, if for no other reason than to change the subject.

He tips his head and I see a smile in his eyes. "How many times are you gonna make me ask you?"

With my arms still pinned, I slowly shake my head and close my eyes. Letting my face plant in his chest, I mumble, "This isn't me."

He transfers my hands into one of his, holding firm when the other comes to my face. "It can be. I'll show you."

His touch on my face disappears, moving down, nimbly unbuttoning my blouse. I drop my head, barely catching a glimpse of his large hand working the delicate buttons before my lids drop. Trying to breathe deep to control myself, I do my best to get it together.

He releases my hands at the same time I feel a wisp of material falling down my arms. My skin is heated, but the silk brushing across my skin gives me goosebumps. I open my eyes when his fingers unbuttoned my pants. My room is silent and the air around us is thick. When he pulls on my zipper, it breaks through the quiet like a freight train.

Followed by my very audible exhale.

Bringing my hands up to his abs, I fist his shirt. "Crew?"

"Shh," he tries to quiet me with his lips on top of my head.

I ignore him. "I don't know if I can do this."

His chin, with new scruff, grazes across my temple. He hasn't shaved since he took me to the White House dinner. Even though it's still short, I like it and it feels even better.

He bows his head, putting his lips to my ear at the same time my slacks fall to the floor. "You can. I'll prove it to you."

I pull on his shirt, trying to bury my face in his chest. At that same instant, my bra goes slack and his fingertips scarcely drift over the bare skin of my back.

Holy shit, how can a barely-there touch feel more intimate than anything I've ever experienced?

He pulls away and slides my bra down my arms with his eyes on his task. Never looking up, he bends a little to reach my now very wet panties. Hardly touching me, he hooks a finger into both hips and pushes until gravity takes over, dropping them at my feet.

Now my breath is shallow. I'm no prude, but no one's made such an event of undressing me before. Especially when he's standing in front of me fully clothed, down to his clompy boots. It's all I can do not to cover myself. I'm not inexperienced in the least, I am thirty-one. He's not even the first man to take my clothes off. He is the first to do it so gently and methodically, it would appear he had all the time in the world.

Crew's not even pretending to make me feel comfortable. His eyes are moving over me slowly. It's all I can do to stand still in front of him and I have to squeeze my legs together, looking for a bit of relief. I've never been turned on like I am now. I'm sure my nipples could cut glass.

"Fuck," he mutters. His eyes finally meeting mine. "Didn't think it was possible to want you more, but I do. Worth every fucking minute of ten years."

Then his arm comes up and reaches over the back of his head. I lose his eyes for a mere second while he rips his t-shirt off and tosses it to the floor. My eyes immediately lower when he reaches for the button of his jeans. He lowers his zipper but stops when he reaches in, adjusting the very large bulge in his pants.

That's when I hear, "Turn around."

I look up, surprised, thinking he was about to join me in my birthday suit. Finding it rather awkward standing here totally naked, I clumsily try to cross my arms and frown at his directive.

He tips his head and gives me half a smirk.

Lowering his voice, he tries again. "Turn around."

I roll my eyes, making him narrow his. Then, for some reason unbeknownst to everything I am—or everything I thought I was—I kick my pants and panties to the side and turn. I do, however, peek at him over my shoulder to see what he's going to do next.

He shakes his head as he steps forward, his chiseled chest warming my back. I feel his hands, low on my hips, wander up my sides when he states, "You're not used to takin' it slow."

I breathe out quickly and don't answer. He should've figured that out this morning.

"It's gonna be good in every way between us, baby. But after this morning, I want to give you something different." His hands glide on me light and easy. "And I want you to let go."

His hands separate on my front, barely stroking my nipple and stomach. I think his idea of slow is going to be my idea of torture.

All of a sudden, he grabs my hips, lifting me. "Knees to the bed."

Startled, I yelp. My knees come to the edge and he quickly steps in between my calves that are thrusting out behind me. His hand at my stomach pulls me back against his chest. I feel the scruff of his jaw at my temple this time where he presses his lips. With one arm locked around me, his other hand is stroking the inside of my thigh.

"Spread your legs."

Oh my.

I inch my knees out.

"Addison." My name comes out as a warning.

I inch farther.

His hand comes up the front of my thigh to cup me firmly between my legs.

"Mmm," I mew.

"Baby. Farther."

I spread, as far as I can. I'm open and exposed, desperate for his touch.

His arms constrict around me as his fingers barely tease. I grab hold of him as my heart starts to race when I realize there's no way I can close my legs. As much as I squeeze my thighs, it's to no avail. I'm cemented.

"Crew?" I call for him, my voice clipped as I try to calm myself.

His fingers shift to my breast, twisting my nipple, making me exhale. It's the most he's given me since he stripped me bare.

His gravelly voice vibrates down my back where he holds me tight to his chest. "Yeah?"

Instinctively, my body is desperate to shift, to turn, to do something. At the same time, I crave his touch in a way that's foreign to me. Leaning my head back on his shoulder, I whisper, "I can't move."

His lips meet the area below my ear, his whiskers scratching my sensitive skin. I feel his tongue dart out tasting me, sending tingles down my spine.

I thought those tingles were intense until his lips come to my ear where his next two words reduce me to mush.

"I know."

Oh. Well, then.

Shit.

"Grab hold of me."

I do, desperate to hold on to something. This pushes my breasts out and he takes advantage, working my nipple, massaging, groping. His hands are rough, callused, and abrasive. I knew he worked on his property, but now I feel it on my sensitive skin. And I love it.

His fingers glide over my clit, but it's not enough. The only thing I can do is arch my back, searching for more.

"You see?" His lips come back to my ear, pulling my hair through his scruff. "When I have you like this, you can let go."

His hand reaches farther and he slides a finger inside.

"Just you and me."

He squeezes my breast as he replaces one finger with two.

"You don't have to pretend. Hide. Be someone you're not."

I say nothing, but turn my head, pressing my forehead in his neck. This is too much, his touch, his words. His fingers keep on, in and out, his thumb circling my clit.

"You're what I get. After ten years of doin' what I needed to do, I settle next door to you."

My breath is coming in short pants—I don't have goosebumps anymore. I'm warmed all over. He's giving me just enough to keep it at bay, my orgasm close, yet nowhere near. I'm heated, rocking against his hand, searching for more as his words cut through me.

"You hand over that control—you don't have to be anyone but you. You don't need it. I can give you back to you. With me, baby, you can be Abby."

I whimper at the sound of my real name, pressing my face tighter into his neck. Even in my frenzied state, my eyes well.

"My Abby," he whispers into the top of my head.

"Crew," I call for him. My voice chokes with a sob and I don't know what I want more, to cry or for him to let me orgasm.

He presses harder on my clit, finger fucking me more vigorously than before.

"Just you and me, Abby."

I arch, pressing my head into his neck and shoulder. It's never been like this before. Ever. I hang on at the same time I search for it, because I'm pretty sure it's going to wreck me.

His arm across my chest turns to a band of steel, holding me steady when he gives me what I want. What I need. What I've never had before.

He was right. I've never had it slow. I've never had it focused on me, and I've absolutely never let go.

But I can do that for Crew.

Because after only a week, he's proven he'll make everything safe for me.

He gives me more pressure on my clit, and I was right. He has the power to wreck me.

I was gone.

My body shook, powerfully and violently, but he held me tight. I couldn't move my legs and I couldn't bend forward. There was no stopping it until he allowed. I whimpered, I screamed, I gasped for air. The whole time, he held me steady.

Finally, when he took me to a place I'd never been, I vaguely felt his hold loosen. I was up, cradled in his arms before feeling the bed at my back.

Trying to catch my breath and lift my heavy lids, I hear a tear. When I'm finally able to force my eyes open, he's over me. I look down and he's forced his jeans down just enough to roll a condom on. His cock is big, bigger than I've ever had, and I want it. I want it more than anything.

"I promise to get creative with you, but after that, I doubt you have the energy for anything else," he says, giving me a hint of the dimple. "That was fucking spectacular."

I can attest to the fact it was spectacular. But I want him, especially while my body's still humming. "Please, Crew."

Coming over me, he takes my hands and raises them above my head. Holding my wrists firmly in one of his, the other plays between my legs keeping me primed. "You want me?"

"I do," I breathe desperately. "Now."

His forearm comes down beside my head and he takes my mouth, kissing me as he gives me his weight. When I pull on my arms, his hold tightens. I do the only thing I can do and lift my legs, wrapping one around his waist and the other over his ass. Gripping him with my legs, I press my hips up, looking for him.

He lifts and I feel the tip of him at my core. He rocks, pressing into me, stretching me. He's perfect, making me want more.

"Yes," I exhale.

"Can you take all of me, baby?"

"Every inch, please."

He pulls out a little and pushes in farther. He does it again, faster, and farther still. More, and it's better than ever.

"Abby." My name seeps from his mouth, strained, his soft breath on my lips.

His eyes sear into mine, and my tears from earlier slide down my temples. I mean it to my bones when I say, "Thank you for giving that to me."

His eyes close and his forehead rests on mine. Then he really starts to move and I get all of him. He is big and it feels better than ever, but really, it's him and all he's given me.

I spread my legs more and he drives into me faster. He hits that perfect spot inside where it's just as good, even though it's different.

"Harder," I plead.

"You gonna come for me again?" he asks, breathless.

I don't answer, but plead desperately, "I want to touch you."

He immediately gives me what I want, releasing my wrists. My hands go to his face, his shoulders, his back, reaching down for his rock hard ass that I couldn't wait to touch again. His skin is heated, every muscle rippling under my fingers.

I feel it coming. "Yes, more."

He gives it to me harder while he takes. When I fall over the edge, I hear him groan, pressing into me deeper with two last powerful thrusts. His breathing next to my ear is heavy, proving he's spent, and I hope that means I gave him just a little bit of what I got.

Leaning back to look at me, his eyes are sated and warm. But it's his words that cut me to the core.

"Worth every minute of ten years. Never thought I'd say this, but I'd do it all again if I knew you were waiting for me at the end."

"Crew."

"My Abby," he murmurs before kissing me.

And those were the last words I heard before falling asleep in his arms later that night. Words that were nothing but a dream and a hushed secret in the back of my brain for most of my life.

It was Crew's way of giving back a little of what I'd lost twenty-five years ago.

It was beautiful.

Chapter Sixteen

Are You Going to Hug Me?

Crew

Standing flush to her back, I hold her hands beneath mine to the shower wall. Then I do what I woke up needing—I slide into her warm, wet pussy.

I left her in bed before five to go home for my run. I ran my property, the trails, and the rough like I always do. Today I extended my run to Addison's vineyard and pasture. It was early enough her cows weren't out yet, but I know her schedule. She walks with them most days between seven and eight.

I finished and was back to her by six-thirty. She was still dead asleep where I left her this morning, on the side of the bed opposite her bedroom door, still naked from our first night together.

Last night was fucking great. I can't get it out of my head and during my run this morning, I thought through every moment. Every touch of her body, her moans, her gasps. She's the best I've ever had. For her to give in to me—especially going against who she is and what she's used to—was even better. I've always liked to be in charge, but I've never demanded it before.

With Addison, it was better than I imagined, and I've imagined a lot over the last week. I got through my run faster than normal. I couldn't wait to get back to her.

But telling her about me, the last ten years, and the life I chose? I didn't think that would happen for a long time—if ever. It's a fucking load off my chest, especially knowing it didn't send her running for the hills. My mom and brother don't even know what I did. I was taking a chance, but just like every decision I make, I knew it was a solid one. Knowing her background and how she's had to live, it was a measured risk, but a good one.

The outcome was good and I couldn't be more pleased. Especially with what she gave me afterward.

I woke her by kissing the back of her neck and she slowly turned her head, her hair a mess over her face. When I brushed it away and kissed her, her face screwed up instantly when she muttered, "You're stinky."

I couldn't help but grin. "I went for a run. Come shower with me."

"I'm gonna go for a walk."

I flipped the covers off her and ran my hand down her bare body. "You can walk later."

Then I pulled her from the bed.

I just made her come on my hand before flipping her around with her palms to the wall. Having to bend to reach her from behind, I slide easily inside. She's plenty wet for me.

Coming up on her toes to accommodate me, I push in farther.

"More." Her voice is breathy, ragged from her orgasm.

I slide a hand down her arm and body, moving lower. Pressing on the small of her back, I demand, "Tip for me."

She arches her back immediately, moaning, "Yes."

"You like that?" It's an unnecessary question. She's pressing her ass into my groin, wanting more.

"Mmm," she hums and tries to move.

I squeeze both beautiful globes of her ass in warning and whisper, "Still."

She stills but complains on an exhale. I slide out and back in completely, adding a little intensity with each thrust.

"I want more, Crew. Harder," she pleads, looking at me over her shoulder with sex laden eyes.

"You'll get it, baby." I grip her hips harder as I give her more. When I eventually give her what she wants, I feel it in my balls. I squeeze my eyes and breathe, not wanting this to end. Needing another drive, just one more second buried in Abby.

When I can't keep it slow any longer, I give myself what I need, and hopefully what she wants. I move hard and fast as she uses the wall to push into me with the water raining around us. When I'm about to explode, I hear her gasp and her pussy convulses around my dick.

I can't hang on another second.

Just as good as last night, I press into her three more times. Leaning forward, I bury my face in her heavy wet hair. Still planted deep, I lean into the wall with one arm and wrap the other around her, cupping her tit perfectly in my hand. I don't move, waiting many long moments to come down from a high I'm learning I've only experienced with her.

"I've never done that," she mumbles through the water.

I tense before moving my lips to her ear. "From behind?"

"No. Ask for more. I've never asked for anything."

Her voice is strained, as if she's embarrassed and can't handle the thought she simply asked for more of what I was already giving her.

I give her a squeeze before slowly pulling out. She stands, but doesn't turn. I take off my condom and tie it before tossing it over the glass shower door.

I put my arms around her from behind with the water rolling over us and sigh. "I don't know what your past was like and I really don't want to know. From what I'm gathering, you've had selfish fucking men in your life. Now, I'm a man and trust me when I say, every man thinks with their dick to some extent when they're around a woman they want. I get off seeing you come for me and the more I play with you, the better that will be. I plan on teasing you and want you in knots before you come apart."

She leans her head back on my chest, mumbling, "I think you've accomplished that."

I smile into the top of her wet head. "You need to ask for what you want. Hell, you can demand it and it'll be even better. You might not get it instantly, but you'll get it eventually. We'll start working on that tonight."

She whispers, so quietly, I almost don't hear her over the water, "It's been a long time for me. I haven't been with anyone in a few years, Crew."

I let go and turn her. Moving her so the water doesn't hit her face, I tip her head and press in close.

I smile when I lower my voice to only half tease, but she doesn't need to know that. "Then I'm lucky. Your body's a minefield for me to play with. I'm gonna make you tell me what you want, how you want it, and then make you beg for it. We'll start tonight when you sit on my face."

I was trying to lighten the moment, even though I'm one-hundred percent serious. She'll be begging to come on my mouth tonight.

She doesn't hesitate, get embarrassed, or shy away at my words. She proved last night she's confident in her skin. Surging up on her toes, she grabs my face, thrusting her tongue in my mouth. When she presses her body against mine, kissing me deep, I can tell she wants it all.

I drop my hands to her ass and pick her up. Turning her so her back is to the tiled wall, she wraps her legs around my waist. Her pussy rubs against my bare dick, something I've never had, but something we might need to fix soon.

I break her kiss and press into her clit when I ask, "You want that, don't you?"

With droplets falling down her face, she says nothing, but she does look straight into my eyes before giving me two small, quick nods. Then I feel her hand in my hair, pulling my lips to hers as she grinds down on my dick.

Yeah. A fucking minefield.

Standing here with Addison in my arms, I take back what I said to her last night. She doesn't make up for every minute of the last ten years.

All that time it took to find my retribution? She's worth every fucking second.

Addy

In my office at the winery, I'm reviewing events for the upcoming week. I didn't get to walk with the cows this morning. After Crew dragged me into the shower, we had coffee and a quick breakfast before he left. He explained he has a full day, since his recruits are arriving early this week for training.

Still trying to get used to all he told me last night, I needed to know more.

I asked how long it took to train a killer. I asked if he taught them everything himself. I asked if they were all sharp shooters or how else would they kill the bad guys. Then I asked a million other questions.

He stopped my line of questioning with a kiss before telling me nothing, but asked if I was okay with it all. Then he asked if I was going to freak out the second he walked out the door.

I told him we'd both harbored secrets a long time and I'd be fine. But I did point out he'd know if I freaked because he'd see it on his cameras.

I got to see him laugh out loud again. It really was something and almost made me forget about the damn cameras.

Then he promised to tell me everything in due time, kissed me, and left to do whatever it is he needs to do before his killers-to-be arrive this week.

Since it's Sunday afternoon and we're at the end of summer, the tasting room is packed. The height of tourism season is coming to a close. We tend to benefit from summer DC tourists who get sick of the city and need to relax with a wine tasting tour of Virginia. The tasting room was full the last time I peeked out my door, and I made a mental note it might be time to hire more help. Part time, at least.

My desk phone rings and it hardly ever rings. I always give clients my cell so I'm easy to reach.

"This is Addy."

"Hey," Evan starts and I hear the buzz of chatter in the background mixed with the bustling noises of the main bar. "You have a call that came across the main line. It's a rush, can I put him through?"

"Sure. I'll come out to help in a minute, I'm almost done in here."

"Thanks," he clips before I lose him.

I hear another beep on my phone and press the outside line to pick it up. "Addy Wentworth."

"Addy," I hear the deep voice come at me from the other end. I still, knowing exactly who it is and force myself to breathe. "It's

Lieutenant Colonel Sheldon O'Rourke. I helped make arrangements for your wine to be served at the White House."

He explains himself like I would forget my time with him. Like I could ever fail to recall him cornering me in the White House, basically threatening me with the knowledge he knew my parents and the real me. Especially threatening me with same demise as my father.

Not knowing what to do, I hesitate, sitting back carefully in my chair. I try to do what I trained myself to do years ago, and focus on something to center my mind. I breathe, trying to think about my response.

But I must have paused too long.

"Ms. Wentworth?" he calls for me.

"Yes," I answer quickly. Focusing on the bowl in front of me, the Laffy Taffy returns to twenty-twenty vision. He knows who I am and I know all about him. Pretending I'm not Abigail Ross would be a waste of time, and honestly exhausting after all that's happened. "Of course, Sheldon. What can I do for you?"

He doesn't miss a beat. "I wanted to reach out, finish our conversation from the other night. You left in haste and I'm afraid you were upset. I want to make sure you're okay and explain."

Rolling my eyes, I try to even my voice. "I think you *explained* quite thoroughly. There's no need for concern, but thank you."

"Please, Addy. I want to clarify how I knew your parents. I do wish I hadn't lost contact with your mother after all she went through. But it does ease my guilt finding you."

"About that." I sit up and absent-mindedly trace the edge of my keyboard with my index finger. "How did you track me down, Sheldon? And please, we both know it's not a matter of coincidence."

It's his turn to pause, probably surprised by my directness. Laying it out there seemed to be my smartest option, it even helps me feel in control. If his intent was to intimidate me, he might have done it the other night, but not today.

"No," he relents, carefully. "No coincidence. I learned your mother passed a while back and wanted to reach out to you. I do apologize for the surprise and façade of your wine being served at the White House."

If anything, his condescending tone pisses me off, no matter how threatening he might be. "No need for apologies, Sheldon. My wine being featured in the most prestigious home in the world is quite the fair trade-off for your masquerade."

I bite my lip after the fact, which always happens too late in my case. If my mother was alive, she'd chastise me for being sardonic right after giving me a hip bump for holding him to his fire.

I hear a low chuckle on the other end. "You are like Anne."

"Is there a purpose to your call, besides taking me away from my work? Sundays are one of our biggest days of the week, things are bustling." I've found my groove and I'm going with it.

If anything, I think my backbone has put him at ease. I'm not sure what to think of that, but it does surprise me when he offers, "Come to the city and have lunch with me."

"I'm not sure what the Army does to keep you busy, but I don't have time to *lunch*."

Suddenly, my office door crashes open right when Sheldon presents his next option. "I'll come to you, enjoy another glass of your finest."

There's Crew, with my doorknob in one hand and his phone to his ear in the other. And he isn't just holding his phone, it appears he's about to crush it.

He's wearing a pair of black cargo pants topped with another white wife beater. But it only shows hints of once being white, because he's filthy from the tip of his head to his work boots. He's swathed in sweat, grime, and dirt. Every muscle I know so well isn't only on display, but taut and tense from what I can only assume is stress. I can't believe I have the mind to think about it, but I lean forward just far enough to look at his feet.

Yep, mud and muck. I'm sure he left a trail. When I look back up to him, I scowl.

He narrows his angry eyes at me and without saying a word, shakes his head.

Oh hell. I'd bet my all the cows' molasses he's listening.

"Addy?" Sheldon calls for me.

At the sound of Sheldon's voice, I swear Crew could bust through his wife beater. His whole body reaches another level of wired.

"Let me check my calendar," I say without breaking eye contact with Crew.

He immediately shakes his head again, even more fiercely than before, narrowing his eyes as if I'm in big trouble.

Shit, he *is* listening. I wonder how that's happening.

I don't have to check my calendar, though. I know my schedule like the back of my hand.

"Thursday? Say, three o'clock?" he offers.

Looking at Crew, I speak into the phone. "I can move some things around, make that work."

"I'm looking forward to it, Addy," Sheldon says before I offer him a speedy goodbye.

The second I hang up my phone, Crew lowers his from his ear, and steps inside my office, slamming the door behind him. I'm surprised pictures don't fall from the vibrating walls.

"What do you think you're doing, Addison?" he demands, towering over my desk.

I try and defend myself. "I didn't know it was him when I took the call."

"You could've hung up," he seethes.

"Crew—"

He bends slightly at the waist when he interrupts me. "You agreed to *meet* him."

"I know, but—"

"A man who's been committing treason for years. A man you know nothing about because I can't tell you. Even I don't know all he's done since I'm officially out of the loop."

"Please, let me—"

"He's dangerous, Addison." Crew raises his voice and goes on to tell me something I already know. "And you're meeting him for a fucking glass of wine."

I sit back in my chair and cross my arms. Strike three. I don't interrupt others and certainly don't appreciate being cut off. Continually.

"What were you thinking?" he belts out.

Saying nothing, I tip my head.

"You were so fucking scared after he approached you at the White House, you were gonna make a run for it. Who knows where you'd be right now if I hadn't stopped you. I don't want him anywhere near you, this property, or mine. After what I told you last night, I hope you can understand the significance of that."

My face falls instantly from his last statement. But keeping on, he gives me no opening to speak.

"And he could've had a hand in your father's death. At the very least, he knew about it, making him an accessory. He had everything to do with framing your dad for shit he was doing, setting your mom on a path of hiding out for the rest of her life, dragging you along for the ride." His next words rumble like thunder through my small office. "This is the man you're gonna meet for a fucking glass of wine!"

I don't say anything, because Crew has lost it. This man, who I've never seen any other way than cool and controlled, even when he is sharp, has lost all control because of me, and that makes me feel terrible. I, of all people, know what it's like to value your control. I can't imagine he loses it often.

When he finally quiets, I let that go on for a few moments, assuring he's done.

When it feels safe to speak, I start quietly. "I'm sorry. I didn't think of him coming here and putting you and your..." I try and find the right word, "...*organization*, at risk."

His brows pull together when he asks, incredulously, "You're sorry about me?"

"Yes," I answer honestly. "Look, his phone call was a surprise, and yes, I was scared and freaked the night he cornered me. I'll even give it to you, I was scared enough to run that night. But you've given me information, and as awful as it is, it made me feel better to at least know something."

"I'm glad you feel better," he spouts, but by the look on his face, he doesn't look glad at all. "Why the fuck did you agree to meet with him?!"

"Quit yelling at me, Crew, and I'll explain."

"Addison, this is not me yelling."

My eyes widen and I lean my forearms on my desk, unable to keep the sarcasm from leaking out. "Then quit talking loudly at me. For the record, I've come to like the way you call me 'Addison,' but not in that tone of voice."

He stands up straight and crosses his arms over his grungy wife beater, saying nothing.

I sigh before finally explaining. "I've no doubt he knew he scared me the other night, he probably meant to since he practically threatened me. But since you were obviously listening, I'm sure you could tell he was taken aback when I didn't insist I'm not who I am. He admitted he knew my parents and what happened to my father. I want to know what he has to say. I wasn't thinking about you or your privacy when I invited him here. I'll reschedule and meet him in the city. I don't want to put you at risk."

I can tell he's shocked by what I'm saying because his frown deepens when he growls, "Have you forgotten what happened on the way home from the White House? There's no way in hell you're meeting him in the city."

"You have to understand." I lean farther and soften my voice. "This is the first time in my life I have the chance to learn something about my dad from someone other than my mom. If he can give me anything—*anything*—I'll take it. Even knowing who he is and what he's done, I need that. I've never known anyone who knew my parents before my dad was killed."

"Addison," he lowers his voice, but his isn't soft. It's still harsh and livid. "He won't give you the truth. Why would he?"

I bite my lip and sit back in my chair. I know he'll probably feed me lies, but my curiosity gets the best of me. I've never had the opportunity to know anyone who knew us before. If he gives me a shred of anything, it'll be worth it.

"He might," I whisper and Crew's face instantly softens into something more of a frustrated acceptance. "He scared me in the beginning because he surprised me. Now that I know everything, I can think with a clear head. If I have the chance to talk to someone who knew us before my dad died, I'll take it. It might seem crazy after what you told me, but that only makes me want it more. This may be my only chance if they finish their investigation soon."

He says nothing, but closes his eyes and drops his head.

I go on, but cautiously. "And, um...for the first time since you told me about them, I'm sort of grateful for your cameras and surveillance. I didn't think it would hurt, seeing as though I'll be meeting with a CIA target."

He looks up at me and simply shakes his head.

"*And*," I pause, wondering how to ask him what I want. "I was sort of hoping you could be there with me?" I tip my head while scrunching up my face, worried about what he'll say.

"Addison," he sighs, my name coming out resigned, even if a bit frustrated when he looks to the side. When his eyes find me again, he informs me of something I already know. "You don't know what you're doing."

"I know," I admit.

"You don't know who you're dealing with."

"I know that, too."

"When you're dealing with someone like O'Rourke, you're not just dealing with him. You're dealing with a group of people you don't even want to know exist, let alone become a blip on their radar."

"Oh." I pause, because he has me there. "I did *not* know that."

He shakes his head. "I bet you've just pissed off a shit load of people at the CIA."

"I guess I should feel a little bit bad about that." I give him a small shrug, because I don't know anyone at the CIA and they really put my mom through the wringer years ago. I couldn't care less about the CIA.

He looks down at me, frustrated. "Come here."

My eyes widen. "Are you going to hug me?"

He shakes his head and a hint of the dimple appears. "I'm gonna do somethin'."

"Well, I'm not sure what you've been doing, but you're dirty and I can smell you from here."

"Addison," he reiterates, the dimple getting bigger.

"I need to help behind the bar—it's a madhouse out there. I can't get dirty," I explain.

"Baby, please."

I sigh and get up, walking around my desk as I warn, "Okay, but you cannot hug me."

When I get close, he reaches for me. He did listen and only reaches for my face, pulling me in for a long, and almost leisurely, kiss.

He pulls away just enough to look in my eyes. "I'll be there when you meet O'Rourke."

I give him a small smile. "Thank you. I thought you would."

"You'll listen to what he has to say. Do not egg him on or ask him questions. I don't want him to have any reason to become more interested in you. You'll take whatever he wants to say and let him be on his way. You understand?"

I bite my lip, not liking him being pushy, but try and appease him for now without agreeing. If I appease him, it's not an official lie. "You *are* the resident bad guy specialist."

He sighs. "You're full of surprises."

"I'm not usually. I'm usually kind of boring."

"It has not been a boring week, Addison."

"No," I agree. "It hasn't."

"I'll be over later. Probably eight or nine. We've got two days to finish some things up."

My eyes go big and a shiver runs down my back thinking of the promises he made me in the shower this morning.

"You've met Grady," he keeps talking. "I need to introduce you to Asa. He's trained a long time, but now he works for me."

I nod, looking forward to meeting the people he works with.

He pulls me in one more time before letting me go with promises of seeing me tonight.

We head to the tasting room together, him holding my hand in his filthy one. There, he kisses me goodbye in front of everyone before leaving to finish whatever dirty job he was doing before he rushed away, spying on my call.

When I get behind the bar to wash my hands, Evan calls for me. "Addy?"

I cringe, thinking he's going to give me shit about Crew.

Instead, he grins when he says, "You've got dirt on your face."

Well, shit. Of course I do.

At least he didn't hug me.

Chapter Seventeen

The Ass-Kicking

Addy

I don't know why I feel weird doing this—but I feel weird doing this.

I mean, Crew did say I was welcome at his house anytime. He said he'd be more than happy for me to see his property, what they've been working on for two months, and all the changes they've made. He told me if he's not at the hardware store or making quick stops for food, he was there.

Actually, his exact invitation sounded like this, "I'm an open book, you know it all. If you wanna come nose around it just means I get to see your beautiful face. All the better for me."

Six of one, half a dozen of the other, right?

It's Thursday and I've known him only two weeks—a life-changing, out-of-this-world, two weeks.

His "recruits" arrived Tuesday morning and I guess they live there while training. He's answered all my questions in the last few days, most of the time while we're lying in bed after ravishing each other. Or more specifically, after he has me where he wants me, he winds me into a sexually induced slinky, practically making me beg for it.

Then he ravishes me. Thanks to Crew and his creativity, I'm usually too spent to do any of my own ravishing.

I never knew it could be so good, but with Crew, it is. It was against my every instinct in the beginning to "comply," but letting Crew have his way with me has by far been the best I've ever had.

Every. Single. Time.

And I swear—it just keeps getting better.

I have my meeting with Sheldon this afternoon. I've been antsy about it all day since Crew left me in the wee hours of the morning, to go do whatever it is he does. I'm not sure where my courage came from when Sheldon asked to meet with me, but it's disintegrated into a pile of dust.

Poof. Disappeared.

I've been bustling around the tasting room all morning, a bundle of nerves, accomplishing nothing, and that's not like me. So I went to the kitchen and threw together a quick lunch for Crew and me, deciding it was finally time to take him up on his offer and come to him. I need to take my mind off this afternoon, and I'll get to see Crew midday, which hasn't happened since he's started training his people.

I slowly drive around the bend where the trees open up into a clearing. His house is much smaller than mine, but mine is huge, especially with the Ordinary. I have no idea if he breaks for lunch, but everyone needs to eat eventually. I grab our lunches and head for his front door when something catches my eye.

Looking to the side toward one of his barns, there's a group of men standing at the entrance, the wide doors all the way open. Abandoning our food on his porch, I decide to investigate.

I see Grady and another man that Crew introduced me to, Asa. They're grouped with a couple of others I've not met, and they're all dressed in workout gear.

Grady turns quickly, sensing my approach. Only he doesn't appear surprised to see me as a slow smile creeps across his face.

Of course he's not surprised, they seem to know everything. I'm sure he knew I was coming, what with all the cameras. I'm about to return his smile when noises from inside the barn distract me.

And those sounds are body parts hitting other body parts with such force—I not only hear the impact, but also the result.

Allowing my eyes to adjust to the dark interior of the barn, the smiling Grady steps aside, making room for me. There, I find Crew battling it out with another guy I don't know, on what seems to be flooring similar to a boxing ring. Crew's in a pair of loose athletic shorts with a fitted t-shirt, and running shoes.

His opponent is maybe an inch or two shorter than Crew, but just as solid, and he's younger, maybe by as much as a decade or more. His dark hair is clipped short, his searing blue eyes are fierce, but beautiful, and if I had a guess, I'd lay money down that he's pissed the hell off about something.

Crew is angled away, his back to me, as his competitor charges. I cringe, but Crew plants his right foot solid when the other guy takes a cut. Crew doesn't miss it. He catches his forearm, yanking the guy toward him, jabbing his other hand in his chest, creating a pained, "Humph."

The guy rallies, not missing a beat. He comes back at Crew coolly, proving the hit did little or no damage. Trying again, he goes for Crew's knees with a spinning kick.

Crew jumps to avoid him, but when he turns, his eyes catch mine. My breath catches from seeing him in action, feeling it down to my toes.

He's exactly what I've come to expect over the short time we've known each other. He's sharp, yet weirdly relaxed, as he battles it out on the mat. His moves aren't exaggerated, but seem to exert the minimal amount of energy necessary to defend himself against his attacker.

An attacker who's not at all relaxed. He's wired and angry, aggression seeping out of his pores.

For the nanosecond Crew takes to look my way, his surprise in seeing me here makes me nervous. I probably shouldn't have shown unannounced, but he said to come, so I came. Now I'm rethinking my visit, positive I've made a mistake.

Surprising even me, a hand connects with Crew's face. He must've sensed it, as he moves, deflecting the worst of the blow. I let out a little yelp, instinctively taking a step forward when he gets hit. Before he swings back into action, I see blood trickle from his upper lip. I'm about to take another step when a strong hand grasps my bicep, pulling me back. Before I know it, I'm tucked tight into a large frame with an arm around me. Looking up to my side, Grady, who's still grinning and not at all worried about Crew bleeding, gives me a shake of his head.

After he fends off another attack, Crew puts a good amount of space between them, assessing his next move. He does this again. Then again. It's almost as if he's humoring the guy.

The whole time, I only have eyes for Crew. Watching him maneuver, how his body relaxes between actions, yet never taking his eyes off his task.

Even I can tell Crew's last jab was harder than the rest, and the other guy growls, "Mother fucker."

I was right. Up until now, Crew was strictly on the defense. The second the words slip through the guy's lips, Crew moves.

As in, *moves.*

For some reason, I can't take my eyes off his hands. Hands that have touched every part of my body. He's comforted me with those hands. He's aroused me, he's gently yet firmly bound me, he's washed me, and he's woken me with his soft touch.

However, right now he's efficiently using those same hands, which have shown me nothing but tenderness, to kick the ever loving shit out of this guy. For some reason—which is completely foreign to me—this creates a surge of wetness between my legs.

He's fluid, quick, and sharp. His opponent is now on the defense and not doing it nearly as well as Crew did. He's almost forced off the mat. When Crew does some fancy footwork, the guy finally crashes to the ground, face first.

Crew, his breath barely accelerated, presses his running shoe into the guy's shoulder blades. I don't know how the guy would get up after all that—he doesn't look to be faring too well. I can tell Crew gives him most of his weight, keeping him where he wants him.

"You might've been a badass SEAL, Jarvis, but this isn't SEAL training. Remember that. You've got a fuck-of-a-lot more to learn and challenging me on the third day was not the brightest idea," Crew growls at the prone body beneath his foot. That body is breathing hard, rasping shallow breaths. Crew looks up at the other three I've not met and bites out, "Anyone else anxious to show us what you've got?"

No one says a word, even though they're all built and undoubtedly know what they're doing. Still, no one jumps in the ring.

Crew shifts away, leaving the guy on the ground and looks straight at Grady. "Get your fucking hands off her, then pick up where we left off."

I hear and feel Grady laugh, but he doesn't listen right away. He gives me a squeeze before finally letting me go. Crew sends him a good glare as Asa tosses him a bottle of water and towel. He presses the towel to his lip, wiping the blood away before twisting the lid off the bottle. When his eyes come to me, they're sharp as usual, but also contain something new.

Uh-oh, he's angry I'm here.

Grabbing my hand at the same time he takes a swig of water, he pulls me out of the barn.

We start up the hill toward his house in a quick clip and once out of earshot, I decide I should try to explain. "Crew, I didn't know—"

He interrupts me, giving my hand a firm squeeze. "Not here, Addison."

I shut my mouth and bite my lip.

When we finally get to his house, he pulls me through a back door and into an old, outdated kitchen—more outdated than mine. But he doesn't stop there. We traipse through a hallway and make a quick turn.

He pulls me into a small room with a huge desk finished in dark wood with a plush black leather chair behind it. There's even a console table between two windows, but what's strange is we're surrounded by flowers—blue, mauve, and yellow, incredibly ugly, flowers.

Without a word, he takes a step back and puts some space between us, leveling his eyes on me. Splashing a little water on his towel, he wipes the sweat from his face and presses it to his lip, where the bleeding has mostly stopped.

He stays silent without taking his eyes off me. I try not to look at his hands, because after watching him in action, they make me want to jump him and rip his sweaty clothes off, even if he is mad I'm here. Just thinking about it makes my nipples hard and I cross my arms over my chest hoping to cover them. Worried what he's going to say, I look away and try to calm myself because I can tell he's upset.

"Addison." His voice is heavy as he takes a step toward me. "I wish I would've known you were coming."

My eyes dart back to his and I try to explain. "I thought I'd bring you lunch. Next time I'll call first—"

"Are you okay?" he interrupts, his eyes searching my face.

I worry my lip, responding quietly. "I was getting nervous about this afternoon and the day was dragging. You mentioned I could come over whenever I wanted, so I thought I'd take you up on it. I had no idea I'd be interrupting, I'm sorry."

When he takes a step, I instinctively step back. This makes him frown and his whole body goes taut.

Oh shit. Yep, he's mad.

Crew

Fuck, I did not want her to see me like that.

She's asked me a million questions about what I've done the last ten years and most of those questions have centered on how dangerous it was. I've most definitely sugarcoated all of it.

I've told her the truth but I also wanted to ease her into it. I've never thought how I might need to handle my past with a woman, but during my time with Addison, I've tried hard not to fuck it up. I sure didn't plan on her seeing me kick that punk's ass.

But when he lipped off about knowing all he needed to know about hand-to-hand combat, I had no choice but to invite him to leave it on the mat. He must not understand we know everything about him. I know what he can and can't do, but I'm beginning to think Asa was right, he's a pain in the ass and might not be worth the effort. He had all the right moves but let his emotions take over when I pissed him off. That's when I decided to make an example of him. He never would've gotten me in the mouth if I hadn't been shocked to see Addison appear out of nowhere.

Now she looks scared, and damn it, I don't like that she's moved away from me.

I hold my hand out low and try to calm my voice. "No reason for you to be sorry. I'm sorry you saw that. You okay?"

"I..." she starts but her eyes dart down and back quickly, trying to figure out what to say. She hugs herself tighter before looking confused. "Why wouldn't I be okay?"

"Because you don't seem okay." I take one slow step closer and try to explain. "I didn't intend for you to see me like that this soon. Or ever."

She tips her head, still confused. "I thought you were upset I was here."

"I am." I reach out, wrapping my hand around the side of her neck. When I do, she immediately lifts her hand to cover mine, pressing it into her skin. There, I swear I feel her shiver when I add, "I had no desire for you to see me like that."

"Why, you didn't hurt him, did you? I mean, permanently?"

"Of course not," I bite out. "The kid has a chip on his shoulder, thought he could come in here and have a dick measuring contest."

She immediately bites her lip. "I have to say, I'm not surprised you won that contest. For more reasons than one."

I immediately release the tension I've been holding onto ever since I saw her in the barn, looking nothing but shocked to see me putting my fists to that kid.

"You're really good at that, aren't you?" she goes on.

I give her another squeeze, and in turn, she wraps her fingers around my hand. "Yeah, Addison. I have to be."

"Well, I knew that." She pulls my hand away from her neck, holding it in both of hers. She weirdly turns my hand over, running her fingers over it when she says without looking up, "I just didn't know how good."

"Addison?"

As soon as I call her name, she looks up. I barely have a chance to catch the look on her face before she surges up on her toes, her mouth hitting mine. Catching her hips to steady her as she presses close, I realize she's running hot.

Holy shit, the woman continues to surprise me.

Pressing her curvy body into my sweaty clothes, she moans into my mouth. Fuck if I don't get instantly hard. I drag my hands up to her waist, lifting and turning her at the same time. She brings her legs up around me and I bend, putting her back to my desk so I can press my cock between her legs where I want to bury myself deep.

Damn. My condoms are upstairs.

"That turned you on, baby?" I ask against her lips.

She exhales on a huff as she buries her hands in my sweaty hair, trying to force my mouth back to hers.

I hold steady, not giving her what she wants until she explains. "Unh-unh. Tell me."

"Yes," she answers, frustrated. "But don't ask me why, because I have no idea. If you're gonna kiss me, then kiss me, Crew. If not, I brought lunch, and it's getting hot on the front porch."

I let my eyes drag over her face, letting myself fall deeper into her dark eyes before I break it to her. "Condoms are upstairs and I've gotta get back."

"Oh," she breathes, her face falling, not hiding the disappointment in her tone. There're no games with her, no pretending. She wants me and she's not hiding it. "I knew it—I did interrupt."

I lean in and kiss her before saying, "I wouldn't've told you to come anytime if I didn't want you here. I'm sure Grady knew you were on your way the second you turned in."

"I'll call next time." She tries to push me away to get off my desk.

I press my raging hard-on into her again and start to move my hands on her body, shaking my head. "You're not goin' anywhere. You run this hot for me, I'm not lettin' you go. You can break in my new desk while I eat you for lunch."

Her eyes go big at the same time her legs constrict around me. I kiss her one more time before flipping off her sandals, tossing them to the floor. When I reach for the button at her waist, she whispers, "I thought you had to get back to the ass-kicking."

I jerk the button and start to rip down her jeans, bringing her panties with them when I smile. "I'll always make time for you, Addison. I have plenty of time to kick their asses. Right now, I want you."

"Well, as long as I'm not keeping you from anything," she breathes.

I toss her clothes to the floor with her shoes. Grabbing her ankles, I bring her feet to the edge of my new desk. Looking down at her spread for me, lying across CIA contracts, recruit backgrounds, and foreign investments, I've never seen anything more beautiful. I see what I never thought possible—my past mingling with a future I never thought to dream of. Never even knew it could exist in my world.

Leaning a hand to my desk, I bury the other in her long, dark hair. I kiss her before saying, "Not once did I think I could be who I am with anyone, let alone someone like you."

She brings her hands up to my jaw, running her thumb over the gash on my lip. Her face goes soft when she whispers, "We're quite a pair, Crew Vega."

"We are." I kiss her again and drag my hand down the center of her body. When I finally reach her bare pussy, her eyes droop as I start to play with her. She wasn't lying when she said she's turned on. She's drenched.

I make my way down her body, not able to wait another second to get my mouth on her. Sliding her up the desk farther, I give her two fingers and circle her swollen clit with my tongue. She moans, lifting her hips for more. I keep at her, fingers pumping, my tongue sucking, teasing. She starts to breathe hard, papers crunching beneath her.

When she moans my name, I've never heard anything better. I give her more, looking for that sweet spot with my fingers and letting her rock against my mouth. She starts to convulse on my hand and I suck her clit a little harder as she comes apart, filling my office with her cries.

When I let her go, she's breathing hard, and I smile from what I see on my desk. Covering her body with my torso, I tease her. "My contacts at the CIA are gonna wonder why their papers have been balled up."

"Sorry," she pants, even though she doesn't sound sorry at all.

I kiss her, loving the look on her face as she comes down from her high. "Why do I think you're not sorry?"

"Probably because I'm not." She barely smiles, but she does wrap me up with her arms and legs. "You're sweaty and stinky. It's rubbed off on me and I'm gonna need a shower. Is this normal for you?"

I give her more of my weight, enjoying the feel of her under me. "My guys ran ten miles this morning. I joined them for eight. We've been doin' drills and other shit before the ass-kicking you saw."

"Wow." Her eyes go big and she shakes her head. "No wonder you're built the way you are."

Running my thumb over her temple, I change the subject. "You should cancel your meeting with O'Rourke. You're anxious and I don't want you around him. There's nothing he can tell you that I can't eventually find out through my contacts."

Her face changes, becoming etched with contemplation and a hint of anxiety. "I need to meet with him. I'm afraid I'll regret it forever if I don't."

I sigh, because even though I'm still getting to know her, I can tell she's not gonna change her mind. "I'll shower and be there early. I don't want you alone with him."

"I feel bad, pulling you away from all the ass-kicking." A small smile takes over her face.

I kiss her quick and move to pull her up. "Get dressed. I've gotta get back."

As she dresses, she oddly tells me something I already know from her background and what she's told me. "I haven't been with anyone in more than two years."

I don't respond because I don't know where she's going with this and I really don't want to talk about it. She finally turns around and I cross my arms, waiting for her to go on.

"I'm on the pill, and I've had doctor's appointments since my last...well, you know," she explains, though, I have no desire to know.

Before she rambles more, I pull her into my arms. "What are you saying?"

"I'm saying, I checked out clean. As long as you've had those same appointments, I'm good to get rid of the condoms."

Surprised, I give her a squeeze and tell her the truth. "I've never had that."

It takes her a second to realize what I'm talking about. "Really? I mean, if you aren't comfortable—"

"I want that," I interrupt quickly. "Never had a reason to want it."

"Really?" she repeats.

"Really. I told you what the last ten years were like for me. I've never had a constant anything, let alone something like this. I'll make an appointment."

She smiles before reaching up on her toes to kiss me. "That means we can have surprise sex on your desk soon."

I smirk back, because she's right. I'm looking forward to that.

"But, Crew?"

"Yeah?"

"You really need to get rid of this wallpaper. It's horrid."

For some reason, that makes me want to fuck her senseless on my desk even more.

Chapter Eighteen

Slimy Chum-Bucket

Crew

Sitting beside Addison with my arm thrown over the back of her chair, I finger a lock of her hair idly. I do this staring across the table at Army Lieutenant Colonel Sheldon O'Rourke, as he feeds a ration of shit to the daughter of the man he had a hand in killing. As far as I can tell, she's soaking it up like a sponge. I do my best to be the relaxed man who's only here to be supportive of his woman, wondering how I'm going to handle giving her the truth.

It's all I can do not to come across the table at him. I also contemplate the fact I regret not being able to do what I've learned to do best over the last ten years on American soil. To hell with the American justice system—there's nothing I want more right now than to put a hole in his head and for him to buy it exactly the way Addison's father did.

O'Rourke was surprised to see me join them. He covered his irritation well enough after I explained I have an interest in everything that has to do with Addison Wentworth.

So far, he's explained how he met her father in the service when she was two and became good friends with her parents. It's plain to see he's a practiced hand at deception. If I didn't know his background of committing treason for decades, I'd have a hard time believing he wasn't completely genuine.

I do know from my contacts at the CIA, he never married, and has only had casual relationships with women. Listening to him spout his bullshit, I don't like where I think this is going.

"I tried to reach out to your mother many times," he explains.

"I'm surprised." Addison leans into the table, listening with rapt attention. "She never spoke of you. I'd remember."

He tries to cover his irritation. "I have to say, that's disappointing."

I do my best to sit relaxed in my chair.

He states instead of asks, "She never remarried."

When Addison shakes her head, a small frown takes over her face. "No. She never looked at another man. My whole life, all she talked about was how he was the only one for her. He was ripped away from her in the worst possible way. She never recovered."

"I wish she would have let me be there for her," he adds, narrowing his eyes.

Yeah, this fucking pisses me off.

"I hope you can understand her need to distance herself," Addison defends her mother. "She explained this to me when I was older. It's what drove her desperation to disappear. It was hard for her to trust anyone after what happened. Especially when they started looking into her simply because she was trying to clear my dad's name."

O'Rourke leans into the table. "I wish I could've cushioned her from that. I was young, very low level. There was little I could do, but I could've offered her comfort. Helped with you. There was no need for her to go it alone."

"She felt she couldn't trust anyone, Sheldon." Addison leans back in her chair and I let my hand rest on her neck. But I give her a squeeze, warning her to shut her mouth when she not-so-innocently asks, "Do you believe my father committed treason?"

Damn her. I told her not to dig.

Sheldon shakes his head. I'm not surprised his answer is obscure and convoluted. "Wes was a committed soldier, loved his country, took his service seriously."

"Then why would they accuse him of such a betrayal?"

When I give her another squeeze, she tries to brush me off by throwing her hair over her shoulder, but I hold firm. If this is any indication of her ability to follow directions, I'm fucked.

O'Rourke shakes his head, faking it like a pro. "I have no idea. It saddens me now as much as it did then. I am relieved, though, I get to see you after all these years. You were a vibrant child. To see you grown and all you've accomplished," he throws out a hand, "your parents would be very proud."

"It's a lot of work, but I learned from my mom hard work pays off," she offers.

"What made you return to Virginia?" he asks.

There it is, the reason he's here.

She goes on to explain about her mother's ashes, running across Whitetail, and taking advantage of a good opportunity. The whole time, he settles in his seat, assessing her answers. He gives nothing away, proving he's a practiced hand.

Picking up his wine glass, he tips it to her before taking a drink. "Your mother would be very proud. Your father, too. You've made yourself into quite a success."

Addison smiles, but ignores his compliment.

"I am curious," she starts before pausing. "How did you find me, and why would you think I'd be nosing around my father's death?"

She just doesn't stop. As I grip her neck again, she brings her hand up to cover mine, faking an intimate touch.

When I look at O'Rourke, his eyes are on his wine. He eventually looks up to Addison, giving her a small shrug. "What happened to your father weighed on my conscience for years. I used my resources to find you, and when I did, I learned you lost Anne. I can't say exactly why I wondered why you moved here. And it makes sense you'd want more information about your father's death. Who wouldn't?"

It's Addison's turn to lean back and she reaches out for me, her hand clutching my knee.

"I'm glad I found you, though," O'Rourke goes on. "It's good to see you after so long. May I call you Abby?"

"No." My voice comes out firm but deep, contributing my first word to their conversation. Folding my hand over hers on my knee, I continue. "You can call her Addy. That's it."

He raises a brow and gives me a curious nod. I certainly don't need any curiosity directed my way, especially from him, but I'm all in now. No fucking way is he calling her Abby. That's mine.

"Fair enough," he relents and downs his last swallow of wine. Looking at Addison, he shifts to get up. "I am sorry to have startled you last week at the White House. My apologies, but thank you for meeting with me today. I hope we can keep in touch."

Addison doesn't agree, but she certainly doesn't disagree. She does stand to shake his hand. Finally, after the two exchange goodbyes, he walks out the door, and she slowly turns to me.

I've known her two weeks and even though I know almost everything, including every inch of her body, I don't know her instincts. I have no idea how her head works—if she bought into his fake sincerity or if she saw him for what he is.

I do know I need to tread lightly. She lost both her parents, witnessing one of them killed violently. I need to proceed carefully, something I have no experience at with a woman.

Crossing her arms, she gives her head a small shake and I'm afraid of what she's gonna say, what she believed from the crap he spewed.

The second I open my mouth, heading into unknown territory, her eyes go big when she spews, "He is *so* full of shit."

I quickly clamp my mouth shut and fold my arms. Surprised, I tip my head, wondering what she's thinking. Finally, I agree. "Yeah."

"Holy shit, did you hear him? I think he was into my mom." Her face screws up, disgusted with what she saw. She throws her arms out to the side. "*My mom.* I don't even know what to do with that. What do I do with that?"

I sigh, relieved she saw what I saw in O'Rourke. I'm also relieved I don't have to convince her of what she's smart enough to see for herself. I reach out for her, giving her hand a squeeze. "There's nothing to do. But you shouldn't've asked what you asked, I warned you not to. You need to let it go and let the CIA do their job."

"I bet that's why he framed my dad," she says, dragging her hands up in her hair, not believing what she just heard. "He wanted my mom. He *wanted my mom*, Crew!"

"Baby—"

"I can't believe I'm saying it, but I'm glad she's not here. She'd feel guilty my dad was framed because some slimy chum-bucket who called himself their friend wanted her." She slides her hands through her hair, shaking her head.

"Addison—"

"Are they close?" she bites out, her voice turning harsh. "Please tell me they're close to taking him down. I mean, what in the hell are they waiting for?"

"They're close, they just need—"

"He must've been doing all his awful stuff since before my dad was killed. That's *forever* ago, Crew. What's wrong with the government?"

"They're—"

"I mean, I know they're slow at everything, but this is crazy." She frowns.

I sigh and cross my arms, letting her finish.

"How long are they going to let it go on? If he's guilty, he's guilty. I'm not sure how guilty one has to be before the CIA finally gets off their asses to make a move. Are there different levels of treason? I would think treason is treason, right? Seriously, though. Are there different degrees, like murder?"

When I wait a moment, seeing if she's finished with her rant, she proves she's lost her patience.

"Well?" Frustration seeps through her voice.

"They're close," I say, leaving it at that.

"That's all? They're close? You won't tell me anything more?"

I reach out and pull her to me. "It's all I know. With the CIA that could mean hours, weeks or months. My guess? Probably not months, more like weeks."

She tries to push me away but I hold steady. "What are they waiting for? How much evidence do they need?"

"Addison," I start and lower my voice, giving her a squeeze because she needs to do the same. "I was never fully in the loop and now I'm really not in the loop. Asa found out O'Rourke's not workin' alone. When they take him down, they want to make sure the entire operation is dead. Not maiming it, only to revive itself. We're gonna have to be patient, let them do their jobs. Trust me—they aren't happy they have traitors in the mix, especially as long as he's been at it."

"He's not working alone?"

I shake my head. "They don't know for sure, but their investigation has expanded. From what I saw today and know from the wiretaps, O'Rourke and those he's workin' for want to know what brought you back to the area. O'Rourke was told to make sure you aren't diggin' around for information on your dad's death. I'm still trying to figure out what happened on the way home from the White House. They haven't heard anything about that on wire. Until they take him down, I still don't want you out on your own. For now, you're good here at the winery, the house, and my camp. I'm curious to see if they intercept any calls about your meeting today."

She looks up at me while raising her eyebrows. "I, um, need to go to Home Depot. Today."

"What in the world do you need at Home Depot?"

"Um, *everything*." Her brows rise like I'm an idiot for not knowing what she needs from a home improvement store. "Morris has cleared out the bungalow and I need to shop for the finishings. My plan was to rent it out and once I recoup the costs of finishing it, it's pure profit. There's plumbing, but it's only roughed in. I need cabinets, flooring, paint, appliances. *Everything*, Crew. I needed it last week, but you've proven to be distracting. I can't put it off any longer, I've got to go tonight."

"What bungalow?" I ask, wondering what in the hell she's talking about since I know every inch of her property.

"Surely you've seen it," she explains. "It's closest to your property, down in the valley."

She can't be talking about what I think she's talking about. "Are you talking about the shack with the broken windows?"

She pushes me lightly and looks put out. "It's not a shack, it's a bungalow. It won't have broken windows after I order them at Home Depot tonight. Like I said, my list is long."

I sigh while looking up, and shake my head. I guess it could be worse. She could want to go to the mall.

I finally look back down and state, "I've worked for months to get my camp up and going, I finally get a group of trainees here, one of them is a pain in my ass like Asa told me he would be, and you think

I'm distracting?"

"I'm not asking you to come with me. Morris can take me, or maybe I can get Evan to—"

"I'm coming with you," I interrupt. No way am I letting her off this land without me.

"But you've got your," she pauses and looks around, lowering her voice, "people here."

"I'll make time to get away," I reiterate. "Please tell me you won't take forever to pick shit out."

"I'm a fast shopper," she says. "Even if I love it, I don't have time for it. I have a list and know what I need. It's a long list, but I plan on having it all delivered. It just needs to be ordered and Morris is managing the contractors for me. They're scheduled to start soon. It shouldn't take long once they get going."

"You're gonna be a landlord on top of everything else?" I smirk.

She shrugs. "I guess. It'll help pay off my business loan, and it's a big one. I've procrastinated since I bought this place. It was part of the plan and I'm overdue getting it rented out."

I lean in to kiss her forehead before letting her go. I really need to get back if I have to go shopping later. "Okay, but I'm running backgrounds on anyone you might rent to. I don't want just anyone on your property. We'll go shopping tonight when the winery closes. Be ready and we'll get it done fast."

She looks up with a small smile. "You haven't seen my list."

"Hey, lover-boy," I hear coming from behind me, and I turn as Addison laughs.

Waddling toward us is Clara, smiling big with a hand holding her belly.

She looks to Addison. "The baby-daddy needs to drop off the hellions. He's gotta go into the office, or so he says. I think he needs a break. Anyway, I'll be done in thirty, they can hang in my office if that's okay. He just called, they're pulling in."

Grinning, Addison pulls away from me. "It's fine. We aren't too busy—they can wreak havoc in the basement inglenook."

Just as Clara's about to answer, something catches their attention and they both turn to the front door.

"Again?" Clara seethes.

"You've got to be kidding me," Addison mutters as she heads toward the front door.

A man is making his way through the tables with his eyes on Addison. He's dressed like a cross between Crockett and Tubbs and someone going to a polo match. Shit, he's even wearing white pants. Not only is he dressed like an idiot who's full of himself, but he pulls a hand through his hair to cover the fact he only has eyes for Addison. Appreciative eyes, dragging over every inch of her. My muscles go taut as I follow, wondering who the hell he is.

When he opens his mouth to speak, Addison interrupts, angrily spitting her words first. "You were asked not to return, Tobin."

Clara butts in, pushing her way into the conversation. "She's not interested in whatever you're offering. Quit expending what few brain cells you do have on trying to buy Addy out."

When I get to the group, I stand behind Addison. The guy holds his hand low, palm out, in a calming manner. He tips his head and his tone is condescending when he placates, "Now, Addy, I only came to congratulate you on being the wine of the White House. I saw it on your website and read a small article featuring the highlighted items from the region. You're impressive as always."

"We're hardly *the wine* of the White House. They featured us at one dinner. Singular—that's it. I'm not trying to impress you. I wish you'd stop with whatever this is. I'm not interested. In *anything*," Addison stresses.

"Who're you?" I ask and put a hand on Addison's waist, pulling her back to me.

"Oo-oo, this is gonna be fun! Let me introduce everyone." Clara claps her hands, all of a sudden excited. Looking to me as she holds a hand out, gesturing to Crockett and Tubbs, she grins as she makes introductions. "This is Tobin McCann, a goopy-glop-of-a-man who runs around in pretty-boy pants with his mama's money, trying to make himself feel bigger than he is," she pauses, raising her eyebrows, "if you get what I mean."

The guy frowns, opening his mouth to argue, but Clara doesn't miss a beat.

"He's been trying to invest in the winery for months as a guise, he's really into Addy. Everyone can see this from a mile away. But since he's goopy and gloppy—kinda like the gross monster in Candy Land where you get stuck and can never get out—Addy's been putting him off." Clara turns to the guy she just demeaned, his mouth hanging open in surprise. Clara notices this, too, and reaches to lightly press up on the bottom of his chin. Her voice is laced with fake concern when she goes on. "I know, I know, Tobin. That was my reaction, as well, the first time I saw Hercules, here. At least he has his shirt on today. Sometimes we refer to him as Zeus, but he's young and virile, so Hercules fits. Oh, and he's also knockin' Addy's socks off in more ways than one. So you see? There's really no reason *at all* for you to return."

"Clara!" Addison yelps.

With big eyes and a shake of her head, Clara replies, "What? It's true."

"Oh, you are really fired this time." Addy's frustrated, and I hide a smirk at the scene playing out in front of me.

Before anyone offers more insults, the front door bursts open. Two blond boys come running in, yelling, and causing a ruckus. Another smaller one follows, dragging up the rear.

"Addy!" the two big ones yell in unison. When they push their way into the middle of our strange circle, I hold firm when they throw themselves at Addison, pushing us both back.

Addison puts her arms around them both. "Hey guys. You come to eat all my Laffy Taffy?"

"No." Clara turns on her mom voice. "No Laffy Taffy or sugar of any kind."

"I don't feel good, Mama," the littlest guy groans, going straight to his mother.

Clara puts her hands to his face, tipping it up to look him over.

Tobin must not like being ignored, because he tries again. "Addy, if I could just have a minute—"

"Babe, Nick's not lookin' so hot," a gruff voice interrupts and I see another man enter the fray with his eyes on Clara. He stands at probably five foot ten in a solid frame with light brown hair. "He doesn't take those hills well."

"He'd take them better if you didn't drive like you're on a rollercoaster." Clara scowls at the man who must be the father of her children. "Look at him, Jack. You've made him sick."

"But it's fun," the biggest boy yells louder than necessary.

"Yeah, there were no other cars, so today we got to go super-fast," the other yells, outing his dad who's frowning at him, probably warning him to shut his trap.

"My stomach hurts," the little guy moans, clutching his middle.

Tobin, demanding attention again, steps toward us. "If I could just have a minute alone, Addy, I can explain the numbers. It'll allow you to pay off most, if not all, of your loan."

And that's where he made his mistake. Because the second he got the words out of his mouth, Clara's youngest turned away from his mom and spewed. Chunks of what looks like half-digested macaroni and cheese mixed with orange juice fly out of his mouth, hitting Tobin's Sonny Crockett pants and stupid-ass loafers, the smell instantly infiltrating the room.

"What the hell?" Tobin jumps back as I move away, pulling Addison with me. Clara hovers over her youngest, consoling him as he starts to cry.

"Ew!"

"Gross."

"Don't step in it."

"Get me away from the puke, it smells."

As Clara's older kids complain, I reach around and grab them by their collars, yanking them away from the mess. Their dad comes around to them, but Clara sees this and growls to her husband, "Don't you dare leave. You did this, Jack."

Addison steps back with us but looks to Tobin, who's standing there with puke all over his white pants and loafers. Trying to hide the smirk on her face, she says like she means it with all her heart, "Thanks for stopping by, Tobin."

His eyes get big. "Addy, my pants and shoes are ruined. Aren't you going to do anything?"

She tips her head while biting her lip, looking down at his feet. "Yes, I agree, they're most likely ruined. I hate to bring this up, because it's not mannerly to say 'I told you so,' so I won't. But I will remind you that if you were elsewhere at this moment, your lovely white pants and shoes would be intact. I do hope this is the last time I'll need to request that you stay elsewhere. Anywhere but here is fine with me."

Tobin's face turns red, and balling his fists, he seethes, "Can I at least have a towel? I can't get into my car like this."

Pressing her lips tight, she gives her head a shake. From the looks of it, I'd say Addy is enjoying every moment of this. "Hmm. Sorry, but no. Please try to tiptoe out, we already have quite the mess here to clean up."

Enraged, he turns—and not on his tiptoes—stomping out the door.

"Addy," Clara calls as she holds her son to her side. I've never seen Clara serious before, but she is now. "I'm so sorry. We'll get this cleaned up and it won't happen again."

Addison's smirk turns into a glowing smile, lighting up her face. "I'm giving you a raise, and paid maternity leave. I really should've thought about that before, sorry. I've never had employees, let alone pregnant ones. Bring the kids anytime. They got rid of that pesky gnat that's been swarming me for months. I couldn't be happier." She turns to look at all three boys. "Come with me. We'll have Laffy Taffy and read the jokes, then we'll go see if we can find the cows. You know the drill—you just can't have the green apple ones."

I catch her hand and when I do, she looks up to me with her big brown eyes smiling. I shake my head when I say, "You're definitely not boring."

If it's possible, she smiles bigger.

"I wanna know all about that guy, though. I'll be here when you close to take you shopping."

She nods and leans up to kiss me as the boys pull on her other arm, wanting candy.

"Save me the banana ones," I say against her lips.

Her big smile softens and she whispers, "From now on, they're yours."

What she doesn't know is I'm claiming a hell of a lot more than her banana-flavored candy.

I turn and step over puke to get back to work so I can get back to her.

Chapter Nineteen
Anything and Everything

Crew

"Asa was right. He's a pain in the ass." I'm standing in the sweltering heat watching the guys maneuver the course we built.

They're climbing walls, balancing logs, climbing cargo nets, and all kinds of other obstacles. The course is long, set in and out of the trees and brush. This is their first time on the sequence. They weren't given any directions and we started them in intervals.

"I hate it when Asa's right." Grady's beside me with a stopwatch in hand, but his eyes are on Jarvis. "Even so, I was right, too. Look at him go."

Grady is right. We worked for months on this course, and I wasn't in the military, but Grady was. He assured me this is harder than anything they had to do, and Grady was a Ranger. I do know it's more than we had when we were trained. The three others aren't slacking by any means, but Jarvis is killin' it compared to them. He's agile and lithe, especially with his bulk.

"As long as he doesn't have to communicate with anyone, he's good. Otherwise, he's a nightmare. We knew he was a loner, but it's been two weeks. This shit is ridiculous," I say, shaking my head while watching Jarvis make the turn to start the second half of the course.

We watch as he makes his way to the end where we're waiting. The kid never loses his pace, nothing in the course slowed him or tripped him up. He kept up the crazy-ass speed he started with, and we're nearing the end of the day. They started out like always, running ten, followed by hand-to-hand, and then the shooting range. He's a machine.

When he crossed the finish line, Grady looks to his watch before narrowing his eyes on the kid and lies, "Fuckin' slow. Get water and hit the showers. You've got language after dinner."

Jarvis is breathing heavy, his hands to his knees, showing his first signs of exhaustion since he started the course. But his head snapped up the second he heard the word "slow" and he shoots Grady the look-of-death we've gotten used to seeing on his face. It's pretty much the only look he ever gives us.

If possible, his glare hardens further before he straightens, and just to fucking rub our noses in it, he takes off in a quick clip, faster than a jog, up the hill.

"I thought you told me we made the course hard enough," I chide. "You must be getting soft in your retirement years."

"That's what I'm worried about," Grady mutters.

We watch the other three cross the finish line, in a respectable amount of time for a first go. I guess this proves we're capable of picking normal badasses, but in the process, got a freak-of-nature thrown into the mix. They're instructed to do the same as Jarvis, but walk instead of run back to camp.

I record their times when I hear from my side, "I wasn't kidding."

I look at Grady. "About what?"

"I'm getting soft."

I start to head back to camp. "You run, lift, shoot, and go to the mat with them. If you want, I'll send you through your own course if that'll make you feel better."

He falls in beside me. "That's not what I mean. I'm getting antsy."

I stop, but it takes him a couple strides to follow suit.

When I glare at him without saying a word, he asks, "You ever get restless?"

I know where he's going with this, but I expected it would pass. He didn't want to quit. I had to talk him into it, but it was time. He was getting closer to the edge with each job, Asa and I both saw it. It can happen, but Grady had a close call, the edge was too fucking close. I've seen men go down because of it, no way was I gonna let that happen to Grady.

He's like me, he could've retired and never worked another day in his life. The money was that good—we're set and could live big if the spirit moved us. There was no way I could hang on a beach for the rest of my life without anything to focus on, and I know Grady would have a harder time than me. Plus, this arrangement was how they let us out when they did, and I took it.

I set this endeavor up for the both of us. Between training new men and making a percentage off their jobs for as long as they work, we'll eventually make as much as we did before. Asa earned off us for ten years, it's the cycle of the beast.

I cross my arms and glare, not liking where I think this is heading. "No," I say firmly. "I'm not restless."

"You wouldn't be," he huffs. "You've moved in with the beauty queen next door. Of course you're not restless."

I ignore his comment about Addison and feel my jaw go hard

because I know it's not about her. "What are you sayin'?"

He looks to the side and sighs for many long moments, crossing his arms. When he finally looks back, he admits, "I've been talking to Carson."

I take a step closer, demanding, "About what?"

"About goin' back. I'm not ready for this like you are. You knew it, guilted me into quitting, and I bit. It's been months, I'm done trying to make it work."

Not able to control my fury, I thunder, "You're not going back."

He knows I'm pissed and lowers his voice. "I am."

I don't even try to control myself, I lose it. With all my force, I put my hands to his chest and roar, "Have you lost your fucking mind?"

He stumbles back a step before righting himself. "Calm down."

"You forget what happened on your last job? Because I haven't. I remember every fucking detail," I yell, not able to control myself.

He takes a step closer and seethes, "I was fine—there was no need for you to step in."

"That's bullshit and you know it." I shake my head and move to turn away from him because I've fucking had it.

"Crew," he calls out for me.

Stopping, I turn and point to him angrily. "You'd better think this through, Grady. Think it through, long and hard, then do it again. You've got tunnel vision and I can't do a fuckin' thing about that. I wish you could see how your life's been on hold for ten fuckin' years. That's a long time, and now you've been given this opportunity and shit on it? I know you're not goin' back for the money, so what, you miss the high? Fuck, I promise you, it's nothing compared to what else is out there, you've just gotta open your fucking eyes and look for it. Don't get sucked back in, Grady. I got you out once. They don't let us go easy, I don't know if I can do it again."

"I never asked you to do shit," he growls. "I'm lettin' you know, when I get assigned, I'll be gone."

"Damn it, Grady. Think about it."

"I've been thinking about it for months," he stresses.

I glare at him one more time before turning to start up the hill. I don't know what I'm gonna do. The one thing I do know is, Grady isn't buyin' it by going back to that life. Not as long as I have anything to do with it. He's had one close call—he's not having another. I'll do anything I can to make sure of it.

Addy

It's been a long day. It's Sunday, we had two small events and the tasting room was busy. It's almost time to shut the place down, I'm helping clean and close the bar. The last customers on the terrace just left. Everyone is gone but Evan and me, and he's in the back restocking from the cellar since we're closed tomorrow.

I plan on going home to get some things done before Crew arrives. We don't even talk about our arrangements anymore. He prefers my house to his, my bed to his, and my shower to his.

Me? I just prefer him, anyway I can have him.

We even tossed the condoms a few days ago when he got his clean bill of health. That's been even better.

It's been a month since he snuck up on me walking with my cows in my pasture. Three weeks since he took me to the White House dinner, and then later that night, saw me at my worst. During all this time, he's proven to be exactly what I need, when I need it.

For the past two weeks, he's been coming to me late since he's busy with his killers in training. He quickly eats dinner and we go to bed.

There, he has his way with me, but in a way I know it's all for me. Each touch, taste, caress—every moment we're together, he makes this clear as crystal. After we're done but before sleep, words are exchanged in quiet hushes, small laughs, and sometimes in my case, silent tears. These are the moments, and sometimes even hours, where he gifts me with everything about him. And during these stretches of time in my darkened room, he's asked everything he wants to know of me.

Everything he doesn't already know on paper from reading my background, that is.

During these times, Crew reminds me I'm his reward for doing what he thought was his duty for ten years. Doing what he believed was right, but after so many years of doing it, knew he needed out. Now he says he knows why he left when he did. Even though he teases me that I was waiting on him and needed a ride to the White House, he's serious as it gets when he says he needs me like his next breath.

I'm not sure about all that.

I do know I've never had a lover like Crew. Someone who's completely focused on my mind and heart, as well as my body. Even though I trained myself years ago to manage my panic attacks, it's hard to describe how I feel now. The fear isn't in my forethoughts any longer. Sometimes I find an entire day has rushed by and I haven't thought about it once.

It's strange, especially since I've lived with it simmering under my skin for as long as I can remember.

It's strange, yet freeing.

Completely, and unequivocally, freeing.

By this time of the day I begin to get anxious. I miss him and can't wait to have time with him again.

I look up when I hear the door creak and see Mary walk in, starting her way through the empty tasting room. "Hey, what are you doing here?"

"Oh." She seems surprised to see me and her step stutters. "Um...I just came by to say hi."

I give her a smile mixed with a curious frown. "Well, hi yourself. Have a glass and tell me your troubles. You look pretty by the way. You going somewhere?"

She does look pretty. Her loose curls are perfect like normal and her makeup is leaning toward smokey. She's dressed as edgy as ever, but today her edge is sporting a side of sexy, suiting her well.

She inhales deeply before sighing dramatically. "I guess."

I frown for real this time, wondering what's wrong with her.

"What are you thirsty for?" I ask.

Pausing to think, she finally slaps her hand on the bar, deciding vehemently. "Tequila."

"Ah...hello? You're at a winery, not a distillery," I offer sarcastically. "You want to tie one on, I'll take you home where I have tequila."

"Holy shit, I don't care. Just give me something that's already open." She's agitated and ill-tempered, definitely not herself.

I let my eyes go big and hold out my arms. "Again—a tasting room. Everything is open, you pick."

"Tie me up and whip me with some silly string, Addy Wentworth. Are you trying to torture me?" She leans forward and demands, "Give me something. Something strong and something red."

I step back, wondering if she's been possessed. As quick as I can reach to my right, I grab the first red I see and set it on the bar. It's a Meritage from four years back, maybe if it's dry it'll be strong enough. Since it seems we have a wine emergency here, I quickly turn and reach for a large rounded glass.

When I look back to her, I'm stopped in my tracks and yell, "What the hell, Mary?"

She's drinking straight from the bottle that was at least half full.

"What's wrong with you?" I keep yelling.

She takes three more gigantic gulps before slamming the bottle to the bar. Through a small wince, she utters, "I have a date."

I'm confused. Mary is practically perfect. She's outgoing, with just the right amount of boisterous to not be annoying, not to mention self-assured. Since I've known her, she's dated her fair share, but I've never seen her like this.

"Why are you so worked up?" I ask.

She gives me a good glare and defends herself before picking up the bottle. "I'm not worked up."

I lean into the bar on my elbows, trying to hide my smile as I watch her gulp down a forty-five-dollar bottle of wine that won awards at the State Fair. If Evan saw this, he'd have a fit. "Yeah, whatever. How are you going to get to your date if you're downing half a bottle of wine in record time?"

She wipes the back of her hand across her mouth, smudging her lipstick. "He's picking me up here. I really don't know why I agreed to this. I didn't even want to go, but he talked me into it. Seriously, I should escape now. I should go home, give myself a conditioning treatment, and apply a mask."

"No, your hair looks great. Better than normal," I offer, trying to make her feel better.

"It does, doesn't it?" She fingers a lock of her turquoise hair and exhales, her whole body slumping on her stool as she throws out a hand to me. "You need a Keratin treatment, by the way. You're starting to frizz."

Running my hand through my hair, I silently agree. "I've been busy. I'll get in soon. Tell me about your date and why is he picking you up here?"

She ignores my question and mumbles with the bottle to her lips before taking another gulp, "I can fit you in next week. You can't walk around frizzing, it'll make me look bad."

I ignore her and demand, "You're not usually a wuss. Tell me about this guy."

I barely get the last word out of my mouth when I hear from in back of me, "You're early."

My eyes widen as I turn slowly, thinking it can't be.

It's Evan, standing at the doorway that leads to the kitchen where he most likely just came up from the cellar. He's got his arms crossed, but he tips his head as a slow smile spreads across his young, handsome face. "You're early *and* you're beautiful. Bonus."

I hear a squeak and a rustle. When I swing my head back to Mary, her bottle is tipped high, almost finished.

"You two are going out?" I ask, not able to hide the excitement in my voice.

"Yeah," Evan answers.

The only answer I get from Mary is her wine bottle being slammed to the bar.

"Really?" My voice goes higher.

"Yeah," Evan repeats.

"Really," Mary grumbles at the same time, but she sounds as excited as one would be about scrubbing the grout behind a toilet, and a public toilet, at that.

Looking to Evan, I have no choice but to play the responsible adult. "She's gonna need some food. Don't let her drive, she just downed a half bottle of the Meritage."

"Mary," he chides. "I'm taking you for Italian. You could've waited."

"No, I needed it." She puts the bottle to her lips again, looking for the last drop of wine.

"You love Italian," I remind her.

She barely catches my eyes before her head falls dramatically to the bar. Resting her forehead there, I hear a muffled, "Of course he's taking me for Italian. What the hell am I doing?"

I look back to Evan. "Where are you going?"

"Girasole's in The Plains."

"Niiiiccce." I grin, letting the word drag out sing-songy, and as I do, Mary bangs her head once on the bar.

I laugh and Evan sighs as he moves out from in back of the bar. Picking up her purse, he grabs her hand in his other. He pulls her gently off the stool. "Let's go. We have a reservation."

"I feel like a proud mama," I announce as they start for the door. Mary turns and gives me her big glaring eyes, but I ignore her. "Or a matchmaker. You two wouldn't be where you are now if I didn't have frizzy hair."

"See ya, Addy," Evan calls.

"You guys coming to poker tomorrow night?" I yell as they get to the door.

"Yep," Evan answers at the same time Mary grumbles, "No."

Evan rolls his eyes as he pushes her through the door. "We'll be there."

The second he does, I'm surprised to see Crew enter as they leave.

I smile, happy to see him before the sun sets. "Hey. You're early."

He barely gives Evan and Mary a nod, his eyes on me the whole time, and not soft eyes. Sharp, intense, and if I'm reading him correctly, a lot angry.

"What's wrong?" I walk around the bar, moving to him.

But he's moving faster. His intensity increasing the closer he gets, making me stop.

"Crew?" I call out, but he doesn't answer.

When he gets close, he grabs my face, almost aggressively but not, crushing his mouth to mine. Our teeth barely scrape and I'm forced to grab his forearms to hold on.

When he finally let's go, I'm breathless. "What's wrong?"

He doesn't utter a word, but his deep, dark eyes sear into mine. Looking around quickly, he grabs my hand, pulling me across the tasting room. When we get to the heavy oak doors of the barrel room, he pulls me inside. The wide door creeps to a close, encasing us in the dimmed atmosphere. The oak barrels—staggered and stacked on risers four-high—surround us.

He presses me up against two barrels, one at my bottom and the other behind my head. Yanking my shift dress up to my waist, I shiver as the cool air hits my bare skin. The room is air-tight and temperature controlled at an even fifty-five degrees. When the backs of my thighs hit the cool wood of the barrel, it's a complete contradiction to his warm hand that dips into the front of my panties.

As much as I love this, I don't understand it. Clutching his wrist, I ask one more time, "What's wrong?"

He stills, his hand in my panties cupping me firmly and possessively. Looking into his eyes, he says nothing while exhaling, giving his head a frustrated, single shake.

I don't know what's going on with him, and I have no clue what the look is in his eyes or the energy seeping from his body means.

But I don't like it and want to do anything and everything I can to make it go away. As much as he's done for me, I want to do something for him.

Crossing my arms at my waist, I grab the hem of my dress that's bunched there and pull—up and over my head it goes. I have to fight not to shiver from the cool, moist air. After I drop it to the side, I reach back and unhook my bra.

For as fast as he claimed me just minutes ago, our actions are now just as slow. Letting gravity take over, my bra leisurely falls down my arms, leaving me bare other than my panties and sandals.

His hand is still buried in my panties where he holds me firmly. I feel myself getting wet—it's the only place on my body that's warm. In fact, the more the heat builds between my legs, the faster I seem to chill. Goosebumps spread over my arms and my nipples harden—erect, overly-sensitive.

His dark, anguished eyes never leave mine. I kick my sandals off, at the same time hooking my thumbs into my panties and push them down.

All through this, he never lets me go, never looks away. I reach up on my toes, putting my hands to his scruffy jaw I've come to love, pulling him to me.

He lets me do all this. Over the past few weeks when it's just us, he leads it. He puts me where he wants me, gives, takes what he wants, and moves us at his speed.

His hand between my legs starts to explore as I kiss him. I glide my hands up his scruffy face into his still damp hair. He smells clean, like he showered just before coming to me.

When I finally let go and come back down to flat feet, I feel small and exposed compared to him, fully dressed, and taller than normal in his big clompy boots.

"You need me?" I whisper, because even though we've only been together weeks, somehow I know.

"Abby." He murmurs his first word. As always when he calls me by my real name, it touches me in a place that hasn't seen light in an eternity. His eyes smolder, and whatever torment that's living inside him, burns deep.

"Take what you need, Crew."

His eyes flare and for the first time since we stepped inside the barrel room, they fall away from mine. They rake over my body, his other hand coming softly to my hip, whispering feather-light up my side, circling my nipple. He never looks away from his touch, giving me more goosebumps and heating me simultaneously.

His fingers between my legs start to move with intent and purpose. If standing naked in the barrel room wasn't titillating, his fingers are. He twists my nipple hard enough for me to beg him not to quit.

But I know him by now. He'll give me what he wants and I'll never be left wanting.

"Crew," I moan, closing my eyes. My body's tingling from him and the cool, moist air combined.

All of a sudden I lose his touch. When I open my eyes, his t-shirt is coming off and lands with my dress on the concrete floor. He rips his jeans open and pulls out his beautiful, rock-hard cock.

Before I know it, I'm up and we're turning. Wrapping myself around him, I hold him close. He's warm and I press my hips in, rubbing my throbbing clit against his hard length. With his hands at my bottom, he lifts me before pulling me down with force. And there he is, filling me up.

I let out a whimper at the same time he groans into the side of my head.

Still without uttering a word, he lays me down on the table in the middle of the barrel room used for tastings. He doesn't start moving like I want him to, he stands up straight scooting my ass to the edge where he remains planted deep. Putting my heels to the edge of the table where I'm spread wide, his hands start to move on me.

I try and press my hips in, to find purchase on his cock, but he gives my hip a squeeze in warning. The other hand goes between my legs, where he's looking down his body to where we're connected. When he starts working my clit, he barely slides in and out.

I'm not cold anymore. I'm warm, breathing hard and trying my best to move against him, but he's holding me still.

When I start to lose control, I grab the edges of the table, hearing my moans and cries echo through the spacious room, bouncing off my barrels of wine.

His strong arm slides under me, around my lower back and up, where he cradles my head. His warm chest is tight against me when he starts to really move.

I don't think he's ever moved like this, not taking the time to work up to anything. I told him to take what he needed and he is. His arm around my waist is pulling me down as he slams into me. I've wrapped my legs around his waist to hold tight, and I need to.

He's holding nothing back, his breathing and groans are all I hear—his face buried in the side of my hair.

Minutes later when he slams into me one last time, his whole body tenses around me. Together we're warm, the cool temperature of the room not affecting us at all.

I slide a hand up from his powerful back, into his hair and pull lightly. Still coming down from his orgasm, he lifts his head to look at me.

"You okay?" I ask.

He closes his eyes and presses into me again. "I was pissed."

I smirk. "I might have to piss you off more often."

I still don't know what's wrong with him, but whatever it was must've faded because he smirks back and raises a brow. "Baby, if I were pissed at you, that would've gone differently."

I doubt I fixed whatever was wrong before, but I am happy he's not wearing his tormented face any longer and challenge, "Oh yeah?"

"Yeah."

"And how's that?" I go on.

The hand around my waist pulls away and he smacks my ass, but not hard.

"Hey!" I yell and try to move, but he has me pinned.

"But it would've ended the same way. You would've liked it." His smirk turns into a cocky smile.

I frown deeply and let my eyes go big. "I doubt it."

I get another light smack. "I'll show you sometime."

"Crew, stop it." I can't help but smile from his change of demeanor.

His cocky smile turns into a devilish grin.

"What were you upset about?" I change the subject since he will *not* be spanking me.

He loses the smile as he closes his eyes, dropping his face into my hair. Taking a deep breath, he mutters into the side of my head, "Work." Leaning up, he keeps talking. "You were right. I needed you."

My face softens. "I'm sorry. You want to talk about it?"

He shakes his head. "I'm good now."

I give him a squeeze. "I'm glad you needed me for a change. Do you have to go back?"

He shakes his head and kisses me softly. "I'm hungry and want a full night with you. Let's get outta here, we didn't even lock the door."

But we didn't think about the door or get out of there. He kissed me again, and then again, both deeply and then tenderly, before he finally let me up to get dressed.

Then, as I walked naked to our pile of clothes in my barrel room, I made a mental note to clean the tasting table tomorrow.

Chapter Twenty

Messages

Marc Whittaker

The lights finally flip on. I've knocked and rang the bell three times. A curtain moves at the sidelight before an alarm is disengaged and the deadbolt flipped.

When Sheldon opens the door of his Falls Church home, he growls angrily, "Why in the fuck are you on my doorstep in the middle of the night?"

I ignore him and barge in, forcing him to step aside in his robe.

"You alone?" I ask, waiting for him to shut the door.

It's his turn to ignore me, and since he's not whispering, I assume he's alone.

My eyes track around the room before looking back at him

questioningly. I point my finger downward, turn it in a circle and raise my brows in question, silently asking if it's safe to speak.

Jerking his chin, he's no less frustrated when he answers, "I did a sweep today, and you know I have cameras on the house."

Wanting to get this done quickly and get out, I lay it out there. "It's been over two weeks since you went to see her. They've been watching her close for months and are not happy her patterns have suddenly changed. She rarely leaves her property, and when she does, she's not once been by herself."

"Why do they want her by herself?" he demands, glaring at me.

Tipping my head, I shrug nonchalantly. I keep my cool, unlike Sheldon, who's been wound tight and on edge since his demons from the past were dug up a couple months back. "Who said they want her by herself? I just noted that they noticed a change."

"They don't *just* notice shit like that," he seethes.

"They're suspicious."

"They don't need to be. She's probably tied up in her business. I doubt her patterns have changed that much and they know she has the new boyfriend," he says.

"They've changed enough," I state.

"It's a coincidence at best," he throws back.

"Maybe. Maybe not," I offer before telling him the real reason for my visit. "They haven't said it outright, but they're becoming leery about you. I'm here to relay a message. You don't need to worry about the upcoming delivery. I'll be handling it. They wanted you to know they'll reach out if they need you."

His face tightens and I can see it in his eyes—realization with a splash of shock, and maybe, a bit of fear mixed in. He regroups quickly when determination takes over, his voice firm when he says, "I'll speak with them tomorrow. We'll see who makes the next delivery, Whittaker."

I tip my head to him in invitation. "I'm sure they'll be happy to hear from you. Convince them who you're loyal to, just like you did all those years ago when your friend, Wes, was suspicious. We all know the last straw was when he stumbled upon you stealing nuclear weapon designs. Even though you did your best to put him off, he was a threat that needed to be eliminated. Now you're trying to protect his daughter—they're not okay with that."

"Get the fuck out of my house," he growls. "Don't come here again or beckon me—I don't care what time of day it is. If they have a message, they can contact me directly. I earned their trust all these years. I don't know what kind of shit you're feeding them, but nothing's changed."

"They see it for themselves, Sheldon. I'm not feeding them anything. Watch yourself. Some might just think you're losing your touch, coming to the end of your career." With that, I turn to reach for the door. When I look back, he hasn't moved from his spot. "See you at the Pentagon, Sheldon."

Descending his steps in the dark of night, I quickly walk around the block to my car. I cross the street and walk one more block west. Assured I'm not being followed—I double back to my car. As I do, I pull my secure phone from my back pocket and hit call.

When it's answered, I speak quietly. "He said he'll be in touch, and like we thought, he was defensive."

I listen for a directive, and exactly as I assumed, I'll be making the next delivery. Sheldon O'Rourke has lost his position, even if the powers that be needed my help seeing it. They'll be making plans soon for a changing of the guard. I can tell it's coming—I just hope it's soon. Then again, I might not know until after it happens.

Ending the call within seconds, I toss my phone on the passenger seat and head back to Arlington. I've got a big couple of days at work and need to get some sleep to be sharp. Creating access to something I've never had access to will need careful planning.

Crew

I got a text less than a minute ago from Rhonda—the first one I've gotten since the day I learned about Addison's past. There's no doubt I'd be right where I am now if that hadn't happened, although it might've taken longer. In some demented way, I'm grateful for the catapult.

I grab the prepaid phone I keep with me and go to the hallway outside Addison's room. I'm tense because I don't like talking to Carson. I prefer Asa be his contact. I'm never happy to get these texts, but especially in the middle of the night, so I bite out his name when he answers. "Carson. What now?"

He doesn't waste any time, either. "Whittaker visited O'Rourke minutes ago. They think the house is clean and spoke openly. Then Whittaker made a call to London after he left. This is good, we're closing in on their European contacts. I wanted you to know we're getting close, but until then, they've got eyes on your neighbor."

Looking back through her bedroom door, my eyes trained to adjust to the dark, I see her sprawled on the far side of the bed. Her back is bare and the sheet's barely covering her ass.

He keeps talking. "Sounds like they've been watching her for a while. They've noticed a change in pattern. She hasn't been out by herself in a few weeks."

"Fuck," I whisper.

"Yeah. But good news, you're just the *boyfriend*," he says, and when he does, I swear he's fucking smiling. "They aren't looking into you, not that they would find anything, you're practically invisible besides clicking away on a keyboard for years creating accounting programs.'"

I shake my head. I'm not worried about me—I can take care of myself. But this means they've been watchin' her a while.

Not waiting for me to respond, he keeps going. "Just want you to know you should continue to keep your *girlfriend* on a short leash, your instincts were right. Then again, they usually are."

"Is that it?" I'm frustrated with this and don't like being on this call for any longer than needed.

"No. Looks like O'Rourke's being cut out. I'm corresponding about this as we speak. We need to move before they eliminate anyone they no longer have a use for. I'm putting a closer tail on him starting tomorrow. We want him alive."

Good. The faster this shit's done, the better.

"You got more?" I go on.

"No. Hopefully we won't talk again," he reiterates my thoughts.

I look away from Addison and back to the large square hallway that's open to the bottom floor with two bedrooms on the opposite side, but see nothing when I change the subject. "You offer a job to Grady, you'll answer to me. Do not pull him back in."

I get nothing.

Silence.

We have no business being on this line sitting in silence.

"Don't make me have to step in, Carson. You know I will. Do not give him an assignment," I threaten.

"You're all independent contractors. You know I can't speak to you about anyone else." Carson's voice is tight, controlled, all business.

"Cut him out," I demand. "I don't care what he wants."

"Crew," he starts before lowering his voice. "An offer's being made tomorrow. They've got a job that fits his skillset. It's already in the works."

I close my eyes and drop my head. I cannot fucking believe this.

"Vega—" I hear, but before he has a chance to say anything else, I disconnect. Then quietly, like I learned how to move so long ago, I walk down the two flights of stairs in Addison's huge-ass house without making a sound, to her garage where I left my tools. I need to decimate this fucking phone.

When I get back to bed, I lay next to Addison, a place I've become addicted to being over the last few weeks. There's no denying it, I don't want to be anywhere else but right here.

I don't roll to her, I don't let myself bury my face in her hair, touch her, giving myself what I want, what I've fucking earned.

I stare at her ceiling the rest of the night while she sleeps, wondering what the fuck I'm gonna do. Or if I can't do anything, how to make sure Grady doesn't step so close to the edge, that this time he doesn't come back.

As I stare into the darkness for hours and contemplate, I've never been more pissed at my friend.

Chapter Twenty-One

The Heavy

Crew

Grady's avoided me all day, and now that the guys are with the language instructor, he's escaped to his barn. He didn't need to work hard avoiding me since I've done the same to him. There's no point in asking Asa to pull any strings, if I couldn't put a stop to him going back, he can't either.

If I can't keep him from going, it makes me fucking sick to my stomach to think about what I might have to do. I can't get it out of my head—it's left a rock in my gut all day.

We're heading into fall where the mornings and evenings are cooler, but some days the humidity can still be a bitch. It's my first fall back in Virginia since I left the Secret Service. As much as I've come to like my property, it's nothing compared to Addison's. The views from her home and business have got to be the best in the region, and set against the rolling acres of her vines, it almost makes me like wine.

But what sets her property over the edge is all her.

My two-hundred and seventy-acre refuge I couldn't wait to settle on has become nothing but a place of work for me. When I'm here, I want nothing but to be there, with Addison.

That's where I'm headed because it's poker night. It's entertaining, to say the least, and her group of strange friends is starting to grow on me. I can tell they care about her, and they not only seem like good people, I know for a fact they are. I've run extensive backgrounds on every single one of them since she's fixed them in her life, and damn it if she didn't give each one of them new keys after I spent the time changing her locks to keep them out. She promised she told them to knock and only use the key if she wasn't home. She was clearly happy she got her way, even if she tried to appease me while doing it.

A long time ago, I might've thought about my future, before my dad was killed. But since then, not once. I've never let my mind wander to what I'd want in life, let alone in a woman. If I had, I can't say I'd ever wish to have one with a backbone like hers. On top of that, she's strong, independent, and smart. Now that I have her, I wouldn't want her any other way. Especially since she gives it all over to me when I want it.

In bed, her barrel room, my desk, and just this morning, her kitchen. The possibilities are endless.

Obsessed might be a strong word, but if this isn't an obsession, it's gotta be something more. I've barely come to terms with being obsessed, anything more is too much to comprehend right now. Whatever "normal" we've created—given both our fucked-up pasts—seems to work, so I'm going with it.

All that makes me pissed at Grady even more, because that rock in my gut is twisting and turning, causing a pain I've never experienced. I don't have a choice—I'm being forced to take action no matter how much I don't want to or how it'll affect Addison.

Climbing out of my truck, I grab the six-pack of beer and head to her kitchen door. It's late, I'm sure they've already started.

No one's in the kitchen but I hear them living it up in the Ordinary. I know I should eat despite the turning in my stomach. Heaping a plate full of food, I head to the poker game.

When I clear the entrance to the Ordinary, Addison's head is thrown back and she's laughing along with the others. Well, everyone but Mary. She's glaring at Addison with a look that could kill. Scowling, she has dark circles under her eyes, and her normally big hair is pulled back into a tie. I think I see what's going on as Evan leans back in his chair and smirks at her. Stretching his arm around her, they're sitting closer than normal as he starts to play with her hair.

"Would you mind lowering your voice when laughing at me?" Mary tries to shrug Evan off as she growls at Addison. "You're not helping my headache."

"Oops, I forgot about the hangover. Most people don't get drunk on their first date." Addison smirks at her friend before catching my eye.

When she does, her face morphs into a content, peaceful affection as her big smile shrinks into a small private one. Her secret smile mirrors the obsession I can't get out of my head. It's one only lovers share, reminding me she takes it any way I wanna give it to her, that she's sucked my dick, ridden my face—even both at the same time—wanting everything I give her.

I ignore the rest of the shenanigans at the table and go straight to her. She leans her head back, looking at me as I set my plate down and cup the back of her head, taking her mouth. I let her go a million times quicker than I want since her poker group is watching.

"Hey," she breathes against my lips.

"Missed you," I say against hers before taking the seat next to her.

She leans into me, bumping my shoulder with hers and fills me in on what was so funny. "I was right, Evan and Mary are officially *a thing*. They had their first date last night, but it was a drunken one for Mary because for some crazy-ass reason, she was nervous and drank too much."

"Never thought you to be the drunk-date type," Van teases Mary.

"I was not nervous or drunk." Mary raises her voice and tries again to push Evan's hand out of her hair, but he won't allow it. She goes on, and as she does, her voice goes frantic. "It wasn't really a date. It was only…dinner. Just because you eat together doesn't make it a date. It was food, and wine—lots of wine—and then really yummy tiramisu, and then I think I had more wine. I wasn't drunk, just happy. Maybe a little tipsy…"

Evan tugs on her hair, getting her attention. "Don't forget about the chocolate martini since you insisted that wine deserves dessert, too."

"Why shouldn't wine get its own dessert?" Bev picks up a glass of her red, tipping it to Mary with a supportive smile. "Hear, hear."

Mary groans.

"Can we play cards already?" Morris grumbles.

"*Two* chocolate martinis. That's when I cut you off," Evan adds.

Mary puts her hands to her face and starts to rub her temples. "Damn, I forgot about the second one."

"*And*," Addison butts in, reaching for my thigh, as if she needs to work at getting my attention. "Evan brought her back here to get her car mid-morning, and Mary was wearing her same kick-ass outfit from last night."

Evan shrugs. "I couldn't leave her alone after all that, so I brought her back to my place to take care of her. Then I made her breakfast."

Addison squeezes my leg as she drawls, "I'm so happy."

"You need a do-over," Bev announces firmly as she puts her glass down. "An old fashioned date. Morrie took me mini-golfing and then for ice cream, I was home by nine-thirty. I don't even know why you're here, you should've had your do-over tonight."

"Tomorrow's your day off," Van says to Evan with a sly smile. "Talk to me after the game, I'll tell you how to do a do-over."

"You will do no such thing." Bev throws a purple Laffy Taffy across the table, but Van catches it just in time. She looks back to Mary and Evan with intent. "Tomorrow night, you'll have your do-over. It needs to be something fun, not involving alcohol."

Evan tips his head and smirks. "I'm good with that."

"Oooh," Mary moans with her eyes closed, pressing her fingertips into her forehead. "My headache is coming back."

Evan sighs and scoots his chair to get up. "Come on. I'll take you home."

"You're leaving?" Van complains.

"No, I'll be okay," Mary insists.

Evan grabs her hand, pulling her from the table. "You don't feel well. We shouldn't have come. I'll take you home and you can lay down."

"You can plan your do-over," Addison sing-songs. Her eyes zero in on Evan not letting go of Mary's hand, clearly in young-love heaven witnessing her friends get together like she wanted.

I shove a bite of food in my mouth and give them a chin lift as they leave the Ordinary.

Van starts to put the chips away, frustrated when he complains, "Let's call it a night. We shot the shit too long—it's too late to start. Maybe next week everyone will be of sound mind and body."

I sigh, grateful to get out of poker. I'm not in the mood.

"Get the cookies, Bevie," Morris bosses his wife and the three remaining groupies gather their things to leave.

As Addison cleans her kitchen, she rambles on about Evan and

Mary, how she's sure Mary will come around eventually, and how she knew it would happen. By the time we make it upstairs, she's moved on to telling me about interviewing tenants for her rental tomorrow since it'll be done in a week. Her chatter doesn't slow as we get ready for bed around each other, something that's become a nightly occurrence, and after only having this for a short time, it's so effortless, it's natural. I still don't understand how it can be, but it is.

Which makes what I have to do even more painful.

Addy

"I have three viewings set up tomorrow morning. I knew you'd go whackadoo about me meeting strangers with the O'Rourke thing still out there, but Morris will be with me. Plus, you've still got all your cameras going, I'll be fine."

I know I'm rambling, but I don't care. Two of my favorite people are getting together and I couldn't be happier. I know they've only had one semi-disastrous, drunken date, but it was because Mary was nervous, and she was nervous because she secretly likes him. Just like I knew all this time.

I *love* being right.

"My appointments are set up back to back. I hope one of them works out, I'm anxious to get someone in and be done with it." I step out of my jeans, yanking my top over my head at the same time and keep talking from my closet. "It would be nice to have someone quiet and low maintenance. The extra money will help pay off my business loan quicker, that won't hurt either. Although, I'm sure Bev will immediately befriend whoever I rent it to, she won't be able to help herself and we'll end up having one more for poker night. We're already up to seven." Reaching for a nightie, I pull it over my head and realize I'm rambling—Crew's hardly said two words since everyone left. I walk out still talking. "Do you think eight is too many for poker?"

When I walk out of my closet, I stop. Crew is standing next to my bed, looking at the floor with one hand wrapped around the back of his neck and the other on his hip, deep in thought.

"Crew?" My voice breaks through the quiet of the room, and as soon as it does, his head pops up, his deep dark eyes aren't soft and relaxed like I've become accustomed to. They're piercing and intense, and I don't like them that way. When he doesn't answer, I frown. "You okay?"

He pulls in a big breath and his arms fold across his sun-kissed, chiseled chest, before he sighs, looking out my window. His shirt is lying near his bare feet. He's all skin other than his jeans, looking nothing short of delicious with the top two buttons undone. It doesn't matter what little time we've had together, I know him well, and he's not the relaxed man I've become enthralled by. The man who possesses me so completely I've allowed myself to let go, let life live itself around me, and for the first time ever, truly relax into it, appreciating it for what it is, and just *be*.

No, he's back to his intense self, but this time he's not hiding it with a relaxed stance. I not only see it in his eyes like I used to, but it's rippling off him in waves.

The sharp is back, and damn it, I don't like the sharp.

"What's going on?" I demand, and he instantly gives me his eyes.

"We all have our specialties," he spouts quickly.

My frown deepens, not understanding. "I'm sorry?"

"In my line of work, we all have our specialties. I told you I'm a good shot. The best."

Really confused now and not liking it, I don't fight the derisive tone in my voice. "I doubt that's something I'll soon forget, Crew."

He keeps on, ignoring my tone. "I got to where I strictly worked from afar, never comfortable unless my finger was lightly resting on the trigger. I've tried other methods but I get antsy—restless. The only way I'm completely solid is behind the barrel of a gun. I think you get from what little I've told you, I can't do my job well unless I'm one-hundred percent solid."

Well then. If that doesn't confirm my suspicions, nothing will. He's held back about his work. I had a feeling he was either sharing half-truths or softening the edges for me. Six of one, half a dozen the other. Any way you paint it, I was right.

And this time, it *sucks* to be right.

But he doesn't give me a chance to respond.

"Grady's not like me. He accepted the job for different reasons." He leans forward, stressing his next words. "He not only needs a challenge—he fucking *thrives* off it. Challenge and change—he likes to mix it up. He doesn't mind interacting with a target before finishing the job. He's also a good shot. He could put down any MMA fighter—he's exceptional and quick at hand-to-hand. But what he's really good at, is disappearing. In a crowd, a quiet home, deserted buildings, and even in the light of day. He can be silent like I've never seen, get close to his target, get it done, and then fade away. He's stealth."

My insides clench from hearing the words *get it done*, and I whisper, "Why are you telling me this now?"

He doesn't hesitate and takes a step toward me. "Grady and I started this shit together, trained together, sometimes worked together. I think you get that this is a lonely fucking business. I have few people in my life because of it, Grady became a brother, just a different kind. A year ago, Asa told me he had a couple close calls. No one knew if he was losing his edge, getting careless, or if it was a case of superhero syndrome—feeling invincible when he absolutely was not."

He takes a breath and I give my head a questioning shake, still not understanding why he's going into all this. But he doesn't make me wait before laying it out there.

"I needed to see for myself, so I worked my way into sharing a job, bein' his backup. It was less than a year ago, and if I hadn't been there to step in, he'd be dead. To this day, he argues that's not the way it went down, but it did. He got too comfortable, ignored the warning signs, and made himself visible. I had to step in and pull my trigger. That was the day I knew he was done with the job and I had to make him done. Not that anyone had to twist my arm, I was fucking thrilled to walk away. That was the day I set the plan in motion that put me here," he growls, pointing to my floor.

I swallow over the lump in my throat because, as much as his words scare me, his extreme emotion scares me more. "What is this about?"

His words come out clipped, angry, and forceful. "He's goin' back and I can't stop him."

I exhale because now I get it. He's worried about his friend. I shorten the distance between us, sensing his hurt, worry, anguish, and I want to touch him. "I'm sorry."

He puts his hand up before I get to him, stopping me when he says in a low guttural voice, "I'm goin' with him, Addison."

I feel like I walked into a brick wall, stuttering back a step.

What?

Oh, shit. Now I *get it.*

A pained look sweeps over his face and he tries to close the distance on me this time, but I take another step back, whispering, "No."

"I have to." He moves in closer and this time I put my hand up, stopping him.

I even surprise myself when I raise my voice, accusing him, "You said you were done."

"Addison—" he starts, but I interrupt.

"You said you'd never go back, Crew. *Never.*"

He shakes his head. "I can't let him go alone."

My tears build instantly and it's coming, it settling in, what I haven't felt in a while. Actually, I haven't felt it since the night of the White House dinner, but this feels different. My breaths start to come quick and shallow as I sound desperate, even begging. "Don't go."

His eyes roam my face, moving over me, surveying what's happening right in front of him. He quickly takes a step to me and pulls me into his warm body. "I'll be back. It could be a week—it could be a month. But I'll be back."

"Please." My tears start to fall. "Please, don't go."

He pulls me in tighter and says into the top of my head, "I have to do this until I can get him to quit for good. I'll never forgive myself if something happened to him."

With my arms squished between us where he's holding me tight, I close my eyes and breathe against his bare chest. Concentrating on my breaths for the first time in a long time, I put into motion what I learned so long ago, doing my best to hold back the weight working its way into my heart.

I should've known this was too good to be true. Having him and all he's given me was too much. I've taken all the security he's offered, and in return, handed him the weight I've been carrying around for twenty-five years. This is what I get.

I understand his job, the dangers and risks. I get that he's worried about Grady, but I'm worried about him. What if he doesn't come back to me?

Oh, that weight is heavy. No one realizes what you're carrying around for so long until it's gone, making you light as a feather—and then crash. It's back, a heftier burden than I've ever experienced.

"Baby, come to bed," he whispers, holding me tight.

When I don't move, for fear the weight will take over, I feel his arm behind my knees and I'm up. The next thing I know I'm back on my feet and he's pulling my nightie up and over my head. Doing everything I can to bury my emotions deep, I turn to climb in bed wearing just my panties, wiping the tears from my face. Moments later, he climbs in behind me on what's become his side of the bed, closest to the door. His fingers dip into the hips of my panties, dragging them down my legs, and hell if I don't let him. I've gotten used to him doing what he wants in my bed and haven't once stopped him.

Fitting himself to my back, he's bare, too, when he says softly into the back of my head, "Nothing between us tonight, Abby. I've got you, baby. I'll be back, don't question that. I don't want to be anywhere but right here. I'm sorry I have to do this."

He pulls me deeper into his large frame, but it doesn't help. As I lay here naked in his arms, I try to pinpoint the moment I trusted him with everything, gave up the control he wanted, handing it over to him. He took it all from me, allowing me to feel light and free for a short time. I can't remember when it happened completely, it just did. I've never felt so free.

I had it for a short time, the normal I've never had. But the heavy is back and it's never felt as oppressive as this.

Crew

Fuck, I knew that was going to be hard, but I didn't know it would be that painful.

I've held her tight, stroking her bare stomach, her thigh, whispering into the back of her hair until she finally found sleep. Her silent tears, still wet on her pillow and drying on her face, were the worst. She never made a sound.

If she falls back into her protective shell and I can't get her back to the good we've been living, I'll fucking kill Grady Cain with my own hands.

Chapter Twenty-Two

Goodbye

Crew

I open my eyes to Addison's barely-lit room. It's early, earlier than she normally gets up, with the sun barely risen. But I don't have the mind space to think about my morning run, my schedule, my fucking best friend, or even the looming issue of O'Rourke.

No, all I can think about is my cock. My throbbing, raging hard-on, which has taken over every inch of my body, mind, and soul.

I groan as a whisper of a touch strokes me from my balls to tip, so fucking slowly. A misery so sweet, I unconsciously lift my hips for more as I turn my head.

She's plastered to my side, her head on my chest but she's looking at her hand, watching her torturous actions. Her single index finger circles my tip so lightly—there's no way she knows the effect she's creating, an ache so intense I already feel like I'm gonna explode.

Forcing her to tip her head to me by fisting her hair, her eyes are alert and awake, yet shielded with something that makes my heart sink. I know it's about what I told her last night, me leaving with Grady.

She moves instantly, pushing her bare body up on her hands and knees before swinging a leg over my lap. Those shielded eyes hold mine as she lifts, and before I know it, she impales herself on my cock. I lose sight of her, my eyes closing, finding relief inside her tight perfection. Just her and me, nothing between us. It's like nothing I've ever had and it's so good, I know for a fact I don't want anything else the rest of my days.

I open my eyes when she starts to move, riding me lazily, taking initiative—my allowing it for the first time ever. Dragging my eyes over her beautiful body, I'm forced to look up when she pulls her hands through her messy hair, pushing it out of her face. She slides up before leisurely sinking on my cock when her hands fall from her hair to her tits, pausing a moment to play with herself.

As much as I love what she's doing, I want more, and reach for one of her hands. Bringing it close, I pull her middle three fingers into my mouth and suck deep, swirling them with my tongue. If possible, when she lifts, she's even more wet, coating my cock with her need as her eyes droop. Sucking one more time before letting go, I direct them between her legs, taking over, showing her what I want.

Just like my Abby, she reads me and starts easily working her clit with her own wet fingers.

If she keeps moving, I might come before her, and there's no fucking way I'd ever let that happen. Lifting my hips, I splay my hands on her ass holding her tight on my cock where she can't move. A small furrow appears on her brow as her objection comes out in a small mew.

I shake my head once and look down my body at our connection.

I know she gets me when she grinds down and her fingers start to move with purpose. Holding her tight with one hand I move the other, pulling her pussy lips wide around her clit, but I don't help her.

As her fingers move faster, her knees widen, and she leans back on my thigh with the other hand to hold steady. I can tell she's close, circling, arching, and breathing shallow. When it happens, I feel her tighten, making my cock jerk. When her climax is rocking her body, I start to move her, finally getting the friction I woke up needing more than anything.

She's still riding her high when her eyes come to mine. Her shield gone now, replaced with a sex-laden contentment, but still wanton. I see how much she hungers for it when she starts to move.

Riding me, she moves fast, grinding down as I thrust, meeting her. She prolongs her climax, her pussy still milking me as I drive into her three last times, finally getting what I woke up wanting after she worked me into an early morning frenzy.

Addison falls forward, her face in my neck, and hair strewn over my chest. Together, we're warm and she sinks into me so deeply, we could become one. Holding her tight at her ass and hair, I turn to kiss her forehead. We lay like this as we both come down, catching our breaths from the best morning sex we've had yet.

As good as it was, after minutes pass it's not hard to feel her tense since she's still wrapped around me and filled with my cock.

"Baby?" I call, finally breaking our morning silence. The word barely falls from my lips when she interrupts.

Her voice is tight and small. "When do you leave?"

I breathe in, smelling her hair before sighing with last night's events surfacing, reality slapping me in the face. I give her a squeeze and continue to hold her tight. "Soon," I whisper into the side of her head. "Probably today, Grady got an assignment. I had to force my way in."

She exhales, her body melting into mine before she eventually shifts away. I'm forced to let her go when she pushes up on all fours and I lose her. Leaning over me, she's shielded, and I force myself not to grimace, masking my features as I reach out to touch her instinctively. No way can I be this close and not touch her.

Her hand comes to my face, lightly falling over my temple, cheek, and lips. She runs her fingertips over my scruff. When she leans to put her lips to mine, it's soft and barely there, but fuck if it isn't the most intimate touch I've ever had, ending centuries too soon.

She pulls away, immediately leaving the bed, and I have no choice but to let her. Without a word, she gives me her shielded eyes one last time before forcing me to watch her walk naked to her bathroom.

Looking at her ceiling, I'm fucking pissed at Grady, frustrated with myself for not being able to let him suffer his consequences, but I'm mostly riddled with guilt over what I've done to her. Her shield is back because of me. Fuck, when I decided there'd be an us, she didn't sign up for me working this job. I'm the one changing the rules at halftime, and I hate myself for it.

Despite what I have to do to keep Grady alive until I can talk some sense into him, there's no fucking way I'm not coming back to her. As I hear her shower turn on, I find myself hoping to God she doesn't think she just gave me goodbye sex, because that's exactly what it felt like. There's no fucking way this is goodbye. Only over my dead body will I let that happen.

Addy

"As you can see, it's all recently finished. The kitchen appliances are new, as are the washer and dryer in the laundry closet," I explain as she stands at the window, running her fingers over the freshly painted white sill. She hesitates, gazing out the window. "It's small, but should accommodate one person nicely. The bathroom and bedroom still need to be painted, but then it'll be done. If you don't mind the smell of fresh paint, it should only be a day or two."

The bungalow is located closer to Crew's home than mine, but the view from the front is nothing but vines. Vines that are lush, in full bloom, and have fully filled out over the trellises at this point in the season. Harvest is in a few weeks and Van thinks this year's crop has the potential to be the best we've had in years. We've had a dry spell, which is a good thing—rain isn't good for the grapes right before reaping. Extra water plumps the grapes, washing out the richness of the tannins wanted in a finished product. Not only will we be able to make better wine if the rain stays away, but I'll also be able to demand a higher price for the grapes I sell to other vineyards.

Needless to say, I'm not doing any rain dances. I need the next few weeks to stay hot and dry. As romantic a notion it may seem to own a winery, when it gets down to it, I'm nothing more than a farmer with cows, completely dependent on Mother Nature.

Today of all days, I'm doing everything I can to bury myself in work. Crew is leaving. I know he's doing what he thinks he needs to do for his friend, but after begging him not to go and realizing he's made up his mind, mine went into overdrive.

Self-preservation.

I've forced myself to revert back to a place in my head where the future is nothing but uncertain. I've allowed myself to get comfortable during a time that should've been the most uncertain with O'Rourke and the events surrounding my dad's death floating to the surface. I gave Crew my worries and let him deal with everything. Then I lost myself in the beauty of us—two souls who lived a long time drowning in death and loss and secrets, but together we were good. Together we each moved past it.

That's all changed.

I know my mind has shifted into protection mode. For now, I won't allow myself to think about the future. What if this assignment turns into another, then another, and so on? What if something happens to Grady, and Crew has to live through another loss? Because the thought of him experiencing more hurt makes me ache. I absolutely can't think about the other outcome—the worst of the worst—where worrying about Crew and me getting back to where we were won't be an issue at all, because they'll be no Crew in this world. That's where my thoughts go—to such a dark place, I simply can't take it.

No, today all I can think about is if we'll get rain, it'll ruin my crops. Renting my bungalow, Evan and Mary's do-over, and how I need to plan a baby shower. I'll get on that this afternoon to keep my mind busy.

But right now, I'm thinking about the woman standing in my bungalow, gazing out at my vines.

Maya Augustine is an inch or two taller than me, maybe five-six or seven. Her dark blonde hair is pulled back into a low pony and she's wearing a pair of faded jeans that fit her so perfectly, if I had to guess, they're her favorite. Every woman has her favorite pair, and when they fit like hers, she'd be crazy not to wear them every day if she could pull it off. She's fit and slim, yet in a healthy way as her tone arms and back are easy to see in her form fitting tank.

"Do you have any questions?" I break through the silence, and when I do, she turns to me.

As healthy and fit as her body appears, her eyes are troubled and I sense a weight there that's heavy. It's plain to see life is hard on her right now. Maya is my third interview. I know from her application she's twenty-eight and is currently working part time at a nearby assisted living center. There's a long, drawn out explanation about her search for full time employment in her application, almost coming across desperate. That desperation was the only thing that made me take the interview. Her part time income will barely cover the rent, she'll have almost nothing left to live on.

Looking around the empty space, she bites her lip before stating on a sigh, "I know you didn't advertise it as furnished, but I was hoping."

"No, I didn't advertise it one way or the other." My curiosity gets the best of me. "What do you need?"

"Well." She pauses, looking around the main room that makes up the living, eating, and kitchen areas. The small bedroom and bathroom are separate off to the side. "I moved here with a couple of suitcases, so...I guess I need everything."

I do a quick mental inventory of my house. Between my mom's and my things from California, not to mention the antiques that came with my farmhouse, everything is eclectic, but in a bad way. Maybe it's time to start decorating. Another thing to take my mind off the future.

And Crew.

Deciding I need something else to focus on—and it might just be internet shopping—I offer, "I didn't advertise it one way or the other because any furnishings I have to offer won't be new, or fancy. I can't promise what it will look like all put together, but you won't be sleeping on the floor. How does that sound?"

For the first time since she arrived, her icy blue eyes brighten a tinge. "Really?"

Right then, I finalize my decision that would not only make my mom happy, but puts the first smile on my face since last night before Crew told me his plans. "Really. Do you know anything about wine?"

She instantly shakes her head. "Just that I like it."

"That's good enough for me. How about we make a deal? You work for me, put in twenty hours in my tasting room a week. The income should supplement you enough until you find the full time job you're looking for. It's not glamorous work, but if you have the desire, Evan can teach you to do tastings with the customers. Other than that, it'll be bussing tables, stocking, helping in the kitchen, and with events. I'll even work around your other job for scheduling. What do you say?"

Her eyes instantly become glassy, and she turns quickly to the window, probably to hide her emotions. I was right, life isn't coming easy right now, and she needs a break. Today of all days, I'm really glad I get to be the one who gives it to her. It makes me feel good.

"Thank you." She nods her head and when she gets it together, turns back giving me a small smile. "I appreciate the job, too. Anything will help. I hope something full time opens up at the place where I work now. I like it there."

I put the other two applicants out of my mind and smile. "This is good. We'll both benefit, I need help in the tasting room and if you moved here with a couple of suitcases, you need to settle. It's a win-win. I'll have some furniture moved in today, you can move in the day after tomorrow. Why don't you come with me now, I can introduce you to Evan and the rest of the crazies you'll be working with."

Maya looks down at herself. "I'm not dressed for work."

"You're not, but you can at least come, meet everyone, and talk to Evan about when you can start so he can put you on the schedule. Come on, it'll be quick."

She takes one final look around the room, taking in her new home before hesitantly following me out the door where Morris is waiting for us on the small porch.

"Morris, this is Maya Augustine. She's moving in the day after tomorrow, and she'll also be working part time for Evan."

Morris sticks his hand out to Maya and grunts, "Hey."

Maya nods with big eyes, having the same reaction most have when meeting Morris. "Um, nice to meet you."

I look back to her and grin. "Morris is my caretaker and manages everything on the property. His wife Bev makes up for his grumpy nature. Watch out for her, she'll adopt you straight away." Morris starts walking ahead of us to the cars when I call to his back, "I'm gonna need some furniture moved, you can get the guys to help."

I hear another grunt and when I look to my side, Maya looks worried.

"Don't worry," I mutter under my breath. "He's a softie—you'll get used to him. Come on, follow me to the main building and we'll get you all set up."

The door opens to my office, and there he is, filling my space the way he always does when he's near me. When he's close, it's only him. But where his presence usually fills me up, making me whole, right now it drains me.

It's afternoon and I forced myself to eat some fruit for lunch when I wasn't hungry. Even though I've done everything I could to busy my brain, I've thought of him all day. I don't know what I thought he would do, but I find myself relieved he's here, even though I dread it. I didn't think he would leave without seeing me, but since he ripped off the bandage that temporarily fixed my fear of the future, I didn't know if I could handle a goodbye.

Of course he didn't give me that choice, because here he is.

"Hey." He steps inside, closing us in my small office.

I lean back in my chair, saying nothing.

He sighs, realizing I have nothing to say. "Asa's gonna stay with you. He can sleep on the couch—he'll want to be on the main floor. I talked to my people today and there's been a hitch in their ops plan with Whittaker—this is puttin' a stall on O'Rourke. Even with the surveillance, I don't want you home alone at night."

The issue of O'Rourke is weighing on me today heavier than normal. I appreciate him arranging someone to be with me at night because it just occurred to me I haven't been alone since before the White House dinner. I ache a little more, knowing I'll be sleeping alone for the first time since he put himself in my bed. So even though I won't be alone, I will. I'll not only missing him, but worrying.

I nod and breathe, getting it together as best I can. "Tell him thanks and I'll have dinner for him."

He lifts his chin and steps farther in the room. When I don't move from my seat, he demands, "Addison, come here."

I don't go there, I stay right where I am and before I know it, the words leave my mouth in a rush. "You'll call me every day, right? To let me know you're okay?"

He doesn't answer with words, but the look on his face says it all, right before he slowly closes his eyes, running a hand through his hair.

When he drops his head to look at his feet, I keep on and hate that my voice is edging toward panic. "Not even a text?"

When he brings his head up to look at me, I see nothing but guilt and remorse in his deep, dark eyes. Even though regret is written all over him, it doesn't make me feel any better.

"Baby." His voice is raw calling for me, pleading this time. "Come here."

Even though I'm scared, hurt, and yes, thoroughly pissed, I need to touch him the way I always do when he's close. He's leaving to go God knows where, to do God knows what, and to God only knows whom. I might know nothing about his plans, but I do know it's far away, dangerous, and there's a chance he might not come back.

So damn it, I can't help myself. I get up and go to him.

Breathing a sigh of relief, he reaches for me and before I know it, I'm in his arms where I realize I want to be forever. Why in the hell am I making that realization now, when the future just became uncertain again? But it's true, I want it forever.

"You stay put on the vineyard, let the others run your errands if you have to. With Asa here at night, I won't worry. Can you do that?" he asks.

I nod into his chest and he pulls my head back, his lips landing on my forehead. Feeling his lips there stirs emotions in me so deep I have to try my hardest to keep it together.

When I finally look up he keeps on, "These things can't be rushed, but I'll be back as soon as I can."

I say nothing, but swallow the lump in my throat.

"Don't worry about O'Rourke or anyone else. You're safe here."

This time I manage a nod.

His eyes sweep my features and he sighs. "Baby, say something."

I knew I'd have to do my best to keep it together, but my best isn't great at the moment, so my voice cracks. "I don't know what to say."

His words come instantly. "Say you'll be here waiting for me when I get back."

Afraid to say what I really want to say, I go with, "Where else would I be?"

His voice dips as he gives me a squeeze. "You know what I mean."

"Come back to me, Crew," I whisper.

"I swear to you, I'm gonna get Grady straightened out and I'll be back. This shit with O'Rourke will be done and we can settle into some type of normalcy. I know you and I, we've never done normal, but I promise we'll find it. Together, we'll figure out what normal looks like for us. We deserve that after what we've both lived through. Focus on that. Look forward to that while I'm gone."

"I don't think I can, not while you're gone. Not until you're done for good," I say honestly.

His face hardens and frustration laces his words. "I'll be back and I'll get us back to where we were, no ifs, ands, or buts. You keep yourself safe here, I'll get Grady squared away, and then it's us. I promise."

I nod, even though I know he can't promise anything.

I'm thankful his lips hit mine when they do, not allowing me to answer. His hands on my face tense, holding me tight. I take it all in until he finally releases me, even though the look on his face tells me he doesn't want to. "I'll see you soon."

I can't answer, I can't move, I can't even nod. Then his lips hit my forehead one last time before he turns, and I watch him leave.

It's then I can't control my emotions another moment as the tears start to fall.

Chapter Twenty-Three

Headaches

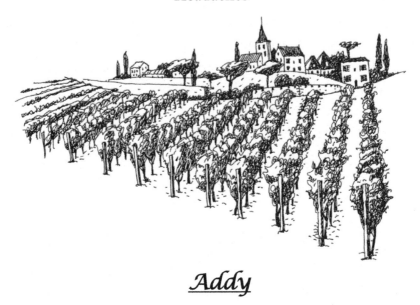

Addy

Looking into the mirror, I drag my hands over my tired face and shadowed eyes.

It's been a long week and a half. The longest I remember in...well...a really long time. As a self-preservation tactic, I decided I needed more than internet shopping to distract me, and threw myself even further into my work, purely to keep my mind off worrying about Crew. Little had I known I wouldn't need a tactic at all, because the business I've come to love has become one pain in my ass after another.

It started less than a week ago when out of the blue, I got a surprise visit from the Virginia Department of Alcohol Beverage Control. Having my liquor licenses current and valid are an underlying necessity of running a business that produces, distributes, and sells wine, not to mention serves it at every function. It's the reason customers choose us as a venue to begin with. My landscape doesn't hurt, but really, it's all about the wine.

So when the VABC showed up last week unexpectedly, informing me they had a tip we were serving minors, my day and my week went to shit. Hell, with all that's happened in the last week, I can pretty much say my life has gone to shit.

My staff and I are overly careful who we serve. We card every single buyer who comes through the tasting room, whether they look eight or eighty. At events, our servers are told to card everyone who appears under the age of forty. This can be a pain in the ass, but if I lose my liquor license, I can't operate, and if I can't operate, I can't make any money. No one comes to Whitetail Farms to drink a Shirley Temple and play with my cows.

The investigating agent was aloof, not giving much information other than it was reported happening at an event that took place over a month ago, and a full investigation would have to happen, but I could appeal if I felt so inclined.

I obviously "felt so inclined" and hired counsel to make sure I didn't miss any loopholes. This isn't something I can screw around with on my own. I know when I'm in over my head and need a professional to get me through. My attorneys advised me to "be on our game" with carding customers since the ABC is notorious for setting up stings like sending in underage guests to test us. This stressed me out all the more and has taken time away from my normal responsibilities of managing the vineyard. If I wasn't already stressed about Crew being gone, why he's gone, and not knowing anything about his wellbeing, my visit from the Virginia ABC put me over the top.

I thought the VABC put me over the top, until two days ago when the Health Department made a surprise visit. They brought in an entire team, disrupting business when they plowed through our kitchen, barrel room, and cellars, doing a thorough inspection of *everything.* I've had visits from the Health Department in the past, but scheduled ones to keep the winery licensed to serve food. We've never had any citations because Maggie's a drill sergeant in there. She knows the ins and outs of her job, making sure we're up to snuff per all regulations.

I was informed one of my employees anonymously reported us for improper storage of perishables.

What the hell?

First of all, it's untrue, and second of all, and most *important* of all, not one of my employees would call us in on anything. Even grasping at straws, there's no way it could even be my new girl, Maya. I was told the allegations came in before she started.

They disrupted my business for hours. Not only did it stop us from serving food, but it was embarrassing to have this going on with customers who were trying to enjoy a relaxing day at my winery. When a couple of customers caught eye of the Health Department, they got up and walked out with disgusted looks on their faces, without glancing at a menu. I didn't even want to think about what was being posted about my winery on the foodie blogs and review sites. It's a business owner's worst nightmare.

Was it only a week and a half ago my life was perfect? That I slept through the night not worrying about the future? It seems like forever ago that Crew was by my side, taking away my fears, and in my bed giving to me in every way. He's even worked his way into my heart, and every additional moment he's gone cements deeper in my soul that I want him forever.

Since Crew left, everything has fallen apart. I'm dealing with an ongoing investigation of the ABC, my newly acquired counsel, the worry of an underage sting operation, and the Health Department threatening to come back at any time for another surprise inspection. Even through all this, I can't get Crew out of my head. I wonder what he's doing, where he is, or if he's safe. If he's not safe or God forbid something happens to him, how will I know? Will Asa tell me?

Asa's slept on my sofa on the main level every night since Crew left. He arrives late, scarfing down his meal while chatting with me. During our first few evenings together, I grilled him for information about Crew.

He put me off softly to begin with, but by the third night he looked at me seriously and said, "Beautiful, you're killin' me with these questions. Wish I could answer you, but I can't. I know very little and what I do know, I can't say. I will tell you that Crew's one of the best at what he does. Grady used to be on top right there with him, but he let his mind fuck with him and lost his focus. We need to let Crew do what he can to get Grady out for good. I know the man better than anyone and after the last ten years, he can't live with regrets. Let him do his thing and he'll be back. He never would've left you if he didn't know you were completely safe with me here on your property."

"I'm not worried about me," I refuted.

"Good." Then he sighed—yet it didn't appear to be a sigh of relief—before he went on. "Don't you worry about him, either."

That shut me up, and after he put an end to my interrogation about all things Crew, I realized Asa and I didn't have much to talk about. Sitting around with him in weird silence before I went off to my bed alone sucked.

I pull my hair back into a low ponytail, and after applying enough concealer to hide my dark eyes, I look away from my reflection. I'm sick of seeing the reminders etched in my face from the last miserable eleven days.

I decide to drive up to the main building, I'm too tired for the short hike. I haven't walked with my cows in days and I'm sure Harry will start to hold a grudge with her only human contact being Morris. He treats them like cows, slopping their food, not talking to them while filling their water, and not gifting them enough molasses. Forget Harry, Scarlett will be downright pissed.

My mind is so boggled with the current messes in my life, I almost forgot about the event we've got going on this afternoon. It's the one Clara landed forever ago, the Eastern Horse Breeders Association. I've got a lot to do. It's time to focus on work and forget about the headaches surrounding me.

My neighbor across the highway, Thomas Kane, is heading up this event. The Kanes are from old money—their horse breeding business has been in their family for generations. When most people put their kids in team sports, their kids specialize in everything equestrian. Even coming from old money, they're not at all pretentious. They've not only become friends, but are also supporters of Whitetail Farms.

"I appreciate this booking, Thomas. I hope everything's the way you wanted." I look to my neighbor who broke away from his counterparts to talk to me. We're on the patio overlooking my acres of vines.

His friendly face turns into a smirk when he lowers his voice. "It's great, just as I told them it would be, Addy. I'm not completely selfless, though. This is right across from my property, everyone had to drive by my ranch to get here. You get the business—I get the exposure. Artificial insemination in horses is barely up-and-coming in these parts. I might need to move farther west, to Kentucky, to really get my share of the market."

"You're moving?" I'm surprised, they have generations rooted in this area. I've learned that when you get this far out of the metro, there aren't nearly as many transplants, most pride themselves as being locals.

"I like to think of my plans as more of an expansion. If I can make it work, I'll sell my land here and buy bigger in Kentucky. Breeding isn't just horse romance anymore—it's technology. To grow my business like I want, I need to be located in a bigger market."

I give him a small smile and try not to look as tired as I feel. "We'll miss you if you go, but I get it."

"Addy!" I hear coming from behind me. When I turn to look, Evan is approaching with a scowl marring his young face, and he's usually so happy. He quickly makes his way through the crowd. "You need to come, now. The IRS just showed."

"What?" If it were possible, my stomach just sank to the ground, taking my fleeting energy with it.

Evan's face tightens as he shakes his head, looking sorry for me. "They didn't say why they're here, only that they need to speak with the manager or owner, whoever's in charge. I'm sorry Addy, I know you've been through the wringer lately, but they don't look very friendly."

What in the hell is going on? First the ABC, then the Health Department, and now the IRS? I'm right there with Evan, I have no clue why they would show up out of the blue.

When my eyes droop from sheer exhaustion, I feel a hand light on my shoulder and glance over to see my neighbor with a reassuring look on his face. "Go, Addy, take care of business. I'm sure it's nothing. Clara has everything covered here."

I offer him a tight smile, because I'm absolutely sure after the last hellacious eleven days, this is anything but nothing.

"Everything bad happens in threes, right? I'm sure this is simply a fluke, nothing like this ever happened to previous owners. If anyone came callin,' it was bankers because they had no clue how to run a business. The tax people will come back tomorrow, quietly finish going through the books, and it will be done. You're not taking cash under the table to avoid paying taxes."

I look across to sweet Bev, whose overly-positive attitude has never annoyed me in the past, but it does now. This isn't the rule of threes, this isn't a coincidence, and this isn't something that's going to blow over quickly. This could go on and on, for who knows how long. But there's one thing I'm certain of.

Someone's fucking with me.

"Bev, you know I love you, but you're wrong." Clara looks from Bev to me. She's just as pissed off as I am, reaffirming my thoughts. "Someone's fucking with you. They're fucking with *us*."

I have a feeling I know who's fucking with me, but I can't tell them. If a certain Army Lieutenant Colonel can commit treason against our country for over twenty-five years, fucking with my little winery has got to be child's play for him.

Today was yet one more thing to add to all my headaches lately. The Internal Revenue Service said they had reason to believe I was accepting cash under the table for our products and services. After a long afternoon of auditors digging through my receivables, I called an emergency company meeting to discuss the issues we've been plagued with lately.

Of course one can't accept cash under the table. Uncle Sam wants his cut of everything. It's illegal and I know it. I'm a business owner who's always gone the distance to walk the straight and narrow. I take it seriously that my mom bought us new identities all those years ago. I don't need any additional attention from the government. So far, I've never had an issue, but the accusations swirling around my business lately are crazy, to say the least. Right now I'm worried about much more than my vineyard.

"Who would do this?" Evan asks. "Maybe a local winery bitter about us getting the White House gig? Sure, it's a competitive local market, but until now it's seemed friendly. I don't get it."

"I'm still angry about the Health Department," Maggie chimes in, not able to get over anyone questioning her ability to do her job. "I invited those dumb asses to eat off my floor—it's that clean."

"Addy," Van calls for me. "What exactly did they say?"

I rub my eyes—positive all my makeup has now been worn off. It's late, the IRS auditors were here until after closing, weeding through my books.

"They said they had reason to believe I was accepting cash for payments of goods and services and not reporting it. My books are usually current, but I'm no accountant and keep them myself, I'm nervous I missed something." I look at everyone around the room with determination. "I report one-hundred percent of our income. I swear, it's all on the up and up."

"We know," Morris says angrily and continues to lecture me the way he would his kids. "Don't question that, you hear me? They can dig all they want. It's time everyone leaves you alone—you work hard enough as it is. We all do."

I sigh and give my grumpy but supportive caretaker a small smile. "Thanks everyone, but you all might have to actually help prove it. They said they might have to interview the team. I hope it won't come down to that."

"Don't worry, Addy. We can handle it." Van gets up and comes over to me, pulling me in for a deep side-hug.

I look to my newest employee, who's been silent throughout the entire staff meeting. "I swear, Maya, it's never like this. I feel badly there's been so much turmoil since you started. I'll understand if you run away and never look back."

Maya, who's proven to be a hard worker, even if she is a quiet one, shakes her head quickly. "It's not a big deal. My dad owns...a company. I understand things happen. I like it here—I won't be running anywhere."

Just then the front door opens and Asa is standing there. Taking in our group first, he eyes me carefully before asking, "You about done for the day? I told Crew I'd make sure you got home."

"Oh, that's sweet." Bev smiles at me big. "When does Crew get back from his business trip?"

Everyone's been asking about him, and the longer he's gone, it's getting harder to put them off. "I'm not sure. He's still working on his project." Looking to the rest of the group, I finish up the meeting. "I know some of you keep your own hours, but if everyone could be here first thing in the morning in case they need to interview any of you, that'd be good. The sooner I get them out of here, the better."

Everyone said their goodbyes, and after I shut down for the night, Asa followed me home. I gave him the rundown of my latest debacle, trying to avoid our weird silence. As he and I sit in the kitchen, I feel a headache coming on. With all that's gone on with the winery and the unknowns about Crew bogging my brain, I've had enough. It's time to deal with one of my biggest worries head on.

I look to Asa and feeling bold, I state, "You know about me."

Asa stops his fork mid-way to his mouth, looking confused. "I'm sorry?"

"Me. My past, my so-called 'background' as Crew refers to it. You know about me."

He sits back in his chair and takes a big breath before answering me carefully. "I pull all the backgrounds."

I guess I'll take that as a yes.

I tell him something he probably already knows. "I have a fake name."

He says nothing, but raises an eyebrow.

"And a fake social security number."

This bought me a chin lift. I guess I'll take that as confirmation of his acknowledgement, too.

"My mom made that happen. She paid dearly for it at the time, but it was forever ago, technology wasn't what it is today. I'd ask Crew if he was here, but he's not. He left me you, so that means you get my questions. With everything that's happened with the winery, all the attention I'm getting from different government agencies, should I be worried?" I ask what's been in the back of my head for days, but I kept telling myself it would all be fine. After today, I'm downright scared it won't all be fine.

Leaving his face void of expression, he tips his head. "Two months ago, I'd say maybe."

"What? What do you mean, 'two months ago?'" Panic laces my voice.

"But not today." He keeps talking as if I didn't say a word. "You're good, Addy. Crew made sure of it."

"What do you mean, he made sure of it?"

"Crew didn't do it, but he gave the order. I was the one who made sure of it. Abigail Ross is buried, as deep or deeper than Crew's real profession. He was worried about it and I personally made it happen." He explained this as if it was as simple as him doing me the favor of picking up my mail while I was on vacation, then digs back into his dinner.

Letting it sink in that Crew's been taking care of me in ways even I didn't understand, I finally form the words, "You did that for me?"

"No." He swallows and takes a sip of his iced tea. "I did it for Crew, but I'd do anything for Crew."

With that, I realize I know nothing about Asa. "How long have you known him?"

"Crew hasn't told you?" He leans back in his chair, leaving his meal be.

I shake my head. "Crew's told me about his job and that you two work together. I assumed at one point you did what he did, but he's never elaborated."

He scoffs when he says on a huff, "I guess that's good. Means he doesn't hold it against me."

"Hold what against you?"

"Recruiting him after his dad was killed. I've known Crew since he was in high school. I worked under his dad—he was my sergeant at the PD when I was a rookie. I was recruited young as well, a few years after I started. But unlike Crew, I didn't break contact with everyone in my life. I stayed friends with his dad, Bruce, and saw him every time I came back to town."

"You've known him a long time." For some reason this warms my heart, because Crew's made it clear he doesn't have a lot of people in his life.

He shakes his head. "Don't do that, beautiful. I'm not the prized favorite uncle. It's my doing he's lived the life he has for the last ten years. He was young when his dad was killed and wasn't dealing with any of it well. I thought I was doin' him a favor, offering him another way to get out of the limelight, away from the attention he didn't want. Not many days have gone by where I don't regret that."

"Why would you have regrets? He doesn't seem to have any." I don't understand his reasoning.

"Addy." He leans forward on his forearms and looks across the table into my eyes. "To do this job, you have to be careful, have a cover, but there's no need to disappear off the fucking earth and not have a life. He chose to disappear. Had I known that would happen, I never would've recruited him. Feel like he lost some of his best years because of me."

"Oh." I look away and think for a moment before responding. "I'm still getting to know him. He's complex, I'd even say mysterious at first. He talks to me a lot—at least it feels like a lot—but regret never comes up. He seems steadfast in his decisions."

Asa leans back, throwing his arm across the chair next to him to stretch out. "I agree, Addy. He's got no regrets. Still doesn't mean he couldn't've had a richer life another way. I will say, he's changed since he met you."

I bite my lip and my heart catches. "Really?"

"Really." His answer comes instantly. "Seein' him with you, bein' with you? He's different. I'm just sorry it took him so long to find it."

I don't like being the topic of conversation, so I ask, "What about you? Who's in your life?"

He gives his head a shake and tries to blow me off. "I'm divorced. As you know, being gone with no communication is hard. She's a good woman, but couldn't handle it. She's since moved on but we've got two kids. I don't see 'em enough, but I'm trying to rectify that."

"I hope you do, Asa."

I know what it's like to be alone, and I hate that for him. Even if he seems a bit closed off to me, I feel sorry for him after getting to know Crew. The life these men chose to lead is difficult, and it's probably harder being a dad. Asa's handsome with his medium brown hair, with only a few flecks of gray at his temples. He keeps his beard full, yet trimmed. I know he's older, but just like the rest of the men in their secret sect, he's built for the job they've chosen.

It's late and it's been a long day, but I don't forget where this conversation started before I got sidetracked with the topic of Crew. "Any update on Sheldon O'Rourke?"

He gives me a smirk like he's on to me. "How much Crew tells you is his business. I'm sure it's more than he's supposed to since you are what you are to him. I like you, Addy, but I'm not putting my ass out there to update you on a CIA investigation."

"Asa, I've had the ABC, the Health Department, and just today, the IRS knocking my door down accusing my winery of a menagerie of wrongdoings. That's no coincidence. I can't think of anyone else I know who has the reach or means to make that happen besides O'Rourke. I like flying under the radar, and as much as I appreciate you making sure my true identity is safe, someone's trying to screw with me, and I think that someone is O'Rourke."

Asa mulls this over, taking another drink before finally giving in. "I'll see what I can find out, but even if I do find something, doesn't mean I can tell you. You looking at me with those big, brown eyes might make me want to tell you everything, but I can't." His smirk grows, creating tiny lines around his hazel eyes, softening his face nicely when he shakes his head. "My boy, Crew. He's fucked."

That makes me feel good, but I ignore it and push on. "So you'll check into it for me?"

He smiles. "Oh, I'll check, just not making any promises on what I'll tell you."

"You know—your mysterious little group of killers are quite resourceful. I'm finding you handy to have around," I tease as I get up, anxious for my bed—even if it is empty—after my very long day. Giving him a genuine smile, I mean it with all my heart when I say, "Thank you, Asa, and thank you for being here. I'm glad Crew's had you all these years." Before I leave the kitchen, I turn to him one more time. "By the way, I have no love for the CIA after what they put my mom through. You can tell them to hurry the hell up, I'm sick of being quarantined. If they could put a stop to O'Rourke and his cronies yesterday, it's too long for me."

His smile turns into a big grin, transforming his face from an all-business killer to a captivating man any woman would gawk at for hours. "I'll relay the message."

I give him a sweet and fake-like smile, before heading upstairs. "Relaying messages to the CIA for me, you're the best."

As I head out, I notice he has a nice laugh and feel sorry for him. The life these men have chosen seems to come with solitude and loneliness. I hope he gets to see his kids more.

Chapter Twenty-Four
Hacked

Marc Whittaker

Fuck, this place is always busy. Today I'm grateful for it because the powers that be are pissed, and I need to talk to him.

I make my way through the morning crowds of the Pentagon City Mall, through the food court to the coffee bar where he's standing in line. A group gives me a dirty look when I cut in front of more than half the line to stand next to him.

I don't beat around the bush, they're angry and waiting for answers. "What the fuck does she know?"

Sheldon turns, surprised to see me and lifts a brow.

"She knows something," I hiss under my breath, not able to control my temper. "They've hacked into her computers and you're all over her search history. She even looked me up a few times, but mostly it's you."

His face remains neutral and he ignores me. When the line progresses ahead of us, he steps forward to order from the barista. "Americano and fill it to the top. I don't need room for anything."

He doesn't glance my way again, but I give him the chance to pay and we move to the side out of earshot.

"You'd better fucking talk to me. They're up my ass about it and think this is my doing. This is not what I signed up for, Sheldon. I want answers."

He slides his hands in his pockets, looking happy when he replies, "This is what you get when you're picked to be the messenger. No one's up my ass, Whittaker. This is what happens when you play with the enemy." Then he cocks his head, narrowing his eyes. "You wanted to be the messenger. If you can't play, you're fucked. Once you're in, they never let you out. I don't think I need to tell you what it means to be fucked."

"Just tell me what she fucking knows and why she's researching us. It's new, been happening for just a few days. And she's combining us on searches with 'treason,' 'KGB,' 'CIA,' shit like that. They don't give a fuck that she won't leave her property, it's open to business during the day, they're ready to move in and take her out."

Finally, his face cements as he turns fully to me, his body tightening. "They'd better fucking not. I don't know what she's searching for, but whatever's goin' on, this is their doing. They opened this fucking can of worms by digging shit up that should've been left buried with her father. Their antics the night of the White House dinner, chasing them down and shooting at them didn't help. They brought on whatever attention they've got all on their own."

"You're not giving me answers," I seethe.

"I don't have any, they need to drop it. I'll call them myself, I could give a fuck who they want to communicate with. They can't take people out just because they get cold feet. It might work that way where they're from, but not here in the States. They start on a rampage here—we'll all get attention we don't want."

"Fuck," I mutter and run my hand through my hair as they call his name to get his order.

He takes a sip of his steaming brew and tips his head to me over the rim. "You need to learn to control your shit, young Marc. This is my last piece of advice to you, you show weakness, they'll know how to get to you. My guess? They already know. This is no more than a game and you've already given up your poker face. You think I'm fucked? You should look in the mirror."

He turns to walk away, leaving me in the busy food court.

He's right, I need to get it together. I need to turn the tables—control them—I didn't sign up to be anyone's puppet. Doing my best to calm myself, I scan the room. For what, I don't know, but I've had a weird feeling lately. Knowing what they're capable of, what they've threatened to do to O'Rourke, I'm getting bad vibes.

Seeing nothing besides tourists, skaters, moms pushing strollers, and suits like me either getting coffee or cutting through to the Metro, I force myself to relax. This shit is so consuming, I'm sure it's in my head. There's no fucking way I'm being followed, I would know.

I move the way O'Rourke did to make my way back to the Metro. It's only one stop to the Pentagon, it'll be faster than walking.

On my way, I pull out my secure cell to make the call I'm dreading. Because I have no fucking answers. I'm gonna have to do what I've been doing—make shit up as I go along.

Asa

I'm on my way to the big barn, the men should be back from their morning run soon. Their times are getting better by the day. Crew and Grady run with them, but I fucking hate running. Always have. I force myself to do it a couple times a week to stay in shape, but I prefer to lift, and at home I've got my rowing machine. I could row for hours, even though the machine doesn't come close to the real thing, but it'll do.

I pull my cell from my pocket and grimace at the name on the screen. He was on my list to call first thing this morning for Addy, but he beat me to it, and I don't like that.

"Yeah?" I answer.

"Whittaker and O'Rourke just had a meet in the mall." Carson doesn't bother greeting me. Then again, he never does. "We've got tails on both of them. It's reported Whittaker is lookin' more tweaked by the day. It was busy, nothing was heard but the one tail who had full view of Whittaker can read lips. He was talking about Addison Wentworth, she's been hacked. If she's been researching them, she needs to stop. She's bringing attention to herself, attention she definitely doesn't want. You need to keep a closer eye on her with Vega gone. My guess, if you secure her system now, it'll tip them off."

I sigh. "How am I supposed to tell her to quit researching them without telling her she's been hacked? She thinks someone's trying to tarnish her business and assumes it's O'Rourke. You know anything about this?"

"I don't even know what the fuck you're talking about. I'll look into it, but he's done nothin' that I've seen and we watch his every move. I don't know why, but if anything, seems O'Rourke's trying to deflect attention from her."

"It's probably why she's looking into him. Check Whittaker, too. I told her I'd look into it, but I doubt it's them. What I didn't tell her is it's not their style to cause small headaches. They'd rather put a hole in your head and be done with it." I watch Jarvis emerge from the forest first, no one on his heels. I pull my phone away from my ear to look at his time, and if it's possible, he's getting faster and more efficient. He's a machine.

I fucking hate it when Grady's right.

"I'll let you know if I hear anymore," he replies, ready to end our call.

"Any word from Vega and Cain?" I ask.

"They're gettin' close, should be wrapping up soon. Cain appears steady, and you know Vega doesn't like to talk to me. I won't hear from them again 'til the job is wrapped."

I shake my head thinking about Crew. From the beginning, he hated working with the CIA, always keeping his communication to a minimum. Less than a minimum, if possible. I hang up immediately after demanding, "Call me if something changes."

I watch the other three recruits appear in close intervals, but nothing close to Jarvis. Crew and Grady had better wrap their job up quick. I signed up for this to work close to Crew, not to babysit recruits all on my own.

I yell toward the clearing where they're cooling down, "You've got two minutes for water, then get your asses to the mats."

Nothing like getting the day started after ten miles.

Chapter Twenty-Five

Not Unusual

Addy

I jerk awake, disoriented since it seems I just fell into a restless sleep—the only kind of sleep I've been getting for almost three weeks now.

Beeps from the keypad by my bedroom door woke me, but not the alarm sounding. Someone has disarmed my security system. Before my feet hit the floor to investigate, my cell rings from the nightstand.

Looking at the screen, I'm not sure if the name of the caller makes me feel better or not. "Asa, what's wrong? Did you turn off the system?"

"The sensors went off," he explains quickly. I can tell he's moving as he speaks. "The recruits are on their way from Crew's camp on foot and I need to communicate with them. Someone's on your property. So far, I only see one, but I'm headed out to look. Stay put and arm your system."

"Can you see—" I start to ask, but realize the line went dead. He hung up on me.

Once I rearm my system, I run to my bedroom window. I see nothing but the dark of night. I don't know whether I should stay here or go downstairs. I should've asked where they were on my land. Ninety acres is a big area. What if it's more than one person? Asa only has his four recruits—do they even know what they're doing yet? Then again, I don't even know what they'd do if they did know what they were doing.

I throw on a robe and decide to go to the main floor. I can't see anything from way up here—the moon isn't even out tonight.

Twenty-five minutes later as I pace the hallway by the front door, my ringtone breaks through the silence. It's Asa and I ask immediately, "Are you okay?"

"Open your front door," he growls.

After disarming my system, I turn to my antique door and when I swing it open, six men are at the bottom of my steps. Asa's standing to the side with three others. He's holding huge cans in each hand by their handles. I immediately smell gasoline, but can't even think what that means. My eyes move to the left and I recognize him immediately.

It's the guy Crew was battling it out with on the mats over a month and a half ago, Jarvis. His hair is longer now, and this time he's wearing nothing but a pair of gym shorts, and tennis shoes without socks, but I know for a fact it's him. He's even more built than I remember, every muscle on display is flexed, tense, and bulging since he's got another man, smaller than the rest of the group, in a hold so tight, it looks painful.

I throw my hand out in front of me and I'm breathy when I ask, "Who's this?"

"We were gonna ask you the same thing," Asa says, looking over to the captive who just groaned when Jarvis roughly yanks his arms farther up his back.

"I don't know who he is." I shake my head because all the men in front of me are looking up at me for answers.

"We found all this on him," Asa says, jerking his chin to one of the three guys standing next to him.

One of the recruits holds out his hands, showing me a flip lighter, cell phone, box cutter, and my eyes widen when I see a handgun. The recruit tosses it to the ground out of reach, and looks up to me with a look mixed with boredom and disappointment. "He was easy to catch."

Huh. I wonder if he's disappointed he didn't get to kill anyone?

I don't get the chance to ponder this this because Jarvis throws him to the ground. Not expecting it, the captive lands face first on the stone of my walkway. Jarvis doesn't stop there. His foot follows the guy down, landing in his side when he demands, "Who the fuck are you?"

A groan emanates from the crumpled body as he rolls into himself when Asa warns, "Watch it, Jarvis."

Now that I think about it, Jarvis is a strange name. I wonder if it's required to have an odd name to be recruited to the killers?

Jarvis doesn't heed his warning. He leans down and yanks him up by the back of his shirt, looking into his bloodied face where he raises his voice. "What's your fucking name?"

The guy groans again, holding his midsection and mumbles, "He said this would be easy."

"Who said that?" Asa asks, stepping closer.

"I just needed to make some extra money, I didn't think it would be a big deal," the guy keeps on.

"Listen, fucker," Jarvis jerks the guy around again. "I'll beat you bloody 'til you tell us your worthless fucking name. You've got two beats to spit it the fuck out."

"D-Dan," he stutters. "Dan Smithson."

"Why were you pouring gasoline on the vines?" Asa asks.

"What?" I scream and start down the steps to them. "He poured gasoline on my vines?" I look at the contents of his pockets and realize what almost happened tonight. When I do, I look right at Dan, lying on the ground and my blood boils. "You were going to burn my vineyard?"

At that, Jarvis pulls his arm back and his fist lands square on Dan Smithson's jaw.

"For fuck's sake, control it, Jarvis," Asa mutters and comes over to block my way so I don't get too close. Asa takes out his phone and messes with the screen as he looks down to Dan. "Who were you talking about? Who said this would be easy?"

Dan doesn't answer, but Asa starts talking into the phone, I guess to nine-one-one, but who knows. Maybe he called some secret society these killers have on speed dial. I do know he reported a trespasser and talked a little about arson.

When he gets off the phone, he looks back at Dan. "You've got the time it takes for the police and fire department to get here to tell us who the fuck you're talking about. If you don't, I'll let Rambo here loose on your ass."

Bruised, bloodied, and in pain, Dan all but gives in when he looks up to us. I wouldn't have believed it if I hadn't heard it with my own ears.

"McCann. Tobin McCann."

I cannot believe he went as far as he did, but after investigations by the police and speaking to the ABC, Health Department, and the IRS, it's confirmed. Tobin McCann was responsible for everything, calling in anonymous tips that were nothing but lies. All the hell my sweet little vineyard has gone through the last few weeks has been at the resentful and wretched hands of a man who wasn't given what he wanted. And like a spoiled child, he threw a fit.

Although, his fit was in the form of false allegations and attempted arson. Local Sheriff's Deputies paid him a visit yesterday and I was told he initially refuted everything. But thanks to Dan-Dan the Pay-Off Man, not to mention further information from all the agencies who have caused havoc the last few weeks, he requested counsel, refusing to answer any additional questions without his lawyer present.

Lucky for me, Asa and his killers got to Dan-Dan the Arson Man before he could do any real damage. He was only able to spread gasoline on a half row of vines—it could've been worse.

Morris and I were worried what the chemicals would do to the soil. First thing the next morning, we hired a hazmat crew to clean it up properly. I hope they got to it in time and the ground hasn't been contaminated, but we'll need to test the soil in months to come. We're close enough to harvest at this point, Van and Morris thought it smart to reap the contaminated row, and a few surrounding it immediately, just in case. Van said he'll use that batch to experiment with some new ideas.

Clara had many choice words about the situation, going on about Tobin's mommy and how she probably wasn't happy about spending her money on his defense, when really, he was just sore he couldn't get in my pants. Of course Bev was sad for Dan-Dan the Misguided-Man, saying he was young and had a lapse of judgment. I'm just glad she didn't see what Jarvis did to him, she'd really feel badly about that. But unlike our sweet, ever-so-positive-Bev, she did not feel sorry for Tobin, rattling off a sting of words I've never heard pass her lips. As sweet as her true nature is, she loves Whitetail as if it were her own.

I found out today Tobin has been charged with attempted arson and filing false statements to government agencies. Asa told me he was released on bail and even though Tobin doesn't seem to pose a physical threat, it was good I was quarantined, just in case.

My attorneys are working at getting all allegations and investigations wiped from our record, which was previously clean as a whistle. I hate that the company I've invested everything in— money, time, and energy—had to endure it all. At least it's over and our slate will be clean. I love my little winery, my employees, and everything that surrounds it. I don't ever want anything to mar it— it's perfect just the way it is.

All the drama is coming to a close. Even as my attorneys are wrapping up loose ends I'd like to say I can breathe easy, but I can't. Just like the last few weeks, Crew is still at the forefront of my every thought, only now I don't have any other annoyances to distract me.

I've done all the internet shopping I can handle. Things are arriving daily by FedEx or special delivery. I kept to the true beauty of my home and went farmhouse, but with an edge. I've even cleared out the room off the main hall that faces the back of my property with rolling, hillside views. Next week, I'm expecting office furniture with an industrial look to fill the space. Now I wonder if it was a mistake, but I ordered everything only a few days after Crew left. If he wasn't on his property with his recruits, he was here, and I wanted to provide a place for him to work. Plus, my room doesn't have horrendous wallpaper, why wouldn't he prefer to work here?

Call it a ploy—or desperate measures, whatever—to keep him as close to me as possible.

But now, after him being gone for weeks, I'm afraid I should've waited. If he doesn't come back, I'll never be able to walk in that room.

"You okay?"

I look up from where I'm picking at my late dinner in the kitchen and see Asa standing in the doorway.

"Sorry." I stand to clean up my half-eaten meal. "Just tired."

My back is to him while I'm at the sink cleaning dishes when he continues. "This isn't unusual, him being gone this long. It can take longer sometimes."

I turn to him but stay where I am. The last few weeks have gotten to me, worrying about Crew and dealing with my headaches. I'm tired and I'm done being polite. "I don't think there's anything usual about this, Asa. Crew is somewhere in the world making sure Grady doesn't get killed while Grady tries to kill someone else, and even though I know this bit of information, I can't know anything else. There's a secret sect of soon-to-be killers training next door, and I have cameras and sensors surrounding me. Don't get me wrong, I'm grateful for them. My property would've burned to the ground otherwise, but still, it's weird. If all this isn't *unusual*, Asa, I don't know what is."

He shakes his head and looks at me like my rant didn't affect him in the least. "You might not've signed up for it in the beginning, but if you want to be with Crew, this is your new usual. Your new normal. I've been at this a long time, Addy. I know you're not used to this life, but you can be—you'll have to be—if you want him. Take it from me, my wife walked away choosing not to live it with me. She might be a good woman, but that also means she wasn't the right one. The choice is yours, but make it quickly for Crew's sake. I was only trying to make you feel better. I wish I could say something to comfort you, but I haven't been in contact with the CIA. We don't call each other just to chat, not that I'd tell you anyway."

He's sort of taken my breath away. I chose Crew when I thought he was done with his job, I never thought about having to make the choice now that he's gone back. Is it really even a choice at this point? I don't think it is. I think I might have to get used to a new normal with Crew, because the other option is too painful to think about.

Putting my dishes in the dishwasher, I turn to him and lay it all out there. "I guess I do have a decision to make, but right now you're not my favorite person, Asa. As long as you have nothing to say to me, I can only assume he's okay. But the second you look my direction, I get the dreaded feeling you might end my dream by telling me something I'm afraid to hear. I hate to be rude, but it's the truth."

He narrows his eyes and nods once. "Don't know what to do about that Addy. I told him I'd be here and make sure you're safe. It's hard to ignore you when I'm sleeping in your house and eating in your kitchen. I'd hate to be," he pauses and tips his head, "rude."

I take a big breath and shake my head at him throwing my words back at me. I move for the door and say when I walk past him, "I'm grateful you're here, but I look forward to the day I don't cringe when you walk into a room or dread you speaking to me."

I hear him chuckle and turn to look at him. There's a sparkle in his hazel eyes when he responds, "You're not the first woman to say that, and I doubt you'll be the last."

He's a frustrating man.

"Goodnight, Asa. I'll look forward to not talking to you tomorrow," I call without looking back.

"Addy," he calls for me. Stopping, I turn to look at him. "Told you I can't say much, but I will tell you to stop with the internet searches."

My eyes go big, knowing exactly what he's talking about.

"Yeah." He's serious when he confirms my thoughts, telling me someone found out I was looking up Sheldon and Marc. "Bad guys can be smart, too. Not often, but sometimes."

Holy shit. That's scary. I don't know what to say, so I say nothing. As I make my way out of the kitchen, I hear him digging through my refrigerator. I guess someone hacking into my internet doesn't suppress his appetite, but I'm sure I'll never be able to sleep now.

My feet hit the floor in the pitch dark. After the last time this happened, my heart speeds, but this time I don't wait for my phone to ring. The beeps from my alarm being disarmed once again broke through the night like a scream.

I don't bother grabbing a robe. In my cotton nightie, I head for my door and race down the first set of stairs. When I round the hall to the second floor staircase, I hear the clunky mechanics of my door clink, and I make it down the last set of stairs just in time to see him step through.

I vaguely notice Asa standing in the doorway to the living room where he's been sleeping.

But I only have eyes for Crew.

I run halfway through the corridor to get to him, but something about him makes me stop. He's back to the way he used to be, a complete contradiction of emotions. He's loose—standing in my doorway casually as if he's back from an errand fetching milk. His beard is thicker and his hair longer, but my breath catches when I see the bruise on his left temple, seeping out over his eye, and cut on his lip.

Even taking in the fact something happened where he had to defend himself, it's his eyes that stopped me in my tracks.

They're piercing and heated, and I hate to admit it, even anguished. There's an underlying pain making my heart clench, and the look on his face scares me more than anything during the past weeks.

I don't call out to him, ask him what's wrong, what happened to his face, or even go to him like I want. And I want to. I need to touch him, make sure he's okay, that he's real.

However, I stop when I hear Asa ask, "Grady?"

Chapter Twenty-Six

Blinding

Addy

Certain moments in life become etched in your soul.

For me, I have merely a handful. Buried deep, they're entwined, tangled, and even disheveled. Living together forever, they create who we are and how we see the world. More so, how we react to it, even live within it. Much like the vines that create my wine, it's hard to see where one ends and the other begins.

My vine was planted the day I saw my dad murdered that cold day in the snow. Since then, these ticks in time have grown together, forming an intricate but beautiful mass of memories, shaping not only who I am, but who I want to be. They're beautiful—every single one. Even if some are ugly. The ugly ones only make the beautiful ones shine so bright, they're blinding.

This is one of those moments, a beautiful one that will live in me forever. To have Crew standing in front of me—home, safe, and returning as promised. And just as Asa demanded I should, I choose Crew.

I don't care if he has to go back to keep his friend safe, or if he decides to go back on his own to take care of justice his own way, ridding our world of threats. Even if this does make him a killer. I'll wait. I'll hate it, but I'll wait because he's mine, and having him back is more perfect than anything I could've dreamed. Because I love him.

As I'm locked in place, seized by only his eyes, I pray my beautiful blink in time doesn't turn ugly.

"Crew?" Asa calls for him when he doesn't answer.

Asa's voice breaks his gaze and he steps through my threshold, tossing his bag, and swinging the door shut. He drags his eyes over me before looking to his friend, his voice rough. "It went to shit. Grady fucked up, but I got him out. The job's done. We're home."

My breath of relief came out as a whimper, drawing Crew's eyes back to me. This time they're heated, fiery, and burning. I feel it in my nipples, down my spine, and between my legs. Without looking away, I know he's not talking to me when he says, "He's not gonna want to see anyone tonight, or even for a few days. I'll fill you in tomorrow—you can go."

After a few beats, I hear a jingle of keys.

From my peripheral, I see Asa go to the door. "See you soon, Addy."

I should thank him for staying with me. For saving my home and business from becoming an inferno. For keeping me safe, for caring about Crew all those years when he withdrew from life before he was mine, but most importantly, for making me realize I needed to make a choice for Crew's sake.

But with Crew looking at me the way he is, I couldn't utter a word.

I guess I'll have to tell him tomorrow.

When the door clicks, he says his first word to me. "Abby."

My eyes instantly well, missing that, like a sweet gift every time he says it. "You came back."

"Told you I would."

"I know." I swallow, trying to control myself. "Still, you're okay and you're back."

Ignoring me, he barely narrows his eyes when he asks, "You wearin' panties?"

I frown slightly. "Yes, why?"

His eyes change and don't ask me how I can tell, but I see the transformation. The sharp is gone and he shifts into my man, the one he is only for me. Just like all the times in the past when he controls it, his voice comes at me soft and soothing, telling me what he wants. "Drop 'em, baby, and come here."

My thighs clench at his demand and his eyes follow my hands that immediately dip up and under my nightie. Hooking my thumbs into my panties, I drag them quickly down my hips. The second they hit my feet, I move, kicking them to the side.

When I close the short distance separating us, I put my hands to his chest, needing to touch him. One of his dives into my hair and the other yanks my nightie roughly above my waist, his hand palming my bare ass before giving me a squeeze when his lips land on mine.

He pulls me into his big frame, his tongue delving into my mouth. When I slide my hands up to his shoulders, we turn. Just when I was thinking he feels better than he ever has, he presses me into my front door.

He shows me how much he missed me with his lips, tongue, and hands. Pushing my nightie up higher, his hands roam my body and I try to pull at his shirt to feel his skin. His finger slides through my drenched core, making me jerk. Forgetting about his shirt, I zero in on his pants, knowing what I really want.

My hands go to the waist of his jeans and I fumble, trying to make quick work of his button and zipper. Finally, he rips the button open, and after efficiently working his zipper, frees himself.

When his beautiful cock springs free, I lick my lips. Putting both my hands on him, I start to rub and knead, feeling a bead of cum on his tip. I drag my thumb over it, massaging it into his silky skin. I need to show him how much I want him, how much I missed him, and I want him in my mouth.

I bend my knees to dip low, but he stops my progress. "Not now. I want to lose myself in you. Up."

The next thing I know I'm being lifted, with my back to the front door, where he's holding me tight. With his arm around me, his other dips and he rubs his tip through my wet pussy.

"Knees up, baby."

When I pull my knees high, my bottom sinks at the same time he surges up, giving me all of him.

He buries his face in my hair and murmurs, "My Abby."

"Crew," I whimper, trying to move, but his arm around my back and hand on my ass keeps me where I am.

He presses into me deeply, and when I arch, I feel it in my clit.

Squeezing my thighs into his sides, he controls it, just like always. His lips dip to my ear and he fills my heart at the same time he moves slowly in and out of me. "Never once had a homecoming. Never had a home to come to. I thought I was traveling, seeing the world between jobs, but I wasn't. I was wandering with nowhere to go."

I move my hand into his hair, holding him close, pressing the side of my face into his. I try to shift to get more, but he barely picks up the pace.

"Never had to work so hard to focus. Ever. Thought of you every single second. I had to fight myself to stay centered for Grady and so I could come back to you."

I tip my head to look him in the eyes and admit, "I was scared."

He exhales, but he doesn't respond. When the word "scared" passed my lips, it must have triggered something, because he really starts to move. Every time he thrusts, he hits my clit and I curve my body to feel it deep inside.

His breath becomes labored against my hair, his arm angled up my back to protect me from the hard door, but he didn't need to. I don't feel a thing besides the heat building in me. Letting go, I'm not sure he's ever fucked me this hard. His thrusts prolong my orgasm and I'm still panting when he groans, pulling me down tight on his pulsating cock.

He holds me tight as we both come down from our high, giving me his weight, pressing me into the door. I've got Crew surrounding me with my nightie above my breasts. I've missed this so much, being utterly consumed by him.

When our breathing evens, he turns to kiss the side of my head and says with his lips there, "I never want you to be scared again."

As much as I appreciate his sentiment, it really doesn't matter. All I can think about is the choice Asa gently demanded I make and look to him. "I love you."

His body stills, yet I feel his cock twitch inside me.

"What?" he breathes.

I give him a squeeze. "I was scared, but it doesn't matter, because I love you. I don't know what went on with Grady, but whatever you do, if you have to leave, if you decide to keep doing what you did, I'll always be here for you to come home to."

I watch his deep, dark eyes slowly disappear as his lids fall. I didn't know it was possible for him to pull me closer, but he does. When he doesn't move, I wiggle my bottom, still impaled on him and call, "Crew?"

He pulls his head back far enough to look into my eyes. "It went south at the last minute, Grady got antsy and moved too soon. I don't want those details in your head, but it was as bad as it could get before it gets permanently bad. He's done and he knows he's done. Even if he was stupid enough to try and go back, there's no way they'd let him. I mean it when I say I never want you to be scared again, I'll do everything in my power to make sure you're not. There's nowhere I want to be but here."

My eyes not only well this time, but they immediately spill over. "You're done?"

He leans in and kisses one of my tears away, whispering, "Done, baby."

I'm so relieved, I don't even know what to say, so I bury my face in his neck.

His hand comes to the back of my head and gently pulls. He's blurry from my tears, but I can hear him clear as a bright, sunny day. "Love you, too, my Abby."

And right now, this moment in time tangles deep inside me, weaving itself together with my past. And it shines so bright, I'm blinded.

Crew

"Farther, Abby."

I'm on my knees, bent over her from behind. All I smell is her hair, a curly mess from going to bed with it wet from our shower last night.

Coming home to her after the longest weeks of my life was everything I never knew to imagine. I never allowed myself to even want it, let alone look for it.

Just like she always does, she gave to me in ways I never expected. Telling me she wanted me even if I planned to go back? Her giving me that was everything. She knows it all and accepts me, my choices, my life, and she did it for me.

I carried her to our bedroom after our time at the front door and we showered. It was the middle of the night and I hadn't slept for over thirty-six hours. As much as I didn't want to lose time with her, I crashed, but not before I told her she was taking the morning off.

I can't remember the last time I slept in, but we did. When she rolled into me this morning, burying herself so close she would've crawled under my skin if she could've, I couldn't wait another second. I needed her again.

I'll always need her.

She did as I asked and spread her legs farther, and I put my knees between hers to keep her where she is. I've been playing with her for a good while, so when I run my fingers between her legs, she's drenched and jerks when I circle her clit with barely a touch.

Leaning with my forearm on the bed, I'm close to her face where she's cheek to the mattress, on her knees with her ass in the air. Her eyes flutter open when I kiss her.

"You want something new?" I ask against her lips.

At the same time, I drag my finger through her wetness and up, circling her other hole so she'll know what I'm talking about. I know she gets my meaning, her eyes go big at the same time her body tenses, trying to bring her legs together.

"What do you mean—" she starts, but I interrupt.

"Shhh." I hush her gently, but put a firm hand on her ass to keep her where she is. I'm surrounding her from above, not that I'd have a problem keeping her where I wanted, even though I never would. "Don't worry, I don't want you to take me. Just my finger."

"Your finger?" she exclaims loudly, surprised, and not in a good way.

"My little finger," I clarify.

I don't know what I expected, she's no prude by any means, but this must be new for her. I like that even more.

"But, why?" Her voice turns breathy.

I tell her the truth as I start to play with her again. "Because I want all of you. Every inch, Addison. Never knew I could want you more than I did before I left, but every day I was gone, I wanted you more. Now that I'm back and we're where we are, I thought we'd try something new, but it's for you, too. I think you'll like it."

"I don't think I'll like it," she shoots back right away. "Plus, I have no idea how big your pinkie is, I've never paid attention to your pinkie by itself."

I shake my head. "I haven't called it my pinkie since probably the second grade. You're not making me feel much like a man calling my little finger a pinkie. Especially with what I want to do with it."

She rolls her eyes before throwing me a bone. "What if I don't like it?"

I spread my knees, in turn, spreading her farther. I do this to make a point. "You ever feel unsafe with me?"

"No," she spouts, giving me a good glare.

"Have I ever given you anything you didn't like?"

She sighs, looking like she might give in. "Of course not."

"We've never talked about this, but you don't like something, you say the word. Any word. I know your body, Addison. I have a feeling if you don't like something, I'll know it in an instant."

"Seriously," she groans. "I can't believe you want to do this...that...whatever you want to call it."

"With you, my sweet Abby," I start as I glide my hand up the small of her back and press down. Her ass tips the way I want it and when I look back into her eyes, I tell her the truth. "I want it all."

Addy

What is it with men and their fascination with anal play?

I've never had any experience with it and certainly none of my past lovers ever asked if they could hang around back there. Then again, I've never had a lover like Crew.

Crew's never let me down, never given me anything I didn't like, and I know he'd never hurt me. Plus, he did ask instead of just doing it. I guess that was nice. I shouldn't speak for the masses, but I wouldn't think anal-anything would be mainstream-cable-television, under-the-covers normal bedroom activity. This is new and different for me.

I mean, I'm already lying here, my ass in the air with my face to the bed, spread for him to do as he pleases. And he always pleases me. *Always.*

My words come out in a rush, because really, this takes it to a new level. For some reason, I think it could be embarrassing.

"Okay, I'll try it. But only because we showered before bed. And you have to promise to stop if I don't like it. Or if it's embarrassing. I still can't believe you want to do this. And by the way, tell me what the fascination is with it? I've never been asked to do it before—I don't get it. And I don't see how it's even going to feel good—"

He puts a stop to my words with his lips to try and quiet me for the second time since we woke up. "You're rambling. I thought you didn't like to ramble."

I widen my eyes. "I think I should get a pass on the rambling since you want to play around back there. Seems like a fair tradeoff to me."

His grin shrinks before completely fading and I lose his dimple. This time he kisses me soft. "Missed you."

His fingers return between my legs and move just enough to make me wiggle. He does it again, drags a finger through my wetness and up. Even though it isn't a surprise this time, I instinctively clench my ass cheeks around his finger.

"Wait." I try and stop what he's doing. "Let me see your pinkie. You're a big guy, your pinkie could be huge."

"No." He flat out turns me down and tells me to, "Relax," before moving away from my face to kneel in back of me.

"What are you doing?" I mumble into the pillow, because this is too much.

Ignoring me, he settles back on his haunches, gently massaging the globes of my ass and backs of my thighs. I can't deny it—it feels good.

"I'm okay with almost anything," I say into my pillow. "But you're massaging my ass. This is embarrassing."

"Don't be embarrassed." His voice dips and his touch has moved from massaging to sensual in no time.

A finger dips inside my pussy, and it does feel a little smaller than it usually does. Maybe it's *the pinkie*. I squeeze my eyes shut, wondering what he's going to do next, when I feel it. His finger, wet and gentle, circling my hole that's never gotten attention before.

He presses in slightly, and I tense.

"Please, baby," he says softly. "Relax."

He pushes again, this time breaking through, and stills.

Holy shit—figuratively and not—he's butt plugged me with his pinkie.

It's definitely weird, but I don't hate it. This surprises me.

He lightly runs his fingers over the skin of my back, ass, and thighs. "My Abby."

I can't say I'm completely tranquil, but I do relax further into his touch.

"There you go," he says and his other hand starts to play between my legs where I'm used to him being.

His fingers, they're barely giving me anything when he starts to move his pinkie. It's weird, foreign, and I'm not sure what I think about it. Every few strokes with his pinkie, he swipes my clit, making me warm and wanton.

"Crew," I complain, fisting the sheets below me. When I push my hips back to find his touch on my clit where I'm burning for it, his pinkie slides in deeper, and I groan.

"There you go." His voice is soft as he slides two fingers inside my pussy, but his next words shock me. "I want you to fuck yourself on my hand."

"No," I breathe. He's teased me enough—I know I'd do it without question if it weren't for the pinkie.

"Yes." His response comes instantly as he starts to finger fuck me and tickles my clit, letting me know where his finger is but giving me nothing. All the while, his pinkie moves minutely and I swear it's deeper than it was.

Everything—it's all so overwhelming. I might like it, but I'm not sure if I really want it. Should I want it? I'm full *everywhere*, it's new and strange and I can't believe myself, but the more he teases me, the more I want it.

"Move, Abby."

Damn, his voice is always so soft when he's this way with me. Like a caress I can't move away from or say no to. There's so many facets to him, I love them all, but I've become addicted to this one. I can honestly say, I've never imagined myself in this position before, my ass plugged with his pinkie and wanting his touch so badly, I'm willing to fuck myself on his hand, making that pinkie do who knows what to me. All the while, he's got a front and center seat for the show. And during the day, too.

Oh, why couldn't he have done this at night?

He tickles my clit one more time. "Move for me."

That tickle. I want more.

Fuck it. Or should I say, fuck me.

I move a little and there he is, rewarding my clit at the same time it forces his pinkie to move inside me.

Holy fuck.

He's right. It does feel good. Really good. Who would've thought?

I'm beyond being embarrassed, worried about his front row seat or where he's got his pinkie. I'm simply beyond everything besides wanting it.

So I do exactly what he wants and move. I fuck myself on his hand, and I love it.

Like every time with Crew, he consumes me. This time I feel it everywhere, and he does it while giving me something new in the process.

Controlling it, he gave me what he wanted, when he wanted, and made me work for it. When I came, I came hard. I'm not sure when it happened during my orgasm, but I lost his hands and he had to prop my knees back up, but I got his cock. Even though I still feel where he's been—pinkie and all—this is so good, I keep moving.

"Fucking beautiful," he growls from behind me where his hands firmly hold my hips.

I might've been fucking myself before, but now it's all Crew. He's not slowly working up to anything this time, he's moving fast and hard. Nothing's ever been so perfect.

When he finally comes, pressing into me the way he does, I hear his familiar sounds I've missed so much. But I'm spent. I let my knees slide out from under me and he comes with me, staying buried deep. He doesn't give me all of his weight but I do feel his warm body blanket mine.

He breathes into the top of my head where his voice is laced with a promise. "Never leaving you again."

I turn my head as far as I can to see him. "Thank you."

He kisses my temple. "For what, baby?"

"For coming back to me. For protecting me in ways I don't even know about. For being everything I need, and I can't believe I'm saying this, but for introducing me to your pinkie. Basically, for everything."

He ignores most of my list and a slow, scruffy smiles spreads over his beautiful, dark features. "You liked my little finger."

I try not to look sheepish and hide my own smile. "I didn't hate it."

He presses his still hard cock into me and grins. "You liked it. I told you so."

I can't help but glare. "Fine. You know everything. You have amazing sexual powers."

"Amazing?"

"If you question it, you'll prove you're merely average instead of amazing. That'll make me question the next kinky thing you want to do to me, Crew."

He kisses me, almost playfully. "Then I'm amazing. Your all-knowing, all-powerful sex machine who now knows I can get kinky."

I roll my eyes and ignore his kinky threats. "We need to get up. I'm hungry."

He kisses me at the same time he slowly pulls out, but doesn't move away. "I hate to leave you, but I need to check on Grady and catch up with the recruits. I'll meet you back here for a late dinner?"

I sigh, happy and content for the first time since he left. He gets off me, but I call for him and he stops mid push-up. When he looks down at me questioningly, I raise my brows and widen my eyes, demanding, "You need to wash your hands. With lots of soap. Maybe even twice."

He starts to do that silent laugh thing before he kisses me quick. I'm still lying in bed, relishing in his homecoming when I hear the sink turn on, and I smile.

Chapter Twenty-Seven

Death

Addy

What a difference a week can make.

I've had Crew back for seven full days. I didn't think it could be better than it was before he left, but it is. It's the deeper kind of better—better because you know what you have since it was gone for a time, and it's the kind of better you know will be there for the long haul. Tomorrow, next week, even next year.

A future.

Imagining my life with Crew is a thing of the past because I know it's real. He's the foundation of my future, and knowing this, I can relish the present and live my life.

My attorneys are finishing up the loose ends of getting all allegations against Whitetail wiped clean from our record. I hope I won't ever have to see Tobin McCann again. I hear he'll probably make a deal for lesser charges and plead guilty to everything. Even so, he made false claims to government agencies, they don't take that lightly. I don't know how Crew found out—or how he finds out anything for that matter—but he said he might get a few months in jail with a couple years probation.

He won't be needing white linen slacks and loafers in the slammer. That shouldn't make me happy, but it does. I'm too happy in general right now to feel badly that it makes me happy.

Good riddance, Tobin McCann.

I'm happy for this headache to be wrapped up. Harvest is in full swing. The weather has cooperated for the most part and Morris has hired outside help for the job. They've been busy in my acres of vines. The grapes are cut by hand, and Van has been here at the crack of dawn every day. We're also shipping to other vineyards in the region. The whole process can take up to ten days, working every minute of daylight.

Even with the harvest, Crew and I have fallen back into almost the same schedule we had before, but we're both trying to work fewer hours into the evening. I'm loving it, but I'm behind on almost everything. If the Tobin McCann ordeal didn't put me behind, the harvest certainly has. It might be time for me to outsource my bookkeeping because it takes a huge amount of my time. I've got a huge stack of mail piled up from the last week and I can't let it go another day.

I pull out a heavy, legal size envelope from the middle of the pile that catches my attention. I frown when I see who it's from because my business loan payments are on auto draft. I don't know what I could be getting from my bank.

When I slide my finger under the flap and pull out the thick pile of papers, the cover letter does a perfect job summarizing the contents. My eyes bug out and I quickly flip through the first few pages where

I find the cover letter didn't lie. It's the details for the loan to my land, home, and most importantly, my business. A business these papers are telling me I own free and clear.

I don't know how long I sit here staring at the papers in my hand, shocked, but mostly infuriated. I have no doubt how it happened.

My disbelief turns red, into a fiery wrath. This winery is mine. I might've gotten the twenty percent to put down from what my mom left me, but I've been paying off my long-term loan faster than planned. At the rate I was going, it would've been paid off in fifteen years, instead of the twenty-year term. If I was really aggressive with my extra principal payments, it could've been paid off in twelve.

Fisting the pile of papers from my bank, I march out of my office. When I get to the tasting room, I wave the papers around as I call to Evan at the counter, "I'll be back. I've got business next door."

I don't give him a chance to say anything. Heading to the front door, I see my newest employee wiping down tables. "Good morning, Maya. Cute dress."

"Oh, thanks," I hear, but don't stop to chat. I'm on a mission.

I pull up his drive quickly. It's a beautiful fall day and it doesn't surprise me to see him standing on his porch waiting. He slides his phone into his pocket, I'm sure he was watching me arrive on the cameras.

I guess I can't be picky, but still find it annoying when they're watching me, even if I was appreciative of them catching my trespasser.

The second my foot hits the ground—Crew tips his head and even as he smiles, his brow furrows. "This reminds me of the day you threw my check in my face. This isn't the way I left you in bed this morning, what's wrong?"

I guess my transparent expression showed over the cameras. It must be a really good system.

"This." I shake the papers in my hand at him. "I got this in the mail today, Crew Vega. What have you done?"

He loses his smile and walks down the steps. "What is it?"

"What is it?" I repeat, raising my voice. "It's only the payoff details of my loan, Crew. For my land, everything on it, as well as my very large, long-term business loan. My loan for two point six million dollars!"

My voice, my yelling, even my anger doesn't faze him. He comes close and simply confirms my tirade with an, "Ah."

"Ah? Ah?!?"

He says nothing, but he does have the nerve to shrug his shoulders.

"What did you do?" I keep yelling.

"Baby, calm down. You were paying a shit-ton of interest."

"Yeah," I agree, exasperated. "Interest is high on a loan for over two and a half million dollars. It's a lot of money."

This time he says nothing, but he has the nerve to tip his head and raise an eyebrow, as if to disagree with me.

"It is!" I argue my point before asking him something I have a feeling I already know. "You paid off my business loan, didn't you?"

He doesn't even seem sorry when he replies, "Of course I did."

"Why?" I wail.

"Because it's not that much money and it was easy for me to do."

"It's not that much money? Are you crazy? I worked hard to get that loan and I've worked hard to turn the business around. It operated in the red for years before I bought it. I did it all on my own and I wanted to prove to myself I could pay it off, too."

"You're not on your own anymore," he calmly states.

"But..." Honestly. I have no words. "Still."

"You and me," he starts and steps forward, closing the distance between us and pulls me to him. "We know death."

My big stack of papers proving I own every blade of grass on my property is crushed between us. His words catch me off guard and I say nothing.

"You were young when you experienced it firsthand. I lost my dad and you lost your mom. I've caused a lot of death on my own over the last ten years. Not everyone knows death, but when you do, you appreciate life."

"What does that have to do with you paying off my loan?"

Again, he ignores me. "When I was gone, I made the decision to start living my life with you. I'm done lamenting death—I want to live. Don't you want to live with me?"

I shake my head, completely confused. "Of course, but you're already practically living with me."

"No, Addison. I mean *live*."

"What are you talking about?"

"I'm ready to live and I want to do it with you. Knowing death like I do—like we do—I've decided I'm living for today. I've put my neck out there, I've worked hard, and got you as my reward. Anything worth anything is an uphill climb. I've climbed it, you've climbed it, now it's time we sit back and live it. You ready for that?"

"But." I sigh, and lean into him, fisting the papers. "This is too much."

"It's not." His answer is firm and resolute. "You don't know what I have or what I'm worth. We need to have that talk. But soon enough you'll be mine officially. You and I both prefer to lay low for obvious reasons. When you take my name, I don't want it tied to a loan when it's easy for me to make that loan go away and save you a shit ton of money in the process. Are you with me?"

My breath catches. "I'll be yours soon?"

He gives me a squeeze. "Yes. I'm ready to live and I think you are, too."

I close my eyes and lean my forehead into the middle of his chest.

His hand dips into my hair when his lips come to the top of my head. "You read those documents?"

"Not really," I mutter into his chest.

"I made it happen when I was gone. Your name's on the deed. Solely. Made no sense you paying all that interest to the bank. Take that money and make your business better than you already have. You might've been on your own before, but you're not anymore."

I look up at him, not knowing what to say. "I don't know what to say."

"Move away from death with me. Let's live."

There's nothing to say. There's nothing I want more than to *live* with him. I push up on my toes and put my lips on his. When he pulls me in closer to take over my kiss, I hear the payoff paperwork to my home and business crinkle between us.

When he breaks our kiss, I ask, "Will you at least talk to me before you do something like this next time?"

He looks confused. "Do you have any other business loans?"

I roll my eyes. "No."

He smiles. "Then yes."

Of course. "I guess I should say thank you, but how do you thank someone for two point six million dollars?"

His eyes warm on me. "I'm sure you can think of something."

Shaking my head, I reach up to kiss him again quickly. "I've got to get back to work. And apparently I need to think of a way to thank you later."

"Love you," he says against my lips. "Looking forward to living with you, baby."

"I love you, too."

Even though I don't want to, I turn to my car so I can get back to work. To a business that's completely mine. I don't even know what I'm going to do with all the extra money.

When I get to my car door, I stop and turn back to him. "Wait, did you pay off my car, too?"

He purses his lips and drops his head, looking at the ground in front of him. He does this while doing his best to hide a grin.

As opposed to him, I look to the sky and sigh. "Of course he did."

"See you for dinner," I hear him call with a smile in his voice.

"I'll have something ready." My voice is resigned, but I like the feeling bubbling up inside of me. I guess this is what it feels like to not be on your own. How can I not like it?

And just like that, with Crew paving the way, we start to *living* together.

Crew

I watch her drive off and am fucking grateful I'm here to see her throw that fit. I was away for only a couple days when I made the changes I did to my finances. What she doesn't know yet is she's now my beneficiary, still leaving a decent portion to my mom and brother. I had to do this in case I didn't come back. Paying off her loans was an afterthought and not a big deal like she made it out to be. I'll need to let that settle with her a while before explaining what's mine will be ours. Or if anything ever happens to me, it'll all be hers.

I had to do this because I didn't lie when I told her it was hard to focus. From the second I left her, I had a bad fucking feeling about the assignment. If something went south—which it did—and I didn't come back, I needed to know she'd be taken care of.

I never knew what it was like to leave someone to go on a job. To worry about coming home to a woman I want, a woman I love, and the hurt I'd cause if I didn't. Maybe that's why it didn't feel right, why the whole thing felt different—off. Or maybe it's because I'd already quit and had no desire to go back. Or, it was Grady.

My guess, it was all of the above, but mostly Grady.

I was on my way to grab lunch, but instead head to Grady's barn. He's barely spoken to me since it happened, even after we arrived Stateside. I arranged for us to land outside of Baltimore on a private airstrip and got him to a doctor at a cash only practice. Grady was fucked up, beyond recuperating on his own. He needed medical attention and there was no way we were going to chance finding it where we were. We couldn't get out of there fast enough, and even in a private jet I chartered to get him out fast, it was a long fucking flight.

I don't knock to alert him I'm here. When I open the door, he doesn't look to me, but tosses his phone to the side. No doubt he knew I was coming. He's laid back on the only piece of furniture he owns besides his bed, a leather recliner, staring out the window.

Exactly where he's been every time I've come to check on him.

I step in and swing the door shut to his makeshift house with its minimal necessities. We've been here for six months—this was supposed to be temporary. I'd planned on him settling somewhere close, but who knows if or when that might happen. At this point, I just hope he sticks around so I can keep an eye on him.

When he doesn't acknowledge me, I ask, "You hungry? I can go to the tasting room and get you something."

He finally looks away from the window and when he does, I see his bruises are fading, and hell if he didn't cut out his own stitches that were lining his temple. That wound was left gaping until we could get back to the States. He still hasn't shaved and he always shaves when he's not on assignment.

He doesn't speak but shakes his head.

"I'll bring you some dinner," I insist. "How are your ribs, the arm?"

He might still be in bad shape, but his eyes waste no time darting to me in record time. "I don't need anyone to take care of me, Vega. Doctor said I'll be fine. Do your business, train your men, go play house. Go do whatever you need to do."

"Speaking of that, let's get you out of this barn. I'm at Addison's every night, you should move into my house. I'm only there during the day. I'll help move your stuff, you'll be more comfortable there."

He sighs and looks back to the window. "I'm good."

"Asa's taking a couple days to see his kids since the recruits have their first days off. Did he talk to you before he left?"

Grady shakes his head. "He tried, but you know he and I don't have the bromance thing going on you two do."

I cross my arms and mutter, "Shit."

He leans forward slowly to get up, looking like he's moving better than he did yesterday. He has a couple cracked ribs and more that are bruised. They dislocated his shoulder when they broke his arm, I had to pop it back in myself. He's lucky it was a clean break and he didn't need surgery, not to mention they didn't fuck with his dominant arm. Although, they were about to. When I got to him, he was hanging by his left wrist with a sack tied over his head, and his right hand was tied to a chopping block. They were trying to make him talk, but he held steadfast, just as we were trained, never uttering a word. For one, it would've given away he was an American and two, if you utter one word, self-preservation could take over and you could utter them all. I've never had to put that into practice and it was a first for Grady.

I'm impressed he's moving as well as he is, even if he's still slow. Though, he's not nearly as slow as I thought he'd be.

Heading to his makeshift kitchen, he opens the fridge and never looks back. "You can go."

He's said more to me today than he has since we've been home, so I'll take that as improvement. When I turn to the door I call to him, "I'll bring you dinner."

He responds, staring into his almost empty fridge, "Don't."

I yell back right before I slam the door behind me, "I'm bringing you dinner."

He'll have to deal with me bringing him a meal. I'm not sure what else to do, but he's gonna need to snap out of this eventually and move on. What's going to make him do that, I've got no idea.

I just got off the phone with my mom, it was time I told her about Addison. At first the line was quiet, and then just as I thought she'd do, she got mom-emotional on me. Once I got her settled down, she asked all kinds of questions. I answered her for the most part, promising her she'd meet Addison soon. I told her I'd get her a plane ticket and she could come here, see my new place but she could stay with us in Addison's farmhouse.

The conversation went well, and I could tell she wasn't only happy, but relieved I'm not alone. I told her I'd call to finalize plans once I checked Addison's schedule, and she was happy to have something to look forward to.

Now it's late afternoon. The day is slow with Asa and the recruits away. I'm in my office looking at new backgrounds. I built out the barn to house ten, we haven't completely fucked up the first group, maybe it's time to add more. Although, Jarvis is still up in the air. He's like a loose cannon that we're waiting to explode.

When my phone vibrates on my desk, I frown at the name showing on the screen. He never calls on this line.

"What?" I demand the instant my phone touches my ear.

His words are rushed. "We don't know where O'Rourke is. Or Whittaker for that matter. Something went down today. I don't know what, but we lost contact with his tail an hour ago. We've been trying to touch base and eventually searched from Whittaker's last reported location. The agent following Whittaker was found a half-mile from there, bleeding out in a ditch. Gunshot wound to the chest. He coded twice in the chopper, but he's in surgery now."

I stand, grab my keys off my desk, putting Carson on speaker so I can check the cameras. "Where's O'Rourke? Don't you still have a tracker on his car?"

"It's still showing at the Pentagon, but our tail followed him from the building two hours ago on foot until a hit-and-run ended his surveillance. Two fucking broken legs. O'Rourke hasn't checked back through security, he's not at the Pentagon. We don't know where he is."

I run through my house and out the front door. "Whittaker?"

"Same. Someone's fucking onto us, both tails were taken out about the same time. The taps have been quiet for over twenty-four hours—we didn't think much of it. Told you they've been arguing, and the way they left it, they were both gonna do their own thing."

"Fuck," I seethe as I gun it down my drive to get to Addison as fast as I can. "Asa's gone and my recruits are on leave, all I have is Grady. Call him, tell him what you told me. I'm headed to the winery now, but left unarmed. I've got to find Addison."

"Call back," he demands, disconnecting immediately.

I pull the cameras up on my phone at the same time I call her cell, putting it on speaker. I pull out of my property on almost two wheels and head for the winery.

Fuck if it doesn't go to voicemail.

Chapter Twenty-Eight
Live

Addy
Fifteen minutes earlier

I look to Bev, who's sitting on the porch of the main building with a book in her lap. This is exactly why she won't let me hire her. If she wants to sit and read while looking out over the countryside, she doesn't want to feel guilty about doing it.

"If anyone's looking for me, I'm going for a walk. I want to see how far they got in the vines today. They should be done in a day or two, tops."

Bev looks to me and smiles. "Okay sweetie. I brought dinner for Morrie and all the workers. You and Crew are welcome to eat if you want, there's plenty."

I turn back and smile after making it down the stairs. "Thanks, we might just do that."

Vines

The workers have made it to the far side of the vineyard and are finishing with the last few acres. This is only my second harvest. I purchased Whitetail in early summer, those first few months here were a whirlwind. I didn't appreciate the excitement of reaping the grapes my first fall here, but I do this year. Watching my vines come to life in the spring after the dead of winter was magical, but I'm still sad. The vines, which have become heavy with fruit, look bare and even a little pitiful already. Soon they'll lose their leaves and be nothing but a ghost of dead, tangled twigs.

I'm almost halfway to where they're working near the far edge of my property when I hear crunching from the side. Turning to see what it is, the noise grows quicker and louder by the second.

I vaguely see someone's legs through the bottom of the vines when I hear my name. "Addy." I freeze, barely having the chance to fully turn to the voice when he appears through the grapevines. His words come out labored and rushed. "I need to talk to you."

I step back instantly, realizing I don't have my phone since I'm wearing a dress without pockets. What is he doing here out in the middle of my vineyard? Crew said he was under constant surveillance. I try not to let my eyes scan the surroundings, wondering where Crew's cameras are. I really should've asked. Damn it. I try not to sound scared when I address him, but it's hard because I know everything about him. What he's capable of and how my dad was killed because of him.

"What are you doing here, Sheldon?"

He takes a step toward me and I unconsciously step back, slipping on the loose ground below me. I stumble into a vine and yelp when the branches tear the flesh on my hand. He stops, puts a hand up, trying to calm me or keep me in place. As if he's in a hurry, he takes a deep breath and says on an exhale, "Your father was my friend. I never meant for anything to happen to him."

I bite my lip to keep my emotions in check, not saying a word.

Looking back and forth, I wonder if I should make a run for it, if he could catch me. I'm in my rain boots, I'm not sure how fast I could even run, let alone get away from him. Then I wonder how he got all the way out here and why those damn cameras aren't doing their job.

"I did my best to keep him safe." He takes another step closer, and this time there's nowhere for me to go. My chest rises and falls quickly, my breathing an erratic mess. He gets even closer when he continues. "I tried to ward off those who knew he was onto something, but your dad was smart. He kept coming at me with his worries about what was going on at work. And then he started asking around, he knew exactly what he was talking about, no matter how much I tried to put him off."

I'm backed up against my vines, feeling them biting me through my dress when I lie, "I have no idea what you're talking about."

"You do," he insists, still in a hurry, and every word that leaves his mouth is more agitated than the one prior. He's losing control as the seconds tick by. When I side-step to try and get away, he closes the distance, seizing my bicep tightly to keep me in place. Gripping me to the point where it's painful, I wince, trying to turn out of his hold, but it only makes him squeeze tighter. "Addy, you need to stop what you're doing because they're questioning your motives. They've hacked into your internet history and are suspicious why you never leave your property by yourself. You're being watched, they've got eyes on your every move. I think somehow you were aware of this since your patterns have changed, but for fuck's sake, quit with the internet searches. Things are so fucking twisted right now, I don't know which way's up. I came to warn you. You're gonna get yourself killed!"

He shakes me, almost violently, when the last words leave his mouth, his anxiety peaking. Holy shit, I was researching Sheldon, and even Whittaker, when I thought it was him who was trying to screw with my business. I can't believe *they* know—whoever *they* are.

Russians, terrorists, aliens? Who the fuck are *they* that everyone keeps talking about?

I try to pull it together, knowing I need to get away from him. I pull my arm again and almost beg when I ask, "Why are you telling me this?"

"These people," he pulls me even closer and pauses, taking a breath. "They're paranoid. When they get this way, they take people out. They did it with your dad and I've seen it done since. The pressure is mounting, Addy. I feel it, and it's never felt like this before."

Another voice comes from our side, I didn't even notice his approach because I was so distracted by Sheldon, but there he is— Marc Whittaker—standing in my vines with a gun pointed at us.

"You fucking traitor. The whole time I followed you out here, I couldn't believe you were coming to her."

Sheldon turns to Marc, letting go of me. I stumble to the side and out of sheer self-preservation, turn as fast as I can, and start down my row of vines. I knew my boots wouldn't serve me well and I was right. I barely make it a few steps when I slide on the twigs and branches.

"Stay where you are!" Marc screams and I immediately stop, letting out a little scream.

"This is between you and me, Whittaker, let her go." Sheldon looks straight at Marc, but he shifts, standing in front of me.

"What is it with her? You still hung up on her mom after all these years?" Sheldon narrows his eyes, but Marc keeps spewing his words. "Yeah, I heard all about Anne Ross. You might've been friends with her husband, but you really wanted her."

Maybe he did have a thing for my mom. Maybe that was just one more reason for her to disappear, creating our new identities.

Sheldon doesn't let Marc's words faze him and looks back to me. "I never had feelings for your mother. I'd never do that to Wes."

Looking back to Marc, he continues. "The Rosses had nothing to do with me. They were innocent victims. I couldn't stop them from taking out Wes all those years ago when he was suspicious, but I'm not going to let it happen to his daughter. This is between you and me, Whittaker. Let her go, we can work this out once and for all."

"She's not going anywhere. I've come to take care of this shit myself. They want her eliminated, she's making them nervous, and you've fucking put them off for months. You're pissing me off, playing games with them, and making it hard for me to do what I need to do. Now I've gotta take care of your shit, too," he spits at Sheldon.

I start to shake. I've got to get away. Doing the only thing I can do, I turn to look behind me. Finding the widest opening in the vines, I take my chance.

I'm only two steps toward my opening when a shot blasts so close to my head, I hear it hit the branches I was trying to move through.

Screaming, I bring my hands to my ears and stumble into the vines. This time they tear through the skin of my arm, ripping my dress. Blood instantly seeps through the material of my sleeve from the gash.

"What the fuck?" I hear Sheldon scream at the same time I turn to see Marc lower the gun in his hand, aiming at me once again.

"I told you not to move!" Marc screams at me.

Barely catching my breath, my voice is edging on hysterical when I beg, "Please let me go. I don't know anything."

"Addison."

I pull in a quick breath and turn quickly to find him. His voice, calm and controlled like always, is coming from the other side of the vines. When he steps through, he doesn't make a noise. Of course he wouldn't, he's trained to be unheard and unseen.

He's loose and relaxed, and if I didn't know him better, I'd think he only happened upon us while strolling through my vineyard. I see it in his eyes—focus and complete awareness of everything. He's at least six feet from me, standing in the middle of the path, but we're separated by Sheldon, with Marc standing across from all of us.

Between the gun being fired in my direction and knowing Marc is here to take me out, seeing Crew is too much. I can't keep my tears from coming, and they instantly overflow. Instinctively, I start to move to him, but Marc approaches me and screams, "I told you to stay the fuck there!"

I freeze, looking into Marc Whittaker's crazed eyes. He's out of control, agitated, and doesn't seem like he has a plan.

"Stay there, baby," Crew gently demands. He might've been talking to me, but he's not looking at me. He's looking straight at Marc. "What's up, Whittaker? You strolling through vineyards now instead of selling State secrets?"

Marc, surprised by Crew's revelation, turns his gun on Crew.

"No!" I scream and start to move to him.

Crew takes another step toward Marc. "You can't see them, but there're cameras everywhere. You might want to stop and think this through. Every move you make is on video, and trust me, it won't make you happy knowing who has the feed to these cameras."

Marc, frantic, not knowing who to point the gun at now, yells, "Everyone stop moving!"

"Addison," Crew's voice turns soft, but he doesn't look away from Marc, holding his hands out low, showing he's unarmed. Even with a gun pointed at him, Crew takes a step toward Marc but keeps speaking to me. "Hang on, baby, and stay there."

"I don't know who you are," Sheldon starts, and when I look over he's addressing Crew. Crew lifts his head, but never takes an eye off Marc's gun that's still pointed at him. Sheldon shocks me, throwing Marc Whittaker to the wolves. "You know more than I gave you credit for. I've got all the information on Whittaker you need. I've kept tabs on him, every drop he's made to the Russians, every piece of information he's stolen and sold over the last four and a half years."

Marc, promptly forgetting about Crew, turns his gun on Sheldon. "You bastard. Like I don't have the shit on you? You taught me everything I know."

I move back a step, the rocks and twigs crunching under my boots.

"Be still, Addison." Crew looks past Sheldon, catching my eyes. His voice gets my attention, steeling me in place because it's not soft anymore. It's firm and the look in his eyes back up his words and tone.

"Really, Marc?" Sheldon continues bravely as if Crew didn't just speak to me. He takes a step toward Marc, and for some reason, I sense he's distracting him. "You have proof of that? You have a timeline, pictures, records of my communication with them? Because I have all that on you and more. You got greedy and wanted all the action for yourself. If you think I didn't see that, you're not smart enough for the task."

Sheldon takes another step toward the weapon and Marc screams, "Stop!"

"Hang tight, baby," Crew says, not moving a muscle.

Neither Sheldon nor Marc give us their attention as Sheldon keeps throwing it in Marc's face. "If you were clever enough to see the big picture, you'd realize everyone's your enemy and you would've kept track. See, I didn't teach you everything, Whittaker. I know how to cover my ass and stay in the shadows. You forget, I've done it for many years."

I look into Crew's dark, beautiful eyes, they're the sharpest I've seen yet. Something about them makes me still, or at least try, as he told me to. I do try, but I can't stop them, my tears continue to fall and he sees it, too. So minutely, I would've missed it had I not been looking into his eyes, he gives me a shake of his head. "Give me five beats, Abby. You'll be in my arms."

I frown instantly, not understanding.

"I go down, O'Rourke, you go down with me," Marc warns.

"Still." Crew's voice softens the way it does only for me right before his next word comes out so differently, I know for a fact it's an order, but to who, I've no idea. "Now."

"What—" Marc's surprised face barely has time to register Crew's order. At the same time, Sheldon advances on Marc as he squeezes his hand around his gun, in what looks like sheer panic.

It happened so fast, that one second there were four of us before the gunfire resounded, and the next, there was only Crew and me.

I'm not even sure if I screamed, if anything came out, but I meant to. My hands come to the sides of my head in pure disbelief as I look down to see Marc Whittaker laying face-first on my land, the back of his head obliterated. I hear something else, someone writhing in pain, but I can't take my eyes off Marc.

Then I see nothing.

Just as he promised, I'm in Crew's arms. Then again, he's never broken a promise.

I can't see anything but I feel myself moving backward. Crew has one hand in my hair and the other around my back, my face pressed to his chest.

Through the ringing in my ears, I hear him comforting me with his lips at the top of my head. "It's over, baby. Calm down."

It's only then do the tears flow on my face, my chest heaving with sobs.

We stop moving and he wraps me up tighter, trying to console me with whispered words into my hair.

When the ringing starts to fade, I hear another voice, a familiar voice. I look over and see Grady, but he doesn't look like the Grady I know. Crew's friend, who's just as built and bigger than life like Crew, has his arm in a sling, and his face is bruised and battered. A handgun is stuck in the waist of his pants and he's talking on the phone, but his eyes are on Crew.

"Whittaker's dead," Grady informs whoever's on the other end of the phone. "Yeah, I did. We need EMS, probably a chopper, O'Rourke's got a gunshot wound to the shoulder. He's hangin' on. You wanted him alive, he's alive for the time being. By the time I got here, Whittaker was about to unload on O'Rourke. I waited 'til I got the all clear from Vega, but didn't get a shot off before Whittaker shot O'Rourke."

Listening to him retell it, I try and breathe deep, sinking into Crew's chest. Grady looks to me and then back to his friend as he ends his phone call. "Yeah, Vega and his woman are good."

With his eyes on Crew, Grady goes on. "Carson said he'll clean this up. I should get out of here. He'll have his people here soon and said he'd take care of local law enforcement."

I don't look up, but feel Crew nod against my head. Then Grady turns to leave, doing it slowly, even gingerly.

"Grady." Crew's voice vibrates through his chest and I feel it everywhere. It takes Grady a moment to turn he's moving so slow, and now I wonder how he got here fast enough to do what he did. When he turns to us, his marred face is intense with its bruises and scrapes. I don't know the details of their assignment and can only imagine how bad it was when Crew says, "You said you'd never be able to repay that debt. But man, you just did." He gives me a squeeze before going on. "You don't know how grateful I am, but someday, I hope you get it."

Grady looks to me and then back to Crew. He lifts his head to Crew right when we hear commotion. That commotion includes a cow mooing and I can tell it's Harry. I can't believe, now of all times, she somehow got through the fence and is wandering through the vines. Besides my cow and Morris calling for me, blades of a helicopter fill the space.

I barely see Grady turn to disappear into my vines when Crew turns me into him, holding me tight. When the commotion gets closer, Crew dips his lips to my ear. "It's over, baby. Time to live."

Even with one traitor lying on the ground with his brains splattered all over my land and the other on the brink, I couldn't agree more. Surrounded by death, another moment in time weaves its way into my soul, this one making the others shine bright as the sun.

I'm so ready to live.

Chapter Twenty-Nine
Cow Daddy

Crew
Four weeks later

With my shoulders against the headboard, I gather her hair in my hands. As much as I love her rich brown hair spread across my lap, I want to see her mouth work me. Some days I think she loves my cock more than me. I feel like I've gone to heaven, won the lottery, and was named the number one draft pick in the NFL all at the same time. How could I have gotten so lucky? I've gotta muster all the control I can to prolong it, to have her mouth as long as I can instead of exploding in two point five seconds like a hormone-raging teenager.

With her hand wrapped around the base of me, her other plays with my balls. Fuck. I breathe deep and pull her head up enough where she only gets the tip. That wins me her beautiful eyes and a scowl.

"Suck the tip, baby."

But she doesn't do as I say. She raises a brow and flicks the tip with her tongue, before mocking me, her voice dipping low and sultry. "Okay, *baby*."

I narrow my eyes, shaking my head. She certainly doesn't comply all the time, but then again, it might become boring if she did. I wouldn't want her any other way.

Her perfect pink tongue peeks out, circling the tip before she asks against my raging hard-on, "Why do you always talk about it in the third person?"

My muscles tense and I have to breathe deep to control myself. Having a conversation with her breath and words coming across my cock isn't easy.

"Because my cock is its own person when it comes to you." I trace her bottom lip with my thumb before dipping my hand into her hair, pulling gently to get her attention. "And it wants you to suck its tip."

"But," she starts before running her tongue up the length, making me crazy and doing it on purpose. She knows exactly what she's doing, she's playing a game I doubt she'll mind losing in the end. "What if I want more," she kisses the tip with her perfect puckered lips, "than *its* tip?"

I soften my voice. "You want more?"

She smiles and when she does, her lips brush across my cock. "I always want more, Crew."

I shake my head slowly before I move. I move so fast—she yelps in surprise. Before she knows it, she's flipped to her back where I've shifted over her, straddling her face. I quickly spread her legs high and wide for me, her bare pussy wet and glistening. I can see everything clear as day since I turned all the lights on before stripping her bare. I wanted to see every bit of what I was in the mood for, but I didn't plan this. This is even better.

I dip my hand under her ass, lifting her hips to my face. Sliding my tongue through her wetness, she drops her knees wide, giving me what I want. When I rub my cock against her cheek, I say, "Take what you want, Abby."

She fists me as she moans, and I don't waste any time pulling her clit into my mouth. Just for teasing me, I don't give her what she wants, and barely offer her the tip of my cock. Her fingers dig into the muscles of my ass and she finally sucks. Fuck, that feels good and I give her more. Her hips start to move, pressing into my mouth, and there it is—her whimper. But this time I not only hear it, but feel it around my dick.

I give her more as I take. Her noises, her pussy grinding against my mouth as I fuck hers, it's a wonder I haven't exploded.

Just like always, I get her there first, and the suction around my cock goes slack when she moans and gasps, breathing hard against me.

I can't take another second.

I climb off her and flip around. When I look at her face, her eyes are closed and her breathing labored, spent from her orgasm. Sliding between her legs with my knees to the bed, I pull her hips to me, and finally, I'm there.

My Abby.

"Yes," she breathes as I slam into her, not able to hold back or keep it slow. There's nothing more beautiful than seeing her take me.

When I finally come, driving into her one last time, I stay deep inside as I drop my body to hers. Giving her only the weight she can handle, I take in the feel of her under me as I kiss her. Her hands slide through my hair and when I release her lips, she breathes against mine, "Wow."

I ignore her compliment and look into her eyes, delivering the truth. "You didn't comply very well."

A knowing smirk floods her features. "If that's what I get, you can count on me not complying more often."

I shake my head and kiss her again. "Love you, Abby."

Her smirk disappears, contentment and happiness taking over. "Love you, too."

Addy

I pop a green apple Laffy Taffy in my mouth, but before I look back to my sales projections, I smooth out the green wrapper on my desk.

I smile. Today's a good day, but then again every day for the last month has been a good day.

I'd say everything's back to normal, but who am I to know what normal is? I've never had normal. When one grows up the way I did, with their real identity buried deep, and they meet the love of their life who happens to be a retired killer one day while walking their cows, that's not normal. Throw in treacherous acts against our country, cold-blooded murder, and deep-seated KGB stalking my internet searches, I know this is not what fairytales are made of. At least not for someone normal.

Which makes me very *not* normal.

Because I would travel my dark road a million times over to be right where I am.

It's been a month since Grady blew Marc Whittaker's brains out in the middle of my vineyard. A month since Sheldon was almost killed on my land and a month since the CIA ended one of its longest running investigations into known espionage against our country. They did their best to try and spin that story, but still, in the end, it didn't look good for the CIA. What wasn't featured in the news was what Crew was able to tell me from his sources—the entire old-school KGB group who were paying O'Rourke and Whittaker are gone.

Gone.

Six months ago, I wouldn't have known what that meant, but that was before I was sleeping with a killer. I'm all *in the know*, now.

Most importantly, it's been a month since Crew and I have fallen into our new normal. A normal where I can come and go as I please, where I wake up and go to bed with Crew, without any dark clouds looming over us. It might not be normal-normal, but it's normal for us, and I love it.

Today is a good day because I struck gold with my Laffy Taffy. A cow joke.

What do you get from a forgetful cow?

Milk of amnesia.

Cow jokes. Who knew they'd make me so happy? Then again, who knew I'd ever own cows?

"Addy!" I hear and I can tell she's in a rush.

Swiveling my chair, I turn to my bulletin board which is designated solely for green cow jokes, and add it to my collection. I don't have a ton, but there are more than you'd think. Finding a green cow joke is like finding a diamond in the rough, but I eat a lot of green Laffy Taffy.

"Addy!" Bev rushes into my office. "Come quick, you'll never believe this."

"What's going on?" I get up and follow my enthusiastic friend who's practically skipping ahead of me down the hall toward the tasting room.

We're halfway between Halloween and Thanksgiving, there's a chill in the air, and most of the leaves have fallen. Even though I'm sad the harvest is over, I love fall. The dry air is really good for my hair.

We make it through my tasting room, which is busy for midweek afternoon. We're ramping up for our annual Thanksgiving Tasting this weekend. Last year was so busy I decided to up my game, have it catered, and take reservations. It booked quickly, the event should be twice as big as last year. If we make in sales what we did last year projected on attendance, November will be off the charts.

"Come on, Addy!" Bev is at the door holding it open for me.

The second the cool air hits me, I stop in my tracks. Not because of the crisp breeze, but because of what I see. Crew's dilapidated truck is again pulled right up to the porch.

I quickly came to love the turquoise beast when he told me it was his dad's and he planned to keep it running forever. When he informed me of this, I had Morris clear out a section of my barn that was only used for storage. It's now protected from the elements every night and Crew has a place to work on it. His brand new black Jag F-Type, though, is parked next to my Audi in the garage. Everything of Crew's now resides in my farmhouse. Most importantly, Crew is here for good, and my home, that's going on four centuries old and listed on the Historic Register, doesn't seem as big and vast as it used to.

However, the sight in front of me is so much more than his truck. Whining and slurping noises fill the air with Bev clapping from my side.

Crew's standing in front of a cattle trailer hitched to his truck. Holding her with a rope around her neck as a makeshift leash, his other is gripping an enormous bottle of milk, and he's feeding the cutest calf I've ever seen. Not that I've paid much attention to calves in the past, but this one is perfect. She's a black baldy, like all my cows, and her markings are beautiful. With a pure white face, she's got a strip of black right across her eyes. She looks like she's on her way to a fancy masquerade ball.

I can't take my eyes off her until Crew's voice cuts into the cuteness. "I got her at the auction, she's an orphan. You'll have to feed her for a while yet."

"She's precious, go see her!" Bev gives me a push and I skip down the steps quickly to meet my new cow.

When I get to her, she startles and leans into Crew to get closer to the one feeding her. I try and pet her, but she wants nothing to do with me.

I smile big and look up to him. "She loves you."

"She should." He shakes his head. "Not very many cows get to be pets. You're never allowed to go to the auction, by the way. We'll end up with a herd."

My smile grows into a huge grin and just when I'm about to name her, Crew must've read my mind. "Batman."

My face falls. "Batman?"

"Yeah, look at her. She's a batman."

"But," I stammer before throwing out my idea. "I was thinking Erik, from Phantom of the Opera."

"Baby, I've never seen that." I open my mouth to suggest we watch it, but he proves to be a mind reader. "I'm not watching anything with the word 'opera' in it. Her name's Batman."

I look down at our new mini masked cow and suggest, "Batgirl?"

"Whatever." He shrugs but does it with a smile. "Batgirl."

I lean up to kiss him, but our new Batgirl doesn't like it, struggling to get between us and closer to her caretaker.

I laugh and give her a scratch before teasing Crew. "You might regret this. I think you're a cow daddy now."

Not caring about our cow baby, he leans down to kiss me. His voice turns dark and even though I know he's teasing, still, he's sort of not when he murmurs against my lips, "I'd rather just be your Daddy."

This from the man who pretty much does what he wants with me—even though I can't deny I've loved it all—makes me laugh out loud. Because there's no way in hell I'll ever call him Daddy and he knows it.

Epilogue

Two years later…

Crew

"Addison?"

I just got back from my run and the house is quiet. She's not in bed and I know she's not at work because she's not supposed to be. Her car is here, so that only leaves one place for her to go. Pulling up the cameras on my phone, I shake my head at what I see. She's definitely within her confines, but she's pushing the limits.

I head toward the rear of the house and through the door to the back of our property. Together, we own the entire section of land, although I only train recruits at my camp. I keep my office here at the farmhouse now, I prefer it here and have since the first day I set foot on her vineyard. We've carved out a little corner of Earth, her and me. Not very many things could make it more perfect, but we're working on it.

I make it down the patio steps and there she is, too far away, near the edge of the yard that backs to the pasture only separated by the aged wooden fence. I look at her across the expanse, almost in the exact spot where I married her, and think about all that's happened over the last two years.

She's talking to her cows, and I can't see from here, but I bet she's feeding them molasses. We should own stock in molasses.

Maybe I'll look into that.

She ignores me since she knows I won't be happy about her being out here, and even though she might not hear me, there's no doubt she knows I'm coming since Batgirl's going ape-shit. I swear I bought a dog in a cow's body. Even at two years old, she's like a puppy, and still gets excited when she sees me.

Standing behind her, I put one hand to the fence beside my wife and cup her belly that's heavy, carrying our baby, in the other. Leaning in, I put my lips to the side of her head. "What do you think you're doing?"

She reaches in the pocket of her sweater for more molasses. "You know the doctor said I could get up a couple times a day to walk around. Surely you haven't forgotten, you were there and argued with him when you thought he was giving me too much rein. I'll go back in a second, I wanted to see cows. It's not like I walked clear across the pasture."

"Baby," I start and gently pull her back into my front and rub the baby. "This is not what he meant and you know it. You walking down two flights of stairs is more activity than he meant. He definitely didn't mean it was okay for you to traipse across an acre to feed the cows."

She leans her head back against my chest and sighs. "Probably not, but she's due in two weeks and I feel good. I just wanted to get outside."

"I would've carried you if you wanted to come outside."

She laughs but looks annoyed. I know she's frustrated being on bedrest, not able to work and keep up with her normal level of activity, but she seems off.

"What's wrong?" I ask.

She shakes her head against me without saying a word.

"What's wrong?" I press.

She sighs again, putting her hand over mine. "Getting so close to the due date, getting to meet her, hold her...it's hard not to think what we missed out on. Do you think about it?"

"Baby." I slide my hand up her body and tip her face to look at me. "Everyday. How can I not? They'll be with us forever."

It's true. Two miscarriages within six months will live in me for eternity. Having two babies we'll never know, watching her go through what she did, and living through that heartache together is something you don't ever get over. We waited months to try again, I even started looking into adoption without her knowing. I wasn't sure I could watch her go through it again.

So when she started having issues this time and had to go on bedrest, I didn't know what to think. Secretly, I'm not sure we should try again. If she wants more kids, I'll press for adoption.

She closes her eyes and leans farther into me.

"Hey." I squeeze her to get her attention. "It's time to focus on the happy. But you need to bake the baby for a couple more weeks and you need to do that from our bed where you're supposed to be. The cows can wait."

She turns, her big belly pushing into me, and gives me a small smile. "I guess, but I have a feeling she'll love the cows. Not every kid has pet cows."

Leaning down to kiss her, I smile and take her hand, leading her to the house where I'll put her to bed myself. "Maybe I should get you a puppy. A house pet, not a farm pet. A big dog that can hang out around the tasting room, sort of a mascot."

"The cows are easy, Crew. I don't think I want to train a puppy with a newborn."

I give her hand a squeeze as I hold the door open to our three story farmhouse. "We'll see. I think my daughter needs a dog."

"Crew," she drawls my name. "You can't over spoil her. Spoil her, yes, of course. I'll spoil her, too. But she can't be overly spoiled. There's a fine line."

We make our way up the first flight of stairs and I'm contemplating carrying her the rest of the way. She shouldn't have even walked down, let alone up. "Does that mean getting her a dog or paying off all her loans? Because if I can help it, she won't ever pay shit high interest rates for no reason."

She squeezes my hand. "I'm serious."

"So am I," I respond earnestly.

We round the second floor hallway to the next set of stairs when she yanks me to a stop. I look back and she's holding her belly, but her face is etched in pain.

"What's wrong?" I ask quickly.

She groans.

"Addison, what's wrong?"

Grabbing her back, she exhales and looks up at me. "I think she's coming."

"Was that a contraction?"

She nods, still in pain.

"But." I try to remember what's next. "Don't we need to wait for the next one? Make sure it's real?"

She shakes her head and looks down where her jeans are wet. "It's real."

"You stay here," I demand. "I'll get your shit and carry you to the car."

"You don't need to carry me."

I ignore her. "Don't move, I'll be right back."

I run up the stairs to our bedroom and grab her bag. By the time I make it down to the second floor, she's not there. I make the turn and she's almost to the bottom.

"Damn it, Addison."

Without looking back, she waves me off as she walks slowly to the kitchen. "I'm about to have your baby, Crew. Don't talk to me like that."

Frustrated she won't do as I say, I calm my voice. "Can you get to the car okay?"

She's already made it to the mudroom and simply ignores me. I close my eyes and drop my head, wondering if my daughter will be just like her mother.

Addy

It went fast, which was a surprise since they prepare you for the worst of situations during those stupid classes. Especially since I was on bedrest for almost three months and we lost two babies before that. It's about time something was easy.

It's the middle of the night and I'm snuggling our daughter who's only a day old. Her daddy, my man, my husband, is asleep in what looks to be the most uncomfortable chair on earth. He won't leave us even though I told him he could go home to sleep. All he had to do was look at me like I'd lost my mind to know that wasn't going to happen.

I don't know how many times he's complained about the hospital, saying he can't wait to get us home. I think he's just ready to get back to the fortress he's created.

"You know." I jump when I hear his voice. Even after years with him, he still finds ways to sneak up on me. "She's getting a puppy on the way home."

I roll my eyes and look back to Vivre who, for a newborn, has a full head of dark hair. But how can she not between Crew and me? "I changed my mind, you're going to have to spoil her rotten so she doesn't hate us. You and your family of strange names. With a French first name followed by a Spanish last name, not to mention all the V's, surely she'll hold that against us."

He gets up and sits on the side of my bed, putting his arm around both of us. "Trust me, it's better than every other language I speak. We'll call her Vivi. Or Vee. What better name could we give our child after what we've been through?"

I agree, but I also have visions of teachers mispronouncing her name. Not everyone will know that Vivre is pronounced *veeve*. It is a beautiful name, if said correctly. Which no one will, but oh well. We'll know and someday we'll explain the meaning to her.

I lean into my husband and look up into his dark eyes. "Time to live."

He looks to Vivi and back before cupping my jaw, pulling me in for a kiss. "Time to live," he agrees. "Love you, my Abby."

I smile against his lips. "Love you, too."

Thank you for reading. Stay tuned for the next Killers Novel, the story of Grady and Maya.

About the Author

Brynne Asher lives in the Midwest with her husband, three children, and her perfect dog. When she isn't creating pretend people and relationships in her head, she's running her kids around and doing laundry. She enjoys cooking, decorating, shopping at outlet malls and online, always seeking the best deal. A perfect day in Brynne World ends in front of an outdoor fire with family, friends, s'mores, and a delicious cocktail.

Made in the USA
Las Vegas, NV
13 May 2023

72029900R00193